MW01610549

THE EXTERMINATORS
TRILOGY

This is a work of speculative fiction. All of the events and dialogue depicted within are a product of the author's overactive imagination. None of this stuff happened. Except maybe in a parallel universe.

Copyright © 2018 by Mark Gillespie

www.markgillespieauthor.com

All rights reserved, including the right to reproduce this book or portions thereof in any form whatsoever.

Cover by Vincent Sammy

JOIN THE READER LIST

Do you love Post-Apocalyptic, Dystopian and Horror fiction? Mark's a busy author and he releases regularly in these genres so if you enjoy what you read here and want to be notified whenever there's a new book out, join the reader list. Just click the link below. It'll only take a minute.

www.markgillespieauthor.com
(*The sign up box is on the Home Page*)

You can also follow Mark on Bookbub.

BLACK STORM (#1)

For Íde, who has saved me from a thousand Black Storms.

CHAPTER ONE

"We gotta run okay? We need to get out of here."

Cody MacLeod kneeled in front of his daughter and squeezed her gently on the upper arms. She felt fragile, like a china doll. "Whatever happens, we can't let the bad woman catch up with us," he said. "She makes people do bad things. You know that don't you?"

Silence.

"Do you understand Rachel?" Cody said.

Rachel nodded her head.

"We've got to stay one step ahead of her," Cody said, pushing a few loose strands of blonde hair off Rachel's face. "Two steps, three steps." His voice was shaking and he took a deep breath before saying anything else. This wasn't a good time to lose it and even if he was on the brink, he couldn't let Rachel see.

They were in the hallway of their house in Spring Branch, Texas. Cody turned towards the front door where two bulging backpacks were sitting. One of them was plain black and the other featured a rainbow colored sky with two silver ponies grazing in a field of green grass.

"All we gotta do is walk out the door," Cody said.

"Are we leaving for good?" Rachel said. Cody saw the confusion in his daughter's indigo blue eyes – the same indigo blue eyes that he'd possessed as a child before the years had dulled them.

He nodded. "Yeah I think so."

Cody heard the Black Storm blowing outside. The wind was howling and moaning – a crude B-movie sound effect that had escaped from the big screen into the real world. Still it was relatively calm, at least compared to the gale force winds that had been blowing the night before when Cody had made the decision to leave home. It was a decision that would either save their lives or seal their fate.

There was doubt in the little girl's eyes. Cody could tell that she wasn't sure he was making the right call and Jesus, who could blame her? He wasn't sure about it either.

"Geez kid," Cody said. "Don't look at me like that. You're looking at me the way other people used to look at me back in the eighties and nineties. That's Grandma's eyes I see in you right now. You don't trust me? You don't think we should go?"

Rachel managed a lazy shrug of the shoulders.

"I'm not on drugs honey," Cody said. "I swear on your Mom's soul."

"I know Dad," she said. I'm just scared."

He pulled her closer. She was so beautiful and innocent – the only perfect thing in his life. And she'd remained perfect – thank God for that. Had Cody stayed in Hollywood to try and claw back his career, the industry would have noticed her. It would have sunk its teeth into Rachel and ruined her like it did for her mother, Kate. No chance – that was one of several reasons that Cody and Kate moved to Texas ten years ago. Cody would die before he gave those bigwig assholes in LA the chance to get their hands on his daughter.

He smiled at Rachel.

"I'm scared too," Cody said. "But we have to go. You've watched the reports on TV. You've heard it on the radio. You know what people are doing to themselves, to each other out there. You know how dangerous it is and you know how dangerous *she* is."

Rachel didn't blink. Despite her saying she was scared, she looked calm –older than her ten years. Sometimes Cody thought, kids did adulthood better than most adults.

"Is it the woman in the long black dress?" she said.

"Yes honey. It's the woman in the long black dress."

Rachel nodded.

"I saw her in my room last night," she said.

Cody's hands fell off his daughter's arms. His mouth hung open and the cold air that haunted the MacLeod residence slid down the back of his throat. He looked at Rachel, his eyes racing over her blue denim dungarees and the white long sleeved t-shirt that she was wearing underneath. He ran a finger down her blue and white basketball shoes, not sure what he was looking for. Damage – but what sort of damage?

With cupped hands, he touched her face.

"She was in your room?" Cody said. "Last night? Did she say anything? I mean, did she try and talk to you – to make you do anything? Did she tell you to hurt yourself?"

Rachel shook her head.

"She was just standing at the edge of the bed looking at me," she said. "Her face *is* like a mannequin. That's what they said on TV. She looks like a giant doll with silver lights instead of eyes."

"Weren't you scared?" Cody said. His heart was pounding.

"No," Rachel said. "Well, not really."

Cody buried his face in the palm of his hand.

"Jesus Christ," he said, almost losing his balance and toppling over onto the hardwood floor. "Tell me something kid," he said. "This is really important. Is that the first time you've seen her?"

"Yes."

"Well then it's definitely time to go," Cody said. "She's starting to pay too much attention to this family for my liking."

Rachel's eyes were wide open. "You've seen her too?"

Cody nodded. "Yeah." *Several times.*

"They've been talking about her on the radio Dad," Rachel said. "People are seeing her everywhere. China, Europe, Australia, Brazil and lots of other places that I've never heard of."

"Yeah I know," Cody said. He was itching to leave. He wanted to grab Rachel and get her out of the house immediately.

"All the people who see her end up dead," Rachel said. "That's what they say, isn't it?"

Cody squeezed tight on her hand.

"Not everyone," he said. "Like I said, I've seen her too."

"In the house?"

"Yeah, in the house. That's why we need to go."

Rachel looked thoughtful. Her eyes darted around the living room before returning to him.

"Is she chasing the world? The whole world?"

Cody straightened the collar of his black cotton shirt.

"Yeah honey," he said. "I think she's chasing the world. And that includes us – you and me. We've got to get away from this house because I'm not going to let anything happen to you. Okay?"

Cody was glad to see that Rachel could still smile.

"Okay," she said.

Outside the Black Storm grumbled. It sounded like it was an angry giant sitting on the roof of their house, waiting impatiently for them to come out.

Cody tugged gently on Rachel's arms. She didn't move.

"Where are we going?" she said.

It was a good question.

Cody nodded. "You remember my friend?" he said. "A big guy called Nick Norton?"

Rachel shook her head.

"Sure you do," Cody said. "You met him once. He works on Alaska Airlines, flies out of San Antonio all the time. He's an old school buddy of mine from LA. He was in the movies too when he was a kid, just like your old man."

"I don't know," Rachel said.

"Big black guy, all mouth and muscle. He was over here about four years ago. You must remember – it's not like we have a ton of guests or anything like that."

"What about him?"

Cody leaned in closer. He felt the need to whisper.

"He's got a plane," he said. "It's a big plane – Boeing 737-800, fully fuelled and ready to go. He's invited us along – some of the other pilots and their friends and family will be there too. I got a text from Nick about fifteen hours ago – the plane is at the airport right now, waiting for everyone to arrive. You understand? We're going to drive down to the airport and get on Nick's plane."

Cody's face darkened.

"Only problem is I can't get in touch with Nick anymore," he said. "My phone keeps jamming up."

Rachel's eyes lit up – a mixture of fear and curiosity.

"Because of the Black Storm?"

"Maybe," Cody said. "But it doesn't matter, not as long as we get to the airport in good time. He'll wait for us, I know he will."

Rachel's expression was grim.

"We're going up into the black sky?" she said, pointing to the ceiling. "What's up there?"

Cody followed her finger towards the ceiling. Kids and their questions, damn it. Who knew what was up there in that black shroud that had wrapped itself over the Earth? Something, maybe nothing. Everything was black these days – even the inside of the MacLeod residence. The curtains were pulled over all the windows, shielding them from the sight of the Black Storm, the mysterious force that had come out of nowhere and robbed the world of sunlight.

"It can't all be bad up there," Cody said. "We gotta try. Anything's better than staying down here on the ground while people go mad and do bad things. I'll bet you it's safer up there. Yeah?"

Rachel looked down the hall towards her bedroom.

"I want to take Bootsy with me," she said. "If we're not coming back."

Cody sighed. He couldn't hide his growing frustration any longer. They should have been gone already. He didn't want to hang around the house one second longer than he had to. He tugged gently on her arm, with more urgency this time.

"You're too big for that teddy bear," he said. "You're ten."

The look on her face stopped him dead.

"Mom gave him to me," she said. "Remember?"

Of course he did.

"I've packed a ton of photos of Mom in the bag," he said. "Lots of photos. We're not going to forget her."

"I want Bootsy," Rachel said. Cody almost smiled – it was like Kate all over again. If she wanted something, she was going to have it.

"Alright kid," he said, letting go of her arm. "Get Bootsy but don't stay in that bedroom one second longer than you have to. I'll grab the bags."

Cody watched her run down the hallway. He felt uneasy watching her go through the bedroom door knowing that the Black Widow had been in there last night. Cody had already seen the ghostly figure several times in the house but there had been no words spoken. That was something to be grateful for at least. And now the Black Widow was coming after Rachel? Any doubts Cody might have been having about leaving had shattered with that revelation.

A few seconds later, Rachel came running back down the hallway with the beat-up teddy bear swinging at her side. She looked content.

"All set?" Cody asked. "Can we go now?" He picked up the two backpacks and flung one over each shoulder.

She nodded. "Just one thing?"

"Oh c'mon Rachel. Let's get out of here."

"Who is she Dad?"

The two backpacks slid down Cody's arm in slow motion. He squatted so that he was almost eye level with Rachel.

"She came out of the Black Storm," he said. "At least that's what people say but we don't know for sure. Everything – the black sky, black rain and the Black Widow – they're all connected. All these things are part of the Black Storm."

"And it makes people do bad things?" Rachel said.

Cody nodded. "Very bad things."

Rachel smiled. It was a great smile – sudden and unexpected.

"We'd better go," she said.

"Right honey," Cody said. "Now you're talking."

He opened the front door and they stepped outside.

It was dark. A permanent state of dusk hung over the world – a rotten, simmering blackness and it was everywhere. It was unending too. Blue skies and sunlight were a distant memory. The air was thick and muggy and scentless. A stiff wind was blowing and the trees that surrounded the remote two-story house were swaying.

They walked towards the car in the driveway. Cody's white 1970 Dodge Challenger was one of only a few references left to his Hollywood past. He was probably the only part-time freelance writer in the world who owned such a vintage car. It was a little much but Cody loved the Challenger with all his heart. It was a perfect replica of the car used in *Vanishing Point*, one of his top five all time movies. It wasn't just an ornament either – he kept the

Dodge in outstanding driving condition and a good thing too – he was going to need it firing on all cylinders if it was going to get them to the airport.

The surface of the car was covered in a thin layer of dirt. Cody didn't have time to worry about it – he opened up the trunk and threw the bags in, pushing them all the way to the back. As he did so, Rachel jumped into the back seat taking Bootsy with her.

"Take me somewhere nice!" she called out. She always said the same thing when she got in the car.

"Sure thing Miss Daisy," he said.

Cody opened up the driver's door. Before he sat down, he reached a hand underneath the seat, checking that the Glock 19 he'd stashed earlier was still there.

It was. He gave the pistol a quick pat and hoped that he wouldn't need it.

Cody climbed into the Dodge and turned the key in the ignition. He heard the 426 Hemi engine growling and hell yes it was a satisfying sound, even under the most trying of circumstances. Taking a deep breath, he gripped the wood grain steering wheel and allowed himself one last look at the house where his wife had died, knowing that he'd never see it again.

Move it mister. That's what Kate would have said.

Cody backed the car down the driveway and onto Rittiman Road. It was a quiet area with houses spaced far apart, but it had never been so desolate as it was now. Was there anyone left around here?

Rachel was quiet in the back – perhaps thinking about her Mom, a woman that she'd barely known and yet someone who had cast a long shadow over her young life. Or maybe Rachel was thinking about the house – it was the only home she'd ever known after all. She was leaving her friends and school behind – but none of those things mattered now. Keeping her alive, that's what mattered.

The Dodge set off, picking up speed.

Cody looked back at the house in the rear-view mirror. One last look.

That's when he saw her.

The Black Widow was standing on the narrow road that stretched north behind them. Her porcelain doll-like skin glowed against the surrounding darkness; it was a nightmarish beacon that offered anything but hope to those who had the misfortune to see it. She was tall – at least seven feet and rake thin like a skeleton with a thin layer of flesh wrapped around her bones. Her bright red hair was styled in an old-fashioned Edwardian coiffure. It was a look that went well with the long black Victorian-style mourning dress that trailed behind her.

The Black Widow's eyes – dazzling silver orbs, devoid of pupils watched them go. She didn't try to stop them but Cody felt little in the way of relief, even as the phantom faded into the distance behind them.

She was letting them go. At least for now.

CHAPTER TWO

The Challenger's headlights pierced through the fog of dark morning. Apart from the lights on the car, the only other light available came from a fierce, reddish-orange glow that loomed on the horizon.

San Antonio was burning.

Cody shuddered. He could only imagine what was going on in the city.

He looked on both sides of the highway. There were few other cars on the road. Cody figured that the traffic would be busier – that people wouldn't just be sitting at home waiting for the shit to hit the fan. Of course there was plenty of shit already dripping off the fan but things were getting worse, not better.

There was some measure of comfort to be found in driving. Movement. It was better than sitting at home, waiting for the end.

Of course most people didn't have anywhere to go. Cody and Rachel at least had the dream of the airport, the plane and God willing they'd find something better. No matter what the radio reports were saying about the Black Storm being everywhere, there had to be somewhere out there still under a blue sky. Even if it was in the remote, inhospitable corners of the country where there were no other people.

"You alright kid?" Cody said.

"Yeah," Rachel said.

They were driving south on U.S Route 281, almost two thousand miles of continuous road that stretched down from the Canadian Border to the humid confines of Brownsville, Texas. To see the highway so dark and empty – it was unnerving. It was enough for Cody to debate several times in his mind whether he'd made the right decision to leave Spring Branch or not. But when he thought about the Black Widow's visit with Rachel – that did it. He knew that leaving was the right call.

Let everyone else sit at home, he thought.

Cody glanced up towards the sky. A few chinks of sunlight were still visible – they'd fought their way through the stranglehold of the Black Storm and it was a meek reminder that it was still daylight, at least according to the clocks.

A few specks of rain landed on the windshield. Black rain – thick, oil-like drops falling from the sky. Cody turned on the wipers and cleared the windshield quickly before he lost sight of the road. He hoped that there wouldn't be a heavy downpour of the stuff that would force them to stop and wait it out on the side of the highway.

"How long till we get there?" Rachel asked, calling out from the back seat.

Cody kept his eyes out front. He racked his brain, trying to recall the precise location of the airport. If he remembered correctly, the airport was about nine or ten miles north of the downtown business district. With any luck, he'd avoid the worst of the carnage and most importantly, the airport would still be intact. Nick had texted him from the terminal building only yesterday so it had to be okay. The worst-case scenario didn't bear thinking about.

"Shouldn't take too long," Cody said. "It's about a thirty-five minute drive on a good day. Maybe a little longer now. I don't want to drive too fast when the visibility is this bad."

She sighed, like it wasn't good enough.

"Hey," he said, glancing in the rearview mirror. He caught a glimpse of Rachel sitting upright with Bootsy on her lap. It looked like she was a ventriloquist and the teddy bear was her dummy. Under normal circumstances, Rachel wouldn't be seen dead with Bootsy, not at ten years old. But these weren't normal circumstances.

"We're going to make it," Cody said.

"I know," Rachel said.

"Let's see if we can get something on the radio," Cody said. Anything to take their minds off this damn road trip.

Cody's fingers turned the dial clockwise. An explosion of static blurted out. He screwed up his face as he tried to find something in the electronic mess – there had to be someone still broadcasting out there, even if it was just a guy sitting alone in his basement.

As he wrestled with the dial, Cody caught a glimpse of his reflection in the rearview mirror. Jesus, it looked like he hadn't slept for days, which wasn't far from the truth. He was forty-two years old but he looked older – at least today he did. His dirty blond hair, which had once been the same bright shade as Rachel's, was long and wavy. His skin looked grey and there was a fine layer of brownish-blond stubble on his face.

"You look like shit," Cody said. There was nothing of the cute, fresh-faced star who'd lit up movie screens around the world back in the 1980s. That kid was long gone.

"Who are you talking to?" Rachel said.

Cody backed away from the mirror. "Talking to myself," he said. "Just acting crazy, it's all good honey."

At last, a woman's voice came through the radio.

"You found something," Rachel said.

"Yes I did," Cody said, with a tired smile. He leaned closer to the radio and turned the volume up.

It sounded like a news report:

Who is the Black Widow?

Sightings of the mysterious Black Widow continue at an alarming rate all over the world. Suicides are through the roof. The murder rate is up. The world is self-harming on a scale never seen before in recorded history. A terrible net of depression and despair has been cast over us.

The Black Fever, some people have called it.

It started earlier this year. Multiple sightings of a tall woman dressed in Victorian mourning clothes were reported but these were treated as a hoax. This started in the United State and later spread to Europe, Africa, the Middle East, Asia and so on. These Black Widow sightings coincided with reports of severe weather anomalies – unusually dark skies that lingered long into the daylight hours, black clouds, black oily rain, and violent winds.

This was the coming of the Black Storm. But we took it lightly and did nothing until it was too late. Even then, what could we have done? Time passed and Black Widow sightings escalated dramatically and spread across all continents – even to sparsely populated research stations in Antarctica.

Our crops began to fail. Had Mother Nature turned against us, like so many were saying? Was the human race being punished for its sins?

Or was it something else?

If it's something else, then what is it? What is the Black Storm? Did it come from another world? Did it originate from deep within the bowels of our own planet? Scientists, the leading experts, and government analysts – you name it, all over the world these people have tried to figure out what's going on. Maybe some of them are still trying even now. Truthfully however, nobody knows what's happening. We haven't got a clue and that's an agonizing thing for an advanced, intellectual alpha-species like ourselves to admit.

We are helpless.

Now all we can do is watch. A permanent darkness has settled over the world – both outside and inside our hearts. Soon nothing will grow. Our water will run out if nothing but black rain continues to fall. There's been a high level of natural disasters, floods, earthquakes, avalanches and more. Most disturbing of all is that the amount of people committing suicide continues to grow at an alarming rate. There can be no doubt that the Black Storm is directly responsible for the obscene spike in suicides, murders, and acts of mass destruction.

Lord knows I'm trying to add something optimistic. To do so however, would be patronizing.

Cody switched off the radio. It was depressing. Amateur or professional, almost everything on the airwaves now was about the Black Storm and the terrible things people were doing. There was no point in switching the radio on anymore and yet Cody always went back to it sooner or later. Maybe he craved the sound of someone else speaking more than he'd like to admit.

"Dad?" Rachel said.

"Yeah honey?"

"Do you miss being famous?"

"What?" he said, looking at Rachel in the mirror. "Where'd that come from? No, I don't miss being famous."

"I think you do," Rachel said. She was looking at Bootsy, still sitting on her lap. "I think Mom missed being famous too."

Cody understood now. Rachel was trying start a conversation about her mother. It wasn't the first time she'd asked Cody a question out of the blue and then flipped the subject – whatever it was – back onto her mother. *Did you do this Dad? Did Mom do that?* Cody always felt that the end goal of these conversations for Rachel was to find out more about her mother's death. She knew plenty about Kate's life but Cody had always spared his daughter the grim details of her mom's last days when drugs and depression had taken hold. It was an ugly ending to a sad story. Rachel didn't need to know any more than that and Cody always took care to steer the conversation away from Kate's death.

"Yeah," Cody said. "Mom did miss being famous. And if I'm honest, I miss being famous sometimes too. We were younger than you when we made our first movies, both of us. Your Mom was such a beautiful kid – she was really something. Knocked me off my feet kid."

"You were beautiful too Dad."

Cody glanced over his shoulder. "Thanks," he said.

Rachel was leaning forward. Cody sensed that she wanted to talk.

"You think Eddie Faldo's dead?" Rachel said.

"Eddie Faldo?"

Cody squeezed down hard on the steering wheel. Eddie Fucking Faldo. Barely a day went past when that name didn't go through his mind at least once. Usually it was more than once. Having said that, Cody would never bring the name up in conversation with anyone. In fact, if anyone started discussing the latest Eddie Faldo movie in a restaurant or in the grocery store and began gushing about how goddamn wonderful it was, Cody would make a point of getting up and leaving the room.

"Why are you asking me that?" Cody said. "A lot of people are dead. Why ask me about Eddie?"

"Because you hate him, don't you?" Rachel said. "It annoys you anytime anyone talks about him. Wouldn't you be happy if he was dead?"

"Whoa now!" he said.

Cody didn't like to hear Rachel using the word 'hate' out loud. Must be his parents' hippy influence alive and well in his mind. Love and peace – that was the foundation of his unusually liberal upbringing. That and the constant round of Hollywood auditions he'd endured as a young child. Then the money came along. Turned out that material things like a shitload of cash weren't off his parents' radar either. What a journey – from beloved child of nature to family cash cow in less than a year. It still made him dizzy thinking about it.

"I don't hate Eddie Faldo," Cody said. "Maybe I was a little jealous of the guy. You know we starred in that big film together?"

"*The Forever Boys*," Rachel said. "Of course I know that."

"Yeah," Cody said. "Well that was our big break into the movies. We were both lined up for big things after it became a huge hit. It didn't quite work out for me. I met your Mom and we fell in with a bad crowd, as you know. Eddie, God bless him, was straight – black coffee was about as dangerous as it got for him. Smart kid, he played the game and look at what happened to him. They groomed him and he turned into an asshole and now he's never off the big screen. Eddie any-shitty-movie Faldo. But I don't hate him."

"You hate him," Rachel said.

"I don't like him," Cody said. "I sure hope he isn't dead though."

Cody was about to say something else when a loud rumble in the distance stopped him in his tracks. At first he thought it was thunder but then he saw a fresh spurt of orange fire appear on the horizon, rising above all the others like it was a cannonball shooting straight for the black sky.

It was coming from San Antonio.

"My God," Cody said. "What's happening over there?"

How many people were still alive in the city? Had they all succumbed to the Black Fever? Cody had always envisioned the end of the world as being instantaneous. A nuclear blast – a fireball, hot blinding light and then nothing. With any luck he'd be vaporized and not feel a thing. It was wishful thinking by the looks of it. If this was the end, if the Black Storm was bringing with it the mass extinction of humankind, then it was taking its goddamn time.

"I don't want to go there Dad," Rachel said.

"I don't either kid," Cody said. "But I'm sure the airport is okay."

But was it? The Black Widow was everywhere, spreading the Fever, putting it into the hearts of the masses, inciting acts of violence and destruction that would bring down human civilization. But why? Nobody had the faintest idea what the Black Storm was or where it came from. As the radio report said, experts from all walks of life had failed to explain what was happening. The military had failed. Anything that had been sent up to the black sky to investigate had either vanished or crashed back to Earth almost immediately.

Cody looked towards the flaming ruins of San Antonio.

That's where I'm taking Rachel?

The back seat squeaked as Rachel sat forward.

"It's so dark," she said. "It's cold too. Can you see the road okay Dad?"

"I can see honey," Cody said. "Don't worry. I'll get us to the airport if it's the last thing I do." Under his breath he muttered: "Which it just might be."

"But we can't outrun her can we?" Rachel said.

Cody's ears pricked up. There was something strange about Rachel's voice. It sounded flat and hopeless, like she'd given up.

He resisted the urge to look back.

It *was* cold in the car though. She was right about that.

"You don't think we're going to make it?" Cody said. "That doesn't sound like you."

"The Black Storm is everywhere," Rachel said, her voice sluggish.

"Hey that's enough of that," Cody said. "We're the MacLeods

from the Clan MacLeod, remember? Just like in *Highlander* baby – we're immortals and we're going to live forever. Ain't nothing going to stop us getting on Nick's plane. Right? You tell me kid, tell me why we can't outrun the Black Widow?"

There was a moment of silence.

"Because she's sitting next to me," Rachel said.

CHAPTER THREE

Cody's heart was hammering as he pulled the car into the side of the road.

He slammed his foot on the brake, pushing the pedal onto the floor and keeping it pressed there. The Dodge Challenger skidded to a halt, missing the cable barrier on the central reservation by inches.

Cody unbuckled his seatbelt and looked in the backseat. Rachel was sitting alone, clutching Bootsy tightly to her chest. She was looking back at Cody, wide-eyed and petrified.

There was no one else in the car.

"Where is she?" Cody yelled. He didn't wait around for an answer. He pushed the driver's door open, jumped out of the car and then pulled at the back door like he was trying to pull the damn thing off at the hinges.

Rachel hurried out of the Dodge quickly, taking the teddy bear with her. Cody could hear short gasps coming out of her mouth as she fought for breath.

"You okay?" he said. "Talk to me."

She nodded. "I'm okay."

Cody stared into the empty backseat area. There was nobody in there. He kept looking for a minute, fixating on the spot where Rachel had been sitting just seconds earlier. He was waiting for the Black Widow to materialize. He thought about getting his gun from underneath the driver's seat but he didn't. No point in frightening Rachel. And would a gun even work against that thing? It seemed unlikely.

"She's gone," Rachel said. "But she was there – I saw her."

"Yeah," Cody said. He took a backwards step away from the car. The adrenaline was still coursing through his body.

"She's gone," he said.

Cody looked at Rachel and tried to smile. He took several deep breaths while the warm air pinched on his skin.

"You believe me don't you?" Rachel said. Her tone was apologetic.

Cody nodded. "Of course I believe you," he said. "But what happened? She didn't try and talk to you did she?"

Rachel was squeezing Bootsy so tight that her fingers were on the brink of stabbing through the bear's fur. Her knuckles were chalk white.

"She didn't say anything," Rachel said, looking at the ground. "I felt cold. Really cold. Sleepy too. I fell asleep for like a second and when I opened my eyes, she was there sitting beside me. And she was staring at me again – I don't like the way she stares at me Dad."

Cody checked both sides of the highway and was satisfied that no other traffic was coming their way. He should have flipped his hazards on when they stopped but that was the last thing he'd been thinking about. It didn't matter – they weren't staying long.

He kneeled beside Rachel.

"I don't like the way she stares at me either," he said. "But she's gone now. It's just you and me little lady. And we've got a plane to catch." He looked up at the black sky and felt darkness wrap itself

27

around them. "It all looks the same now doesn't it?" he said, pointing a finger at the sky. "You'd never believe it was morning right now, huh?"

"I miss the sunshine," Rachel said, not looking up. "The feel of the sun."

"That's your Californian blood talking," Cody said with a smile. "We'd better go kid. Now if you see anything else in the car or if it starts to get cold like that again, you tell me. Got it?"

She nodded. In the gloomy haze cast by the Dodge's taillights, Cody saw Kate in her eyes and felt like he couldn't love his daughter any more. Of all the people in Cody's rollercoaster life that had come and gone – and there had been a lot of people – Rachel was the one good thing that had lasted.

The Black Widow wasn't going to take her away from him.

Rachel smiled. "We could pretend all this is just a movie," she said. "That it's make-believe."

Cody raised an eyebrow. "You think that'd help?"

"Yeah."

"Yeah, that's the spirit," Cody said. "Clan MacLeod. The immortals."

"And we're the good guys?"

"Of course," Cody said. "What else? And the good guys always make it. Hey, you know what else kid?"

She shrugged. "What?"

Cody leaned over and kissed her on the forehead. "All movies end," he said, standing up and checking the highway for traffic again.

Rachel looked up. Her blue eyes roamed the sky, as if searching for the lost stars. "Where will this movie end?" she asked. "Up there?"

Cody shook his head. "No," he said. "When we find a new home."

"You really think there's somewhere?" she said.

"There's always somewhere."

Cody pointed to a small dot of yellowish-white light in the black sky. It was nothing and yet it was everything. It was a freckle of hope. It was a chink in the armor of the Black Storm and a hint that the sun, stars and the moon were still up there. The old things hadn't been eradicated. The Black Storm had locked them out.

Rachel looked up at the faint speck of light, her eyes wide with hope.

They stood there for a few seconds, both of them hypnotized and looking towards the sky.

"Thirsty?" he said, scratching at the stubble on his face.

Rachel nodded. "Yep."

Cody went over to the car and opened up the trunk. There were eight multipacks of bottled water in the back, sitting next to a huddle of reusable shopping bags full of food. Canned food mostly, along with the water and several large bottles of multi-vitamins.

Bullets were another priority taking up space in the trunk. Cody had stocked up at the local arms supplier when things had gotten worse and he wasn't the only one. What a day that was. It was like Black Friday for gun fanatics. People were grabbing guns and bullets off the shelves like they were reaching for life preservers on a sinking ship. The events of that day only fell short of anarchy because almost everyone appeared to be paying for their goods before leaving the store. Cody had grabbed as many boxes of 9mm ammo as he could carry and he'd gotten the hell out of there before stocks ran out.

He pulled out a small bottle of water, unscrewed the cap and handed it to Rachel. She took a long drink, wiped her mouth dry and handed it back to him. Cody finished the bottle and felt a little better. He tossed the trash back into the trunk and looked at the food bags stacked up in the corner. His stomach grumbled, despite all the excitement. It had been at least ten hours since he'd last eaten anything. There was a loaf of bread and a jar of peanut butter sticking out the top of the nearest bag. He could always rustle them up a quick roadside breakfast. The bread wouldn't last long – it had been in the freezer until the electricity went off. Maybe this was a good time to use it up. Cody didn't know how long it would be until their next meal.

"Hungry?" he said, turning to Rachel. "Want me to fix you something quick?"

She shook her head. "No."

He nodded and looked down both sides of the highway. Best to keep moving. It wasn't safe stopping on the side of the road, not for too long. When he was on the plane he would sit back and eat as much as he wanted – a mountain of bread and peanut butter and whatever else he could get his hands on. Shit, it was something to look forward to. That and sleep.

"How far to the airport?" Rachel said.

"Didn't you ask me that already?" Cody said.

"I asked how long it would take to get there."

Cody laughed. "Alright smart ass," he said. "From home, it's about twenty-five miles to San Antonio airport. We've chopped off a couple of miles already. Won't be long now. We're doing okay."

Rachel looked up at him. "But we can't drive too fast?"

"No. It's too dark. It's dangerous."

"Let's go then."

Cody looked at her, his eyebrows standing up.

"Who made you captain of this expedition?"

She smiled and walked over to the car. Cody slammed the trunk shut and slid back into the driver's seat. He looked at the road that stretched towards the San Antonio. It looked like the Northern Lights had settled over the city, except this colorful display was violent and man-made.

He turned the key in the ignition. At the same time, he could feel the heat travelling up the highway towards him, scalding his face from afar.

The next few miles were quiet. There were no other cars on the road and no further disturbances over San Antonio.

Cody kept both hands on the wheel. Drowsiness was creeping in fast. He tried to shake it off, to stay sharp. Sleep later, he told himself. But for now, get to the airport and get on that plane. In a normal world it was the simplest of tasks and this time he didn't even have to remember their passports or paperwork or worry about putting their liquids into a little quart-sized bag and taking it through security.

He looked in the rearview mirror. Rachel's head was resting on the back of the seat. Her eyes were closed and her mouth hung open a little. Cody smiled – she always fell asleep in the car without fail and nothing, not even the end of the world was going to stop that.

A cool breeze crept up Cody's arms.

"That's nice," he said.

The constant muggy temperatures had been wearing him down all morning and it wasn't helping him to stay awake. The breeze was welcome but it got colder quickly. Cody rolled up the window and pulled the crumpled sleeves of his black shirt over his forearms.

He saw something out of the corner of his eye. A shape, emerging in the passenger seat.

"Cody it's me."

Cody's fingers clamped down on the steering wheel. He was paralyzed by a sudden onslaught of fear.

She was sitting in the passenger seat.

Cody shook his head.

"No," he said. Don't speak to her. Don't look at her.

"Cody it's me."

Something about the voice. It was familiar.

"Cody it's me."

He looked in the rearview mirror and saw that Rachel was still asleep in the back. Thank God.

"Cody."

He felt his foot sliding off the gas pedal. The car was slowing down. A moment later, they were crawling down the highway at about 15-miles-per-hour.

"You're dead," he said. "You're not real."

"It's me," she said.

Cody plucked up the courage to look at what had appeared in the car.

Kate MacLeod, his deceased wife and the love of his life was sitting in the passenger seat. She looked like she'd done in the last year of her life – beautiful, but damaged like a flower in the early stages of wilting. Her long blonde hair had lost its youthful shine but her magnificent face – the broad forehead, almond-shaped eyes and full lips – they were still exceptional. As it had been in those last years, her cheekbones were so prominent that the word 'addict' might as well have been tattooed onto her forehead.

She'd sat in the same passenger seat many times before. So many warm evenings spent racing along Mulholland Drive in the Dodge Challenger, speeding past the Santa Monica Mountains and glorious orange-red sunsets to die for. Those were some of Cody's happiest memories of his life with Kate.

"What's happening?" Cody said. He spoke quietly, desperate not to wake Rachel up. "It can't be you. You're dead."

"Of course it's me," Kate said, staring at him. She blinked slowly, like a reptile. "It's so good to see you again Cody."

God how he'd missed her. It felt so much longer than ten years.

"It's you?" he said.

He looked at her and she nodded.

"I'm here for *you*. Only you."

"Only me?"

"That's right."

Cody gave a little snort of disgust and snapped out of whatever daze he'd been in.

"You're forgetting something," he said. "Aren't you? You haven't even looked at Rachel once. You haven't asked about *our* daughter, not once. That's her sitting in the back seat by the way. She's ten years old now and she's spent her entire life trying to understand why her Mom wasn't there for her when she was growing up. Thanks for leaving me with that problem."

"I'm so lonely," Kate said. "Over here, on the other side – it gets so lonely. Won't you come back with me?"

"Bullshit," Cody said.

He glanced at her. Her marble-like eyes were empty.

"I know who you are," Cody said. "I know what you do. Sometimes you come to people disguised as friends and family members – even dead ones because people want to see their loved ones so much that they'll believe it. Then you whisper in their ear, do your sweet-talking and they off themselves. Sometimes you convince them to take others with them. Burn the house, burn the street, burn everything. Right? You sick, twisted bitch. Get the fuck out of my car."

"You don't know what it's like over here Cody," Kate said. "It's so beautiful."

"Well I know one thing," Cody said. "I know that I've sunk about as far as any human being could sink in life without dying or going insane. I know that I fought off a hundred Black Storms in my head when you died. But I learned to live with it. I had to for Rachel. So why don't you just fuck off? Please."

A massive explosion lit up the sky behind them. Cody gasped and looked over his shoulder.

A towering fireball was shooting towards the stratosphere.

He looked at Kate, his eyes wide open in horror.

"Was that...?" he said.

"Spring Branch," she said. "Is that what you were going to say?"

Cody's voice was shaking. "Did you just do that?"

Kate's face was expressionless. Doll-like.

"You did it," she said.

She vanished like a ghost. The bitter cold disappeared with her and everything inside the car felt normal again – at least as normal as could be expected.

Cody sat in stunned silence, looking at the smoke plumes billowing in the north. The black sky had lit up under the wreckage of Spring Branch; it looked like a fireworks display that had gotten out of hand.

"What did you do?" he whispered.

Cody thought about the everyday faces he'd encountered in Spring Branch – good people, big hearts and friendly Texan greetings. He envisioned them all, caught up in the Black Fever, driving around town in their cars, pouring a trail of gasoline in their wake and destroying everything that they'd helped build.

He thought about their home.

In a daze, Cody reached for the radio. With any luck, it would at least distract him from the carnage that was unfolding in the rearview mirror.

His trembling hand found the dial.

CHAPTER FOUR

I saw her at the start – a tall woman dressed in mourning clothes.

The Black Storm was in its early days back then. There was no Black Fever, no black rain, and the sky was still kinda blue. We were living a normal day to day routine. Work, jobs, life – you know?

I was on my way to work in Bismarck, North Dakota. I'm in marketing. I was standing at the train station, not far from the platform edge when I heard a woman's voice whisper in my ear – I heard it as clear as I can hear my own voice now. Jump, she said. You have nothing to live for. That voice pushed me forward, taking me closer to the edge of the platform. A train was coming – my train. And the closer the train got to the station, the louder the voice in my ear was.

Jump.

And I nearly did because you know what? She was right, I didn't have anything to live for. Have you ever heard of something the French call L'appel du vide – the call of the void? That's what they call it. It's a strange phenomenon where we feel the urge to do terrible things to ourselves. You might be holding onto a kitchen knife and think what would it be like to stab myself with this? What if I crashed the car? What if I leaned over the cliff just a little further? That sort of thing. The call of the void.

She kept whispering in my ear. I don't know how I fought her off that day. Others haven't been so fortunate. She's already taken my wife and children and grandchildren so I know she's coming back someday.

I won't resist next time. When she comes...

Cody turned off the radio. It sounded like another private broadcast from somebody holed up in a house somewhere. It was like listening to the last ramblings of the doomed.

Wasn't there any hope left?

The horizon to the south was on fire. Cody leaned forward in his seat, taking in the view with both fascination and horror. San Antonio looked like it was under attack. Looking at the city reminded Cody of an old Second World War newsreel that he'd seen about the Allied bombing of Dresden in 1945. The German city had been turned into a firestorm by the Allied bombs over the course of several nights and it looked like something similar was happening in San Antonio. Cody looked up to the sky, half-expecting to see a fleet of fighter jets flying overhead and making towards the city.

A voice in his head told him to turn around. Take Rachel back north, the voice said. Take her into the less populous areas where the destruction wasn't so intense. Where there were less people. Spring Branch might be gone but there were other places they could try.

No, he couldn't do that. Nick was waiting for them at the airport. The plane was waiting. They had to get off this sinking ship somehow, even if there were no guarantees that it would work out once they took off.

They had to at least try.

Cody's eyes followed a distant plume of smoke as it drifted towards the black sky. "Just let me get her to the airport."

He was distracted by a tapping noise at the windshield. Seconds later, the black rain came down in buckets and Cody, cursing quietly, knew what he had to do. He pulled the car to a halt at the side of the road as the sudden downpour of black rain laid siege to the Dodge Challenger.

The heavy oil-like drops crashed to Earth in a furious, machine-gun rhythm. The windows were covered in running black liquid and in a matter of seconds it was impossible to see anything outside the car.

Cody wasn't too concerned about being off the road for long. He knew that as ferocious as these downpours were, they didn't tend to last more than a few minutes. This was sprinter rain, not marathon rain. It was a pain in the ass though, forcing him to take precious minutes out of their journey while they sat on the side of the highway. On top of that he'd have to wipe the car down when it was over and that would eat into their time even more.

"Shit," he said.

He looked behind him. Rachel was still asleep in the backseat. Not even the Spring Branch explosion had woken her up so a little black rain wasn't going to disturb her. She was getting used to the chaos.

"Good for you kid," Cody said quietly.

The rain lasted for about three or four minutes. When it was over, Cody opened the door, stepped into a thick black puddle and ran towards the trunk. Opening it up, he took out one of the large bottles of water and walked around the car, pouring it over the windows. He emptied the bottle onto the roof and doors of the Dodge too, trying to soak through as much of the black rain as possible.

When he was finished, he put the empty bottle back into the trunk. Back inside the car, he turned on the windshield wipers at full speed, clearing the murky glass screen as quickly as he could. When he was satisfied he could see okay, he put his foot to the floor, turned the steering wheel to the right and rolled the Dodge onto the highway.

After the fury of the black rain it was quiet. It was so quiet that Cody flipped on the radio. It was a habit he couldn't seem to break. Not the worst habit he'd ever acquired by a long shot. As he turned the dial, Cody was greeted with blaring static and he brought the volume down to a whisper. He glanced over his shoulder. Rachel was still fast asleep.

Turning the dial a little more carefully, a familiar voice came floating out of the speakers.

"It's so lonely over here Cody," Kate said. "We can be a family again – you, me and Rachel. It doesn't matter, none of this matters anymore. Look at San Antonio and tell me that you're not scared. Well you don't have to be scared. You don't have to go there. There's only pain and death waiting for you if you go there. There's no pain here Cody – only love."

"Get the fuck outta here!" Cody said. His eyes went back and forth between the radio and the road.

"I miss you," Kate said. "I miss Rachel too."

"Now you remember she exists, huh?" Cody said.

"Let go Cody," she said. "Let go of the steering wheel and drive off the highway. End the pain. Take off your seatbelt. Take off Rachel's seatbelt and come to me. Drive fast and hard. I promise I'll be waiting on the other side. Do the right thing for all of us."

Cody felt a bead of sweat running down his forehead. He shot a hand out and turned the radio off. But it was no use – the voice kept coming, like a siren beckoning to him from distant rocks.

"Stop fighting," Kate said. "Stop running. End the pain."

"No," Cody said. "Go away."

"I'm so lonely," Kate said. "Oh how I long for Rachel, my dear baby girl. I need to hold her in my arms again. You know how much she needs her mother. Don't you? Would you deny her a mother's love?"

Cody looked onto the road. Was it really Kate talking to him after all? How could anyone else know how much Rachel yearned for her dead mother? Maybe Kate, wherever she was, maybe she knew and...

"Jesus Christ," he said. "Kate. It can't be you."

There was a lot of sense in what she was saying. Things *were* bad. Look at the world burning on all sides. Maybe there was something better and it wasn't with Nick and his magic plane. That's if the plane was still there. A long shot. A pipe dream. Nick had probably gotten bored waiting for them to arrive. For all Cody knew, Nick Norton and his pals had taken off and now they were up there, sitting on that giant metal island in the sky, drinking champagne and toasting their future in an unknown paradise. Meanwhile Cody was risking everything, driving to an empty airport on the outskirts of a city that was spilling over with people infected with the Black Fever.

Was that fair on Rachel?

"Yes," Kate said. "You know what you have to do."

Cody felt like crying. Poor Rachel. It would crush her. Would she ever forgive him for letting her down if they turned up at the airport and the plane was gone? He looked at her in the mirror. She was asleep – a perfect and innocent child in this god-awful world. She could stay that way – asleep. What sort of father would allow his child to wake up in Hell?

It was so cold in the car.

"Drive fast and hard," Kate said.

Cody looked through the windshield, up at the sky. It was rotten and purplish-black, like a bruise.

"No," he said. "You don't know what you're asking." But his voice was weak. And he found himself wanting her to speak again.

He craved the texture of her voice – telling him, reassuring him that it *was* the right thing to do.

"Kate," he said. "Where are you?"

"I'm here," Kate said. The voice was soft and soothing. "And I'll be there on the other side, waiting for you both. It's so beautiful here Cody – it'll be the three of us, driving around the Santa Monica Mountains, surrounded by the California sun. Forever. You'd like that wouldn't you?"

"Yes," Cody said. He sounded sluggish. "I'd like that."

"Drive fast and hard," Kate said.

Cody nodded. "Yes. Fast and hard."

He knew she was right. And yet there it was – this voice, somewhere at the back of his mind trying to fight her off. It was screaming from a distance, like the voice of someone falling into a deep hole.

"No," he said. "No I can't do it."

He pointed a stabbing finger at the radio.

"I don't quit," he said. "You're the one who quit. You're the one that let us down. And why? Did being a big star in Tinseltown really mean more to you than being a mom to your little girl? More than being a wife? You just couldn't accept it could you? We blew it baby! We drank and snorted our way to the bottom of the Hollywood dung pile. Rachel was our last chance at happiness. Real happiness. A family – we were supposed to be an ordinary family. But you couldn't do it. You brought Hollywood with you."

The words gushed like hot lava out of a volcano.

"I don't quit," he said, looking at the radio. "That Hollywood golden couple label was on both our heads. I was drowning in the same ocean Kate but I swam out of it. You think it wasn't hard for me too? And when everyone tried to get me to stay in LA, telling me that perfect comeback role was right around the corner, don't you think I was tempted? We had a baby on the way – a real baby.

The only way we were going to give her a chance was to get the hell out of Los Angeles."

He'd said the same things to her so many times in his mind.

"This is our chance to start all over again," Kate said. "I can't come to you. But you can come to me."

The voice sounded closer. Like she had her lips pressed up against his ear.

Cody looked in the rearview mirror and saw Kate sitting in the backseat. She was looking at Cody while stroking Rachel's hair with a long pale finger.

It wasn't her sudden appearance that shocked him the most. More than anything else, he was taken aback at the sight of them together – mother and daughter, like it was supposed to be. Rachel hadn't even been a year old when Kate died. He'd imagined so many times what it would be like to see them together had Kate lived.

"My family," she said, not taking her eyes off Cody.

Cody's eyes returned to the road. "Family," he said.

He looked in the mirror again.

Eddie Faldo was sitting in the backseat next to Kate and Rachel. It was the young Eddie Faldo, eleven years old, looking exactly like he'd done in 1985 when he'd starred in *The Forever Boys* alongside Cody. His jet-black hair was slicked back in a greasy fifties style. His olive skin was smooth and flawless, and he wore the same stripy red and white t-shirt and skin-tight jeans that his character, Ziggy, had worn in the film.

"Just do it man," Eddie said, talking in Ziggy's wise-ass Brooklyn accent. In *The Forever Boys*, Cody had played a character called Jared – a shy kid with a stutter and the exact opposite of Ziggy's confident street kid persona. Actors loved stutters – they were Oscar bait and indeed the role had netted the young Cody his first and only Academy Awards nomination. He'd lost out to some old fart actor who'd played a dementia patient in a care home.

Eddie was holding an Oscar statuette in his left hand. The 24-karat gold-plated award was looking at Cody or at least it seemed to be. *Look at what you could have won.* Eddie Faldo had won an Oscar in his early twenties playing an on-screen junkie, a role that Cody had been perfecting in real life around the same time.

"A-a-asshole," Cody said. "Get the f-fuck out of my car."

"Do it Jared," Eddie said. "Drive fast and hard."

Cody felt like he was falling into a deep hole. It felt like his mind was slipping beyond his control. He saw no future. No point in going on, not when it was this hard.

"You're right," he said. "I can end this."

His eyes roamed the side of the highway. There were plenty of trees lined up along the 281 but most of them were tucked in behind a short metal fence. If he drove the car into that little fence, even at high speed he'd be lucky to get whiplash. The utility poles however, those caught his eye. They stretched out along the highway very nicely. Slamming the Dodge into one of those babies, now that would cause some damage.

Cody had already unbuckled his seatbelt by the time he'd decided to go after one of the utility poles. He slowed the car down and stopped in the middle of the highway. Turning around, he reached a hand into the back seat area. Quickly, he found the buckle at Rachel's waist and unclicked it.

Cody checked to see if she was awake. She was still out of it, bless her. Kate and Eddie Faldo, still sitting beside her, urged him onwards with eager, gleaming eyes.

"Do it," Kate said.

"Do it," Eddie said.

Cody turned on the engine and put his foot down on the pedal. The 1970 Dodge Challenger roared as it built up speed and charged forward down the lonely 281.

No more pain. It was for the best.

If the utility pole didn't finish them off there was always the gun. As long as he was still conscious, Cody would reach for the Glock and put both of them out of their misery.

They would be a family again. Driving around the Santa Monica Mountains forever.

The car raced down the highway, picking up speed. The road was like an empty runway, allowing Cody to bring the Dodge up to top speed, almost one hundred and forty miles-per-hour. It was going to be the ultimate takeoff when he hit that pole.

"Dad?"

Rachel sounded far away.

"Don't worry about a thing," Cody said. "It'll all be over soon. I'm taking care of it."

"Dad!" Rachel's voice was louder this time. She was getting closer. "Why are you driving so fast? Slow down. I'm scared."

The voice pulled him back. Cody looked in the mirror and saw Rachel sitting alone in the back seat. There was only Bootsy keeping her company now. He saw the fear and confusion in her eyes and his foot immediately released the accelerator. The Dodge, which had been speeding along at over a hundred miles-per-hour, slowed down quickly.

"Oh my God," Cody said. It felt like he was opening his eyes after a deep sleep only to find that he was lying on the edge of a tall cliff, inches from toppling over the side. "I was going to..."

He wiped the sweat off his face. His skin was burning.

"Rachel," Cody said, trying to pull himself back together. "Put your seatbelt on okay? I think it came off by accident when you were asleep."

"Okay."

As he spoke, he fastened his own belt. Quietly.

"Did you see that?" Rachel said, fixing her seatbelt.

"What? See what?"

"There was someone standing at the side of the road," Rachel said. "I think it was a hitchhiker. We just passed her by a second ago."

Cody looked in the side mirror and saw someone standing at the edge of the highway. A woman was holding a thumb out, looking towards the Dodge with hopeful eyes.

It was not the Black Widow.

Cody pressed the brake and the Dodge slowed to a stop in the middle of the road. Now that the engine was quiet he could hear his heart thumping. He wanted to shout, to punch a hole in the roof of the car – to do something. His head shook back and forth as he tried to understand what had taken place just moments earlier. What happened? It had felt so real – Kate, Eddie, and the certainty he'd felt about killing his daughter, not to mention himself.

Rachel leaned forward in the back.

"Are we giving that woman a ride?" she asked.

Cody looked in the side mirror again. The woman was walking down the road towards the car. The Dodge's bright taillights allowed him a good look at her. She was between fifty and sixty years old with long red, wavy hair that fell down past her shoulders. Her face was pale with strong, handsome features. With her plaid shirt, blue jeans and knee-high boots, she looked the part of a stranded country and western singer. All that was missing was the guitar case in hand.

She had no bags.

"Yeah," Cody said. "Let's help her out. As long as she's going our way." What he didn't tell Rachel was that he would welcome the distraction. That was his main reason for stopping. With any luck, there'd be less interference from malevolent forces if someone else was in the car.

Cody glared up at the black sky. *Fuck you.*

"But you said nobody else was going to be riding with us," Rachel said.

"We can't leave a woman on the side of the road like that," Cody said. "She's likely to get run over or worse. Look she won't interfere with our plans honey. We're going straight to the airport and if she wants, we can drop her off somewhere along the way. That's the best we can do. Okay?"

"Okay," Rachel said.

Cody smiled at Rachel. Then he listened as footsteps approached the driver's side of the vehicle. As he waited for the hitchhiker, Cody closed his eyes and saw Kate's gaunt and waiflike face in the back seat, begging him to die. Begging him to kill their daughter.

CHAPTER FIVE

Cody rolled down the window and the hitchhiker leaned in.

"Going my way?" she said. She was smiling, showing off a set of large front teeth – massive ivory monoliths that glowed in the dark. Her eyes lit up when she noticed Rachel sitting in the back of the car. It was as if the sight of the child reassured her that Cody wasn't an axe murderer and that it was safe to approach.

"Depends," Cody said. "What's your way?"

"Oh Lord," she said, leaning in closer. "Whatever way you're going is my way. I just want to get off this damn highway for starters."

"We're going to the airport," Cody said. "No further. Sorry."

The woman's eyebrows stood up, turning her face into a question mark.

"Well I ain't going *that* far," she said. "I live in one of them cute little suburbs further down the highway. Came up to Spring Branch to see if there was any food or water left in the stores. Figured it was quieter up there – thought they might have some supplies lying around, you know? Came out empty-handed as you can see. Ah sure as hell wasn't walking into San Antonio though.

46

That city's gone up in hellfire and I hear they're all batshit crazy or fleeing in droves. Don't know about the airport though."

Cody looked towards the horizon where a blip of violent color lingered over San Antonio.

"The airport is okay," he said.

The woman pointed a finger at the sky.

"So you're getting on a plane?" she said. "That might be the craziest thing I've heard yet."

"Staying on the ground is crazier," Cody said. "You got a better idea?"

"Nope," the woman said. "I do not. Crazy ideas in crazy times are probably the sanest choice. God speed my friends. All I'm looking for is a little haul further down the highway, that's if you don't mind. I've seen some selfish assholes driving up and down this road and you're the first kind-hearted people who've stopped to help a lady out. What do you say? Can you help old Mary Jane get home?"

Cody smiled. "Mary Jane?"

The woman offered a hand to Cody through the gap in the window.

"That's me darling," she said. "Mary Jane Labelle. Housewife and part-time adventurer. Just trying to get through the Black Storm so I can get back to my man and kids who're probably worried sick." She winked at Rachel. "And my dogs of course. I probably miss them most of all."

Rachel giggled in the back.

Cody took the woman's hand and shook it. Her skin was like sandpaper and the grip was strong.

"I'm Cody," he said. "That's my daughter Rachel."

"Well hello there Rachel," Mary Jane said. She reached through the window and greeted the young girl with a warm handshake. "How are we doing this evening? Is it evening?"

"It's morning," Rachel said.

"Right you are."

Mary Jane, still smiling, turned back to Cody. He saw the hopeful look in her eye.

"Mind if I search you for weapons?" Cody said.

Mary Jane nodded. "Absolutely not," she said. "You'd be crazy if you didn't."

She stepped back from the car and Cody got out. Mary Jane stood on the side of the road. She held her arms out, waiting for him to begin.

Cody hesitated.

"Don't be shy Cody," Mary Jane said. "I ain't going to accuse you of trying to cop a feel or nothing like that. You got a beautiful little girl there and it's only right you want to protect her. Go on and search me. I ain't armed but I understand you gotta find that out for yourself."

"Alright," he said. "Can you put your hands on your head? Fingers interlocked if you don't mind."

"You a cop?"

Cody shook his head as he patted her down. He wasn't a cop but he'd played one in several straight to DVD movies back in the nineties. Thanks to a short spell of research undertaken with the LAPD he knew exactly what he was doing when it came to conducting a standing search.

He started the search from Mary Jane's back because doing it that way reduced the risk of an attack. He asked her to widen her stance, which she did. Afterwards he thoroughly searched the areas on both sides of Mary Jane's body – those parts where it would be easy for her to reach for a weapon if she had one stashed away.

Now it was time to search the more delicate areas. Once again, she seemed to sense that he was uncomfortable.

"C'mon," she said. "This is the most fun I've had in years."

Cody ignored her and got on with it. He felt around the

perimeter of her breast using the side of his hand. When it came to the breast's underside he used the outside of the thumb like he'd been taught to – he recalled this was done to avoid accusations of cupping. He didn't get the feeling that Mary Jane was going to accuse him of anything.

He could feel Rachel's eyes watching him from the car.

"You're pretty good at that," Mary Jane said in a deep, almost masculine voice.

Cody's hands dropped to his sides.

"All done," he said. "You ain't packing."

"I can get in?"

"Sure."

She looked at him, long and hard. Cody got the feeling that she was trying to flirt with him. Maybe he *was* better at conducting a standing search than he realized.

He backed off towards the driver's door.

"Alright let's go," Cody said.

He climbed back into the car and waited. Mary Jane walked at a leisurely pace and eased her way into the passenger seat.

"I like your style," she said to Cody, looking around the inside of the car. "Is this an old-school Dodge Challenger? Or is it a Charger?"

"Challenger."

"Man, these cars rock."

Mary Jane turned around and smiled at Rachel.

"Going on a plane sweetheart?" she said, buckling up her seatbelt.

Rachel nodded, then looked away shyly. "Yeah."

"How exciting," Mary Jane said. When she turned back to the front, Cody saw her glance nervously at the black sky.

"Alright," he said. "Let's go."

Cody drove the Challenger back onto the highway. He barely bothered to check for oncoming traffic anymore because the roads were so quiet and empty. Maybe that would change as they got closer to the city.

An uncomfortable silence lingered. It felt weird having somebody else in the car and Cody didn't like it. But the risk of another encounter with the Black Widow was greatly reduced in company. And with no cup of coffee likely to appear in the near future it would help him stay alert too.

Fortunately the silence didn't last long.

"Say you look familiar," Mary Jane said. She was looking at Cody, her eyes gleaming like he was something sweet and sugary sitting on a supermarket shelf. It was a little unnerving but it was a look that Cody had encountered many times during his film career from giddy fans.

Cody shook his head. "Don't know about that," he said. Ever since moving to Texas a decade ago, he'd heard those four words all lined up in that exact same order, more than anything else.

Say you look familiar.

"What did you say your surname was?" Mary Jane asked.

"I didn't," Cody said.

But Mary Jane didn't seem like the type of woman to take a hint. Her eyes were bulging with curiosity.

"I do know you though," she said. "I'm sure of it."

"Maybe I've just got one of those faces," Cody said. "I probably look like someone you knew once."

Silence followed but he could hear Mary Jane's brain at work. She was sizing him up from the passenger seat. It was something he'd gotten used to a long time ago – strangers gawking at him. At first, back in the 1980s, it had been glorious but as things had gotten worse in his private life, those starstruck eyes had been replaced by looks of pity and the occasional look of disgust. Nowadays he was happy with being Mr. Invisible.

"You're famous," Mary Jane asked. "Am I right?"

"He used to be," Rachel said.

Cody threw Rachel a dirty look from the front.

"Thanks a lot," he said.

Rachel screwed up her face. "What? What did I say?"

He sighed and turned back to the road. "Never mind."

Mary Jane watched this exchange between father and daughter from the passenger seat. Slowly, her eyes lit up and with a deep sigh, she fell back into her seat.

"I know who you are," she said. "Holy sh...sugar!"

Cody looked at her. "Congratulations."

"Who do you think he is?" Rachel said. She was laughing now. If nothing else, at least all this was entertaining her.

Mary Jane glanced over her shoulder. Rachel, putting shyness to the side, leaned closer to her.

"I think," Mary Jane whispered to Rachel, "that your daddy is the blond kid from *The Forever Boys*," she said. "The stutter kid. Which means that your daddy is Cody MacLeod. Am I right?"

Rachel's giggling was all the answer Mary Jane needed.

"I love that movie," Mary Jane said, turning back to Cody. She smiled, showing off her dazzling white teeth. "Always has me in tears at the end. Good Lord, you and that other kid nailed it man. What's his name? Eddie Faldo, yeah. We all watch that movie in my house. Even my kids love it. You know how it comes on TV all the time during the holidays? Well if *The Forever Boys* is on TV, no matter what else is going on in the Labelle house, we'll drop everything and watch it. It's that damn good. Wow – I can't believe the stutter kid just picked me up on the side of the road."

Cody was only half-listening. As Mary Jane talked, he was staring at the raging red sky over San Antonio. He was still wrestling with the possibility that he'd made a mistake in accepting Nick's offer. It wasn't too late to turn around and start driving north. What chance did they have up there in a plane?

"You don't like talking about the past," Mary Jane said. "Do you?"

Cody gave her a lukewarm smile. "Don't worry about it," he said. "Where am I taking you Mary Jane?"

"Stone Oak," she said, pointing a finger at the windshield. "You know it?"

"Sort of."

Cody wouldn't have picked Mary Jane as the Stone Oak type. Not in a hundred years. All those big houses, picturesque views of downtown San Antonio, swimming pools and country clubs – it sure as hell wasn't cheap to live down in that neck of the woods. He'd envisioned Mary Jane as being more of a trailer park type. Or maybe somewhere with a little wooden shack in the backwoods with the confederate flag poking out the top.

He scolded himself for being an asshole.

"That's where you live?" Cody said. As hard as he tried, he couldn't keep the surprise out of his voice.

"That's where my brother lives," she said. Her voice was harder this time around. Colder. Cody wondered if she'd taken offence. "We've been staying with him since all this started."

Cody nodded. That made sense. A lot of families had been sticking close together since the Black Storm.

"You ain't that far from the airport," he said. "If Stone Oak is still standing then maybe the airport is too, right?"

"Sure. I guess."

Cody looked in the rearview mirror. "You okay kid?"

"Uh-huh," Rachel said.

Mary Jane pointed towards the dark road.

"Listen Cody," she said. "You'd better come off the highway before we get to Stone Oak. I ain't seen it for myself but I heard the 281 is a little wild on the outskirts of the city. That's me putting it mildly. There's a lot of human traffic moving this way and that means carjacking, robberies…"

She looked at Rachel briefly, turned back and lowered her voice. "And a whole lot worse," she said.

Cody had heard the same rumors. "Yeah."

"Stick to the suburbs as far as you can going south," she said. "That's the best plan. Might take you a little longer but it'll get you there alive. Get off at Bulverde, travel down the back roads – down Bulverde Road, keeping south till we get to Stone Oak. After you drop me off there, take the 1604 back onto the 281. You'll pass the worst of it. After that, you put the foot down mister and don't slow down or stop for anyone until you reach the airport, you hear me?"

"Yeah I got it," Cody said. "I don't really want to come off the highway though."

Mary Jane nodded.

"I get it," she said. "But there's a lot of distressed city folks spilling out of San Antonio. Some good people for sure, most of them just trying to get away. But there's some bad ones too. You know, the type of people who see opportunity in disaster. Some of them will be coming north. You're driving straight into the eye of the storm Cody. You gotta take care of yourself – you got a little lady here to protect."

As Mary Jane was talking, Cody saw the exit sign for Bulverde at the side of the road.

"Yeah," she said, pointing at the sign. "That's the one. We're going to jump off here and I'll give you directions that'll take us straight to Stone Oak. After that, you're almost home."

Cody didn't want to come off the highway. But he didn't want to run into a gang of violent opportunists spilling out of the city either. They'd be all over the Dodge in seconds. All over Rachel. Mary Jane was right. The quiet roads were his best chance of finding smooth passage to the city. He saw the sense in it but he still didn't like it.

"Alright," he said. "But before we turn off I'm going to pull over so I can take a leak. Might as well get it over with."

"Sure thing," Mary Jane said. "I might even go myself."

"Rachel," Cody said, glancing over his shoulder. Rachel was

sitting upright with Bootsy at her side. "We're going to take a little detour in a minute. Narrow roads, less people. I don't really want to stop once we get on them. You need to go?"

"Okay," she said.

"Good girl."

Cody pulled the Dodge into the side of the highway, a little short of the ramp that led down to Bulverde. He got out the car and Mary Jane and Rachel did likewise.

"Is there a ladies room?" Mary Jane said, her lips curving into a half-smile.

"Over there," Cody said, pointing to the stretch of central reservation at the back of the car. "Little boy's room is up here at the front."

"Sure thing. Let's go Rachel."

Cody walked in the other direction, unzipped his pants and peed. Further down, Mary Jane and Rachel were huddled somewhere out of sight.

He stared into the distance.

To the south, orange fire-clouds and black smoke plumes spewed out of the city. It was neverending. There was however, at least from afar, a strange serenity to be found in that moment. While he was by himself, Cody felt like he was the last human being in the world.

"Say what you will," he said, shaking out the last drops. "But if that's the end of the world, it's kind of beautiful."

CHAPTER SIX

Cody was the first one back in the car. While he waited for Rachel and Mary Jane to finish up, he turned on the radio.

Static. Of course.

He persevered and turned the dial back and forth. After about ten seconds of electronic hissing and spitting, he found something. A brief spurt of electric guitar, a stabbing rhythm, and a familiar Irish bluesy voice sang out to him. Cody knew the song. It was 'Moonchild' by Rory Gallagher. The first time he'd heard that song was ten years ago when he and a pregnant Kate had undertaken the long drive from California to Texas to start their new life away from Tinseltown. They'd insisted on driving to Spring Branch because somehow it would feel more real than hopping on a plane and just landing in Texas a few hours later. They wanted to feel the wheels turning underneath them. They wanted to look over their shoulders and watch as Los Angeles faded into the background.

The music didn't last long. The static returned and the memories slipped away inside the white noise.

About a minute later, the front door opened and Mary Jane

squeezed back into the passenger side. Rachel climbed into the back seat.

"Oh man," Mary Jane said. "I needed that."

"All aboard?" Cody said.

Rachel picked up Bootsy and put the scruffy-looking bear back on her lap.

"Yeah," she said.

Cody looked at her and shook his head.

"You haven't given that bear a single glance since you were five years old," he said. "Now you're best pals again?"

Rachel's eyes scowled at him.

"We all need our vices Cody," Mary Jane said, tossing a wink in Rachel's direction. "Lord knows when my cigarettes run out there's going to be hell to pay. My poor Harry and the kids. This Black Storm ain't gonna look much worse than a stiff breeze compared to what I'm going to put them through when the tobacco dries up."

She made a mock angry face at Rachel.

Rachel laughed.

Cody saw the way they were looking at each other. It wasn't a bear that Rachel needed – it was a mom. He'd tried his best to be both a father and mother to her over the years but there were some things a young girl needed that only a woman could provide.

With a sigh, Cody turned the dial on the two watt Music Master radio. He was chasing after that lost piece of music. He wanted the others to hear it too. He wanted them to know that there were still people out there putting music on the radio and that it was something to be hopeful about. At the very least, let them hear it again. When was the next time they'd be able to listen to music?

But he couldn't find it.

Cody was about to give up fidgeting with the radio when he caught onto a woman's voice amidst the static.

Anybody out there getting this? I'm in Arkansas and things are real bad here, especially with planes going missing or falling out the sky. Seems to be happening all the time nowadays. I heard this morning that another flight has been reported missing out of Little Rock. It's the third one this week, another small private passenger aircraft and that makes it the ninth this month that has seemingly vanished into thin air. That's not counting all the planes that have crashed into buildings, highways and into the Arkansas River.

All commercial passenger flights have been suspended, we know that much. Still, private jets and light aircraft are venturing up into the sky at great risk not only to themselves but also to those on the ground. Yeah I get why they're doing it. I know a lot of people are stranded far from home. It must be horrible to be so far from your loved ones. Especially with all this going on. These latest incidents aren't expected to stop people from trying to make private arrangements with local pilots to get home but my advice to you all is to stay on the ground. Look at what's happening for Christ's sake. You think it's bad on the ground? Trust me, it ain't much better up there. The Black Storm will spit you out of the sky. The Black Widow will show up in the cockpit, whisper into the pilot's ear and then...

Cody turned the radio off. He was about ready to take a hammer to that damn thing.

The silence that followed was excruciating.

Cody?" Mary Jane said, after about a minute. "Are you sure you know what you're doing? That ain't the first time I've heard about that kind of thing – planes crashing into buildings, roads and whatever. Up in the sky – that sounds like a bad place to be if the pilot gets a dose of the Black Fever."

"We're not going on a Lego plane," Cody said. He kept his eyes on the road but could feel her looking at him. "There's a fully-fuelled Boeing 737 waiting for us at the airport. It ain't exactly a ten-seater job."

Mary Jane lowered her voice.

"Used to be the big planes that went down first," she said. "Before they grounded them."

Cody hoped Rachel wasn't listening in. He had a feeling she was.

"Nick's taking seven or eight pilots with him," he said. Damn it, he didn't want to talk about this right now. "Anything weird goes down, it's covered."

"Yeah maybe so," Mary Jane said. "But where exactly are you going to go? You got fuel, you got pilots – you got a destination?"

Cody looked through the windshield and pointed to a break in between the dark sky. A speck of white-golden light shone back at them, piercing through the black sky like a laser cutting through metal.

"Up there," Cody said. "Somewhere..."

"Over the rainbow?" Mary Jane said. "That's nice but..."

"Have you looked at San Antonio lately?" Cody asked. "You really want to hang around and be a part of that?"

"No I don't," Mary Jane said. "But where are you going to go where it ain't the same thing happening?"

Cody bit his lip. "Nick's a great pilot – he'll find a way."

Mary Jane sighed. "I'm all for hanging onto hope," she said. "And I don't mean to bring you down. But honestly, it sounds a bit like out of the frying pan and into the fire to me."

Cody put his foot down as they approached the ramp to Bulverde.

"You know I saw her tonight," Mary Jane said. "I saw the Black Widow. On the road, not long before you guys showed up. Jesus, I thought my time was up. I thought she was bringing me some of that Black Fever. Thought I was going to end up stepping out in front of the next car that came speeding along the highway at a hundred miles per hour. She wasn't far away, about fifteen or twenty meters. Those eyes man, or whatever you call them – they were looking right at me. *Through* me – like she was drilling down into my soul."

She smiled but her eyes were fearful at the recollection.

"Tell me something Cody."

"What?"

"You think all this is real?" she said. "You think the Black Storm is real? Or do you think we've all gone crazy? What is it they said? That some military-constructed virus has gone airborne and we're all having the same mass hallucination. What's going on?"

"Don't know," Cody said. "I've stopped trying to make sense of it."

He drove the Dodge towards the ramp and down into Bulverde. Cody knew little about the area he was going through. He knew that Bulverde was a tiny city with a population of less than five thousand and that it was located on the outskirts of San Antonio. He wondered if they'd see any people once they got into the suburbs to drop Mary Jane off. What he'd give to see something humdrum and ordinary right now. Kids playing in a park, people jogging on the sidewalk – boring suburban activities like that. Where was everyone? Were they all hiding indoors, listening to the radio and waiting for the all clear? Or were they dead already?

Off the highway, the roads were darker and quieter.

"Stay on this track for a little bit," Mary Jane said. Her voice sounded louder in the stillness of the back roads. "There's a right turn coming up that'll take us onto Bulverde Road," she said. "After that we're on our way down to Stone Oak. It's easy when you know how."

"Alright," Cody said. "Just tell me when."

"This one here," Mary Jane said, pointing straight ahead. Cody could barely see the turn until he'd almost driven past it.

"Bulverde Road," Mary Jane said. "Right there."

"I see it now."

Cody turned the steering wheel to the right. He felt uneasy as the car drove onto the narrow and claustrophobic Bulverde Road. Only the Dodge's headlights prevented a total blackout from swallowing them up. Large trees stood on both sides of the road, swaying menacingly in the wind.

"Wow," Cody said. "It's creepy down here. Right?"

Mary Jane didn't answer. She was a dark, faceless shape, sitting like a statue and staring out at the road. He looked over at her. Conversation wasn't exactly Cody's thing, but it would at least take the edge off things.

"Right?" he said.

Nothing.

Where was that soft, jovial Southern humor when you needed it? Of course she had good reason to be quiet. It was scary as hell around these parts and who wanted to talk about it? Just shut up and get through it. Maybe she was worried about her family.

Cody wished he'd never left the highway. The airport felt further away than ever since they'd left the house.

Several minutes passed. Only the humming sound of the Dodge's Hemi engine could be heard.

Rachel sat forward in the back seat. Quickly, like she'd sat on something sharp.

"Dad, what's that?"

Her slim figure squeezed in between the two front seats. She was pointing at something on the side of the road.

Cody looked over that way.

Movement.

Dark shadows were emerging from behind the trees. They were stepping onto the middle of the road, spilling out from both sides. On the left hand side, two white tunnels of light appeared. Headlights, beaming across the road. A monstrous engine growled and seconds later, a red Chevrolet pickup truck lurched its way forward and then stopped in the middle of the road, blocking the path ahead for the oncoming Dodge.

Cody felt sick.

"Dad!" Rachel screamed. "What is it?"

There were about ten or eleven people out there. They came forwards, creeping like skulking demons. Their faces were hidden behind homemade balaclavas – large knitted ski masks with crude eyeholes, a pointed nose and an oversized hole torn at the mouth, which made it look like the mask was smiling. Cody figured they were mostly men. Most of the waistlines were crudely spilling over the rim of their pants. He did notice at least one large-breasted, overweight woman standing amongst them. She was one of five people pointing a shotgun at the Dodge.

Cody turned to his right and looked at Mary Jane. He wanted to grab a hold of her bird-like neck and throttle the bitch until her face turned purple. She'd led them down here to the slaughter and Cody had let her do it.

There was no expression on her face.

"What's happening Dad?" Rachel said. Her chest was heaving up and down as her little lungs grasped for air.

The masked strangers were standing at the hood of the car. Five pump action shotguns were locked onto the driver's seat.

"I'm sorry Rachel," Cody said.

Poor Rachel – she deserved so much better than this.

CHAPTER SEVEN

"What is this?" Cody said.

He looked through the windshield and his blood ran cold.

The masks plodded forwards like a lumbering ghost army. Their feet made no sound on the surface of the road and only a chilling silence accompanied their approach. Cody watched them, feeling very much like a man being buried alive. The car was a coffin. His arms and wrists were taped and he was listening to the sound of the earth being shoveled on top of him.

Mary Jane rolled down the passenger side window. She leaned her head through the gap and held out a hand like she was stopping traffic. The masks halted their approach. The little fat woman in the mask nodded and gave the thumbs up signal. At the same time, the red Chevrolet rolled forwards on the road. It crawled into the left hand lane and the masks shuffled to the side, making space as the truck drove past the Dodge Challenger. Seconds later it stopped again at the rear, spreading itself out on the road and turning into a four-wheeled roadblock.

They were shutting off all escape routes.

"I said what's going?" Cody said.

Mary Jane pointed at the steering wheel. "Turn off the engine Cody."

He did as he was told.

"Boy oh boy," Mary Jane said, shifting towards the driver's seat so that she was facing Cody. "First and foremost, it ain't nothing personal. Truth be told, I like you both, I really do. You seem like a good guy Cody – not the sort of spoiled brat junkie asshole the papers made you out to be. And you're just the sweetest thing Rachel. The sweetest thing."

"Please don't do this," Cody said. "What do you want?"

"We want the car," she said, screwing her face up like it was a dumb question. "Take a look. World's gone to shit and we gotta take care of our own. These folks out here, they might look all Halloween-like with those masks on but these are some of my dearest friends and family. They mean the world to me and I don't want anything bad to happen to them."

"And Rachel means the world to me," Cody said. "You know that."

"I do."

"Then don't do this."

"I need two or three cars to get my people somewhere safe," Mary Jane said. "Good cars. See I want to find a place where there ain't no Black Storm too. We're the same Cody. I might have been acting skeptical about your escape plans but truth is I believe the same thing you do. Gotta be somewhere. So we've been working on the transportation side of things – we got the pickup earlier today and now we've got ourselves a 1970 Dodge Challenger. Almost a full tank of gas in it too."

"I don't believe this is happening," Cody said, his hands dropping off the steering wheel.

"Didn't your momma ever tell you that it was dangerous to pick up hitchhikers?"

"My momma told me to be kind to strangers," Cody said.

Mary Jane laughed softly. She looked at her companions outside.

"C'mon," she said. "You think a good-looking lady like me would be out there hitchhiking on a night like this? On a morning like this? We all got our little plans and schemes. You got yours, we got ours. We're just trying to stay alive."

Cody shook his head. "Please don't do this," he said. "I've got to get Rachel to the airport. There really is a plane waiting for us down there. Let us go please. For Rachel."

Keep saying her name.

Cody watched the razor sharp outline of Mary Jane's face melt into the darkness. For a second, he thought he might have reached her.

She smiled and his hope was crushed.

"You're breaking my heart Cody," she said. "Truly. But there ain't no place in this world for that sort of goodness anymore. Certainly not for strangers. Your mom's advice is out of date. Look here, that plane you keep thinking about – try and put it out of your mind. Seriously, there ain't no need to torture yourself about it. You ain't getting on it."

"Please," Cody said. "She's all I've got in the world."

Mary Jane looked at Rachel and paused for a second.

"I know that," she said. "This is *not* personal. Hurting you is not our goal here. It's just a consequence of that goal. This is how things get done in the world right now and maybe in the world to come. It don't matter who you are. Don't matter how much money you've got or how many movies you starred in. All that matters is what you can take."

"Take it then," Cody said. His left hand slid down the side of the driver's seat. "Take the car but leave us alone."

Mary Jane turned towards Rachel. There was a hungry look in her eyes.

"I'm taking the car," she said. "But that's not all I'm taking."

Cody almost grabbed her by the throat. He could and would have killed her with his bare hands but fortunately he still possessed enough self-control to hold back. He looked outside at the masks, standing like a flock of ghoulish scarecrows at the front of the car. Their shotguns were all over him.

"No," he said. "Whatever it is you're thinking, please don't."

"She's a great looking kid," Mary Jane said, turning back to Cody. "Just perfect for what we have in mind."

"Please," Cody said.

"Don't worry we're not going to hurt her," Mary Jane said. "We need her alive and well and healthy. We're just planning for the future Cody. When all this passes we'll need breeders like her – young mothers to bring more babies into the world. We're just doing our part, trying to get this wheel called humankind spinning all over again. And if we have a big family, we'll be so much stronger."

Mary Jane smiled at Rachel, who shrank into the back seat. Rachel's fingers clung to the teddy bear's tattered fur like it was keeping her afloat in deep, dark water.

"God she's adorable," Mary Jane said.

She leaned closer to Rachel, her eyes probing the little girl like she was examining a doll on a shelf.

"Dad," Rachel said.

Cody turned around. He saw the fear in his daughter's eyes.

"I want to stay with you," she said.

"Oh my Lord!" Mary Jane said. A short bark of laughter transformed into a coughing seizure and she turned her head away, putting a hand over her mouth to block the air shooting out of her lungs.

"Sorry little girl," Mary Jane said. She coughed once more into the back of her hand. "But there ain't no need for no has-been actors in the new world. Space is tight in our little convoy, you get it? Especially if we can't get another car to stop. You understand little darling?"

She turned to Cody. "*You* understand don't you, deep down?"

Cody's left hand was underneath the seat. His back was pushed up tight against the car door while his right hand remained on his lap.

His fingers were inching towards the Glock.

But what about all the other masks? There were fifteen rounds of ammunition, plus one in the chamber in the Glock 19. Was that enough? There was more ammo in the trunk but he had zero chance of getting there and reloading without at least one of those shotguns plugging him on the way. The odds were stacked against him but taking a shot in the back was better than letting them take his daughter away. They wanted to turn her into a breeding animal for God's sake. What did that mean? Being locked in a filthy, cockroach infested room day and night? Being raped and impregnated by fat rednecks until her body finally gave out? And then what?

He could do this.

Cody knew how to fire a gun. One good thing he'd taken away from his two forgettable cop movies was a set of impressive shooting skills. On both filming locations, he'd earned special praise from his firearms instructors and regular trips to the shooting range were something that he'd kept up over the years.

What about these redneck assholes? Could they shoot? Could they even see under those grotesque masks?

"You won't get away with this," Cody said.

Mary Jane pointed a thumb back to the large pickup truck that was blocking the road behind them. Its bright headlights, pointing slightly to the side, looked like the eyes of a nocturnal monster.

"The guy who owned that truck said the same thing," she said. "He was still saying that when we led him over to those trees at the side of the road. You want to know something Cody? The police don't care about your problems. They've got more pressing concerns right now wouldn't you agree? Like saving their own families."

Cody's fingers crept towards the gun.

"Welcome to New America," Mary Jane said. "Where people don't give a shit. Not altogether different from the old version – we're just admitting it this time around."

"Where will you go?" Cody said. "You're taking my daughter and my car? What's your plan?"

His fingers found the plastic grip of the Glock. It was a snug fit. He was well aware too that there was no safety to switch off either, not on this type of pistol.

Cody glanced at the masks standing outside. He couldn't see their faces but he could tell they were getting restless. They were shifting on their feet, mumbling to one another quietly, and looking over their shoulder for any other traffic on the road.

"There wasn't much of a plan," Mary Jane said. "Not really. But then you told me about this plane of yours waiting at the airport."

Cody shook his head. "C'mon," he said. "I saw your face when you heard that report about planes falling out the sky."

Mary Jane leaned closer to Cody. "Yeah but it's a big plane," she said. "A Boeing 737 with seven or eight pilots on board. That's what you said, right? Shit, that's a good bet. Probably a ton of food and water and medical supplies on board too. Sounds a lot better than anything else I've heard so far."

"Nick won't let you anywhere near the plane," Cody said.

"Sure he will," Mary Jane said. "We're Rachel MacLeod's guardians. We'll tell him the whole story. We'll tell this Nick all about the tragic accident that claimed the life of her father – how poor Cody got caught up in a human stampede on the 281 as people were fleeing San Antonio. You got crushed to death. Bummer. And we'll tell him that we were with you at the end.

How you instructed us to bring her to the airport, your dying wish and all that crap. Rachel will stay quiet, we'll make sure of that."

"There's not enough room on the plane," Cody said.

His fingers were locked around the handle of the gun. He squeezed tight.

"Rachel will get us close," Mary Jane said. "Our guns will take care of the rest. Some of those other folks, they're just going to have to catch a train to New America."

There was a moment's silence.

"What about me?" Cody said.

"Daddy," Rachel said. Her voice trembled.

"It's okay honey." Despite everything, he sounded calm. "I'm just talking to Mary Jane."

Cody saw a flicker of something in the older woman's eyes. It might have been empathy but it didn't last long.

Mary Jane looked at the masks standing outside. Her face was somber.

"It's time," she said. "I've been sitting with you long enough. I did that to try and explain – to tell you why we're doing this. Because I like you both."

Cody swallowed hard.

"Rachel," he said, keeping his voice quiet. "I want you to do me a favor okay? I want you to close your eyes and keep them closed. It's just for a little while."

Rachel was crying softly in the backseat.

"Do it honey," he said, turning around to look at her. "Please close your eyes. Can you do that for me?"

She closed her eyes.

Mary Jane's eyes were glistening and she smiled. "You're a good Dad," she said. "Ain't no doubt about that. Now I promise you this much – she won't see anything that happens out there. And don't worry – you won't feel a thing Cody."

"Mary-Jane!" a raspy male voice yelled. "What the hell is going on in there? What's taking so long?"

Mary Jane leaned her head out of the window.

"We had some talking to do," she said. "Don't you recognize this man Hank? This here is a bona fide movie star. Ah seen some of his films back in the day, back when he was young and beautiful. Think maybe I'm a little starstruck. He's got a real pretty little girl sitting in the back seat too. Think she'll be coming with us."

"C'mon woman," Hank said. He was holding a shotgun and he took an impatient step towards the car. "We don't have all night for Christ's sake."

"It's morning Hank," Mary Jane said. "Alright we're coming out." She turned to the driver's seat. "Let's go Cody. Outside."

"Dad!" Rachel screamed.

"Keep your eyes closed honey," Cody said. "Do what I said."

"C'mon man," Mary Jane said. She was all business now. "Don't make it any harder than it already is. Get out the goddamn car, step outside and let's get this shitty thing over with."

Cody lifted the gun off the floor. Mary Jane didn't seem to notice his arm stretching underneath the seat.

The darkness was good for some things.

"We'll take care of her," Mary Jane said. "Outside, now."

"Keep your eyes closed Rachel," Cody said.

"Let's go Cody," Mary Jane snapped. "Get out the goddamn..."

He whipped out the Glock and squeezed the trigger. There was a deafening crack that sounded like fireworks going off outside the car. Mary Jane gasped as the bullet pierced her chest at close range and tore through her heart. Rachel screamed in the back seat. When Cody glanced at his daughter, her eyes were still closed.

Good girl.

"Keep 'em shut Rachel. I'm okay. We're going to be fine."

Mary Jane fell back against the window, both hands grasping

at the blood gushing out of the wound. It looked like she was trying to catch the blood and scoop it back into her body. Her eyes were getting cloudy. She looked at Cody and opened and closed her mouth like a drowning fish. She tried to say something but there wasn't enough time. To Cody's horror, when she died, her eyes were staring straight at him.

"Oh fuck!" one of the masks yelled. "He shot her! He shot her!"

There was a moment of panic and confusion amidst the spectators.

Cody dropped the Glock onto his lap and turned the key. The Dodge Challenger snarled at the masks like a waking dragon. The sound of the 426 Hemi engine snapped the would-be kidnappers and murderers out of their daze.

"Kill that son of a bitch!" the female mask cried out. "Kill his baby too."

Welcome to New America.

"Dad!" Rachel screamed.

"Keep 'em closed baby," Cody said. "And get down in between the seats."

He heard her drop down, squeezing into the space between the front and back seats. Cody slammed his foot on the pedal and the Dodge hurled itself forward like it was on the starting line of a drag race. He plowed straight through the masks, hitting one of them square on like the car was a bowling ball and the mask was a fat pin. There was a sickening thud as the car pushed the big man backwards, his hands outstretched like he was dying on the cross.

"Motherfucker!" somebody else yelled. "Kill them."

Cody didn't slow down. He kept his foot down as the Dodge built up speed.

The masks shot at him – loud shotgun blasts that sounded like cannonball fire. Cody kept his head low as he sped the car along Bulverde Road.

He drove like it was the devil on his tail.

Glancing in the rear-view mirror, he saw the faint glow of headlights.

"Shit," he said.

The Chevrolet was coming after him.

Cody turned his eyes back to the front and pressed the gas pedal to the floor. The road was narrow and there was no light anywhere apart from the Dodge's headlights. Traveling at speed, he couldn't see the turns coming until he was practically on top of them and this forced to slow down. It was either that or risk coming off the road.

There was a gurgling sensation in his guts and Cody knew he was going to puke sooner or later. Hopefully it would be later. Once or twice he glanced at the fresh corpse sitting in the passenger seat.

Mary Jane was a goner but she was still gawping at him like a creepy mannequin.

He heard Rachel sitting up again. She'd stopped crying and when he glanced in the mirror he saw her eyes looking ahead at the dark road.

"Daddy. What's happening?"

Rachel only called him Daddy when she was scared. Really scared.

"We're going too fast," she said. "I thought we weren't supposed to be driving so fast in the dark."

"I know," Cody said, catching a glimpse of two dazzling head-lights appearing in the side mirror. The Chevrolet was catching up. If he was going too fast, they were going *crazy* fast. Revenge was obviously a bigger priority for the masks than road safety at that moment.

"Seat belt on?" Cody said.

He heard a clicking noise in the back.

"Yeah."

"Good girl," he said.

He checked the side mirror again.

When he looked back out front, the Black Widow was standing on the road. She was almost invisible; her tall frame, wrapped up in the long black, flowing dress, was cloaked by the surrounding darkness. Only her bright red hair and glowing silver eyes stood out.

"Holy shit!" Cody yelled.

He slammed the brakes but it was too late. The Dodge went through the Black Widow like she was a cloud of mist. Cody looked in the mirror and then over his shoulder, not sure what he expected to see back there. There was nothing – nothing except the angry headlights of the Chevrolet coming after them.

"What the...?" Cody said.

Hitting the brakes had cost him time. The Chevrolet wasn't slowing down, which told Cody that the Black Widow hadn't appeared to anyone else. Rachel couldn't have seen her either – she hadn't even asked why Cody had hit the brakes so suddenly.

Cody checked the mirror. The Chevrolet was gaining fast. He could see four people sitting in the cargo bed of the truck. One, maybe two more were in the cab.

He put his foot down but the road was too dangerous. The Dodge picked up speed but not enough to put any significant distance between the two cars.

Only one option remained.

"We're going to have to fight them off," Cody said. "Rachel, do you hear me? We're going to have to stop."

"I want to go home," Rachel said.

"No," Cody said. He didn't tell her that home wasn't there anymore. That everything she'd ever known back in Spring Branch was a smoking pile of rubble. That was a conversation for another time. "The only way to get rid of these people is to stand up to them. Alright?"

72

No answer.

"Just sit tight kid. We're getting on that plane."

Cody slammed his foot down on the accelerator. The plan was to open up enough of a gap between the Dodge and the Chevrolet to allow him time to stop and get ready. He raced the car down a stretch of welcome straight road, building up a handy lead on the pursuing Chevrolet. But it was a temporary escape – there would be no outrunning the masks tonight.

"Alright you bastards," he said. "Let's do this."

He hit the brakes and turned the wheel to the right. Rachel screamed as the Dodge skidded to a halt on the far side of the road. Cody spun the car around so that the driver's side was facing the oncoming pickup truck.

He turned off the engine and grabbed the gun. The he opened the door and at the same time, he could hear the pickup truck charging down Bulverde Road behind them. The bright headlights were coming into view as the Chevrolet swerved around a slight corner in the road.

"Rachel," Cody said, pulling the door open. "Get out. Now!"

She unbuckled her belt and hurried out the car.

Cody kneeled down and embraced his daughter. He squeezed her tight.

"I want you to do something for me," Cody said, letting go of her. He wiped a single tear off her cheek and pointed to a wall of trees at the side of the road. A short wire fence ran along the road in front of the trees. If Rachel crossed the fence in good time and ran into the open fields behind the trees, she had a good chance of getting away.

"I want you to jump that fence," Cody said. "Take off into the trees. Run and don't stop running until you find somewhere safe, you hear me?"

Rachel shook her head. "I want to stay with you."

The Chevrolet's headlights raced towards them. The engine eased off as the pickup slowed down to a stop.

Cody pushed his daughter towards the fence. "I love you," he said. "Everything will be okay."

"Dad."

"Go now," he said, raising his voice. He pushed her again. "Go!"

She looked at him one last time. Then she ran.

CHAPTER EIGHT

Cody ran over to the trunk of the car. He'd planned to grab some extra ammo before the shootout but it was too late. The pickup truck had already stopped in the middle of the road. Four masks jumped out of the cargo bed and quickly took cover on the other side of the truck. The driver's door fell open and a dumpy little figure in a mask spilled out onto Bulverde Road.

"You motherfucker!" the fat woman yelled. She hurried around to the back of the pickup, joining the others.

The loud crack of shotgun fire forced Cody to dive behind the Dodge. He pressed his back against the tire while the masks fired in anger from across the road.

In between shots, Cody heard a chorus of click-clacking noises as the masks reloaded their guns and ditched the empty shells.

They fired again.

It didn't take long for Cody to realize that the masks were lousy shots. Either that or they couldn't see under those creepy masks and in such dark conditions. Bullets sprayed everywhere but they weren't hitting anything. The majority of gunfire strayed off into the wilderness and even the Dodge wasn't taking much damage. At least Rachel had gotten a decent head start before the gunfight began. One of those stray bullets could easily have caught her in the back.

She would be far away now.

"You bastard!" someone yelled during a pause in the gunfire. "You're going to die now. And then we're going to take your little darling too."

Cody peered out from behind the car. He could hear them reloading – shoving bullets into the magazines as fast as their fingers could work. They were mumbling to each other. Sounded like they were arguing.

Cody leapt out and fired three shots. Four of the masks were in plain sight and three of them ducked behind the pickup at the sound of gunshots. The fourth one wasn't so quick. Cody's third shot landed flush in the big man's forehead and down he went.

"Frank!" the woman's voice screamed. "Frank, oh my baby boy. No, Jesus God no!"

Cody ducked behind the Dodge. Uh-oh – who had he shot this time? If the fat woman hated him for killing Mary Jane, what was she going to do now that he'd taken out Frank, her baby boy?

The masks retaliated with anger. The shotgun fire came hard and fast. In between the masks' reloading and another attack, Cody jumped to his feet and fired two shots, hitting nothing but air. As he took cover again, a massive explosion rang out from far away. Cody felt the ground beneath him shake, just for a second.

It sounded like a volcano had erupted in San Antonio.

The noise of the distant explosion faded and Cody heard footsteps running towards him. He peered out and saw that all four of the shotgun-wielding masks were making a charge at the Dodge.

"Oh shit," he said.

They came out all guns blazing. The fat woman led the charge, shooting and cursing at the top of her voice.

"You fucker!" she screamed. "I'm going to watch you die. Slowly, you son of a bitch."

The other masks were running beside her. All four of them sped towards the Dodge in a clumsy zigzag pattern, trying to present as difficult a target as they could.

Cody dropped onto all fours, rolled out from behind the car and lay on his chest. It was a maneuver he'd learned on the set of *Midnight Trooper* – a straight to DVD cop movie he'd made in 1995. This was prone position – shooting from the ground. The cops he'd researched with told him this was the most stable field position and although he'd practiced with a rifle on the movie set, he was confident enough with the Glock.

He pointed the pistol and fired. One shot – the fat woman dropped like a stone. Second shot – he missed. The third one pierced the chest of the tallest man who dropped his gun and screamed like a dying pig.

He fell onto his knees beside the body of the fat woman.

"Fuck you!" the dying man said, spitting out blood. He fell onto his back and a moment later, he stopped moving.

The remaining two masks had seen enough. They turned around and fled back to the safety of the truck, but not before stooping down to grab the two vacant shotguns that were lying on the road.

Cody watched them disappear around the back of the truck. Jesus, he'd killed four people now. Maybe five if the guy he ran through with the Dodge hadn't made it. Five people. How long before that sunk in?

"Hey!" a screechy male voice called out from behind the Chevrolet. "Alright now mister. Let's work out some kind of deal, huh? Nobody else has to die here tonight."

"It's nine o'clock in the morning asshole!" Cody yelled back.

"That ain't the point!"

"What's the deal?" Cody said. "I'm listening."

There was a pause.

"How about this?" the screechy voice said. "We let you keep that car of yours but you hand the girl over to us. How'd that be?"

Cody laughed out loud.

"Holy shit!" he yelled. "Are you fucking kidding me?"

He heard two male voices arguing behind the truck.

"Shit, I didn't mean that," the screechy voice said. "I'm all fucked up man – you just shot my sister for Christ's sake. I meant, how about we let you keep the girl and you let us take the car and we'll be on our way? Huh? How about that?"

"You don't need the car anymore," Cody said. He peered out from behind the Dodge but couldn't see anyone in the dim light cast by the Chevrolet's headlights. The two stiffs lying in the middle of the road looked like toppled statues.

"This might have escaped your notice," Cody said. "But you're down at least four people. That truck is all you need."

Another pause.

"Nah, we're still going to need that car of yours."

Cody sat up straight, his back pressed against the rear tire. He looked at the black pistol in his hand. How many shots had he fired so far? There'd been fifteen rounds in the magazine to start with, plus one in the chamber. Had to be at least six bullets left at most. Right? That was enough to take the last two masks out. But he couldn't afford to miss anymore.

"How about this for a deal?" he called out. "I let you get in that truck of yours and you drive the hell out of here. Take your guns. Take your dead with you if you want to. I'll even give you Mary Jane back."

Bang! Click-clack. Bang!

Cody ducked out of sight as they answered with gunfire. He waited for the firing to cease before he came back with three shots of his own. The drivers' window on the pickup exploded and glass shattered everywhere. Two more shots landed in the cargo bed.

Three bullets left, if he was lucky.

What was he going to do when the gun was empty? Was there any chance he could reach the trunk and reload in time without getting shot?

Cody heard hushed voices behind the red Chevrolet.

About a minute passed and nothing happened. An eerie silence lingered over Bulverde Road.

Then he heard the sound of footsteps. They came quickly, trotting over a carpet of broken glass.

Cody sat up straight, bracing himself for the final shootout. Three bullets – he'd use them well. At the very least he'd given Rachel the head start she deserved.

But instead of gunfire he heard the truck doors open and slam shut. Peering out, Cody saw the two masks sitting in the cab up front. The Chevrolet engine growled and the truck did a swift U-turn on the road, only barely avoiding the dead bodies lying scattered nearby.

"Thank God," Cody said.

He leapt back to his feet and watched the taillights disappear into the darkness. When the truck was gone, Cody surveyed the damage. The road was littered with three dead masks and a large number of spent shotgun shells. He patted himself down, checking for any wounds that he might have missed. He didn't have a scratch on him.

Cody turned to the trees at the side of the road.

"Rachel," he said.

He ran over to the fence and stared long and hard into the dense foliage. It looked so bleak and lonely out there.

"Rachel!" he yelled. "Can you hear me?" How far had she gone? He'd only sent her into the trees because the odds had been stacked against his survival. He'd tried to give her a fighting chance. Cody hadn't even thought about the possibility that he'd see off the masks.

Where was she?

"Rachel!"

He was about to jump the fence and chase after her when something stepped out from behind a large tree. Light footsteps tiptoed on the grass and Cody knew right away. Seconds later, he saw the shape of blue dungarees and a white long sleeved t-shirt. He saw the bright blonde hair, in contrast to the dark world that held them in its vice-like grip. She looked perfect. Even Bootsy the teddy bear, hanging at her side, looked brand new.

"Dad? Is that you?"

"Rachel. Thank God."

Cody vaulted the wire fence and ran over to his daughter. When he reached her, he wrapped his arms around her and buried his face in her soft, warm neck. He could smell the scent of wild flowers and grass on her skin. Her heart was pounding, just like his.

She squeezed him tight.

"What happened?" he said, checking her from top to bottom for wounds. "You were supposed to run away as fast as you could."

"I wanted to stay with you," she said. "You need me, don't you?"

Rachel spoke with all the assuredness of an adult.

"Yeah," Cody said, dropping his hands, satisfied that she hadn't taken any damage. "I do need you."

"Are we still going to the airport?" she said.

Cody stood tall and offered her his hand. "You bet kid."

They walked back to the car, hand in hand. Cody pointed Rachel towards the back seat and then opened up the passenger side and dragged Mary Jane's blood-soaked body out onto the road. Her eyes were wide open, staring up at the black sky. The bullet had gone straight through her body and was now embedded in the car door.

With a grimace, Cody gripped the corpse by the forearms

and dragged it away from the car. As he brought Mary Jane towards the other dead masks, her legs scraped along the road and it sounded like a sharp knife tearing through cloth. Cody laid her body down next to the others. For a moment he was tempted to remove the masks' balaclavas so that he could see their faces. But he didn't. Deep down, he knew what was underneath those masks – normal faces, unspectacular, everyday people.

It would have been easier if they'd been monsters.

"Are they all dead?" Rachel asked. She was standing beside the car. Her face was expressionless as she surveyed the lifeless bodies sprawled out in the center of the road.

"Yeah they are," Cody said. "I had to do it. They were going to hurt us."

"Maybe they deserved it."

Rachel turned away from the bodies, concentrating instead on the Dodge Challenger. "Did they hit the car?"

Cody walked over and inspected the damage. "She took a few to the body but they were hitting air mostly. We'll be alright, it'll get us there."

He kneeled down and his fingers probed one of the bullet holes on the side of the car. There was nothing to worry about. Thank God, they'd...

His stomach gurgled.

Cody stood up straight, knowing that he was going to be sick.

"Rachel," he said, sounding groggy. "I'm just going to take a leak down by the trees. Will you wait for me in the car?"

"Okay."

Cody hurried back over to the side of the road. Then he jumped the wire fence and ran towards the trees like his life depended on it.

Five people. Dead.

He ran into the dark fields, doubled over and threw up. Afterwards, he felt faint and had to sit down on the grass. His head was spinning, like he'd just stepped off a fast-moving roundabout.

"Nothing personal," he said.

He was sick again.

When there was nothing left to throw up, he spat twice and wiped his mouth with the back of his hand. Then he took a deep breath, devouring the fresh air like it was water for a thirsty man.

They still had some miles to cover before they reached the airport.

"C'mon," Cody said. "Keep moving."

He jumped the fence and walked back to the road. Standing at the car door, he took one last look at the red-haired body lying on the road.

Her eyes were still pointing up at the starless sky.

"So long Mary Jane," he said.

CHAPTER NINE

Cody turned the Dodge Challenger back towards the 281.

He knew he was taking a risk going back the way they came. The masks might still be there but the alternative was to find some other route back onto the highway and Cody didn't know the roads well enough for that. It was dark too, which only added to the likelihood of them getting lost.

It was a tense journey back. Bulverde Road was a long, winding desert in the middle of nowhere. At any moment, Cody expected the masks to leap out from the side of the road and attack the car. He didn't dare to blink. One hand was on the steering wheel, the other wrapped around the handle of the gun.

But they made it. They reached the highway without further incident.

Now they were back en route to the airport. Things felt as normal as they could possibly feel. The horizon was a reddish-orange glow once again, thick plumes of smoke billowing skywards.

Cody could literally feel the heat pouring out of San Antonio. As they got closer to the city, they passed several other cars on the road, all racing in the opposite direction like rats fleeing a sinking ship.

There were people walking on the other side of the highway too, migrating north with the flow of traffic. But there wasn't enough human traffic on the 281 for Cody's liking. Where was everyone? Not everyone was migrating north, of course. He guessed that others coming out of the city were heading south, east and west too. But there should have been more people traveling north. San Antonio had a population of one and a half million souls. It was the second most populated city in all of Texas. If people weren't getting out, they were still trapped in the city.

Maybe they couldn't leave. Maybe it was too late.

There should have been thousands of people on the road.

Cody glanced at some of the faces. He saw one middle-aged couple walking down the grassy strip along the middle of the highway. They were walking with a sense of urgency. They had no bags in their hands, nothing but the clothes on their backs. They looked at Cody as he drove past with a look of bewilderment in their eyes. Maybe they were in shock, or maybe they were wondering what the hell anyone was doing driving south.

He took the Dodge into the center of the highway, not wanting to get too close to those traveling on foot.

"How we doing kid?" he said, glancing over his shoulder.

"I'm okay."

"You sure about that?"

There was a long pause.

"Rachel?"

"Did you have to shoot Mary Jane?" she said.

Cody eased off the gas pedal.

"Yeah I did," he said. "I had to shoot her. Look I'm sorry you had to see all that bad stuff Rachel. I know it wasn't easy for you."

"It wasn't easy for you either. Was it?"

"No," Cody said. "It wasn't. But it was self-defense. It was them or us."

"Is there any blood in the car?" Rachel asked.

Cody looked to his right. There were a few dark stains visible on the black vinyl passenger seat – not as much leftovers as he'd expected to see. Most of the blood had stuck to Mary Jane by the looks of it. Didn't matter – Cody was past caring anyway. He knew that he'd have to leave the car behind at the airport. Keeping the seats clean was the least of his concerns.

"Not much," he said. "Just a little.'

Rachel leaned forward in the back. "She seemed nice. Didn't she? Before she took us down that dark road."

"She was just pretending to be nice to us," Cody said. "She did that so we'd trust her and take her where she wanted to go. Where those people were waiting to steal our car and..."

"And steal me?"

Cody tugged at his sweat-soaked shirt.

"Yeah," he said. "Guess we learned a valuable lesson today, huh? Even if people seem nice assume they're not. Don't trust strangers. They might not have the Fever but they're still desperate in other ways."

Rachel put a hand on his shoulder. It was an unusually adult-like, reassuring gesture that surprised Cody.

"What about Nick?" she said.

"What?" he said. "What about Nick?"

"Can we trust him?"

Cody smiled.

"We can trust Nick," he said. "Nick Norton and I go way back. I'd trust him with my life – with *your* life. We met at the auditions for *The Forever Boys* in the eighties and hit it off right away. I saw Nick at a lot of auditions back in those days. We became friends, good friends. I trust him. Don't worry about Nick."

"He's a pilot now?"

"Yeah," Cody said. "Acting wasn't for Nick Norton, not long term. He left Hollywood when he was still a teenager and took to the skies. He became a pilot. Air force at first, then he got married – several times I might add – and eventually went into commercial flights. Only Nick Norton would have come up with a plan that involved stealing a commercial plane, filling it up with friends and family and taking a chance up there in the black sky. He's a hell of a pilot too. If anyone can find something out there, it's Nick."

Rachel took her hand off Cody's shoulder and sat back in her seat. There was a sharp clicking noise as she buckled up again.

Cody switched on the radio. Part of him was still chasing after another snippet of that lost music. Rory Gallagher, where are you? Anything was better than endless reports and commentary on the Black Storm.

After a brief search, a man's voice fought its way through the static.

...and I'll tell you another thing. Strange things have been happening everywhere – it's not just suicides and mass murders and crashing cars and falling planes we've got to worry about. It's all gone to hell, even in the already strange realm of the Internet and social media. People think I'm crazy but listen to this. What would you say if I told you that dead people were setting up Facebook accounts? This was when it all kicked off back in the early days. When nobody knew much about the Black Storm. What do you think about that? Don't believe me? Well listen to this – about five months back I logged onto Facebook and saw a friend request waiting from my dad. My dad's been dead for ten years. Ten years! Well I didn't know what to think. I accepted of course. Right after I did that he sent me a private message. 'My dear boy, You're so lonely, aren't you? I know you keep a gun in your drawer. I can't come to you but you can come to me. Save yourself. Your mom and I will be there to greet you.'

Well I'll tell you this folks – to anyone who's listening out there. I've never been so scared in all...

Cody switched the radio off.

"Shit," he said under his breath. That was it – no more radio. He'd said it many times before and he always came back. Not this time. These people – whoever they were – weren't telling him anything he didn't already know. The world and everything in it was screwed.

He heard Rachel shifting in the back seat.

"The Black Widow did it," she said.

"What's that honey?" he asked, forcing a smile in the rearview mirror.

"The Black Widow pretended to be that man's dad on Facebook. Didn't he?"

"I don't know," he said. "I guess so."

"How come nobody knows what she is?" Rachel said. "Or what the Black Storm is?"

"We've talked about this Rachel," Cody said. "Many times. Nobody knows for sure. The Black Widow came out of the Black Storm, like all the other things – the rain, the winds, the Fever, you know? All of it – we call it the Black Storm. You know that already."

"Yeah but what is it?"

Great. All the easy questions.

"Some people think the Black Storm is a part of nature," Cody said. "They believe that nature has turned against us as a species. We've overpopulated the planet and so Mother Nature is cleaning house. Like a mass extinction event."

"Yeah but what do *you* think?" Rachel said.

"Nature can be cruel," Cody said. "But if Mother Nature wanted to, she could wipe us out with floods, earthquakes, whatever she wanted. But not this – this feels like something else. This doesn't feel natural to me."

"What do you mean?"

"It feels like something *infiltrated* nature as we know it," Cody said. "Something from the outside."

"What does infiltrated mean?"

"It just means something got inside nature."

Rachel paused. "Something bad?"

"I guess."

"Like what though?"

"That's the sixty-four thousand dollar question kid," he said. "The greatest minds on the planet have been trying to figure that one out since this mess started months ago. And you're asking me? Hey, you keep thinking it over honey and if you find out the answer you'll be the next President of the United States. I guarantee it."

Cody dabbed at the fine layer of sweat gathering on his neck. It was muggy inside the car and he pulled at his shirt again – it felt like he'd smothered himself in glue before getting dressed. He thought about opening a window but he didn't – not with all the smoke drifting out of the city.

He heard Rachel sitting forward again. When she spoke this time, he felt her warm breath on the back of his neck.

"Mary Jane's eyes were still open," she said. "After you shot her."

"I know," Cody said. "But she was dead."

"Were Mom's eyes open?"

Cody hesitated. "I don't remember."

A pause.

"You think Eddie Faldo's eyes are open? Right now?"

Cody's foot leapt off the accelerator and he brought the car down to a steady speed.

"Eddie Faldo?" he said, looking at her in the mirror.

"Eddie Faldo's dead," Rachel said.

"Since when?"

"I heard it on the radio yesterday," Rachel said. "I was going to tell you when we were talking about him earlier. But then you said you didn't hate him. Still, maybe you want to know. Somebody in Los Angeles was talking about Hollywood Hills and how all the houses over there were on fire. *All* the houses – that's what they said. Somebody's been going around and starting fires, burning everything to the ground. That's where he lives right?"

"Yeah," Cody said. "That's where he lives."

Eddie Faldo did indeed live on Hollywood Hills. Cody had seen pictures of his house on the Internet – a lavish three and a half million dollars of Mediterranean themed property, tucked neatly inside the heart of Celebrity La-La Land.

Damn nice.

"That doesn't mean he's dead Rachel," Cody said. "It just means the houses are on fire. You never know, people might have gotten out in time. It happens."

"But would you be sad if he was dead?" Rachel said. "Seeing as how he won the Oscar and all? He took that away from you, didn't he? He hurt you. I don't like it when other people hurt you Dad. It makes me want to hurt them."

Cody glanced back at her. Rachel's facial expression was oddly serene.

"Eddie didn't hurt me," he said. "Look I get it Rachel – you're curious about death and all that but don't forget that we're alive right now. And we're trying to keep it that way. That's all that matters. We'll talk about those things another time."

Rachel sat back in her seat with Bootsy resting on her lap. She pulled gently at its tattered ears.

"Were you and Mom bad people?" she asked.

Cody bit his lip. It always came back to Rachel's mom.

"No," he said quietly. "We weren't bad people. We were just lost and because we were hurting, we did stupid things. Like making some really bad movies."

He was surprised to hear Rachel giggling in the back seat.

"Like *Attack of the Skeleton People?*" she said.

Cody looked in the mirror and laughed. "Right," he said. "Exactly like *Attack of the Skeleton People*. Didn't like that one huh?"

"It's probably the worst film ever made."

"Zero percent rating on Rotten Tomatoes," Cody said. "I don't know, I'm kinda proud of that. At least I got good money for doing that movie. We wouldn't be sitting in this 1970 Dodge Challenger right now if it wasn't for crappy movies like that."

"Did Mom make bad movies?"

Cody had only ever shown Rachel the good ones.

"One or two," he said. "Not as much as me though. I'm the undisputed champion in this family when it comes to making crappy movies."

Cody winked in the rearview.

"Hey you wanna know why there was never an *Attack of the Skeleton People* 2?" he asked.

"Why?"

"I made a decision in the hospital," he said. "Ten years ago. Right after you were born, when you were still in the incubator. Looking at you for the first time, man you were so tiny. I knew I'd never go back to my bad old ways. No

more drugs, no drinking, and definitely no more crappy movies. I was done with all that. This new life we'd made in Texas – I knew I was going to stick with it. Being a dad, that was my job now. You were our baby."

"And Mom?"

Cody shook his head.

"She tried kid," he said. "She really tried. But I guess it was harder for her to let go. And well, it turned out if you look hard enough you can still find drugs in the middle of nowhere."

"Were her eyes open?" Rachel said.

Cody pursed his lips tight together. "Yes."

Rachel didn't ask any more questions after that.

Cody leaned his head back on the seat. With a sigh, he looked through the windshield towards San Antonio – what was left of it.

Hard to believe he was taking their baby closer to that.

CHAPTER TEN

There were a lot of people spilling out of San Antonio.

They were traveling north, seeking refuge in the outer edges of the city and beyond. They came in groups, large and small. Solitary figures were spotted on occasion too. Some hurried up the grassy median strip that separated opposing traffic lanes, looking over their shoulder every few seconds as if they were being chased by something unseen. Others plodded up the highway, their stride slow and labored, as if the bags they carried in their arms or strapped to their backs were weighed down with heavy rocks.

A few cars drove north alongside them. The drivers in these vehicles ignored the countless pleas of those standing on the roadside, their arms waving frantically as they begged for a ride. The Dodge Challenger was still the only car driving south. Some people on the median strip stuck out their thumb as the Challenger raced by. Cody had a feeling that once they were in the car, these people would try to get him to turn around and take them north, by force if necessary.

They probably thought he was crazy for driving into the eye of the storm. Maybe he was crazy, but he wasn't crazy enough to pick up any more hitchhikers.

"Some of them look so sad," Rachel said, staring out at the procession of travelers.

"They are sad," Cody said. "And tired and frightened. They've lost everything."

"But we can't give them a ride, can we?"

Cody looked in the rearview. He saw a pair of bright head-lights in the distance and couldn't tell what side of the highway they were on. It would have been a relief to see at least one other car traveling in the same direction as they were.

He shook his head. "No," he said. "We can't give anyone else a ride. Look what happened last time, right? We've got to be strict about that now. Anyway, these people are all heading in the opposite direction. We're the only ones going south."

"Not the only ones," Rachel said.

"What?"

"There's a car behind us." Rachel said, looking through the rear window. "I can see the lights."

Cody leaned closer to the side mirror. Sure enough, those high beam headlights he'd seen in the distance were on the same side of the highway after all. The Dodge wasn't the only crazy car left on the road. It was a miracle.

The car was little more than fifty meters back and it was catching up with the Challenger at a rapid rate. The headlights were so strong that Cody screwed up his face and recoiled from the mirror.

"Thanks a lot buddy," he said, blinking furiously. "Better let them have the passing lane before they blind me."

Cody pulled the Dodge into the right hand lane. He eased off the accelerator, slowing down just enough to let the other vehicle pass safely. When it didn't overtake right away, Cody slowed down to fifty miles-per-hour.

The other car pulled into the right hand lane.

"What the hell?" Cody said.

His eyes went back and forth between the side and rearview mirrors. Once again, he winced at the high beam headlights, unable to shake them off his eyes. It was because of the headlights that he couldn't see anything of the vehicle behind him. He couldn't tell what make it was or anything like that. All he could see was those damn bright lights.

"C'mon man," he said, gripping the steering wheel tight. "I'm giving you the road for God's sake. You trying to blind me or something?"

The other car came closer. Still it didn't overtake the slow-moving Dodge Challenger. After a while, it pulled back into the passing lane. Cody said a silent hallelujah and waited for the car to pass.

It came back into the slow lane.

Cody's face screwed up in confusion. "What the...?"

The vehicle accelerated until it was right up against the Challenger's tail. There was only a few inches of space between them now. The headlights dipped to low beam and at last, Cody was able to see what was behind them.

A red Chevrolet pickup truck.

Crack. A loud shotgun blast made Cody and Rachel jump in their seats.

"Rachel get down!" Cody yelled. "Get down. Back into position. Go, go, go!"

She knew exactly what to do. Before the second shotgun fired, Rachel unbuckled her belt and dove into the space behind the driver's seat.

"Dad!" she yelled.

"Stay down."

Cody kept his head low. Every muscle in his body was taut and alert. The bastards! So the rest of the masks had come to finish what Mary Jane and those other goons couldn't finish back in Bulverde. Now that the high beams were off, Cody saw some of them standing on the cargo bed at the back, trying to retain their balance while pointing shotguns at the Dodge.

Crack!

"Take that you murdering son of a whore!" somebody yelled.

Cody ducked his head down further. He could barely see the road through the windshield and so he pushed himself up again until his eyes were able to keep track of what was in front of them.

Crack!

With as much force as he could muster, he swung the Dodge to the left and then back to the right. Then repeat. He was trying to present his assailants with a moving target in the middle of the highway. To put that lousy shooting of theirs to the ultimate test.

Another glance in the mirror. The masks weren't even wearing masks anymore. Cody could see their faces this time around and just like he'd thought, there was nothing unique about any of them – they were just a gang of men, ordinary men, beer-bellied rednecks, ranging in ages from about thirty to fifty years old. He wasn't sure how many were in the truck, both standing on the cargo bed and sitting inside the cab.

The refugees walking along the highway screamed at the sound of the first shotgun blast. They fled for their lives. Most ran north in the direction they were traveling. Others however, in a state of fear and confusion, turned around and ran back towards San Antonio.

Cody slammed his foot on the gas and the Dodge raced down the highway. He opened up a small gap between his car and the pursuing Chevrolet.

"You okay Rachel?" he said. "Talk to me."

"Yeah," she said. "I'm okay. Is it the mask people again?"

"Yeah. It's the mask people."

"Why have they come back?" she said.

Cody was reaching for the pistol that he'd dropped under the driver's seat. He scooped it up and put it on his lap.

"Because I killed their friends," he said. "And now they're mad at us."

The Dodge kept up a steady lead on the pickup. Cody knew he had a chance of outrunning them this time. They weren't driving down the narrow back roads of Bulverde where taking sharp corners at high speed was a life or death maneuver. The center of the 281 was empty and Cody could keep the pedal pressed down for as long as he wanted, which meant the Dodge would easily outrun the heavier Chevrolet.

So why was it such a bad idea?

Cody knew that the masks would stay on his tail all the way to the airport. They weren't going to stop chasing him even if the Dodge raced far ahead and built up a strong lead. The last thing Cody wanted was these bastards turning up at the terminal building and screwing things up at the last minute. There were a lot of people putting their faith in that plane. It wasn't just about Cody and Rachel. Given the seriousness of the situation, Nick might even be forced to take off without Cody and Rachel, rather than run the risk of the rampaging masks getting anywhere near the aircraft.

Crack!

The Dodge Challenger weaved back and forth between lanes at breakneck speed. The masks might not have been the best shots but there were still four guns letting loose on Cody's car. They only needed to get lucky once. If they hit him, it was over for Rachel. She'd either be dead in a car crash or she'd survive and the masks would take her.

Dying was the better option.

"Shit," Cody said.

One other thing he had to consider. Cody wasn't familiar with the route to San Antonio International Airport. He hadn't flown anywhere in years and he'd have little chance of finding the airport at this speed, especially with the masks and their shotguns riding up his ass all the way down the highway.

He knew what he had to do. He had to get rid of them.

There was a brief lull in the volley of gunfire behind them. The driver beeped the horn of the pickup several times and it blared angrily in Cody's ears. It sounded like a madman playing the trumpet. He even heard laughter, high-pitched redneck guffawing, coming from the cargo bed. The masks were enjoying themselves. They were excited. They probably had a plan of sorts too – a hideous, agonizing death in mind for Cody, that's if they didn't kill him with the shotguns first.

"Damn it," he said. He punched the steering wheel like he was trying to hammer something into it.

"Rachel," he said. "You listening?"

"Yeah."

"Look we're going to have to face off with these guys again," Cody said. "You hear me kid? Just like last time. It's the only way to get rid of them for sure."

"No!" Rachel yelled from her hiding place. "What if they kill you?"

"They won't," Cody said. He didn't sound convincing. "But we can't go to the airport like this – with these people on our backs. You understand? We have to shake them off and we can't lose them on the highway."

"What about me?"

"You're going in the trunk. No arguments."

"No way," Rachel said.

"Yes way," Cody said. "I said no arguments. Now listen to me. Here's the plan - we open up a little gap between the two cars like last time. Remember? Now when I stop you're going to get out and jump in the trunk as fast as you can. You gotta run Rachel because we won't have much time to get ready. I'm going to reload the gun and then I'm going send these assholes back to Hicksville. Got it?"

She didn't answer.

"Alright," Cody said. "Here we go, ready or not."

He put his foot down on the gas, slamming the pedal to the floor. The Dodge accelerated down the dark highway, moving quickly up to ninety, then a hundred miles per hour and even faster. The world went past in a shadowy blur, as did the scores of northbound refugees walking along the grassy center.

Some of the travelers stopped to look, their jaws hanging open at the sight of the vintage car racing down the highway. Some of them pointed at the Dodge, like they were standing wide-eyed on the sidelines of the Indy 500, trying to keep up with the leading car.

The Chevrolet slipped further behind. Cody kept his eyes on the road ahead, trying to judge the right time to stop.

The headlights in the rearview mirror got smaller. It was tempting to keep going however, because another shootout was the last thing Cody wanted. But standing up to the masks was the only way to shake them off his tail. He had to show them that he wasn't the prey animal here. And after the Bulverde Road encounter, he'd grown in confidence with the realization that these people weren't exactly the greatest shots in the world.

He could do it. With any luck he'd discourage them permanently this time.

"You ready?" Cody said. "We're about to do this."

"Ready."

He swung the car to the right. The tires screeched until the Dodge went full circle and skidded to a halt with its headlights facing the oncoming Chevrolet.

"Now," Cody yelled. "Into the trunk."

He turned off the engine and grabbed the Glock off his lap. Then he reached for the door handle.

Rachel leapt out of the back seat as quickly as she could. Cody led his daughter to the trunk and opened it up. As he did so, he glanced further down the gloomy highway. The Chevrolet was coming at them fast. He could hear ecstatic pig-like squeals coming from the cargo bed.

Cody grabbed his backpack and pulled the front zip open. Keeping his hands steady, he pulled out a box of spare ammo and the speed loader too, which attached to the magazine and made reloading the Glock easier and faster.

He released the magazine. Then he attached the speed loader to the top of it, clicked down and slid the rounds in as fast he could.

"Hurry up Dad," Rachel said. She was pointing to the monster truck hurling itself down the highway. "They're coming."

"I know," Cody said, not looking up.

He inserted the magazine back into the gun. Then he looked at Rachel, whose chest was heaving up and down at an incredible speed. She was trying to be brave but he could see that she was petrified. He knew exactly how she felt.

"Okay," he said, gesturing inside the trunk. "Ready?"

She nodded.

"Go," he said.

He helped her climb into the trunk and watched as she curled up into a tight ball next to the food supplies. She clung onto Bootsy, burying her face in the teddy bear's tattered fur.

"I'll leave the door ajar," he said. 'If anything happens to me you can get out by yourself. Just push the lid up and run. I'll try and signal if things go bad. Listen honey, there are lots of other people traveling north on the highway. Find the good ones and stay with them. Okay?"

Rachel's eyes were glistening but the tears didn't come. There were no tantrums or protests. She'd accepted this terrible new way of life. It was both admirable and heartbreaking to see such hardness forming in the eyes of one so young.

"Okay," she said, laying her head down.

Cody tried to smile as he closed the trunk over. All he could manage was a grimace.

"I love you," he said. "See you soon."

"I love you too."

He pulled the lid down and made sure that it wasn't locked. Then Cody dropped into a crouch and crept around to the side of the car.

The Chevrolet came to a sudden halt nearby.

Cody peered round the side of the Dodge, watching as five men jumped out of the cargo bed of the pickup. Four of them had shotguns pointed at the white Challenger. Cody saw three other people sitting in the cab up front. Two of them jumped out of the passenger side door. The driver stayed where he was. The two men coming out of the passenger side were wielding iron bars in their hands.

Eight people.

The masks didn't take cover behind the pickup, not this time. They weren't here to settle in for a long gunfight, not with such superior numbers. Cody didn't know whether that was impatience, drunkenness or strategy on their part. What he did know was that they were walking straight over to the Dodge, their shotguns primed and ready to turn Cody into a piece of human roadkill.

Cody's heart was racing – what were they thinking? Were they really just going to walk him down and annihilate him? It sure looked that way.

All four shotguns exploded at once. It was as if the masks were responding to some unseen cue on the sidelines telling them to shoot.

Crack-crack-crack!

This was followed by a high-pitched, rapid click clacking as the masks readied their weapons for another assault.

There was a loud shattering noise. It came from the front of the Dodge. The masks had taken out one of the headlights, not far from where Cody's head was positioned. He winced as if he'd taken a shot to the gut.

They were coming fast and hard, leaving little window of opportunity for Cody to get a round of return fire in.

But he had to – he'd have to take risk it.

"Fuck it."

Cody leapt to his feet, pointed the Glock at the huddle of masks and fired. He tried to stay calm and make his shots count. There were plenty of bodies coming his way. As long as he held his nerve, he was going to hit something.

He aimed at those with the shotguns first.

Bang! The man at the front – a middle-aged, leathery faced son of a bitch dropped like a lead balloon. So did his gun, which spilled out of his dying grasp and landed on the road.

Bang! Cody missed with the second shot.

Bang! Another one went down. This time it was a younger man – a rake-thin twenty-something who'd been barreling forward with hatred in his eyes. The shotgun was locked in his grip as he fell onto the road. As he lay there, a bloody hand reached towards Cody, clawing for a revenge that would never come.

The other masks weren't deterred by these setbacks. They hurried forwards in a shambling run. The two men wielding the iron bars stopped to pick up the shotguns of the deceased.

They fired at Cody, who ducked behind the car.

Cody wondered if the shotguns were being used as a distraction. Maybe they didn't want to shoot him – maybe they wanted to get close enough to get their hands on him. After that, they'd do something much worse than just put a hole in him.

What sort of torture were these rednecks capable of conjuring up?

And what about Rachel?

Cody leapt out from behind the car and fired again. He hit nothing. He tried and missed many times over. The red mist had taken over and he was shooting angry now.

"Damn it," he said.

He extended his arm, took aim and was about to fire again.

Something stopped him. Out of the corner of his eye, he saw a blinking light in the sky. Red and green lights. But whatever it was, he couldn't afford to investigate. Not now.

Cody stood there, pointing the pistol at the masks, his trigger finger paralyzed with fear. They were too close. There were too many of them.

"We've got you now you son of a whore," one of them said. "Hey where's your pretty little girl at Mr Hollywood? Oh boy! I can't wait to get my hands on that little piece of celebrity meat."

"Fuck you," Cody hissed.

He squeezed the trigger. When he heard the clicking noise that told him the gun was empty, his heart sank.

"Oh shit," he said, looking at the pistol.

"Looks like you shot your load boy," one of the masks said, laughing.

They all laughed.

Cody was beaten. He'd come into this second gunfight too confident after his victory over the masks in Bulverde. He was so sure that he'd dispatch them again that he hadn't even pulled any extra ammo from the trunk. Now the Glock was empty and he'd only dropped two of the eight masks.

Why hadn't he tried to outrun them in the Dodge? What the hell was he thinking playing at cowboys in the middle of the goddamn road?

The masks lowered their weapons as they walked towards him.

They didn't seem in the slightest bit bothered about their dead companions lying on the road. It was party time.

Cody held his hands up in surrender.

"C'mon guys," he said. " Let's work something out and..."

A roaring sound in the distance cut him off. It sounded like a giant, angry wasp in the sky. Cody listened closely – it was the sound of an engine in trouble or something like that. Instinctively, he looked up and saw a small plane making a rapid descent towards the highway. The blinking red and green lights that had caught Cody's eye were on its wings. With each second, the lights were getting bigger. The buzzing noise got louder.

There was no doubt that it was coming down. The plane didn't appear to be in any obvious trouble – there was no smoke or visible signs of damage trailing off the aircraft.

If it wasn't in trouble, it was coming down deliberately.

But the masks weren't looking at the plane. They were circling the Dodge Challenger, cutting off all of Cody's escape routes.

"Rachel," Cody said, backing off. He wanted to yell at her – to tell her to get out of the trunk and run as fast as she could. But he was hypnotized, both by the presence of the encircling masks and the strange commotion unfolding in the sky. There was also a chorus of high-pitched screams in the distance. Further down the highway, scattered groups of refugees were standing on both sides of the road, as well as on the median strip in between. They could see what Cody saw up there. The plane was coming towards them and they didn't know which way to run.

Cody's heart nearly stopped.

"Oh shit," he said. He pointed towards the blinking lights in the sky.

"That's a plane coming down fellas," he said. "Will you look behind you for Christ's sake?"

"Bullshit," a stocky-shouldered, bald-headed man said. There was a murderous glint in his eyes. He was leading the slow charge coming after Cody.

"He's aiming for the road I think," Cody said. "That plane's going to go through those people like a bowling ball. And we're not exactly standing in a safe zone here."

The sound of the roaring engine in the sky got louder. Finally one of the masks turned around to check it out.

"Holy shit!" the man squealed. "It *is* coming down Hank. Coming straight out of the sky like this highway was a runway."

The bald man turned around and his jaw dropped.

"Oh Lord Jesus!" he said. "Not another one."

The five masks turned around and watched as the small plane descended towards the 281. For a moment, they were hypnotized just like the refugees were further up the road. It was as if no one could believe what they were seeing. They'd all heard about planes coming down elsewhere, but to see one – it was both mesmerizing and horrific.

Sensing his chance, Cody crept backwards towards the trunk. The incoming plane drowned out the sound of his footsteps.

The bald man called over to the driver sitting in the pickup. "Randall! Look at that! You see it?"

The fat, white-haired man in the cab was leaning out of the Chevrolet, watching the plane speeding towards the highway.

"See it? You think I'm blind?"

"What do we do?"

"Get back here!" Randall yelled, ducking his head back into the pickup. His voice was shrill with fear. "We've got to get off the road. Now! That's another kamikaze and it's coming straight towards us."

Cody reached the trunk and pulled it open quietly. When Rachel, still lying curled up in a ball, saw him standing there her eyes lit up. She was about to say something but Cody quickly pressed a finger to his lips and she did the same, letting him know that she understood.

Reaching inside the trunk, Cody grabbed a handful of ammo and the speed loader. He went to work fast and in a matter of seconds, the Glock was fully loaded.

"What about this cocksucker?" Cody heard the bald mask say to the driver. "What do we do with him? And what about the girl?"

"Grab them and put them in the truck," the driver yelled back. His voice was by now hoarse with panic. "But we've got to go — hey! What the...? Where is he? Where is the bastard?"

"Son of a bitch is trying to sneak off."

"Never mind him, let's get back to the truck!" a frightened voice yelled. "There's a plane coming down on the highway for Christ's sake. Who cares about that asshole?"

"We ain't leaving without him. He killed my sister."

"He's over there at the trunk trying to run," Randall said. "Grab him. Grab the girl. But quick."

Cody was biding his time. He was standing behind the open lid of the trunk. He winked at Rachel.

He heard footsteps rushing towards him.

Cody took a deep breath. Then he closed the trunk and started firing.

He shot the bald mask first. The nine-millimeter bullet ripped a dime-sized hole through the man's skull and a gargled gasp was all he could manage before he fell. The four other men panicked when they saw that Cody was back to shooting at his best. Survival instincts kicked in. The plan to seize Cody and Rachel was abandoned and they all fled back towards the Chevrolet in a disorganized mess.

The light coming off the plane was getting closer. The noise of the engine was louder. It felt dangerous just to be there. People on the highway were jumping off the road on either side, taking their chances in the trees and in the open spaces that lay beyond the 281. Others were racing down the highway back towards San Antonio, convinced that the plane wasn't going to land on the road.

They were too close to it. From where he stood, Cody was certain the plane was targeting the road.

The masks hurried back to the pickup. Cody knew that he couldn't let them go, not this time. There was every chance that the bastards would find him again further down the highway and try their luck. Maybe they'd find him at the airport. It would just go on and on until they killed him and took Rachel. Or until he killed them.

He had to protect her. That was his job, no matter how grim.

He chased after the fleeing men, dropping them one at a time like skittles. He felt nothing as he watched them go down. Meanwhile, Randall the driver saw what was happening and in a state of panic, he slammed his foot down and the red Chevrolet began to roll down the highway.

Cody pointed the pistol at the cab. He had a solid lock on the old man's head and all it would take was one more shot. Squeeze the trigger and wipe them out. One big happy family, all dead and spared the horrors of Mary Jane's 'New America'.

But Cody didn't shoot. His arm fell to the side.

It wasn't that kind of world yet.

The Chevrolet sped down the 281, charging towards San Antonio at high speed. Cody looked over his shoulder at the plane descending towards the highway. It might have been a Cessna. He saw the small wingspan, the twin turbofan engines – it probably held no more than five or six people inside.

"Holy shit," he said.

Those poor people on the road were trying to get away. But they were caught like a flock of rabbits in the plane's headlights. Their high-pitched screams filled the air and Cody saw the inevitability of the situation. It was a horrifying sight that was about to get worse.

He couldn't help them. Nobody could. He only had enough hero left inside him to save his little girl – he hoped.

Another glance at the plane. The Black Widow – she was up there, whispering in the pilot's ear and telling him to do it. But who else was in that plane with her and the pilot? Was it another case of someone paying an extortionate amount of money to charter a private aircraft in order to get home? Maybe they'd taken their family members aboard. Was there a child on the plane?

"Dad?"

Rachel's voice pulled Cody back, reminding him of the urgency of the situation. Turning around, he hurried over to the car and stood by the trunk. The lid was slightly ajar but he couldn't see inside.

"It's me," he said, knocking on the lid. "I'm okay. The masks are all gone."

"I want to come out."

Cody looked at the plane coming towards them.

"I want you to stay in here for a little longer," he said.

"Let me out!"

"Trust me," Cody said. And with that he slammed the trunk shut, ignoring her cries as he climbed back into the Dodge.

When he turned on the headlights he realized that one of them had indeed been shot out by the masks. A one-eyed car – it didn't matter. He wouldn't be on the road for much longer.

He turned on the engine, spun the car around and raced back down the highway towards San Antonio. His foot pushed the gas pedal all the way to the floor. As the car picked up speed, Cody's eyes darted back and forth between the road and what was happening in the rearview mirror.

Down it came. Lower. Losing altitude at a dramatic rate. Now it really did look like an authentic kamikaze plane speeding towards its target. But unlike the World War Two planes, the target this time wasn't an enemy warship; it was a group of human beings who'd been trying to escape the tragedy in San Antonio. It was almost there – God, it was coming in so fast.

Cody couldn't take his eyes off it.

"Oh Jesus Christ," he said.

The small aircraft crashed into the center of the 281. There was a massive explosion and a fireball engulfed the plane and burned through everything and everyone in its path. Thick plumes of black smoke gushed out of the wreckage and raced towards the sky.

It was a massacre.

The ground trembled underneath the Dodge Challenger.

Cody wanted to scream at the top of his lungs. He wanted to cry but his eyes were dry. He wanted to do something to acknowledge those people who'd been vaporized on the road. All they'd wanted was something better, for themselves and for their families – it was the same something he was searching for now.

He drove on in stunned silence. As he did so, he kept the gas pedal pinned to the floor, convinced that the fireball was chasing down the highway after them.

It was a while before he heard the noise. When he snapped out of his daze, he realized that Rachel was pounding on the roof of the trunk.

"Let me out!" she screamed.

"Just a little longer," Cody said. He scratched at his arm through the sleeve of his shirt. His skin was prickly hot, as if the heat of the explosion was all over him.

He looked at the massive fireball in the mirror.

How would anyone ever know what happened to those people? What if they had loved ones waiting for them somewhere?

More thumping from the back.

"Dad!" Rachel yelled from the trunk. "I want to get out of

here."

Cody knew that he couldn't keep her in the trunk for any longer. She'd heard the blast and there was no way he could hide the aftermath from her. It was too big. He slowed the Dodge to a stop and wiped the sweat off his face. Then he stepped outside into the warm air.

He tried to take a deep lungful of air. Breathing had never been so hard. It felt like someone was trying to smother him with a pillow on a hot summer's night.

Cody opened the trunk and helped Rachel climb out onto the road. She stood up straight and gasped as she looked at the fireball blazing in the north.

"What happened?" she said. "I heard the noise but..."

"A plane crash," Cody said.

Rachel stared at the smoking horizon.

"What about all those people?" she said.

"Some got away," Cody said.

They stood with their backs propped up against the Dodge Challenger for a minute or two. They were two spectators with front row seats to the end of the world.

Cody put his arm around Rachel.

"Want some water?" he said.

She didn't take her eyes off the wreckage. "Uh-huh."

Cody handed her one of the large bottles out of the trunk. Rachel held it with both hands and took a long drink. Then she passed it back. Cody drank the lukewarm water, letting it spill down the sides of his mouth.

"Are you ready?" he asked, wiping his mouth dry with the back of his hand. He screwed the lid on the bottle and put it back into the trunk.

"Ready," she said.

When they got back in the car, Rachel climbed into the passenger seat.

CHAPTER ELEVEN

They drove south.

Cody tried his best to ignore the wreckage that lingered in the mirror. He shut his mind off to what had happened – the masks, the plane crash, and most of all the fate of those people who'd got caught on the highway. He couldn't allow himself to get caught up in a tidal wave of emotion or it would overwhelm him. That would come later.

It was hard to forget however, when San Antonio was going up in flames to the south. There was nowhere to turn to escape the calamitous events triggered by the Black Storm.

"Bad things are happening everywhere," he said.

The road – that was all that mattered. That and the airport.

"Are we still getting on a plane?" Rachel said. "After...*that?*"

Cody looked at her sitting to his right in the passenger seat. It was a novelty seeing her there; it was as if a little woman now possessed the body of his ten-year-old girl. A little woman with a teddy bear.

"Are you scared?" he said.

"Aren't you?"

"Yeah," he said. "But I asked you first."

"I'm not that scared," Rachel said, eyeing the dried bloodstains on the passenger seat. She was doing her best to avoid sitting on them, so much so that she was only using about half the seat. "Not as scared as you."

Cody nodded. "It's not a bad thing to be scared," he said. "It happens to everyone. You wanna know what the scariest time in my life was?"

Rachel looked at him. "What?"

"When you were born," Cody said. "You were so weak. It was because of all the bad things that your mom put in her body. I was so scared – I kept thinking the worst was going to happen and we didn't really know anyone down here in Texas – we had no close friends and family. You and Mom were in hospital and I was alone, just thinking all the time."

"You told me I had trouble breathing when I was born," Rachel said.

"Yeah," Cody said. "Well it was a bit more serious than that."

"Thanks for telling me."

"Well you didn't need to know before," Cody said, glancing over at her. "Maybe you do now though."

Rachel had her arms folded and she was scowling at him. "Why?"

"I don't know," he said. "To remind you...to remind us that bad times don't last forever."

Cody shook his head. It sounded like he was reading from a bad script. And he'd read his fair share of those over the years.

Her eyes were restless. She looked back and forth between Cody and the road. "What happened?"

"Thought we'd lost you a couple of times," Cody said. "But you didn't quit kid. You knew how to keep fighting and look at us now. Still fighting to stay alive. Look I don't really want to get on a plane either but we're running out of options. Take a look around you honey, it's not safe on the ground around here."

"But it's so dark," Rachel said, looking up at the sky. "What if we crash too?"

Cody pointed a finger at several cracks of light – white specks like a glint of gold sliding around a prospector's pan. They were pushing back against a tide of darkness.

"There's gotta be something…"

His voice trailed off. It was a meager hope and they both knew it. The alternative however, was to give in.

Cody kept his eyes on a smoke-filled collage of red, orange and yellow on the southern horizon.

"We're going to be okay," he said.

They drove past Stone Oak, then the westbound and eastbound flyover bridges that connected the 1604 and the 281. Cody knew he had to stick to the 281 all the way, at least until he saw the first signs for the airport.

That should be anytime now. They were getting close.

Rachel held Bootsy by a single arm. The teddy bear was hanging over the edge of the seat, its legs dangling in midair and on the brink of falling into the abyss. Cody knew she was still worried – who could blame her? But he didn't know what else to say to reassure her. Everything that came out of his mouth sounded forced – like he was giving the big chest-swelling inspirational speech prior to the third act of the movie. He was playing that guy – the hero who picks up his fallen comrades and who instills hope and enough juice to carry them home to victory.

It was a demanding role.

"You want to listen to the radio?" Cody said, reaching for the antique Music Master on his right. Despite insisting that he was done with the radio, Cody was still curious about who was out there. "Now that we're closer to the city maybe we'll pick up something interesting. What do you say?"

Rachel shook her head.

"I don't want to listen to any more of those stories," she said.

Cody yanked his hand away from the radio like it was rigged with explosives.

"Gotcha," he said.

"How long till we get there Dad?"

"Ten minutes honey," he said. "We're almost there."

"Where is everyone?" Rachel said. "What happened to all the people leaving the city?"

Cody shrugged. "My guess is that anyone who was traveling north saw the plane crash and took off in another direction. Or at least they saw the smoke rising from a distance. Being the cautious types, they had a change of heart and went east or west instead. That's what I would have done."

Rachel was looking at him. She opened her mouth to say something but then stopped herself.

"What?" he said.

"Nothing."

"Spit it out."

"What do you mean?" she said.

"Something's on your mind kid. Tell me, please."

She looked at Bootsy.

"What were those people going to do to me?" she said. "The mask people."

Cody gave the steering wheel a little squeeze. "They were going to take you away with them," he said.

"What for?"

"When you were older they were going to..."

"What?"

"Use you."

She was quiet for a second.

"Use me how?"

"You know, to make babies for them. To be a mom."

Rachel screwed up her face in disgust. "Why?" she said.

Cody shrugged. "Because of the way things might go in the future," he said. "We don't know what's happening with the government, the police and army – those things might not even be there anymore. People are going to have to figure out how to look out for themselves. The way Mary Jane was telling it, people are going to do better with a big family behind them. I guess. They wanted you because you're young and healthy and you would have given them lots of sons and daughters."

"That's disgusting," Rachel said.

"It is disgusting," Cody said. "Listen to me kid – from now on ask yourself this question every time you meet someone new – what does this person want from me? Everyone's getting desperate out there. Food supplies are low. There are water shortages. People are scared and they're doing bad things, not necessarily because they're bad people but because they're desperate."

Cody reached a hand out and ruffled Rachel's blonde hair.

"You'll be alright," he said. "I won't let anyone hurt you."

"And I won't let anyone hurt you," Rachel said.

Cody smiled. "Sounds like we're going to make it then."

The steady hum of the Dodge's Hemi engine was constant and soothing as the car traveled south. Cody's eyelids were getting heavier. Once he got on the plane, he wanted nothing more than to sit back and drift off into a deep sleep. And to dream – to dream of anything except the Black Storm.

"I'm going to miss Spring Branch," Rachel said. "All my friends are back there."

Cody thought about the explosion from earlier – the one that happened during his encounter with Kate, aka the Black Widow. Had they turned the car around and drove north back up the 281 to Spring Branch, what would they find instead of their home? Fire and smoke? Or maybe nothing at all.

And what of Rachel's friends?

"You were happy there," Cody said. "Weren't you?"

"It was alright."

"I know it wasn't the most exciting life," Cody said. "But the most exciting lives aren't always the happiest. Take it from somebody who knows."

"You were happy there too," Rachel said. "You liked writing your articles for the magazines and the websites. You liked being boring."

Cody smiled.

"It was the best home I ever had," he said. "Hands down kid. When I was a boy – younger than you are now – your grandparents moved us around a lot. Hippy communes, trailer parks – that kind of thing. Real colorful existence. Sometimes it was fun. We'd meet new people all the time but sometimes it was tough too. My brothers and sisters and me – we had to work hard, busking, doing lame tricks and telling crappy jokes on the street, just so we'd have enough money to eat that night. It was a lot of work being free. And we never hung around the same place for long. I'd start making friends and then my dad would make an announcement, telling us that we'd be moving on soon. We didn't really stop moving, not until I got the part in *The Forever Boys*. And look at me now, huh? On the move again."

Rachel lifted Bootsy onto her lap. She pushed a piece of loose stuffing back into one of several holes on the teddy bear's body.

"Why didn't we bury Mom in Spring Branch?" she asked. "With us."

Cody looked over at her.

"Your mom wanted to be cremated," he said. "I took her back to California."

"I know," Rachel said. "But where is she? Exactly?"

"I scattered her ashes near the Hollywood Reservoir," Cody said. "Went up there disguised in a hat and dark sunglasses. It was just me and your mom. It's real pretty up there and your mom loved it. On a sunny day, the lake and the trees are just beautiful. You can see the Hollywood sign too – I think your mom would have gotten a kick out of that. I'd always hoped to show you that spot someday. Maybe I still can. Someday."

Rachel didn't say anything else. She sat in silence, doing repairs on Bootsy, her fingers frantically trying to keep him intact. As the car traveled south, she worked furiously, trying to seal up all the holes in order to prevent the teddy bear's polyester guts from spilling out all over the car.

CHAPTER TWELVE

The Dodge raced along a desolate, lonely stretch of road.

The highway began to open up as they got closer to the city. Cody now had a choice of five empty lanes to choose from instead of the two he'd been traveling down so far. If nothing else, it was a little less claustrophobic. They spotted several other cars on the road but none of the bright headlights that came into view were pointing towards San Antonio.

Occasionally a few people appeared, walking along the center of the highway. Refugee sightings were few and far between. After the plane crash, north apparently wasn't the most fashionable of directions.

Cody followed the signs on the highway:

'Downtown'.

'San Antonio'.

'The Alamo'.

This last one seemed to pique Rachel's interest. She leaned forward in her seat, studying the words on the sign carefully.

"The Alamo?" she said. "I've heard of that. Haven't I?"

Cody nodded. "Of course you have. Remember the Alamo?"

"What?" she said.

"Wow," he said. "And you've lived in Texas all your life? Remember the Alamo!"

"What do you mean?"

"I'm talking about history," Cody said, looking over at her. "The Alamo is Texan history with a capital 'H'. Hey did you know there was a time when Texas wasn't even part of America?"

"No."

"It's true," he said. "Texas used to belong to Mexico. Then it became an independent state in 18...I don't know, the late nineteenth century or something like that."

"You don't know?" she said. "Some history lesson Dad."

"You want to hear this or not?" Cody said.

"Not," Rachel said.

Cody kept talking anyway while his eyes roamed the highway looking for any more signs to the airport.

"The Mexicans weren't too happy about Texas going off and doing its own thing," he said. "You can imagine. So they laid siege to a little mission located not too far from where we are right now. Bet you can't guess what that mission was called."

Rachel lifted a bored eyebrow. "The Alamo?"

"Right," he said, drumming his fingers on the steering wheel. "Thousands of Mexicans fought against two hundred men who were defending the Alamo. Two hundred – that's crazy right? So the two hundred fought their hearts out and they held out for like two weeks before the Mexicans finally overpowered them. Two weeks man, that's pretty impressive. Ever since then, for Texans and a lot of other people, the Alamo has become a symbol of heroic resistance. Fighting against the odds. And that's exactly what we're doing – you and me. We're like the two hundred."

Rachel turned away, unimpressed. "They all died," she said. "Didn't they? What's so great about that?"

Cody's shoulders slumped in defeat. The Alamo was a great

historical example of courage and bravery, no doubt about that. But Rachel was right – they'd all died in the end.

"Yeah," he said.

He concentrated on the road instead of trying to give any more pep talks. And at last, he saw the sign he was looking for:

'*San Antonio*

Int'l Airport

EXIT 1 MILE'

"Here we go," Cody said.

He merged onto the McAllister Freeway. Soon after that, he followed a sign taking him left towards the airport. Cody's heart was galloping as they got closer to the destination. All the worst-case scenarios that could still happen were playing around in his head on a constant loop. What if he'd taken too long to get here? What if Nick and the others had already gone? What if that mask he'd let go on the 281 appeared on his tail again, all guns blazing and with more of his shotgun-wielding redneck pals standing on the cargo bed?

And what about the refugees? What if they'd been flocking on foot towards the airport? They were searching for a way out the city. Why wouldn't they try the airport? It was possible wasn't it? What if Nick saw them coming – hordes and hordes of people who may or may not have been infected with Black Fever? He would have been left with little choice.

Was the plane still there?

The sweat was running down Cody's forehead.

When at last he reached the airport, he followed the signs towards Terminal A, just as Nick had instructed him to do. The area was dimly lit and there were no other cars and no people in sight.

Cody pulled up outside the terminal building. He let go of the wheel and his head fell back onto the seat with a quiet thud. With a sad smile, he turned the Dodge's engine off for the last time. He gave the steering wheel an affectionate pat.

"We did it," he said.

"You talking to me?" Rachel said.

"I was talking to the car honey."

"You're weird."

Cody closed his eyes. He felt like he'd been on the road for days, as if he'd just completed a cross-country trip from one side of America to the other, non-stop. In reality, he'd driven about twenty-six miles from Spring Branch to San Antonio International Airport. Twenty-six miles that felt like twenty-six hundred.

Now all they had to do was find the plane.

Cody had memorized the next part. Once they got inside the terminal, they had to follow the signs for departures and make their way down to Gate A5. Walk through the door of the gate and onto the apron. That's where the white and blue Alaska Airlines plane would be waiting for them.

Cody pulled the key out of the ignition.

"Dad," Rachel said. "Look. Do you see that car over there?"

She was pointing at a police car parked further down outside the terminal building. Cody had noticed it as he'd pulled up, assuming it was just one of thousands of abandoned vehicles lying scattered around the San Antonio area.

He leaned forward in the driver's seat.

It was a Ford Explorer Police Interceptor. The passenger door was lying wide open, pointing towards the terminal entrance. Upon first glance it looked like someone had exited the car and ran into the airport in a hurry. Poking his head through the Dodge's open window, Cody saw the words 'San Antonio Police – Protecting the Alamo City' written on the side of the car.

"That's the real deal," he said. "SAPD. I wonder what it's doing there."

"Do you think the police are in the airport?" Rachel asked.

"I doubt it," Cody said. He sure hoped not. He didn't want to have to walk in and explain to anybody what he was doing there with his daughter and a couple of heavily packed backpacks. But what if some do-gooder asshole had snitched on Nick and told the authorities that a black man had laid siege to San Antonio airport and was at present trying to steal an expensive Alaska Airlines plane?

The police were too busy downtown to care. Weren't they?

Cody took another look at the black and white Explorer. It looked empty. He glanced at the terminal, searching for any sign of activity taking place inside the building.

"Don't see anything," he said. "You?"

"No," Rachel said.

"Maybe somebody just left it here," Cody said.

"Maybe it broke down," Rachel said.

Cody nodded. "Come to think of it," he said. "Whoever left it there is probably one of Nick's friends. Yeah that's gotta be it. Nick knows a few cops downtown. Looks like whoever it is, they're getting on the plane too. Everyone else must have parked in the car park, apart from us latecomers."

Rachel looked satisfied with that explanation.

"Anyway," Cody said, pushing the driver's door open. "We've got to go kid. Let's grab the bags out the back and get moving."

Cody got out of the car, opened up the trunk and threw the two backpacks onto the ground. They took out some of the plastic water bottles and crammed as many as they could into what little room was left in their bags. Cody had already put some food items into the bags back at the house – fruit, sandwiches, potato chips, nuts and chocolate. Anything he could think of that would fight off the hunger pangs while they were up in the air. There were some books in there for Rachel to read too. Thin ones.

Cody packed the ammo and speed loader into his bag. He

zipped up the bulging backpack and checked that Rachel's bag, also crammed to bursting point, was closed too.

He stood up straight.

"Ready?" he said.

"What about the car?" Rachel said, taking a step back from the Dodge.

Cody looked at his beloved 1970 Dodge Challenger with a heavy heart. His stomach felt like it was tied up in a tight knot. It wasn't just the car – it was the many memories associated with it. Some of them bittersweet. A decade ago, he'd undertaken the journey of his life in the Dodge when he'd travelled from California to Texas with Kate. And with Rachel too, who would have been about the size of an apple in Kate's womb at the time.

"This is where we say goodbye," Cody said.

"I wish we could take it with us," Rachel said.

Cody smiled. "Me too."

He looked at the car key, which was fastened to a small Swiss Army Knife keyring. It was sitting next to the house key, which opened the door to a house that he'd never see again either. He tucked the keys into his pocket. At least he'd be able to take a little piece of the house and the car with him on the next stage of the journey.

Cody gave the car a final pat on the hood. "Thanks old buddy."

He took a step back.

"Let's go Rachel," he said, throwing another wary glance towards the abandoned-looking police car in the distance. He walked to the front of the Dodge, grabbed the gun out of the driver's side and checked there were still plenty of bullets in the magazine. When he was satisfied there was enough, he tucked the Glock into the waist of his jeans.

"Got your passport?" Cody asked.

Rachel held the teddy bear up. "I've got Bootsy."

"Guess that'll have to do," he said.

Cody walked over to the two backpacks lying on the ground. Rachel held a hand up.

"I want to carry my bag," she said.

"It's heavy," Cody said. "It'll slow you down."

"I want to carry it. It's my bag."

He sighed. "Alright."

Cody handed the backpack to Rachel and she swung it over her shoulder. She grunted slightly under the weight.

They turned around and walked into Terminal A.

"So what now?" Rachel said. She was looking at the display boards next to the check-in area. All the boards were switched off. Although the lights inside the terminal building had been left on, it looked like the airport hadn't been in service for weeks, maybe even months.

Cody looked up at the ceiling. "I sure hope that was Nick who put the lights on."

"What did you say?" Rachel said.

"Nothing kid."

"So where are we going?"

"Gate A5," Cody said. "Alaska Airlines."

"Alaska?" Rachel said. "It's freezing up there."

Cody shrugged. "Yeah but maybe it's too cold for the Black Storm," he said. "You ever think about that? If so, I'll take it."

As he spoke, his eyes darted back and forth around the terminal. It was so quiet inside the building.

They walked further inside and found a sign for departures. Cody led Rachel across the building, suppressing the urge to take out his gun. Even though he'd have been more comfortable with it in his hand, he kept it tucked in at the waist. He wanted Rachel to feel safe – to think that they'd made it. She'd already gone through a lifetime of worry that day.

They both had.

The terminal's interior was sleek and modern. The color scheme was mostly white and cream, the style tasteful and minimalistic, at least just enough to avoid an aura of blandness. As Cody and Rachel walked towards the departure gates, large digital display screens were scattered throughout but like the other boards they'd encountered, none of them worked.

It wasn't long before they found a sign for Gate A5. They hurried off in that direction, looking out for subsequent signs to the gate.

Cody was beginning to believe that this last part of the journey would go smoothly after all. It was about time something went their way. Both sets of footsteps were light, echoing around the deserted airport. There was even a spring in their step now.

"Do you think the car's okay?" Rachel said, looking up at him.

He nodded. "Yeah I think..."

Cody stopped dead in his tracks. He grabbed a hold of his daughter's arm and pulled her back.

There was a man standing further down the terminal.

It was a cop.

The cop was walking towards them. His face was curious but he remained silent as he closed the gap. There was no friendly greeting and no rapid-fire, robotic cop jargon to try and intimidate them either.

The man's shoes made a loud clicking noise on the hard floor.

"Good evening sir," said the cop. "Ma'am. How are you both?" He spoke with a stereotypically overdone West Texan accent – it was a lousy John Wayne impression that didn't fit neatly with the boyish face. He couldn't have been more than thirty years old. The cop possessed a pair of striking, emerald green eyes. He had long sideburns and he was handsome in a delicate, almost feminine way. The most striking thing of all was his skin – it was a sickly, pallid gray, which hinted of a lurking illness beneath the surface.

Cody looked at the man's uniform – the dark blues, the silver badge and the equipment belt wrapped around his waist. He wondered what the cop was doing at the airport. There was a lot of valuable equipment in the building. Had he been sent to patrol the area, to guard it against looters?

Cody was glad that he hadn't taken out his gun after all. The cop's pistol was drawn and hanging by his side as he walked. The man looked ready to go. Things might have gotten ugly if Cody had been carrying his gun.

"Good evening officer," Cody said, despite it still being mid-morning. "My name's Cody MacLeod and this is my daughter Rachel."

The cop smiled, showing off a row of white, slightly crooked teeth.

"What are you doing here at the airport Cody and Rachel MacLeod?" He spoke playfully, like he was talking to two young children instead of one.

The man took a step closer. Cody recognized the gun in the cop's hand as a police standard, a Smith & Wesson M&P40. He found himself thinking back to the black and white Explorer sitting outside the terminal building. That was a real cop's uniform the guy was wearing. That was a real cop car parked outside. And that was a real cop's gun in his hand.

But something didn't fit.

"We're here to meet a friend," Cody said. "That's all."

"You shouldn't be here mister," the cop said. He pointed the gun at Cody and Rachel. In a split second his tone had shifted from playful to pissed off. "The city's in big trouble and we need all hands on board downtown putting out fires and helping people. You know what I mean?"

Cody nodded. *Yeah? So what the hell are you doing here?*

"I hear what you're saying," Cody said. "Really I do. But I gotta meet my friend first. I said we'd be here."

The man laughed – a sneering adolescent cackle that made Cody's blood run cold.

"You're fleeing the sinking ship aren't you mister?" he said, putting a hand to his mouth, trying to suppress the giggles. "I know what's going on here."

"What do you mean?" Cody said.

"You think I don't know about that plane out there?" he said. "Gate A5, right? It's a big plane, Alaska Airlines. It's like a modern day Ark, ain't it? All set to fly up into the sky and escape the drowning world. That's what you're here for right? You've got a ticket to ride with black Noah. The animals went in two by two. Hurrah! Hurrah! Tell me mister, what animal are you? The elephant? The kangaroo?"

The plane was still there. Despite the tense situation, Cody's heart leapt with joy when he heard that.

"Look man," he said. "I'm just trying to keep my daughter safe, you know?"

"And yourself," the man said, pointing the gun at Cody in a stabbing motion. "Don't forget that. Don't you go pretending to be some sort of saint now."

Cody nodded. "Yeah," he said. "You're right."

The cop grinned and looked at Rachel. His dazzling green eyes lingered on her in a way that made Cody squirm.

"She's a pretty girl," the man said. "Damn pretty."

Cody clenched his jaw.

"Are you really a cop?" he asked.

The man grinned. "What do you think?"

"I think I'd like to see some ID please."

"You see the badge don't you?" the cop said.

"How do I know it's yours?" Cody said. "Show me something else man. You got a wallet on you? All those doughnuts you cops eat don't come cheap. You gotta be carrying a wallet on you."

The man looked at Cody with dead eyes.

"It's in the car," he said. "Parked outside. Are you going to be difficult sir?"

"No I'm not *sir*," Cody fired back. "I'm a law-abiding citizen. But as you can see, these are hard times and I gotta wonder what an officer of the law is doing holed up in an abandoned airport when the city he's supposed to serve is going up in flames. I'm talking about the Black Fever. There are people out there losing their minds. They need your help."

There was a slight twitch at the corner of the man's mouth. He was still looking at Rachel with ravenous eyes.

"Pretty girl," he said again.

Cody did his best to stay calm. Time was running out and they had to get past this guy.

"Lot of people out there talking about starting anew," the man said. His green eyes were staring into empty space now. "They're looking for pretty girls. You hear it on the street all the time these days. People are thinking about the future – they're talking about hauling ass out the city. Everybody thinks there's gotta be some-where the Black Storm don't reach. Not so sure about that myself. Anyway these people, they want breeders, you know? Girls, good looking ones, to start over their families with. A big family – it might be the difference between life and death in the New Eden. Between being strong and being weak. That's what they say."

He pointed at Rachel.

"A little golden-haired beauty like that? They'd pay a lot of money to get their hands on you princess."

Cody took a deep breath.

"You're not a cop," he said, keeping his voice low. "Are you? You stole that Ford Explorer out front. Didn't you, *mister*? You stole the uniform and the gun. What I want to know is what happened to the cop you stole them from – did you kill him? Is he still in that police car out there? In the trunk?"

The man's smile faded.

"Do you really want to know?" he said.

"I do," Cody said. *As long as you stop looking at Rachel.*

"Wait till you hear about the day I've had," the man said. "First thing, I went over to my parents' house to see if they were still alive. Hadn't heard from them in a long time. Guess I should've checked up on them sooner. Some son I am, huh? Turns out they weren't alive. My best guess is that my dad had the Fever. He'd bludgeoned Mom to death with a golf club before hanging himself in the living room. Who knows? Maybe it wasn't the Fever that got him. He was always teetering on the edge of crazy, the old bastard."

"I'm sorry man," Cody said. "Really I..."

The man held a hand up, indicating that he wasn't finished.

"Anyway," he said. "I was sitting in the backyard after that, trying to process what I'd seen and that's when I heard them talking."

"Who?" Cody asked.

"The couple next door," the man said. "Tom and Linda Wagner. Well they had a plan, didn't they? The city was toast but that's okay because Tom and Linda had a plan. Whoopee-doo! And they were talking it over, unaware that I was listening on the other side of the fence. Somebody they knew, I guess it was Black Noah, had invited them to the airport. Apparently there was a plane – a big one, not one of those paperweight deathtraps falling out of the sky. It was going to get them out of San Antonio. Yes sir, Tom and Linda were being offered a free ticket for the Ark. The select few, middle-class and beautiful, had been chosen."

The man wiped his nose with the back of his hand.

"I thought about asking them," he said. "Straight up. Can I come with you please? My family are dead and I ain't got nothing anymore. But I knew what they'd say – limited space and all that crap. They always thought I was bit weird. But it didn't matter because I heard everything I needed to hear – Gate A5, Alaska Airlines – come as quickly as you can."

He tapped the barrel of the gun off the silver San Antonio police badge. It made a loud clinking noise.

"Now here's the good part," the man said. "I knew that whoever was organizing this escape pod wouldn't take me. So I thought to myself, what if I turned up at the party dressed as someone else? Let's say an authority figure, someone they wouldn't dare refuse."

He laughed like it was supposed to be funny.

"So I took my old man's car and I drove downtown," he said. "Holy shit, it's bad there. Like there's some real fire and brimstone biblical shit going on. Place was swarming with cops, still acting like they were king of the hill. But hold on I say, because the hill is on fire! Well those cops were so scattered and disorganized that it was easy pickings. Nobody cares about their authority anymore. Found me a crowbar, sneaked up on this old boy about my size and build, and WHACK! Took the man's uniform and drove here as fast as I could. Yes I did."

"The cop's dead?" Cody asked.

"Oh yeah," the man said. "If you'd seen him you wouldn't be asking."

Cody hesitated. "But they didn't let you on the plane, right?"

The man lowered his gun.

"You're a smart guy," he said. "Black Noah took one look at me, pointed his shotgun at my head and told me to get-the-fuck-outta-here. Cop or no cop, he said – you ain't getting on my plane. *His* plane? There were several guns on me. Not what you'd call a warm welcome."

"Look," Cody said. "I'm real sorry about your folks. It's tough to lose your family like that, I know. But I'm trying to protect my daughter from the Black Storm. You wouldn't begrudge her a way out of this mess, would you?"

The man looked thoughtful for a second.

"You know something pal," he said. "Yes I would. Why should I be the only one getting screwed today?"

Cody ran a hand through his sweat-soaked hair.

"You're not well mister," he said. "You're not thinking right. Please just..."

Cody gasped. He saw something over the man's shoulder.

The Black Widow was in the terminal.

She was approaching the young man from behind. She came slowly, floating down the terminal building like a ghost traipsing through the corridors of a haunted house. There was no life in her features – only those silver orbs, gleaming on her deathly pale face.

Her long black mourning dress trailed behind her like a vast, sprawling cloak.

Rachel must have seen it too because she dug her fingers deep into the back of Cody's hand, her nails slicing through his skin.

Cody wanted to say something – to warn the man. But it all happened so fast. The Black Widow glided towards the young man and entered his body.

She vanished.

"Dad," Rachel said. "Do you..."

Cody gave her hand a squeeze. "Yes."

The man whimpered like a frightened child. His emerald eyes lit up, his body stiffened, and for a second it looked like he was about to keel over in shock. Then his shoulders drooped as he appeared to relax. Slowly, he lifted his head and looked over at Cody and Rachel.

His green eyes had dulled to charcoal black.

The man's expression had also darkened. His pallid grey skin was dry and wrinkled, making him look much older than his thirty or so years.

The gun was pointing at Cody and Rachel again.

"Why won't they let me on the plane?" he said. His voice was shaking, like a little child on the brink of tears. "They sent me away. What am I supposed to do? I'm alone. My parents are dead. Why doesn't anyone want to help me? And now you want to leave me alone too. What is it with you people? You think you're so much better than everyone else. Aren't we supposed to stick together at times like this?"

Cody let go of Rachel's hand. His fingers moved towards the gun tucked into his waist.

"Hey man," he said. "It's the Black Fever talking, you understand? You gotta fight it."

The young man laughed. He was pointing the Smith & Wesson back and forth between Cody and Rachel like he was playing eeny, meeny, miny, moe.

"No I'm just tired," the man said. "Tired of being treated like shit by everyone. Tired of living. Aren't you sick of it all? You look exhausted mister. Well I can help you with that. I'm going to do you a favor. Ain't nobody going to take your little girl from you. No breeder mob will touch her, I'll make sure of that. Yeah, how about this? How about we stay together forever in this airport – all three of us? One shot each, that's all it takes."

He smiled at Rachel, baring his teeth like a wild animal.

"I'll do you first little girl," he said. "Close your eyes."

The gun stopped moving. It was pointing at Rachel.

"No!" Cody yelled. He threw his hands up in the air, pleading with the man to stop.

Cody pushed Rachel as hard as he could. He possessed the superhuman strength of a parent witnessing their child in extreme danger. In that moment, he was sucked into another world where time slowed down, where colors were brighter and more intense, where sound was clearer, and the entire universe was inside him.

Bang!

Rachel dodged the bullet. She fell out of range of the gunfire, rolling onto her side and curling up into a tight ball on the ground.

When Cody saw that Rachel was safe, he returned to the lesser plane of existence. This was where pain still existed. Almost immediately, he felt a searing heat coming from his side and when he looked down he saw blood pouring from a wound at his side.

"Shit," he said, dropping onto one knee.

He heard the fake cop walking towards him. Cody looked up at the man and saw that his eyes were like two black moons stuck to his head.

"It'll be alright," the man said. "I'm here. I'm here."

Cody kept his hand pressed against his left side, applying pressure to the wound. He was leaking.

His fingers fumbled at his waist, trying to reach the Glock tucked underneath his shirt. But he was grasping at nothing – his hands couldn't keep up with his brain.

"It's going to be alright," a voice said.

The man was standing over him. Cody looked up and saw the black pistol pointing at his head.

"I'll see you on the other side brother," the man said. "I won't be far behind. And neither will your little girl. It's better this way."

Cody closed his eyes. His head dropped, like he was baring his neck to the blade of a sharp axe. He didn't even have the strength to beg for his daughter's life anymore.

Rachel. I'm sorry.

There was an explosion of noise. It sounded like something else blowing up in San Antonio. Had the end of things come at last? Maybe the old city would go into the history books at exactly the same time as ex-Hollywood superstar, Cody MacLeod.

He waited for the darkness to envelop his mind. But nothing happened.

Cody dared to look up and just as he did, the man in the police uniform toppled over like a falling statue. There was a trickle of dark blood pouring out of his mouth and running down his chin.

One hand was reaching towards a massive, bloody hole that had been ripped open in his chest.

"Die motherfucker!" a booming voice yelled.

Cody heard somebody running. Footsteps came closer. It sounded like a Greek God striding over the clouds on Mount Olympus.

"Cody!" a man's voice yelled. "Are you okay man? Talk to me."

Cody felt himself being dragged up to his feet. He wasn't sure he'd be able to stand but once he was back on two legs, he leaned on the other man's shoulder for support while he regained his composure.

He looked at the man's face and grinned.

"Nick?" he said. "Is that you?"

"Hell yes," the man said, laughing. It was a deep glorious rumbling sound that shook the floor.

It *was* Nick Norton. He was standing there in all his splendor – six foot five, two hundred and eighty pounds, and built like a linebacker with boulders for shoulders. His black skull was shaved almost to the bone and he was sporting a pencil thin goatee that Cody immediately loathed. Cody had expected to see Nick strutting around in his beloved pilot's uniform but to his surprise, the big man was wearing a navy blue t-shirt and dark pants. He looked like he was about to head off for a round of golf with the boys.

A black and tan rifle was hanging at Nick's side.

"What took you so long asshole?" Cody said. "You had to wait till I got shot before riding to the rescue?"

Nick wrapped his arms around Cody and squeezed him tight. Cody yelped. It felt like he was hugging a grizzly bear.

"Good to see you!" Nick said.

Cody winced under the weight of the man's tree-trunk arms. "You too," he said. "Although that beard is ugly as hell man."

"Fuck you too," Nick said with a grin.

Like Cody, Nick Norton had been a beloved child star in the

1980s. But in the man's own words he'd 'grown pissed off with playing the token black kid in all those coming of age movies about white kids and their stupid white problems'. Acting wasn't a man's game anyway, not according to Nick. As a result of his dissatisfaction with the industry, he'd bailed on Hollywood, went to college and eventually joined the air force.

"Dad!"

Rachel ran over and wrapped her arms around Cody's neck, nearly strangling him in the process. He'd just survived a near death encounter and now the two people he loved most in the world were trying to kill him with hugs.

"Oww!" he yelped, pressing a hand against his wound.

"My God!" Nick said, taking a step back and looking at Rachel. "Little Rachel MacLeod, is that you? The last time I saw you, you were about the size of my thumb."

Rachel laughed.

Cody kneeled down to inspect the damage on his side. Nick stepped forward and beat him to it. He lifted Cody's shirt and took a good look.

Nick looked unimpressed, like he was staring at a shaving cut.

"The bullet grazed you, that's all," he said. "Just a flesh wound."

"It hurts man," Cody said.

"Don't be a pussy," Nick said. He looked at Rachel and his face was instantly apologetic. "Sorry Rachel."

"She's heard a lot worse than that," Cody said.

"Can we go now?" Rachel said, looking at them both. "Is the plane ready?"

"It's ready now you're here," Nick said, holding the rifle across his chest. "Fashionably late I might add – so much so that I decided to come looking for you guys. Good job I did, right? I see this dead asshole wasn't in any hurry to leave."

CHAPTER THIRTEEN

Cody, Rachel and Nick set off towards Gate A5. They'd been walking in that direction no more than ten seconds when a strange, shuffling noise stopped them in their tracks.

They turned around.

The corpse on the floor was twitching.

The three of them stood there, watching in horror as a spasmodic jerking of the dead man's muscles proceeded to throw the lifeless body back and forth across the blood-splattered surface. It looked like his soul was a prisoner, trapped inside the mortal flesh.

Cody knew better. The man's soul – if he'd had one – was long gone.

Nick pointed his rifle at the convulsing corpse. "What the...?" he said. "He can't be alive. I just put a hole in that guy the size of West Virginia."

"He's not alive," Cody said.

The body stopped moving. A spray of black mist shot out of it, like steam rising from a kettle. It hovered in mid-air, lingering above the dead man.

"You've got to be kidding me," Nick said.

The dark mist swayed gently, like it was dancing to soft music. A statuesque woman was reborn out of the cloud – the black vapor at the edge forming the arms, while legs sprouted out of its underside. Two silver orbs materialized at the top, along with last but not least, a deathly pale head. It was a graceful, artistic formation of life. In any other context, it might have been beautiful.

"It's her," Rachel said.

The Black Widow's face was a blank canvas. There was no emotion, no sign of anything resembling life. She was a seven-foot doll. Yet she didn't need facial features to express her intent towards Cody, Rachel and Nick.

She glided slowly towards them.

"This is bad," Cody said.

"I'm going to shoot the bitch," Nick said. He rolled the rifle to the side, the muzzle still pointing at the Black Widow. He checked the magazine, then ran the action and rolled the weapon back onto his shoulder. All in a matter of seconds.

"Don't," Cody said, putting a hand on the muzzle of the rifle. "It's a waste of time. You can't hurt her with a gun."

"You got a better idea?" Nick said.

Cody shook his head. "No."

"Dad," Rachel said, taking a forward step. Her eyes were locked onto the Black Widow. "She's coming for you. I can...feel it."

"Rachel," Cody said, putting a firm hand on her shoulder. "Come on, we're going to have to make a run for it."

"No," she said.

Rachel looked at Cody. He saw the defiance in her eyes – bravery, foolishness, hard-headedness, call it what you will. It was a familial trait, passed down from mother to daughter. Kate had been a stubborn mess of a woman in life – the drugs, the glamour, the neverending hope of making a comeback and reclaiming the spotlight once again. She wouldn't let go of the dream. She chose her path and it was to walk the road of excess that supposedly led to William Blake's palace of wisdom.

The Black Widow glided forward. Rachel stood her ground.

"Rachel," Cody said. "Do you hear me? We have to go now."

He grabbed a hold of her arm and dragged her away.

"No Dad," she said. "She's coming for you."

"C'mon Rachel! She's coming for all of us."

Cody tried to pull Rachel back but a sharp pain flared up in his side. He winced and was forced into loosening his grip on Rachel's arm. He doubled over in pain and Rachel took advantage, managing to wriggle free of Cody's weakened grip.

She ran towards the Black Widow.

"Rachel!" Cody yelled. He pressed a hand to the wound on his side. It was bleeding profusely.

Rachel didn't listen or turn around. She kept running towards the Black Widow, the teddy bear swinging at her side.

"Stop!" Cody yelled. He was about to chase after her again but Nick threw a heavily muscled arm out, blocking Cody's path. Nick pointed to the rifle in his hand.

"You're no use right now partner," he said. "Let me take care of this."

Nick gently shoved Cody out of the way. With the rifle in hand, he watched Rachel running towards the Black Widow. Slowly, he took aim.

"Don't shoot my kid," Cody said.

"I'll try not to," Nick said. His index finger teased the trigger. Then he fired.

Crack!

The first shot went through the Black Widow like an arrow flying through the mist. The Black Widow kept coming forward and Nick fired again but with the same outcome. He was shooting at a ghost.

"Damn it," Nick said, lowering the rifle. "How are we supposed to fight?"

Rachel stopped running. She looked over her shoulder at Cody and Nick, as if to make sure nobody was trying to catch up with her. Then she stood her ground, waiting while the Black Widow came to meet her.

The red-haired phantom's long ghoulish arms were outstretched.

"Rachel!" Cody yelled out. "Run!"

"She's not going to take you away," Rachel said.

The little girl took a step forward. She thrust her head forward, like someone leaning out of the window of a tall building to look down below onto the street. Then she screamed. It wasn't the scream of a frightened ten-year-old child. It was an angry scream and it echoed around the airport, forcing the end of the world, which was taking place outside, to take a back seat.

The Black Widow was pushed backwards by the weight of the scream. She was like a butterfly caught in a hurricane. Rachel walked forward, still screaming, pushing the Black Widow away from her father.

Cody and Nick watched from afar, their mouths hanging open.

Rachel stopped screaming and the Black Widow bobbed around in mid-air, like a piece of flotsam caught in treacherous waters. The little girl swung her arm back and with all her strength, threw Bootsy at the Black Widow. The teddy bear flew through the air like a guided missile, striking a direct hit on the Black Widow's lifeless face.

Two silver orbs flickered on and off like a faulty television screen.

The Black Widow put her hands to her face like she'd been doused in acid.

"Look!" Cody said, tapping Nick on the arm. "Outside."

Both men looked through the window. The black sky that had smothered their lives for so long blinked on and off like a broken light bulb. It did this several times and in between Cody saw a miracle – he saw the blue sky and a scattering of cotton ball clouds. He saw the sun. It was glorious as it reached for its zenith in the sky.

Nick saw it too. "Holy shit!" he said. "Cody..."

"I see it," Cody said.

But the miracle was short-lived. Seconds later, the world reverted back to darkness.

There was no sign of the Black Widow in the airport. Rachel was standing alone where the confrontation had taken place moments earlier. The only hint that the ghostly woman had been there at all was the dead man in the police uniform lying on the floor, his body soaking in a pool of fresh blood.

Rachel turned around. In that moment, her eyes were as blue as Cody had ever seen them. They were practically glowing, every bit as blue as the sky that had appeared outside during the short-lived miracle.

She walked over and picked Bootsy off the floor. With a half-smile on her face, she dusted him down with the back of her hand.

Cody ran over to her and dropped onto his knees. He grabbed Rachel by the shoulders. There was blood all over his hands and he was getting it on her clothes.

He tried to ignore the gnawing pain at his side.

"What the hell were you thinking?" he said. His voice was cracking as he spoke. "I could have lost you."

Rachel shook her head.

"She was coming for you Dad," Rachel said. "I wasn't going to let her take you away from me. Not you."

"What do you mean?" Cody said. "How could you know she was coming for me?"

Rachel shrugged. "I just did."

Nick walked up behind them, laughing like a man who'd just found the winning lottery ticket sitting on his doorstep. "Well, well, well," he said. "Ain't nobody as badass as daddy's little girl."

"What did you do?" Cody said, looking at Rachel.

"I don't know," she said. "Something just happened..."

"What do you mean? Something happened inside you?"

Rachel nodded.

"Whatever she did the girl just embarrassed us both," Nick said. "She did with a teddy bear what I couldn't do with an AR-15 semi-automatic rifle. No matter what happens, I'll never doubt that kid again. Now what do you say folks – are we going to catch this plane or not? I for one, would like to get the hell out of here."

Rachel looked up at Nick and nodded.

Cody tried to wipe some of the blood off Rachel's dungarees. He was only making it worse.

"Sorry," Cody said, taking his hands off her. "Look what I did."

"Are you hurt?" Rachel said, pointing to his wound.

"It's not as bad as it looks kid," Cody said. "You ready to keep going?"

She nodded. "Okay."

They hurried towards Gate A5. Nick led the way, guiding them through the gate door and out onto the apron.

The plane was waiting for them. Cody almost wept with relief at the sight of it. Despite everything that had happened on the road and in the airport, they'd made it. It was like looking at a giant mechanized angel. It wasn't the biggest plane Cody had ever seen – it was about a hundred and thirty feet long but it was a damn sight bigger and sturdier than all those private planes that were dropping out of the sky. This plane wouldn't let them down – he was sure of it. Not with Nick Norton sitting at the helm.

There was a large face printed on the tail of the blue and white aircraft – an Eskimo's face. It had a welcoming smile.

They walked forward. The plane was humming in anticipation as bright white light flooded onto the apron from the floodlights.

"We made it," Cody said, squeezing Rachel on the arm.

Nick laughed. "You sure did," he said. "And we're getting out of here, you better believe it folks. This plane is *my* baby. She's going to take good care of us up there, trust me. The Black Storm can kiss my black ass."

Rachel giggled.

Cody saw several other planes parked further along the apron. They were all Alaska Airlines, about the same size as their plane. They sat there in the dark, like giant, expensive toys that somebody had gotten bored with.

"Hey Nick," Cody said, pointing to their plane. "Is that thing ready to fly? Straight up man?"

Nick slung the rifle over his shoulder. His eyes stared out into the blackish-gray gloom of morning. "Don't worry about the plane," he said. "What do you think we've been doing all day while you were cruising down the highway in that 1970 Dodge Challenger of yours? We're on it. We've got oxygen, electricity, food and water – everything we need to get up there. And stay up there for as long as we need."

"So it really is the Ark then," Cody said.

Nick screwed up his face. "The Ark?"

"That's what that loon in the cop uniform called it," Cody said. "He called you Black Noah by the way."

Nick threw his head back and laughed. It was deep and bellowing – the laugh of someone who hadn't quite given up on the world yet.

"Black Noah," Nick said. "I like that." He looked at Cody and slapped him gently on the arm. "Glad you made it bro," he said. "Boy you sure cut it close though. San Antonio is a goner – they're ripping it to pieces. Blowing cars and buildings up like they were toys – you have to see it to believe it."

"Yeah," Cody said. He pointed at the plane. "Did everyone make it here?"

"They're all here," Nick said. "Some of them have been here for a long time. They've been sitting on the plane and they won't get up for anything. Some of them have been getting restless, bitching and moaning about still being on the ground. Told them we were doing safety checks, all that bullshit. Sounded better than telling them the truth – that we were waiting for your slowcoach ass to get here. Anyway, this is Nick Norton's party and it ain't starting till all the guests have arrived."

"Thanks for waiting," Cody said.

Nick smiled. He led them towards a set of airstairs at the back of the plane. With no ground services to assist takeoff preparations, they were using the stairs that folded and stowed under the floor of the back door.

Rachel climbed up first. Cody was right behind her with one hand pinned to his side, applying pressure to the wound. He glanced up at the smiling Eskimo and felt reassured by the serene expression on the man's face. The Eskimo was saying 'everything's going to be okay'. At least that's what Cody hoped he was saying.

Nick walked up the airstairs behind them. "You guys are sitting at the back," he said. "First two seats on your right. Row 31."

"Not first class?" Cody said, looking over his shoulder.

"Spare me the prima donna movie star bullshit," Nick said with a wicked glint in his eye. "This ain't Hollywood and judging by the last few movies you made you should be sitting in the crapper."

"Fair enough," Cody said.

They walked into the cabin. It was a full house. While Nick stayed behind to pull the airstairs in, Cody and Rachel found their seats, located at the rear of the fuselage. There was a young man, perhaps in his early twenties, sitting at the window seat in their row of three. He looked at Cody and Rachel and smiled. Then he noticed Cody's wound and bloodstained hands.

The man's face turned a ghastly shade of white.

"Don't worry," Cody said. "It's not contagious."

The man turned away – he looked less than enthralled at the prospect of sitting next to the MacLeods for the rest of the journey. That was alright with Cody – he wasn't in the mood to talk anyway. Especially not to strangers.

Rachel squeezed into the row and took the middle seat. As she sat down, she propped Bootsy up on her lap.

Cody sat down on the aisle seat. Almost immediately he felt lightheaded, like his body was teetering on the edge of exhaustion.

He caught sight of other people looking at him. Maybe it was the blood on his hands and shirt that drew their attention. Or maybe they recognized him – after all, he was the stutter kid from *The Forever Boys*.

Cody heard the hatch door closing behind him.

Nick walked down the aisle seconds later, his footsteps like cannon fire.

"Alright boys and girls," he said, stopping in the center of the aisle. "Now I know a lot of you have questions so now's a good time to spit 'em out. Right now, before we take off. Don't be shy."

An old lady sitting in an aisle seat raised her hand. She had a plastic crate on her lap and Cody saw two black and white cats moving around inside. Now it really did feel like he was on the Ark.

"She's got cats," Rachel said, pointing that way.

"I see them," Cody said.

"Shoot," Nick said to the old woman. "What's your question?"

"Will there be other planes up there?" she asked. "How can we fly anywhere without air traffic control watching over us?"

"Don't worry about it ma'am," Nick said, flashing her a toothy grin. He pointed a thumb over his shoulder. "We've got all that good avionic shit going on in the cockpit back there – everything's working just fine. TCAS – that's traffic alert and collision avoidance system, that's working too. Other planes won't be a factor because well, there ain't going to be any. We're pretty much alone up there. Let me reassure you – all of you – that this plane is fully fuelled and that the equipment is in good working order."

A young man – mid thirties, shot his hand in the air. He was dressed like a grunge rocker from the early nineties, with Kurt Cobain hair and a plaid shirt with ripped jeans. He was sitting beside a woman and a restless young boy who was about four or five years old.

"Go," Nick said, pointing at the man.

"What about the Black Widow?" the man said.

There was a murmur of discontent amongst the other passengers.

"Look I'm sorry," the man said, turning towards the grumbling. "I know nobody wants to think about it or talk about it but what if she gets in here? How do we stop the pilots from getting the Black Fever and taking us down? I'm still not sure I've done the right thing coming here. I just..."

Nick held up a hand, cutting the man off.

"That's an excellent question sir," he said. "Let me tell you something. We've got seven pilots on this plane. *Seven* damn good pilots. Anyone starts acting weird, getting all morbid and singing Radiohead songs at the top of their voice, it ain't going to go unnoticed by the rest of us. Another thing – the cockpit will not be locked. Never. We have multiple keys on board, just in case anyone tries any funny shit. All guns are locked out of reach in the hold. There are no sharp objects. Precautions have been taken so let me assure you, this plane is as Black Widow-proof as we can possibly make it."

Nick looked around the cabin. "Any other questions?"

"Where are we going?" somebody yelled.

Nick pointed towards the ceiling.

"Up there," he said. "Let me tell you something ladies and gentleman. Today I saw a miracle – I saw the blue sky for the first time in a long time. Now that's another story and we can talk about it later. But trust me – this baby's gonna take us through that black shroud, I know it is. We'll find something better than this. Somewhere that ain't burning up like San Antonio."

"So you don't know where we're going?" the same voice yelled.

"Sir," Nick said, fixing a hard stare on the man. "You know as well as I do that this is not a normal flight. Nobody here is going on vacation to Hawaii for two weeks. Do you see anyone wearing a grass skirt? Or wearing one of those flowery shirts? The other pilots and myself, we're going to figure it out. Nothing is guaranteed BUT you got a shot here. Now if anyone wants to leave and take their chances in what's left of San Antonio you're more than welcome. I'll open the doors for you right now. Let me know because this is your last chance to walk away. We're taking off in a few minutes."

Several discussions broke out amongst the passengers. Heads leaned in close to one another as opinions were shared back and forth.

But nobody raised their hand.

"Alright," Nick said. "The human race ain't beat yet. Am I right?"

The response was sluggish.

"AM I RIGHT?" Nick yelled.

The passengers were livelier second time around.

Nick signaled over to Cody, pointing at his wound. "We'll get someone to take a look at that."

Cody gave a sluggish thumbs up gesture in return.

Nick disappeared down the fuselage towards the cockpit.

"I'm tired," Rachel said.

"Me too," Cody said, squeezing her hand. "Been a long day kid."

"You got blood on me again," Rachel said, looking at her hand.

"Sorry kid."

A few minutes later, a young dark-haired woman came walking down the aisle. She stopped at the rear of the cabin and knelt down beside Cody. She had a black satchel in hand, out of which she started taking some bandages and other medical equipment, laying them on the floor next to Cody's feet.

"Nick says you've got a scratch that needs my attention," she said.

"Nick's a funny guy," Cody said.

The woman smiled. She was tan-skinned with chocolate brown eyes – kind eyes, and a beautiful smile to go with them.

"My name is Jessica. I'm going to clean the wound and give you something for the pain."

"Great," Cody said.

As Jessica cleaned the wound, Cody drifted in and out of consciousness. He could feel Rachel holding his hand.

"Don't worry Dad," she said.

"That's right. Don't worry Dad," Jessica said.

The woman's voice floated into his ear. "You're going to be fine," she said. "We're going to need to keep an eye on you – make sure you're hydrated, keep you moving about a little bit too to keep the blood flowing. You're in good hands. And I see you brought your own little nurse with you too. Is that your daughter? Isn't she just the cutest?"

"Yeah she is," Cody said. "The cutesssht." His voice sounded far away. Inside his head, everything felt warm and fuzzy. Whatever Jessica had given him was working fast.

He closed his eyes.

"I think I'm a little high," he said.

The desire to sleep was overwhelming. And why not? After all, he deserved a nap.

Just a quick one.

Cody sat bolt upright in his seat, his fingers clamped around the armrests on either side. Something wasn't right. He felt drunk – rip-roaring, high as a fart drunk and that was something he hadn't been in a long time. The plane's engines roared and it took him a moment to adjust to the drastic noise levels all around him.

He leaned over Rachel, trying to get a look at the window. Both Rachel and the young man to his right paid him little attention as he clambered closer. They were apparently transfixed by what they were seeing outside.

"Jesus," Cody said.

The city was on fire. Hot colors spewed out San Antonio, reaching up to the sky like thousands of flaming sharp claws. It looked like the plane was trying to escape out of the jaws of a hungry volcano.

The plane tilted as it climbed towards the black sky. Inside the cabin, a lot of people were whooping with delight, making celebratory noises, and giving high-fives to the person sitting next to them. They were even getting the champagne, the Scotch, and the beers out. It was a strange time to have a party but the relief inside the fuselage was palpable. Whatever else happened, they were at least getting away from *that*. San Antonio wasn't a place that anyone wanted to stick around in for much longer.

Cody turned back to the window.

The plane was climbing at a steep angle – but was it too steep? He could hear the whirring and bumping noises coming from the hydraulics. There was a clunking noise. Something that sounded like the landing gear retracting.

Cody felt sick. It was the drugs – it had to be. His stomach was swirling around like a washing machine drum. Maybe everything that had happened that morning was catching up to him at last – Mary Jane, the masks, the plane crash, the fake cop, and the confrontation with the Black Widow in the airport – it was sinking in and now it felt real. Those people, those encounters, were going to stay with him for a long time.

So much had happened. It didn't feel right, watching those people celebrate further down the cabin. Clinking glasses, laughing and joking, patting each other on the back like they'd done good.

Cody looked towards the window. Not everyone had gotten out after all.

"Assholes," he said, glaring at the party people.

Several faces turned around and looked at him. Their expressions were strangely blank. Cody looked across the aisle to his left. A young family was sitting over there – a man, woman and two little girls. The man looked confused and scared. The woman had a distant look in her eyes, like she was thinking about something she'd left behind. Or someone.

Several rows down, a baby started crying.

Cody leaned back in his seat.

"Jesus kid," he said to Rachel. "I think she gave me a real humdinger dose of something. I don't feel too good."

Rachel squeezed his hand.

The plane climbed further into the sky. Outside it was blacker than black. Inside it was cold – the cabin felt like it had been slotted into the compartment of a giant freezer.

Cody's eyelids were heavy. It was time to go back to sleep.

Before closing his eyes, he turned to his right.

Rachel was looking at him, smiling.

To Cody's surprise, Kate was there too, sitting in the window seat. She was looking at him. The young man who'd been there just moments earlier was now gone.

Kate MacLeod was young and alive. She was at the height of her beauty and it was 1986 all over again. The MacLeods were on top of the world. They were the perfect couple going on a family vacation with their perfect daughter. With any luck, they'd see the Santa Monica Mountains again.

Kate's silver eyes were dazzling and bright. She leaned forward. Slowly, she opened her mouth to speak.

Everything went black.

BLACK FEVER (#2)

CHAPTER ONE

Cody MacLeod thought he was dead.

Why wouldn't he be dead? Just seconds ago, the Black Widow had been sitting beside him at the back of the plane.

She'd come disguised as Cody's ex-wife, Kate. Like she'd done several times before. She'd leaned in closer, her silver eyes shining bright. She'd spoken to him, although her blood red lips hadn't moved. Cody couldn't remember the precise words that she'd uttered. All he'd heard was the soothing and familiar sound of his wife's voice, floating around the cabin like a distant siren's song, drowning out everything else.

Seconds later, the roaring engine of the Boeing 737 had degenerated into a choking whine. The engine sputtered, stalled and then cut out altogether.

They were going down. Fast. When Cody looked to his right, the Black Widow was gone. All traces of Kate's voice had extinguished and the only sound left in Cody's ears was the chilling, high-pitched screaming of the other passengers.

The Boeing plummeted nose-down to the ground.

Cody grabbed a hold of his daughter Rachel, sitting next to him in the middle seat. He pulled her close and squeezed tight. He looked around at the growing scenes of panic unfolding within the plane.

A burning smell seeped into his nostrils and nearly choked him. The screaming inside the cabin increased. The passengers sounded like trapped animals locked inside a burning barn, banging their heads against the walls with no way out.

Cody looked straight ahead.

A raging fire roared around the tube of the fuselage. Like a hungry monster, it consumed the last of the oxygen and soon there was nothing left to breathe, nothing except thick plumes of swirling black smoke.

Everything went gray at the edges.

Cody couldn't see very well but he could literally feel the plane disintegrating underneath him. He was suffocating. The air was heating up but it didn't matter anymore.

It would be over soon.

Rachel looked around the cabin. Her fingers clamped down on Cody's arm, like somehow he was supposed to keep her afloat while the plane sunk to Earth.

They wouldn't escape the Black Storm. After everything they'd gone through on the road to the airport, it was a bitter pill to swallow. But it had always been a fool's hope. In the end, they'd be like all the other poor lost souls down there in San Antonio. Mad or dead. They wouldn't even be a statistic because nobody was counting anymore.

Cody braced himself for impact.

Jesus Christ, he was about to die in a plane crash and so was his daughter. He held Rachel tight, kissed her and spoke in her ear, telling her that he loved her over and over. He couldn't say it enough, not now that words were all he had left for her.

He closed his eyes and stroked Rachel's hair. She was locked in his arms, rigid and motionless like a mannequin.

At least they were together at the end. Nobody had taken her away from him. And now nobody ever would.

Cody opened his eyes. He gasped.

It was gone.

There was no fire, no screams, and no roaring engine. The cockpit hadn't ripped away from the rest of the fuselage and neither had the tail. The plane was intact. Everything was normal and yet the experience of falling through the sky was still surging through his mind. It had been so real – the feeling of helplessness, of despair.

"What the hell?" Cody said.

Was this it? Was he dead?

He looked at Rachel sitting to his right. She was holding onto Bootsy the bear with one hand, while rubbing her tired eyes with the other. There was a look of confusion on her face.

No, he wasn't dead.

The engines were silent.

Somebody groaned further down the cabin. Muted voices could be heard from all directions – more confusion in those voices.

"What happened?" somebody said.

Cody looked down the aisle. As he leaned to the side, his body creaked like it hadn't moved for weeks. The other passengers were slowly waking up from what looked like a deep sleep. They were sitting up straight, rubbing their eyes and yawning and stretching their limbs. Some of them looked like they'd woken up from a nightmare – their eyes were wide and their mouths sucking at the air, like a dying fish.

A woman's voice screeched from further down the aisle.

"Oh my God!" she said. It sounded like she was having trouble breathing. The words spilled out in between a series of violent gasping sounds. "We're alive."

Cody looked at Rachel.

"Are you okay honey?" he said. His voice was deep and raspy.

She looked at him.

"Are we dead?" she asked.

Cody shook his head. "We're not dead," he said. "At least I don't think we are."

Rachel looked further down the cabin with a wary look in her eyes.

"She was right there where you're sitting," Rachel said. "The Black Widow. The plane was going down."

Cody felt a cold shiver run through him.

"You're okay," he said. "She's gone now."

"But where are we?" Rachel said.

He shook his head. "Sounds like the engines are off. I think we've landed somewhere. I don't know kid."

"Did we crash?" Rachel said. "That's what she does to planes isn't it?"

"I don't think we crashed," Cody said, looking around for anything inside the fuselage to indicate otherwise. "We're in good condition if we did."

"Why are the all the windows closed?" Rachel said.

Cody had already noticed that the shutters had been pulled down over the windows. Nobody had dared to open one yet. The lights inside the plane were switched on and everything looked normal. Back in the Hollywood glory days, Cody had regularly gone on wild drink and drug binges that would last for forty-eight hours and sometimes longer. When the party was over, he'd always wake up on the floor in a strange house or apartment surrounded by empty beer bottles and overflowing ashtrays. The world would be a foul-smelling blur. Nothing made sense.

That's what it felt like now.

Cody glanced over at the young man sitting in the window seat next to Rachel. His skin was a ghoulish white. Thick beads of sweat dripped down over his scrunched up features.

"Are you alright?" Cody said. "Hey mister, can you hear me?"

"I saw her too," the man said, turning towards Cody. "She was right there, sitting in your seat for Christ's sake. It was my mother, with silver eyes. She spoke to me but I can't remember what she said."

The man looked up and down the cabin like he was frantically searching for something he'd lost.

"We didn't crash?" he said. "It was so..."

The man stopped talking. He looked like he was about to pass out.

"She *was* here," Cody said. "But I don't know...she's gone now."

"Why aren't we dead then?" Rachel said.

Another man's voice cut in. "That's what I'd like to know."

Cody glanced over his shoulder. The voice belonged to a man sitting directly across the aisle. He was leaning in closer, as if he'd been listening in on their conversation for some time. The man, a portly thirty-something with round, wire-rim John Lennon glasses, had a dazed look in his eyes. A blonde-haired woman sat beside him, trying her best to comfort their two young children who were groaning as they sat on her lap.

"The Black Widow should have killed us," the man said.

"Did you see her?" Cody asked.

The man's expression was grim. He nodded.

"My little girl," he said, leaning further across the aisle so that his wife and children couldn't hear what he was saying. "She spoke to me but it was her, the Black Widow. Those eyes, for God's sake."

The man sighed and turned his attention back to his family. Cody looked at the little girl spread out in her mother's arms. She was about one year old and it was hard to imagine her with silver eyes. Cody didn't want to imagine.

"Somebody open one of those damn shutters!" a voice yelled.

"After you asshole," somebody else replied.

There was a chorus of metallic clicking noises. People were unbuckling their safety belts. One by one, they forced themselves out of their seats. They moved slowly, like freshly unwrapped mummies stepping out of their tombs. The sound of cracking limbs was everywhere.

"Where are we?" a man said, standing in the center of the aisle. He was looking towards the windows. The other passengers shook their heads and continued to talk quietly amongst themselves.

"Stay here Rachel," Cody said. "I'll be back in a minute."

He unbuckled his seatbelt and tried to get up onto his feet.

"Oh Jesus," he said.

His body was stiff and disobeyed the command being sent by his brain. Cody fought through it, staggering into the aisle like a drunk, his legs not quite fully underneath him. Once or twice, he had to grab onto the headrest of the nearest seat to retain his balance.

"Wait a minute," he said, calling over to the huddle of people who'd gathered in the center of the aisle. The passengers ignored him and kept talking to one another. Cody cleared his throat and tried again, this time yelling at the top of his voice to make sure everyone heard him.

"Did everyone see the Black Widow?"

They stopped talking. All of them.

Some of the passengers nodded right away. Some didn't have to – the frightened look in their eyes was enough. Most people ignored the question and turned away.

A middle-aged man nodded. His face was pale and somber.

"She was here," he said in a deep, rumbling voice. "But we haven't crashed. That's what I don't understand."

"Maybe we did," a woman sitting nearby said. "Maybe this is what happens when she brings down a plane – everyone on board gets stuck in limbo."

The man shook his head. "I don't think so."

An older woman stood up in her seat. Rachel had pointed this woman out to Cody earlier because she had a cat crate sitting on her lap when the plane took off. The woman yelped at the stiffness in her legs as she straightened up. She was still clutching onto the handle of the crate while the two black and white cats inside were in a crouching position, peering outside at the unfolding drama.

"Will somebody just look outside for God's sake?" the old woman yelled. "I want to know where we are. Somebody open those shutters."

Cody saw the hesitation in the passengers' faces – especially those who were sitting next to the shutters. It wasn't a good time to have chosen a window seat.

At last however, a few hands tentatively reached for the closed shutters.

Everyone held their breath.

There was a clicking noise as the first shutter was pushed up. Others followed quickly.

Cody leaned over from the aisle, trying to get a better look through the nearest window. It was dark outside, which didn't come as a surprise. That was about all he could see. He'd have to go in closer if he wanted more detail.

Those who'd lifted the shutters pressed their faces tight up against the window.

"Well?" the old woman said. "Where are we?"

"Well we ain't floating in the ocean," a man said. "We ain't sinking in it either or we'd be swimming by now. Looks like we're just sitting in..."

"We're back!" a woman's voice cried out. She was looking through a window on the left hand side of the cabin, pushing her face tight up against the plexiglass, twisting left and right in order to get a better look at their surroundings. "I don't believe it."

"Holy shit!" someone else said. This voice was coming from the back of the plane. "We're at the airport."

Cody frowned. "What?"

Other people hurried over to the windows to see for themselves. Soon dozens of faces were pressed up against the side of the cabin. Some turned back around, a look of bewilderment etched on their faces. Others walked away in shocked silence.

"San Antonio?" the old woman holding onto the cat crate said.

"It's true folks," a booming voice called out. "We're back."

Nick Norton was standing at the cockpit door. A grim expression was stamped onto his rugged features.

"Damnedest thing I ever saw," he said.

A crowd of people quickly gathered around Nick. It looked like a flock of groupies trying to get their favorite rock star's autograph. They hurled a barrage of questions at the pilot like they were throwing bricks at glass windows. Nick did his best to try and address each one but it was impossible to keep up.

Cody hurried down the aisle. He stopped at the back of the crowd.

"Nick!" he said, raising a hand in the air. "Hey Nick, over here."

There was a glimpse of relief in Nick's eyes when he saw Cody. With a curt nod, he pushed through the crowd of passengers and walked over. He gave his old friend a brief bear hug.

"You okay?" Nick asked, looking Cody up and down. "How's Rachel doing?"

"Yeah we're both fine," Cody said. "Confused but alive. You?"

"Same," Nick said. "I don't know what the hell happened up there man."

"Tell me about it," Cody asked. "You saw her then?"

Nick nodded. He lowered his voice so the other passengers couldn't overhear.

"She was sitting in the co-pilot's seat," he said. "Get this – she was only disguised as my grandma. My evil old grandma for Christ's sake. The only person on this planet who ever put the fear of God into me. All of a sudden, I was a five-year-old boy sitting at the controls of an airplane. The other pilots were gone. It was just me and that bitch. Boy she laid into me good – told me I was a waste of space, digging deep into all the worst mistakes I ever made. And you know as well as anyone Cody, there's been a lot of mistakes. All those marriages and no kids to show – that always used to piss my grandma off."

"That's what she does," Cody said. "Hits you where it hurts."

"I don't know what happened after that," Nick said. "The plane was coming down and there was nothing I could do to stop it. Not a goddamn thing. Next thing I wake up in the cockpit and I'm looking out at San Antonio airport."

"She brought us back," Cody said.

"Yeah," Nick said. "But why didn't she kill us?"

Cody shrugged.

"Maybe it's a Purgatory thing or something like that," Nick said. "Anytime we try to leave San Antonio she brings us back. That's worse than death, ain't it?"

There was still a crowd of people hovering at Nick's back. It was clear by the way they were encroaching on his personal space that they wanted to talk to him further. He looked back at them and nodded, indicating that he hadn't forgotten them.

"Good luck with your fan club," Cody said.

Nick turned back to Cody and rolled his eyes. He pointed at Cody's waist.

"How's your wound?"

"What?"

"You got shot remember?"

"Oh yeah," Cody said. He put his index finger to the location of the wound at his side and poked at it. He raised an eyebrow. "It feels fine. Better than fine actually."

"Well it *was* only a graze," Nick said.

Cody grinned sarcastically. "Because you'd know how I feel after I get shot, right?"

Nick didn't answer. He was staring at the people who were huddled over by the windows.

"You looked outside yet?" he said.

Cody shook his head. "No."

"Go ahead," Nick said. "Looks like they trashed the airport while we were away. At least we missed that."

"Alright," Cody said.

He left Nick to deal with the mob and their endless questions. Cody turned around and fought his way past the crowds who were gathered in the narrow aisle. He found a row of empty seats and scooted his way down to the window. Then he pressed his face up against the cold surface.

"Oh shit," he said, looking outside.

The terminal building was sitting on scattered patches of barren, charcoal colored earth that stretched back as far as the eye could see. It looked like a war had been fought out there.

Cody twisted his head to the left.

He saw three massive objects sitting in the distance. Cody recognized them as the three Alaska Airlines planes he'd seen sitting on the apron outside Gate A5, just before they'd taken off.

Nick was right. They'd gotten away just in time. The Black Fever had probably sent thousands of crazed people to tear the airport to shreds, to lay waste to everything in sight. They must have worked fast. How long had it taken to cause such horrendous damage?

Cody suddenly remembered that the Dodge Challenger was sitting outside the airport. His heart sunk.

"Bastards," he said. What hope was there that they'd left his car untouched?

From further down the aisle, Cody heard the mob letting loose on Nick.

"You told us she wouldn't get on this plane Nick Norton," a woman's voice said. "What was that big speech you gave us before we took off? You said this plane was Black Widow-proof. Now what the hell do we do?"

"You're alive aren't you?" Nick said. "Count your blessings."

"So much for your great escape plan Nick," a nasally voiced man said. "Real good job."

One distressed passenger – a man of about thirty – pounded his fists off the side of the fuselage as hard as he could. He was like a man trapped inside a sinking ship with nowhere to go but down. Nobody knew what to say to him.

"There's something else out there," a woman's shrill voice cried out. She was peering out of a window on the opposite side of the plane from where Cody stood. "You see it?"

Cody spun around, alerted by the surprised tone in her voice. He hurried back into the aisle and squeezed down a vacant row of seats on the other side of the plane. He pressed his face up close to the window.

He was looking towards downtown San Antonio. To his surprise, it was no longer a city under siege. There was only a vast, sprawling darkness out there. No more fire. No smoke lingering above the city.

"The fires are out," Cody said. He screwed his face up. "How long were we up there Nick?"

Nick took several steps down the aisle, moving away from the mob.

"Honestly man," he said. "I don't know. Everything's a bit foggy upstairs."

Cody turned back towards the window. Now he could see what the woman with the shrill voice had pointed out just seconds earlier. From somewhere in the distance, a small circle of blue light was flashing in the sky. It was a lonely beacon, switching on and off every two or three seconds. It was a solitary neon light, blinking in the wilderness.

"What is that?" the woman said. "It's coming from the city ain't it?"

"That's a signal," Cody said.

Nick took up position at a nearby window. He looked outside. "You think?"

"What else could it be?" Cody said.

The blue light blinked on and off against a black starless canvas.

"It's the army," a man's voice said from a few rows down. "They're looking for other survivors. What do you guys think?"

"Yeah," another man said. "We gotta get over there people. It's our only chance of getting some help. Thank God, there's somebody out there."

Cody straightened up and turned back towards the terminal building. The airport reminded him of a ruined castle out of a fairy tale – it was sad and grotesque. It was a dead place, with a subtle hint of evil surrounding it.

He felt a finger tap him on his back. He turned around and saw Rachel standing behind him. Bootsy was hanging by her side.

"Is it the army?" she asked. "Is it help?"

"Yeah," Cody said. "Well, maybe. It looks like there are some survivors out there."

Cody kneeled down and squeezed his daughter's arm gently.

"It's going to be alright," he said. "This just another setback."

Rachel was about to speak but the sound of loud footsteps marching up the aisle cut her off.

Cody looked up and saw a tall woman in her thirties standing in front of Nick.

"I want off this plane," she said.

There was a fierce look in the woman's eyes, one that challenged Nick to say no. "That signal out there is our ticket to safety," she said. "For all of us. Thanks anyway, but you had your chance Nick."

The woman turned around to address the other passengers.

"Does anyone else think that the Black Storm is over?" she said. "I mean, look outside – there's no more fire out there. The city isn't burning. Somebody's signaling us towards them, so maybe they really are looking for survivors. Maybe that's the authorities finally getting their shit together."

The other passengers' eyes lit up in hope. The woman spoke with conviction, like she truly believed what she was saying. Her conviction was contagious.

"Yeah," a bearded man said. He took a cautious step forward, pushing a mop of long greasy hair off his gaunt face. "It makes sense. Maybe that's why we're not dead. The Black Widow couldn't finish us off because the Black Storm is over. Just in the nick of time as far as our asses are concerned."

"But it's still dark outside," another man said. "How can the storm be over if it's still dark?"

"Maybe it's just night-time," the woman said. "Remember that? I'm serious folks. I mean look at it – I don't think the sky is anywhere near as dark as it was before. Right?"

"Yeah she's right," the bearded man said. "Something's different."

"I want to get off the plane," the woman said, turning back to Nick.

"Oh God please, let it be true," someone said from the back of the plane. "Let it be over."

Nick held his hands up, calling for attention.

"Take it easy folks," he said, looking around at the flock of eager faces standing in the aisle. The passengers were shifting back and forth, twitching with excitement.

"We've just been through a very strange experience," Nick said. "Maybe we should take some time out and..."

"Open the door Nick."

"Let us out!"

"Open the door," the fierce-looking woman said. She spoke with a fire in her belly, like she was giving a speech at a political rally. "You can't keep us on this plane against our will. If that's the authorities out there then we've got to get to them. Now! Some of these people have a family to protect."

"Open the door!"

More and more voices chimed in. All calling for the doors to be opened.

Nick took a backwards step and sighed.

"Alright," he said, his voice cutting through the noise. "Have it your way. I'll go open the airstairs but you gotta wait a couple of minutes. Think you can handle that?"

Cody watched as Nick walked through the crowd towards the back of the plane. His shoulders were slumped like a pair of worn out beach balls.

While Nick opened the airstairs, the rest of the passengers, those who'd been sitting on the fence about leaving, gradually became giddy with excitement. Most people didn't waste any time in getting their things ready. They were running down the aisle, opening their lockers, and grabbing their bags and other belongings.

Cody and Rachel watched from an empty row of seats.

Rachel looked up at Cody.

"Is it true?" she said. "Is it over?"

Cody shrugged. He was looking at one middle-aged man, who was pulling a small suitcase out of the overhead locker. The man was crying and laughing at the same time. His wife was standing in the aisle beside him, giving him a comforting pat on the shoulder as he took their bags out. Her eyes were damp and glistening.

They looked overjoyed. They'd made it.

CHAPTER TWO

Nick walked back into the cabin. He pointed a thumb over his shoulder towards the rear exit.

"Alright then," he said to the throng of passengers who'd been impatiently awaiting his return. "The door's open. The airstairs are down. Now listen up people – if you have weapons in the hold, I'll be opening it up in about five minutes. Think you can wait that long?"

There was a general rumble of approval from the crowd.

Nick stepped to the side – an indication that the passengers could leave if they wished to. The pilot furrowed his brow as the long procession began to shuffle down the aisle. They moved indelicately, bumping into one another like they were trying to get out of a haunted house. Anxious parents dragged their kids by the hand. Suitcases were either wheeled or scraped off the floor.

"C'mon guys," Nick said. "Take it easy, huh? Nice and slow. Don't crush the little people. You've survived the Black Widow today – no point in killing each other trying to be first off an airplane. That's it. Take it slow."

Cody and Rachel stood at a distance watching the passengers go.

"Why are they in such a hurry?" Rachel said.

"Guess you can't blame them," Cody said. "If that blue light is a signal for survivors, we have to go to it."

"Shouldn't we be going then?" Rachel said.

"First things first," Cody said. "Before we go anywhere we're getting out of these dirty clothes. Damn bloodstains, they're everywhere. Let's change first. Okay? It's going to be a long walk into San Antonio. No need to stink up the highway."

Rachel looked at a splatter of bloodstains on her long-sleeved t-shirt and denim dungarees. It was Cody's blood, which he'd accidentally wiped on her after the encounter with the fake cop in the airport.

"Okay," she said. "Good idea."

With his hands on her shoulders, Cody guided Rachel towards the aisle. They cut into the procession of departing passengers and moved towards the back of the plane. When they reached their seats, Cody opened up the overhead locker and pulled down their backpacks. He pulled out some fresh clothes for Rachel – a red sweater and a fresh pair of jeans. Adding some clean underwear to the pile, along with a bar of soap, he handed her the items and pointed to the bathroom, just a short distance from their seats.

"Go on kid," he said. "Be quick. Toss your dirty clothes into the trash when you're done, okay?"

Rachel took the pile of clothes and nodded. Turning around, she cut out into the aisle and walked over to the bathroom.

Cody watched her go. Then he unzipped his backpack and took out some clothes for himself – a white shirt, a pair of light brown khaki pants and some underwear. With the clothes in hand, he went into the vacant bathroom and locked the door. Inside, he pulled off his clothes, expecting his gunshot wound to sting as he lifted his arms up. There was no pain. The white bandage was still there, strapped to the left side of his body. A small circle of faded red splatter, like a Rorschach inkblot, had formed in the center of the bandage.

Cody poked at the wound again but felt nothing. It felt like he hadn't taken any damage.

Slowly, he peeled back the bandage.

"I'll be damned."

There was a hint of a crooked scar where the bullet had grazed him.

Cody squinted his eyes as he looked at the wound. He stepped forward, bringing the scar closer to the mirror.

"Doesn't make any sense."

He continued to probe at the wound, which had healed over almost entirely. There was no time to try and make sense of it. Rachel was out there waiting for him and they'd have to get a move on if they were going to keep up with the crowd. And they did want to keep up with the crowd. Traveling to San Antonio on foot in small numbers was a bad idea.

Cody put on the fresh clothes and stuffed the old bloodstained ones into the little trash basket. Working quickly, he washed his hands and face and ran some cold water over his dirty blond hair.

Rachel was waiting for him back at the seat. Cody smiled. He was pleased to see that his daughter was no longer wearing clothes that had been spray-painted in blood. *His* blood. Her long blonde hair was loose and fell down her back. It looked like she'd soaked it under the tap like he'd done. Rachel's cheeks and forehead were glowing as if she'd been scrubbing them with soap for hours. Cody could almost see his reflection in her face.

"You feel better?" Cody asked.

"Yeah," Rachel said, grabbing a hold of her backpack. She wheezed as she tried to haul the heavy bag over her delicate shoulders. It took several attempts to lock it around her arm and when it was done, she squatted down and picked Bootsy up off the seat.

"Can we go now?" she said.

Cody nodded. He glanced over his shoulder towards the rear exit. Nick and a young, dark-skinned woman were standing at the top of the airstairs, watching the last of the passengers descend towards the apron.

"Yeah," Cody said, securing the bigger backpack's strap over his shoulder. "We can go. You want me to carry your pack?"

Rachel shook her head. "No. I can do it."

"It's heavy Rachel."

"It's fine."

"Alright," Cody said with a sigh. "Tell me when it's too much."

They walked over to the rear exit. Cody lifted his chin in silent greeting to Nick and the young woman standing beside him.

Nick nodded back and pointed to the passengers, all of who were gathered down on the apron. They were trudging forward, making slow progress towards the terminal. It didn't look like anyone was in such a hurry anymore. The apron was a ghoulish sight – it looked like the passengers were trekking inside a deep meteor crater, craggy and cavernous. This was a dead place where nothing flew or crawled or walked. Nothing except two hundred people.

"Ungrateful assholes," Nick said. "Even the other pilots couldn't get away fast enough. That's the thanks I get for trying to save their lives."

"Lighten up," Cody said. "They're scared."

Nick raised his eyebrows and sighed. "Yeah," he said. "Who isn't?"

The young woman standing at Nick's side laughed. She patted him gently on the back.

"It's never boring when you're around Nick," she said. "You don't get this sort of drama on any other airlines."

Nick pointed a finger back and forth between Cody and the young woman.

"Cody MacLeod," Nick said. "This is Crazy Diamond. She's the niece of one of the other pilots. One of those swift-legged assholes down there making a quick getaway. Cody's an old friend of mine from the acting days. And the pretty little girl standing beside him is the lovely Miss Rachel MacLeod."

The young woman smiled at Cody and Rachel. She was about twenty years old with a pretty face, adorned by striking high cheekbones and almond-shaped, almost oriental looking eyes. Her natural, elegant beauty was at odds with a casual, almost scruffy dress sense – dark jeans and a tight fitting denim jacket with a black Pink Floyd t-shirt poking out underneath.

"I know you," Crazy Diamond said to Cody. "You're the stutter kid from *The Forever Boys*. When I was growing up we'd watch that movie all the time. I loved it – especially the little stutter kid. You were *so* cute."

Cody managed an awkward smile. "Yeah that's me," he said. "Real cute."

Nick let out a barrage of muffled laughter into the back of his hand.

"What are you laughing at Norton?" Cody said.

Nick held up a hand. "Take it easy man," he said. "I just find it funny sometimes that nobody ever remembers you for anything other than that one part. You're the *stutter kid* man. To millions of people."

Cody flashed his middle finger to Nick.

"That's one part more than you're remembered for," he said. "Token black kid."

"Whatever," Nick said, still laughing. "Stutter kid."

Crazy Diamond kneeled down closer to Rachel.

"Wow, I love your hair," she said. "It's so pretty."

Rachel smiled shyly. Cody noticed that she was trying to hide Bootsy behind her back.

"It's dirty," Rachel said, putting a hand to her hair.

"Nah," Crazy Diamond said. She smiled, showing off a set of perfectly straight teeth. "You're good."

"Crazy Diamond," Cody said. "That's an unusual name."

"Yeah," she said, standing back up again. "It's a nickname I've had for about six years. My real name is Winona. I'm Oglala Lakota, just like our great warrior Crazy Horse. I'm also a big Pink Floyd fan. As a matter of fact, I play drums in an all-female Pink Floyd tribute band called Wish You Were Her."

Cody smiled. "Now who's cute?"

Rachel tugged on Cody's arm.

"What's up kid?" he asked.

"We could give her a lift to San Antonio," Rachel said, pointing a finger at Crazy Diamond. "If the car's still there."

"Well that's very kind of you Rachel," Crazy Diamond said. "But I'm not sure any cars around here are still intact. This place is toast, which means we're going to be walking to San Antonio."

Cody nodded. He looked down at Rachel. "She's right," he said. "Don't get your hopes up about the car."

Rachel scrunched up her brow. "The Dodge?"

"Yeah," Cody said. "The Dodge. Now c'mon, are you ready to start walking?"

"Ready," Rachel said.

"You guys coming?" Cody said, looking at Nick and Crazy Diamond.

There was a duffel bag lying at Nick's feet. He bent down and picked it up.

"Don't feel right," Nick said, looking back down the cabin. "Leaving her like this."

Cody reached over and tapped Nick on the arm. "How do you think it felt leaving the Dodge back there?"

Nick nodded. "Yeah I hear you," he said. "Stupid ain't it? Grown men getting emotional over a heap of metal."

"Yeah it is stupid," Crazy Diamond said, throwing a small

173

backpack over her shoulder and turning towards the door. "So let's go and you boys try to forget about your toys. Okay?"

Cody looked down towards the apron. The passengers, still apprehensive, were making slow progress towards the terminal building. They might as well have been wading through mud.

One man, with a shock of thick black curly-hair and dressed in a dark suit jacket, pulled his family forward at a slightly faster pace than the others. Several times, he turned around to face the slow-pokes at his back.

"C'mon people," the man yelled over. "What's everyone so worried about? You saw the signal over the city. It's over. There's a major relief effort going on in San Antonio right now."

He clapped his hands together, like he was rounding up a pack of dogs.

"Let's go! C'mon people."

A few stragglers, either emboldened or embarrassed by the man, moved forward at a quicker pace. They closed in on the terminal building.

"That's it," the curly-haired man said, beckoning them forward. "Let's go. It's going to be alright. Now listen up – if anyone's struggling to carry their bags, let somebody know and we'll find someone to carry them for you. But we've got to keep moving whatever else happens. Chop-chop!"

"What about our guns?" somebody yelled.

The curly-haired man raised a hand in the air.

"The worst is over," he said. "Nick's going to grab a couple of guns out of the hold – we won't need any more than that or they'll weigh us down. What we need right now is for people to start walking. Movement. As quick as you can. I don't want to make it all the way into San Antonio only to find that whoever's setting off that signal is gone."

The man turned around and steered his family towards the terminal. Others followed, apparently buoyed by his enthusiasm.

"Guess we'd better go," Cody said, standing at the door of the plane. He took Rachel's hand in his. Then he paused to let Crazy Diamond walk down the airstairs before him. Nick then gestured for Cody and Rachel to go before him.

"Better grab those guns," he said.

Cody and Rachel stepped onto the stairs. The air was warm and fresh outside. As they took the first couple of stairs, Cody felt the wind picking up-tempo.

Something landed on his head. Something wet.

Cody flinched, like he'd felt a giant spider crawling up the back of his neck. He touched the top of his head and looked at his fingers.

A drop of oily dark liquid ran down the palm of his hand.

He felt a stabbing dread in his guts.

"That's black rain," he said. "See that?"

Rachel tilted her head back and looked up at the dark sky.

"We shouldn't be out here," she said. "Dad..."

Cody was about to say something when a noise cut him off. It was a shrill, tearing sound – it sounded like a giant piece of cloth being shredded inside their ears. It was so loud that everyone on the apron, in the midst of their initial shock, was forced to cover their ears and wince in pain.

Everyone was looking around in wide-eyed panic. Some of the passengers turned to the curly-haired man for guidance. But he was frozen to the spot, his earlier assurance obliterated by the sudden noise. Cody saw him screaming in agony – the man's face was grotesquely contorted, as if the tearing sound was a sharp blade slicing its way down the tip of his skull.

Cody saw something – a flicker of movement on the ground.

"Jesus Christ," he said. He pointed towards the apron. "Look!"

Hundreds of black shapes shot out of the earth. They were tall, humanoid figures and each one appeared directly in front of a horrified looking passenger. Cody's jaw dropped. It was as if a multitude of invisible holes had materialized on the ground, out of which a secret phantom army had emerged from.

Cody and the others looked on in horror from the airstairs.

The black ghosts were tall and faceless. There were no features at all – no eyes, nose, mouth or ears – it was as if they'd been built out of black mist to resemble a human shape and nothing else.

The phantoms bolted at the person standing nearest to them. They didn't walk, they moved at a rapid speed like they had fast-moving wheels attached underneath.

They slid inside the nearest passenger, like keys fitting into a lock.

Cody grabbed Rachel and spun her around. He tried to bury her head in his shirt but to his surprise, Rachel resisted, wriggling free of his grip and turning her head towards the apron.

The passengers convulsed immediately. They were caught in the grip of a violent seizure that took over their bodies and Cody assumed, their minds. He didn't want to watch but he couldn't close his eyes or turn away either. It looked like the passengers had received an injection – a ten thousand gigawatt speedball that had turned them into a set of violent human jumping beans. They shook back and forth, possessed people – no longer themselves.

The curly-haired man dropped onto his knees.

Blackness seeped into his eyes.

An overweight, middle-aged man grabbed another man by the hair. He started hitting the other man on the face, using his closed fists like hammers. During the struggle, they both fell to the ground and the other man came out on top. Now it was his turn to throw a barrage of punches from top position, while the older man on bottom put his thumbs to the man's face and tried to claw his eyeballs out of his head.

It was as if a murderous rage had infested their minds. They were slamming each other's heads off the ground like they were basketballs. Husbands were strangling their wives and vice-versa. The air was filled with a violent shrieking noise – a sound that would never be forgotten by those who heard it.

Some of the passengers didn't bother with anyone else. They were slamming their own heads into the ground.

Cody's stomach lurched and he knew he was going to be sick. If not now, then soon. He looked down and saw three passengers – an old man and a younger couple – who'd been close to the plane, running back towards the airstairs.

"Get back here!" Nick yelled to them. "Quick."

The horrific scene seemed to last forever. In reality however, it was over quickly – probably less than a minute and a half before there was only one passenger left. A young man, around his late twenties, he dropped to his knees and proceeded to slam his bloody head off the ground.

Then he stopped.

A chilling silence swept across the airport.

Cody took a step backwards, almost tripping over his feet. Instinctively, he pulled Rachel towards the door of the plane.

"Get inside," Cody said to the others. His voice was trembling.

The three survivors on the apron leapt up the stairs and followed the others back inside the cabin.

Nick stood at the door, waiting until everybody was inside. When the old man and the young couple had caught up with them, Nick pulled up the airstairs as fast as he could, folding it below the door. After that, he ran back into the cabin.

"Is that door locked?" Cody yelled to Nick, pointing to the back of the plane. "Is it locked for Christ's sake?"

"It's locked," Nick said, holding his hands up. "It's locked. Ain't nothing or no one getting in here Cody."

The old man dropped onto his knees in the center of the aisle. He crawled into a row of seats and once there, fell onto his stomach and wailed pitifully into the back of his hands like a child.

The young couple who'd made it back with the old man slid down onto the floor outside the rear cabin bathrooms. They were shaking in manic spurts and clutching onto the other's hand for dear life.

Wide-eyed panic filled their faces.

Cody, Rachel, Nick and Crazy Diamond were standing in the center of the cabin. At first, they were too shocked to speak. All they could do was look at one another.

Eventually it was Nick who broke the silence.

"What the hell was that?" he said. "What just happened out there?"

Cody couldn't answer. He was thinking about running to the bathroom and being sick when Crazy Diamond made a gagging noise beside him. The young woman turned around and running at full speed, beat Cody to it. She went into the vacant bathroom opposite where the young man and woman were sitting on the floor, still shaking uncontrollably.

Everyone heard Crazy Diamond retching violently. Cody tightened his grip on both Rachel's shoulders and the contents of his stomach.

Nick fell back into one of the aisle seats with a crashing thud. His brown, haunted eyes stared into empty space.

"Why did she bring us back?" Nick said.

No one answered.

CHAPTER THREE

Cody looked down the cabin.

Crazy Diamond, after having spent a long time in the bathroom being sick, was now sitting a few rows down from where Cody sat with Rachel perched on his lap. The young woman was hunched over in her seat. Her skin was a ghastly yellow color, like that of a wax doll. She looked like someone trying to quietly endure the worst hangover of their life.

The old man's muffled sobbing was a constant background noise. He'd said nothing to anyone since getting back on the plane. The young couple hadn't spoken either – they were still sitting on the floor by the bathroom. They continued to cling onto each other in terror. Their eyes were doll-like, swimming in the fresh horror of recent memories.

"We can't go back out there," Cody said. "Not with those things running around."

Nick was sitting opposite Crazy Diamond. He was staring at the floor, head in hands.

"Those things," he said. "And what the hell were those things?"

Before Cody could say anything, the couple on the floor jolted in unison. It was a sudden, spasmodic movement that caused almost everyone else to jump in fright. The woman tried to say something to the man but the words appeared to clot on the tip of her tongue. All meaning was lost in the gargled mess that spilled out of her mouth.

Cody looked over at Nick.

"We've got to figure this out man," he said. "We can't go outside but we can't stay in here forever."

There was a distant look in Nick's eyes.

"This is my fault Cody," he said, looking up at his friend. "I told those people that I'd get them out of San Antonio. I told them they'd be safe with me – that their families would be safe with me. Their children."

"Don't you dare," Cody said, pointing a finger at Nick. "You're not going to blame yourself for this, okay? Those people couldn't get off this plane fast enough."

Nick closed his eyes. He grimaced slightly.

Cody was about to say something else but a strange noise interrupted him. It was coming from outside the bathrooms again. The two people on the floor were making rattling noises with their teeth – a click-clacking sound – as if their mouths were percussive instruments.

Cody shot them a furious look, wishing they'd shut the hell up. They looked like nice people. College educated, nice sweater, nice blouse, neat and inoffensive haircuts – the type of people you'd see sitting around the dinner table at an upper middle-class dinner party, strutting around the tennis club bar, and driving the latest BMW. The man was skinny and his wife was verging on the plump side.

They weren't paying any attention to anyone but themselves.

The man's head fell onto his wife's shoulder. He was shaking violently and she struggled to keep a hold of him.

"Hey guys," Cody said, calling over to them. He couldn't hide the irritation in his voice. He slid Rachel off his lap and she dropped onto the seat. Cody stood up and took a couple of tentative steps down the aisle. He didn't want to get too close to the couple. He didn't know why, it was just instinctive.

"You're safe now," he said. He wanted to sound firm without seeming callous. "Please just try to calm down. It's going to be okay – we're going to figure it out."

They didn't even look at him.

"Nice people," Crazy Diamond said. "I'm so glad they're here."

Cody looked at her and shrugged.

"Tell me about it."

He turned around – perhaps a little too fast. Cody saw flashing images in his mind – lightning fast, vivid and bloody memories of people attacking one another on the apron. The blood in his vision was black.

Cody put a hand on the nearest headrest. He swayed on unsteady feet.

"You okay?" Nick asked.

Cody nodded but didn't talk.

"You want to sit down?" Nick said.

"I'm good," Cody said, as the feeling passed. "Look, we need a plan. I think we should stay here at least for now. There's food, water – there's a bathroom. We're okay I think as long as we just keep ourselves inside the plane. If nothing else, it'll give us some time to think."

Crazy Diamond nodded. "Yeah. I got nothing better."

"Yeah," Nick said.

Crazy Diamond stood up slowly. She looked at the old man a few rows along and walked over there. The man was sprawled out on his front. He was sobbing into the back of his hands.

There was a look of curiosity intermingled with concern on

Crazy Diamond's face. She kneeled down at the edge of the aisle. The soles of the man's stylish brown shoes were just inches from her face. His head was pushed tight against the side of the fuse-lage, like he was trying to bury it inside the plane.

"Sir," Crazy Diamond said. "Excuse me sir. Is there anything I can do? Bring you a glass of water? Something stronger? I'm sure there's some whiskey around here somewhere."

The old man didn't respond.

Crazy Diamond stood back up and walked down the aisle. She unzipped her bag and pulled out a small bottle of water. Then she went back to the old man, unscrewing the lid as she walked. She took a sip and then offered it to him.

"Some water?" she said. "Sir?"

The old man didn't answer but Crazy Diamond wasn't deterred. She stayed beside him and although it took her asking several times, eventually he turned around, picked himself up and sat up straight in the seat. Cody looked at him and guessed he was about seventy years old. He had an impressive head of hedge-like white hair and a large, matching beard that covered most of his face. He was wearing a gray tweed blazer and sweater, with a pale shirt collar poking out at the neck. Cody thought the old man looked like a history professor who'd wandered far from the campus grounds onto the set of a horror movie.

The old man looked at Crazy Diamond with bloodshot eyes. Cody knew that look well. He'd seen it in the mirror plenty of times.

"Marianne," the old man said. His voice was deep and quiet.

Crazy Diamond offered him the bottle of water. The old man looked at it and shook his head.

"No thank you."

"Your wife?" Crazy Diamond said. "Is that Marianne?"

He nodded. "She was out there. She's still out there."

"I'm so sorry," Crazy Diamond said.

She sat down on the floor and crossed her legs.

"What's your name sir?" Crazy Diamond said. "What do we call you?"

The old man looked puzzled by the question. Like it didn't matter.

"Richards," he said. "John Richards."

"Nice to meet you John," Crazy Diamond said. "I'm Winona, but they call me Crazy Diamond."

"I'd prefer it if you called me Richards," he said. "If you don't mind."

She smiled. "Sure."

Richards looked at the bottle on the floor. A trembling hand reached for it and Crazy Diamond handed it to him quickly. Richards unscrewed the lid and took a long drink, letting some of the water spill down the side of his mouth and soak into his massive beard.

"Thank you," he said, wiping a hand across his lips.

"You're welcome," Crazy Diamond said.

Richards leaned his head back against the seat.

"She walked ahead of me," he said. "She was always walking ahead of me and I was always dragging my heels behind her. Everywhere we went it was the same. Oh Marianne, she wouldn't take her time, not for anything. Not even me. When those *things* came out of the ground...I heard her scream. I couldn't see her – it was too dark but I heard her over everyone else. Screaming my name. I was supposed to help her but what did I do?"

Crazy Diamond shook her head. But Cody knew the answer and he had a feeling she did too.

"I ran," Richards said. He spat the words out like they were phlegm clinging to the back of his throat. "Like a coward. I didn't even stop to think about what I was doing."

Crazy Diamond put her hand on the man's arm.

"You were scared," she said.

He shook his head.

"But I heard her," he said. "Yes of course I was petrified but I was in my right mind. And if I was in my right mind that means I abandoned her."

"If you'd turned around," Cody said. "You'd be dead too."

Richards looked at Cody. There was a hint of surprise in his eyes like he'd forgotten there were other people in the plane.

"And would that be any worse than this?" Richards said.

Cody looked at the floor. It was a damn good question.

"I don't know."

"I'm a coward," Richards said. He took another half-hearted sip of water and then handed the bottle back to Crazy Diamond.

"It's very kind of you to try and comfort me young lady," he said. "But there's none to be found."

A long silence lingered in the cabin.

"Dad."

It was Rachel's voice, coming from further down the aisle.

Cody turned around. "What is it honey?"

Rachel was pointing towards the bathroom.

"Those people are acting weird," she said.

Cody looked at the couple sitting on the floor. They were both shaking violently. It was something else now – something other than fear. It was as if they were badly ill and caught in the grip of a disease-ridden fit. Their arms were wrapped around one another. Their faces were pressed up tight, their noses touching.

"Oh for God's sake," Cody said. He couldn't hide the anger in his voice anymore. "Think you can cool it a little over there? You're scaring my..."

Cody's blood ran cold. This time they both looked at him.

Their eyes were black.

"Oh shit."

The woman unlocked her arms from around the skinny man's waist. In a flash, she sprang onto all fours like a cat. Then she maneuvered herself around so that her head was pointing at the bathroom door. To the horror of the onlookers, the woman charged forwards at an unnatural speed and slammed the top of her skull against the door. The crunching noise was sickening and Cody's insides lurched – it was like the sound was coming from inside his head, that's how close it felt.

She hit her head off the door again and again. It sounded like someone was slamming a battering ram into the side of the plane.

"Stop!" Crazy Diamond yelled. She clapped a hand over her mouth.

Crazy Diamond grabbed Richards by the arm and pulled him into the aisle. They hurried over to where Cody, Rachel and Nick, were watching events unfold with a look of horror in their eyes.

Cody pulled Rachel tight towards him, keeping her close.

"Don't look," he said to her.

But Rachel looked.

It took the woman less than twenty seconds to end her life. After a furious assault on the bathroom door, she dropped face-first to the floor. A splattering of blood slid slowly down the door. There was a high-pitched wheezing noise that came out of the woman's mouth – the last sound she'd ever make.

The skinny man leapt to his feet. With breathtaking speed, he ran down the aisle towards Cody and the others. He was like a rabid animal on the loose. He lunged at Crazy Diamond, grabbing her by the collar of her denim jacket.

The man dragged Crazy Diamond back down the aisle. He pulled her hair, forcing her head back. Crazy Diamond shrieked in pain and tried to fight him off. She aimed a knee at his balls but the blow fell short. The man dragged her down quickly with a wild grin on his face. He was about to slam Crazy Diamond's head off the floor when Nick ran over and tackled him, pushing the man backwards.

Crazy Diamond jumped back to her feet. She kicked the man on the leg as hard as she could. Then she kicked him everywhere.

"Asshole!" she cried out.

Nick tried to seize control of the wriggling body underneath. It shouldn't have been too hard for him to gain the advantage, judging by appearances. Nick Norton weighed well over two hundred pounds, compared to this slightly built man who probably weighed no more than a hundred and forty at most.

That made it all the more shocking when the skinny man jerked his hips and tossed Nick backwards down the aisle.

Nick landed on the floor with a crashing thud.

"Nick!" Crazy Diamond said.

The skinny man sprang back to his feet and leapt at Nick. He pinned the big pilot to the floor and threw punches to the body and head. His black eyes, like cold marble, stared through Nick like he wasn't even there. The evil grin was still on his face.

Nick tried to fight him off but the Fever had given the skinny man a freakish hit of strength.

"We've got to help him," Crazy Diamond said, turning to Cody.

Cody grabbed Rachel and scooped her up in his arms. Clutching her tight, he ran back down the aisle, dropping her off in a row of seats at the other end of the plane. Far from the action.

He kneeled down and cupped her face in his hands. Her wide, frightened eyes looked back at him.

"Keep down," he said. "Got it?"

She nodded.

Rachel dove down to the floor and curled up into a tight ball. It was a maneuver she'd practiced in the back of the Dodge on their way to the airport and now she had it down to perfection. She made herself small. Her arms were locked around Bootsy.

Cody ran back down the aisle as fast as he could. "Give me my bag," he called out to the others.

Crazy Diamond and Richards looked at the floor, their eyes searching for the right backpack amongst the pile of luggage. It was Crazy Diamond who found it and she picked up Cody's bag and handed it over to him.

Pulling open the zip, Cody found the Glock 19 sitting at the top of a pile of badly folded clothes.

There was a gargled choking sound. Cody looked up and saw that the skinny man had his hands wrapped around Nick's barrel-like neck. He was throttling Nick Norton like a rag doll.

"Quick!" Crazy Diamond said. "He's killing him."

Cody checked the magazine for rounds. Then he walked down the aisle, pointing the pistol at the man's chest.

"Get off him!" Cody yelled.

The skinny man paid Cody no attention. He continued to strangle Nick, whose bulging eyes were rolling to the back of his head. His massive, linebacker body looked almost limp and it was obvious that whatever fight he had left in him, it was fading fast.

Cody waited for the skinny man to straighten up a little. When that happened, Cody took aim and fired a shot at the man's chest. That skinny body, wrapped up in a cream woolen sweater, jerked backwards as the bullet struck.

But he didn't fall. If anything, the man was no more perturbed than somebody who'd just been bitten by a mosquito. He continued his brutal assault on Nick.

"Fuck," Cody said. What the hell was he dealing with here?

He aimed again. The crack of gunfire exploded in the cabin.

The second shot made the skinny man take notice this time. His long, well-manicured fingers released their grip on Nick's neck at last. Upon letting go, Nick's entire body made a loud gasping noise as his lungs begged for air.

The skinny man stood up, looking at Cody. At the same time, a blotchy red stain was forming on the center of the cream-colored sweater.

He walked down the aisle towards Cody.

"Don't," Cody said. He knew the words were useless, long before they'd left his lips.

The skinny man burst into a sudden sprint. He charged at Cody like a reckless bull. Cody squeezed the trigger and another loud crack exploded inside the plane.

The bullet pushed the man back and tipped him off balance. But he stayed on his feet, his face twisted in an agonized rage.

He ran at Cody again.

Cody stood in the center of the aisle, his heart pounding furiously. He squeezed the trigger again.

Crack.

This time the skinny man dropped onto his knees. His sweater was soaked with blood – it was more red than cream now. And yet his limbs still twitched and jerked; the Fever was trying to pull him forward.

But his body wasn't up to it. The skinny man fell to the floor and started wriggling like a worm that had just been pricked by a sharp stick.

"Jesus," Cody said. He walked up to the man, kneeled down and pressed the barrel of the pistol against his temple.

The man's breathing was slow and labored.

Cody glanced over his shoulder. He wanted to see if Rachel was looking. He couldn't see her and hoped she was still hiding on the floor.

Crazy Diamond was standing in the aisle, next to Richards. The old man's eyes were wide with horror. Cody had to wonder – was he thinking about his late wife?

Crazy Diamond nodded to Cody. She knew what had to be done.

Cody nodded back. He pressed the gun harder onto the man's temple. With a grimace, he squeezed the trigger and this time it was over.

For a moment, Cody was lost in a daze. He stood up straight and looking down, he noticed a few droplets of blood splattered on his pants. Perfect, he thought. Just after I changed them.

Nick was back on his feet. His mouth hung open and one hand was wrapped around his neck, rubbing at where the man had tried to strangle him. A trickle of blood ran down his nose.

"Damn," he said, looking at Cody. "I was just getting the better of that asshole."

Cody looked at Nick and managed a weak smile. "Sure you were."

Nick winked at Cody.

"Thanks man," he said. "You saved my ass right there."

"Guess that makes us even," Cody said.

"Yeah," Nick said. "I guess so."

Nick's expression turned to one of sudden surprise. He pointed to the Glock in Cody's hand.

"Wait a goddamn minute MacLeod," he said. His tone leapt from grateful to pissed off in a heartbeat. "What are you doing with a loaded gun in the cabin? I specifically told everyone that all guns were to be locked in the hold during the flight. You had a gun in your bag the whole time?"

Cody looked at the gun in his hand and shrugged. "We were late remember?" he said. "Guess I must have missed that part."

Nick stepped over the fallen corpse like it wasn't even there.

"Oh really?" he said.

Cody nodded. "Really," Cody said. "And I was shot – you gotta admit, I had other things on my mind man."

Nick's face was deadly serious.

"You listen to me MacLeod," he said. "The next time I tell you to do something..."

Nick charged forwards and then stopped. His face burst into a massive grin. He reached out and grabbed Cody, lifting him off the ground. Then he burst into a fit of raucous laughter.

"The next time I tell you to do something you just ignore my stupid black ass," Nick said. "Got it?"

Cody was about to answer when he heard a rattling sound at their backs.

"What the hell was that?" Nick said, putting Cody down.

They both turned around at the same time.

"They're moving!"

It was Richards who spoke. He was walking down the aisle, his arm outstretched, a finger pointing at the two fresh corpses sprawled out on the floor. They were twitching. It looked as if conducting rods had been inserted into the bodies, shooting a high dose of electricity into the nerves and forcing the limbs to move, even though the owners were beyond this world.

The dead man's fingers were going up and down like he was like tapping at a typewriter. The woman's legs flinched like someone had pinched her.

"They're still inside them," Cody said.

"This doesn't look good," Crazy Diamond said, staring at the reanimated corpses. "We have to get rid of the bodies. We've got to throw them out of the plane. Quick!"

Cody shook his head. "You saw how strong they were," he said. "And besides, what if those things get inside us if we get too close?"

"So what do we do?" Nick said. "I'm not too happy about leaving these people inside the plane with us. You know what I mean?"

Cody looked over his shoulder to the opposite end of the fuse-lage. Rachel was sitting up in her seat, watching events unfold with keen eyes.

"We can't stay here," Cody said. "We've got to get a long way from this airport. Everything's fucked up. We can't risk staying anywhere near all these bodies."

"Where are we going then?" Nick said.

Cody turned sideways to face his companions. There was a look of resignation on their faces, like they already knew the answer.

"Downtown," Cody said. "There are people there and they're signaling for a reason. Let's go find out what that reason is."

CHAPTER FOUR

"Grab your bags everyone," Nick said. "Let's get the hell off this plane."

Nick ran to the tail end of the plane to let the stairs down again. When he came back this time, he ran down the cabin, past the twitching corpses, and stopped beside an overhead locker near the cockpit door. He looked sheepishly over at Cody and pulled a small silver key out of his back pocket. Nick unlocked the overhead door. Without a word, he reached in and pulled out an AR-15 rifle and a black Berretta pistol, placing them onto the seat below the locker. Several boxes of ammo followed. Nick crammed the ammo into his sports bag lying on the floor.

"You asshole," Cody said, shaking his head. "No guns in the cabin? That was Nick Norton's big rule, right?"

Nick shrugged. "Later MacLeod," he said. "You really want to talk about that now?"

"Yeah."

"Yeah," Nick said, running back up the aisle with the sports bag and guns. "Well I don't. C'mon everyone. Let's go. We got a couple of weapons. We got enough food and water in our bags to

keep us going till we get there. Leave the rest of your luggage in the
hold. We'll come back for it."

Cody lifted Rachel's backpack off the floor as well as his own.
He threw the bags over a shoulder each.

Rachel reached up for her bag. "I can carry it," she said.

"Maybe later kid," Cody said, grabbing her by the hand. "We
gotta be quick getting out the airport."

Cody led her towards the back of the plane. They walked
down the airstairs together as fast as Rachel's legs would allow
them. Crazy Diamond and Richards were close at their backs.
Cody could hear the urgent, rhythmic tap-tap of their footsteps
hitting off the stairs.

Nick was the last man out – the reluctant captain leaving the
sinking ship with a heavy heart. He was carrying a flashlight in one
hand, pointing it ahead of the others to guide their step.

"Good God," he said, as he caught up with the others at the
foot of the stairs.

Nick pointed the flashlight straight ahead.

The apron was littered with bodies. They looked like macabre
works of art, sprawled out in a variety of tragic shapes, their wide-
open eyes staring up at the black sky. Only a short while ago they'd
been people, full of hope. The Black Storm was over – and to think
they'd believed it. Now they were so *dead*.

Cody and the others crept forward, their sights set on the
terminal building just a short distance away. Their steps were slow
and light. Cody felt an immediate chill in his bones. It felt like
they were entering hallowed ground, intruding upon the aftermath
of a terrible battle in which there had been no victor.

It wasn't long before Richards abandoned his sense of
caution. There were no monsters and the bodies weren't
twitching like those in the plane – these corpses were well
behaved, still like the dead ought to be. Whatever had
infected them was gone. The old man hurried ahead of the

pack, staggering towards the terminal building on unsteady feet.

"Marianne?" Richards whispered. "Marianne?"

Cody watched him go and cringed. What the hell? He didn't like the thought of hanging around while Richards looked for his wife. It felt dangerous to linger here. He was certain that the others felt the same as he did but no one it seemed had the heart to interrupt Richards as he diverted from the straight path to the terminal, searching the bloody site for a glimpse of something familiar.

"Dad," Rachel said, squeezing his hand.

Cody kept his eyes on Richards. "What is it Rachel?"

"Do you hear that?" she said.

Cody shook his head. "Hear what?"

"It's cats meowing."

Cody took his eyes off Richards for a second. He looked at Rachel and heard it – a faint, high-pitched sound coming from somewhere nearby. He remembered the old woman with the cat crate who'd been on the plane. The cats sounded like they were in distress.

"Do you hear it?" Rachel said.

"Yeah I hear it," Cody said, his eyes going back to Richards.

Nick and Crazy Diamond caught up with them.

"Crazy Diamond," Nick said, holding the Beretta aloft. "Know how to use this?"

Crazy Diamond looked at the gun and hesitated. She shook her head.

"I've shot a gun before," she said. "But guns just aren't my thing. Sorry Nick."

"Yeah that's what I thought," Nick said, tucking the black pistol into the waist of his pants. He threw the AR-15 carry strap over his shoulder and looked at Richards in the distance. "I doubt the old man has ever picked up a weapon in his life. Don't matter. Looks like it's you and me leading the charge Cody."

"Fine," Cody said. "Speaking of the old man, we need to get moving."

They walked on, hoping that Richards would notice them moving and come back over. There was a wet squelching sound under their feet.

"Don't look down," Cody said. "Keep your eyes straight ahead and concentrate on the terminal."

"Good idea," Crazy Diamond said.

Cody looked at her.

"You thinking about your uncle?" he said.

"A little bit," she said. "I didn't know him that well but he was the only family I had left and vice-versa."

"I'm sorry," Cody said. "He sure as hell didn't deserve to go out like that."

He tried to smile for her. But smiling here felt like a sin.

"Look over there," Nick said, pointing a finger at Richards in the distance. "I'll be damned. The old man found what he's looking for."

Richards was about twenty feet away from the group, kneeling down beside what looked like a pile of mangled remains. That was all Cody saw of the old man's wife before he pulled his eyes away – it was all he wanted to see.

They walked closer, but not too close. They heard Richards talking softly to the remains, whispering something that nobody else could hear.

Nick was looking back and forth across the apron. Cody saw the worried look on the pilot's face.

"We'd better go," Nick said. "I don't like this place."

"Right," Cody said. He looked at Rachel.

"You alright kid?" he asked. "Want me to carry you or something?"

195

Rachel was only half-listening. She was staring out across the apron, her eyes searching for something.

"You're already carrying my backpack," she said. "I'll walk just fine."

"Yeah but you don't have to," Cody said. "I mean, if it's hard to…look down. Okay?"

"I've already looked down," she said. "More dead people."

She stopped walking before the last word left her lips.

"Dad."

"What?"

"Do you see the cats anywhere? They sound scared."

Cody sighed. "I can't see anything Rachel," he said. "All I'm doing right now is looking at the terminal over there. Getting to it – that's what I'm thinking about."

"Two hundred people," Nick said.

Cody spun around and saw Nick looking back at the Alaska Airlines plane sitting on the tarmac. He wasn't sure if Nick was talking to anyone in particular or if he was just thinking out loud. Or maybe he was talking to the two hundred ghosts lying on the apron. It was possible.

"Five people left," Nick said, turning back to Cody. "Wasn't supposed to be like this man. Why did she bring us back? Doesn't make any sense to let us live only to butcher us out here."

"C'mon," Cody said. "Just keep walking."

Nick pointed over at Richards.

"I think the old man would be happier if we left him behind," he said.

"Well we're not going to," Crazy Diamond said. "No matter what he says."

They walked over to Richards. Cody heard the meowing again. Louder this time. There was also a high-pitched clawing sound, which suggested the cats were scraping frantically at the door of their crate.

"It's the old lady's cats," Rachel said.

"I know it is honey," Cody said.

"We can't leave them in the box," Rachel said. "They'll die."

Cody felt his patience wearing thin. It wasn't so much with Rachel as with the situation. Why the hell weren't they out of that place already? They should have been long gone. And why did he feel a pulling sensation in his mind, a voice that kept badgering him to look down at the butcher's yard at his feet? He didn't want to see it.

"Rachel, we..."

But Rachel had already let go of Cody's hand. She was walking off, trying to locate the meowing cats.

"Kitty kitty," she said.

"Rachel!" Cody hissed at her. "Get back here."

He caught a glimpse of a bloody female corpse lying at his feet. A cold metallic smell shot up his nostrils. The woman's dead eyes, half-open and glassy, were looking straight at him.

Cody stumbled forwards, keeping his eyes closed to block out the carnage. Without the sense of sight, the squelching noise underfoot got louder. When he opened his eyes, Rachel had found the cat crate. She was kneeling down just a short distance away from Cody. He could hear her talking in a gentle voice, comforting the frightened cats. Cody walked towards her. His feet connected with bits and pieces of the dead. They felt soft and squishy, like human slush. He wasn't looking forward to taking his shoes off anytime soon.

"Rachel," he said. "What are you doing?"

"They're scared," she said. "I'm just trying to help them."

Cody looked inside the crate. The black and white cats were anxiously pacing back and forth, clawing at the plastic gate. Cody found himself thinking about the old lady. Where was she? Had he stepped on her remains on his way over?

"Let's go Rachel," he said. "This is giving me the creeps."

"We've got to let them out," she said. "It's not their fault this happened."

"Alright," Cody said. He didn't want to kneel down and touch the crate. That meant getting closer to ground.

"Lift the lever on the door and pull it open," he said.

Rachel's face was a mask of concentration as she studied the front of the crate. She lifted up the metal lever and the door squeaked hideously as she pulled it open. Both cats hesitated for a second, as if they could sense something was wrong.

"C'mon," Rachel said.

They dashed outside, side by side, their sharp eyes taking in the sights as they galloped away from the carnage.

"You're free," Rachel said, watching them disappear.

"Can we go now?" Cody said.

She nodded and got to her feet.

Cody took her hand. They navigated their way back through the sea of dead bodies. Cody kept his eyes straight ahead, ignoring the endless wet sounds under his feet. Looking further along the apron, he saw that Nick and Crazy Diamond were standing over Richards, who was still slumped beside his dead wife's remains.

"You've got to be kidding," Cody said under his breath. "Hurry up old man."

"You're not watching your feet Dad," Rachel said. "You nearly fell over something there."

"Keep walking," Cody said.

They caught up with Nick and Crazy Diamond. Richards was on his knees, tight up against the remains. Cody caught a brief and unfortunate glimpse of Marianne Richards' green cardigan, still buttoned up neatly at the front. Her hands were covered in blood and lying stretched out at her sides in a crucifix pose.

Cody stood sideways on, so that he wouldn't catch sight of her face.

"Can we go now?" he said.

"He doesn't want to come with us," Crazy Diamond said. "We've tried talking to him and he won't listen."

Nick squatted down beside Richards. It looked like he was giving it another try.

"Listen Richards," he said. "I'm sorry for your loss. Truly I am, but we've gotta go now and I'll be damned if I'm leaving you behind. Whatever passengers I've got left I'm hanging onto. That includes you."

Richards glanced over his shoulder at Nick.

"Go away," he said. "There's nothing more you can do here."

Nick looked at Cody and Crazy Diamond. He shrugged his shoulders and straightened back up again.

"I'll drag him out of here if I have to," Nick said. "By the beard."

"Can't we just cut him a little slack?" Crazy Diamond said. "Give him a few minutes. I don't think anything else is going to happen here or it would've happened already."

"I've given him plenty of slack," Nick said. "Every second we stand here is a second too long."

"I'm with Nick on this one," Cody said. "We should be walking."

Richards called over to them.

"I have to bury her," he said. "Help me bury her and I'll go with you."

Nick shook his head. "There's no time Richards," he said, talking through clenched teeth. "Ain't none of these people out here going to get a proper burial. But how about this? If we find the army in San Antonio then we'll get back here and take care of her. You have my word – we're not going to leave her here for long."

Richards' expression darkened. "No," he said.

Cody saw Nick's body stiffen. It looked like he really was

bracing himself to grab the old man by the beard and drag him through the airport.

Crazy Diamond stepped in between Nick and Richards. She kneeled down beside the grieving widower, getting close but keeping a respectful distance.

Richards glanced at her briefly.

"John," she said. "Please come with us."

"Richards," Richards said. "Not John."

"Sorry," she said. "Richards, please come with us."

Crazy Diamond put a hand on the old man's tweed sleeves. She tried to guide him back up to his feet but Richards resisted. He grunted, then moved closer to his wife, taking a hold of her bloody hand.

Cody and Nick were both getting restless. They were trapped in an open graveyard against their will. The reek of death was everywhere and all they had to do to get it out of their nostrils was to walk away. But the old man's guilt and stubbornness was holding them back.

"I insist you come with us," Crazy Diamond said in a calm, gentle voice. "We're not leaving you here."

"But I have to bury her," Richards said, his eyes still on his wife. "I can't just leave her lying on the ground like this. Not like I left her to die."

"We'll come back for her," Crazy Diamond said. "But right now, we've got to go and check out that light in San Antonio. It's our only chance and we can't go if you don't come with us. We *won't* go. "

"I'm a coward," Richards said. "You're better off without me."

"You're not a coward," Crazy Diamond said. "And you're not stupid either. That's why you're coming with us. Because you're smart enough to know that our best chance of giving Marianne a proper burial is if we find someone to help us. You know that's right don't you?"

She tried to encourage Richards back to his feet again. This time the old man didn't resist. His wrinkled hand remained locked around his wife's fingers until his arm ran out of reach.

Cody rejoiced quietly at the sight of the old man standing up.

"Let's get moving," Crazy Diamond said. She put an arm around Richards's shoulder and guided him towards the terminal. Cody hoped that Richards wouldn't turn around for one last look.

The five survivors walked through the ruins of San Antonio International Airport. It was too dark to see much inside the terminal building. It felt like they were walking through a haunted house with no lights, waiting for something to reach out and grab them by the leg. Fortunately Nick, who'd been through the airport many times, knew his way down to the front entrance with no problems.

They approached the front doors of the terminal.

Cody looked through the entrance and stopped dead.

"Oh no," he said. "Don't let it be true."

"What is it?" Nick said. "What are you talking about?"

Cody didn't answer. He was already running forward, still holding onto Rachel's hand and taking her with him. She ran alongside as he hurried through the open doorway and outside into the balmy air.

Rachel let go of his hand.

"Dad," she said. "Is that...?"

"Yeah."

Cody dropped the two backpacks onto the ground with a thud.

Father and daughter stood in silence.

Cody's 1970 Dodge Challenger was still parked outside the airport. But it was a burned out wreck. It was a rusting, decaying monument from another lifetime. The body, which had been classic white, was now covered in ugly splotches of metallic gray, red and yellow. The doors were lying wide open, as was the trunk, which suggested the car had been ransacked before it was torched.

Cody trudged forwards. He felt lightheaded.

"What happened?" Rachel said, walking behind her dad. Bootsy the bear swung at her side.

Cody shook his head. "They got her," he said. "They well and truly got her."

"Who?"

He shrugged. "Somebody. It doesn't matter."

Cody could only imagine what had happened. Some mad bastard, their brain swirling with the Black Fever must have torched the car during the attack on the airport. Either that or it was the Black Widow herself – she could have done it after their last encounter in the airport just to spite him.

Either way, his beloved Dodge was a wreck.

"Damn this fucking city," Cody said.

He looked at Rachel.

"Sorry kid. Your old man's not supposed to swear, I know."

Cody sighed and took a backwards step from the car. It had been hard enough leaving the Dodge sitting outside the airport. It had been like abandoning an old friend. But to come back and see it burned out and looking like a piece of scrap, barely fit for a junk-yard – that was tough.

He touched the pocket of his pants. The car key was still in there – it was attached to the Swiss army knife keychain along with the house key and a few other remnants of the past. Useless items, all of them.

Nick, Crazy Diamond and Richards caught up with the MacLeods outside.

"Oh shit," Nick said. "I'm sorry Cody. That's gotta hurt man."

Cody turned to face the other three adults.

"Don't suppose any of you guys got a car?"

Crazy Diamond shook her head.

"I carpooled here," she said. "Came in my uncle's car with some other people. He's got the keys on him somewhere back there. We weren't super close or anything like that, but I don't think I want to go back there and start rummaging through the bodies. If I found him..."

"I know," Cody said. He looked at Richards. "What about you?"

"We shared a ride too," Richards said. "Nick set it up for us."

Nick stood beside Richards and nodded.

"Some of the other pilots were using my car to shuttle their families to and from the airport," he said. "I thought an armed escort would be a good idea, seeing as how crazy things were getting in the city. I guess I should have gotten the keys back off them."

Cody felt the black sky pressing down on top of his head. Pushing him down.

"Looks like we're walking to San Antonio," he said.

Cody turned around and touched the hood of the Dodge. It felt rough and alien to his skin. Rachel copied her father and put a hand on the car. It was a silent moment – a farewell to a dear friend, like touching the lid of the coffin that was about to be lowered into the ground.

Cody picked up the two backpacks. He slid the straps up both arms and around the shoulders. They were already starting to feel heavy. It wasn't going to be pleasant hiking downtown with those weights strapped to his body.

He turned back to the others.

"We're all agreed then?" he said. "We walk to San Antonio. Find whoever's flashing that blue light and hope they're on our side?"

Nick adjusted the rifle strap on his shoulder.

"I'm game," he said, stepping forward. "What choice do we have anyway?"

"Agreed," Rachel said, looking up at her Dad.

Crazy Diamond walked over and put an arm around Rachel's shoulder. "I'm with Rachel on this one," she said.

Richards was the most reluctant. He kept looking back over his shoulder like someone who suspected they were being followed. "I don't know," he said. "I don't know if I've got it in me."

"Sure you have John," Crazy Diamond said. "You can't walk any slower than me. I'm like a slug for God's sake."

Richards smiled. For a moment, his eyes forgot his troubles.

"Marianne always insisted on calling me John," he said. "Fifty years of marriage – fifty years of asking her to call me Richards. My father – he was John, but I was always Richards."

"Good for her," Crazy Diamond said. "Sounds like she didn't take any of your shit."

"No," Richards said, with a sad smile. "She didn't take any of my shit."

Crazy Diamond walked over to the old man.

"How about this *Richards*?" she said. "We walk to San Antonio together, nice and slow. And on our way downtown we can talk about how awesome Marianne was. Alright?"

Richards nodded. "I'll try."

Crazy Diamond bent down and picked Richards' satchel up off the ground. She slung it over her spare shoulder while the other carried her own backpack. With a nod to the others, she led the old man away from the terminal building.

Cody heard her talking to Richards.

"So how long were you guys married for?" Crazy Diamond asked.

CHAPTER FIVE

The five survivors walked down the McAllister Freeway towards downtown San Antonio.

They passed several abandoned cars on the road. Upon closer inspection of some of these vehicles, Cody and the others found the occasional rotten corpse festering in the back seat. Usually there was a small army of flies buzzing around furiously in the glare of Nick's flashlight, scavenging upon the shriveled human remains.

It was a strangely hypnotic sight, too devastating to fully comprehend with a single glance. How many other bodies were lying in between them and the rest of San Antonio?

It smelled terrible. They didn't linger around the cars for long.

The surrounding area was a desolate sight. The three-lane highway, both northbound and southbound, was empty for long stretches in between these scattered four-wheeled tombs. Several looping overpasses towered above the group as they walked towards the city. The trees that lined the side of the road were tall and overgrown, some of them spilling over onto old advertisement signs that would have been hard to miss under a blue sky. Whatever great deal was being offered on these billboards was lost underneath the ravenous foliage.

Cody and Nick walked at the front of the group. Rachel was walking by herself in the middle, a couple of paces ahead of Crazy Diamond and Richards, who were bringing up the rear.

Cody looked over his shoulder at Rachel. She didn't look tired; on the contrary, there was a spring in her step as if the walk had revived her.

"You okay kid?" he said, trying to sound cheerful. "Getting tired?"

She shook her head. "Fine. Apart from the flies."

"Yeah," Cody said. "Hopefully it won't be so bad in the city. You warm enough?"

"I'm fine," Rachel said. She looked at him with an irritated frown.

Crazy Diamond and Richards walked at a slower pace. The old man's body was limp, his arms long and ape-like at his side. His eyes were distant – his mind far from the grim reality of the McAllister Freeway. Cody had heard Crazy Diamond talking to him, valiantly trying to keep the conversation going. Even Rachel had joined in, doing her best to raise the old man's spirits. Asking him about anything and everything – his work, where he lived and other aspects of his life. But it didn't take Richards long to tire of conversation – his answers had become more blatantly gruff and grunt-like. At that point, Crazy Diamond and Rachel decided it was better to leave him alone.

"You guys okay?" Cody said.

Crazy Diamond waved over. "All good."

Richards didn't look up.

Cody turned back to the front. A black horizon stretched out before them. Nick's flashlight was a feeble speck of light in its presence, a flimsy blade of yellow trying to cut through a towering wall of darkness.

"So this is what feels like," Nick said.

Cody raised an eyebrow. "What do you mean?"

"To be the last man."

"Huh?"

Nick was staring into the emptiness.

"Don't you feel it?" he said. "It's like we're hanging on by a thread. Humanity, civilization – all that crap."

"Maybe," Cody said.

"Strangest thing," Nick said, his fingers locked around the rifle sling that hung from his huge shoulder. "I always thought it would be great. No one else around to tell me what to do. Just me, myself and I in the Garden of Eden. Because we live in the Garden of Eden, don't ever doubt that Cody. You fly as much as I have, look down on the world – it's Paradise. Except for us. But yeah, I thought it was going to be great. No people."

"Changed your mind?" Cody asked.

"As a matter of fact I have."

A hint of sadness crept into Nick's brown eyes.

"You know I got married don't you?" he said. "Several times in fact."

Cody's lips curled into a half-smile. "I was at your weddings Nick," he said. "Every last one of them."

"Right," Nick said. "And you know I never had kids from any of those marriages. I didn't leave anyone behind to carry on my name. No little Nick Nortons running around out there – not that I know of anyway. My ex-wives all hate me and my folks and Grandma are long gone, thank God for small mercies."

"So what are you saying?" Cody asked.

Nick let out a long sigh.

"I've got no family," he said. "So why do I give a damn if the world falls apart? I should be celebrating. Why do I feel so bad? I keep thinking about the little things you know, everyday things that we don't notice at the time – people taking their kids to the play park, first dates, watching the sunset on a hilltop, sitting in the backyard with a cold beer...you know? I sound like an asshole, don't I?"

"Maybe you're not quite as misanthropic as you thought," Cody said.

"Misanthropic?" Nick said. "You mean one of those miserable sons of bitches who hates everyone? That sounds like you Cody. You're the one that turned your back on everything and became a recluse in Texas."

Cody laughed. "With good reason," he said. "LA was chewing me up man. And Kate. We didn't want Rachel to be born in a toxic environment."

Nick sighed. "Yeah I know man. I didn't mean anything by it."

"Hey guys!"

Crazy Diamond was calling to them from the back.

"Any sign of that blue flashing light?" she said.

"Not since the airport," Cody said, looking over his shoulder.

"Are you sure it was coming from downtown?" she said. "What if we're walking in the wrong direction?"

"Downtown is as good a place as any to start looking," Nick said. "Don't worry so much CD. Whoever it is, we'll find them."

They continued walking south along the freeway. Cody passed the time by checking out the sights – those that he could make out amongst the blanket of darkness that pressed down on them. He noticed a large public car park off to the left with few cars taking up a fraction of the space. Most of the cars were burned out wrecks, not unlike Cody's Dodge Challenger outside the airport. Further south, they passed a large wooded area at the edge of the freeway, which appeared to stretch in a westerly direction for miles. Cody was aware that some of this scenery – the car park, the woods – was starting to look familiar. If his hunch was right, they were close to Alamo Heights, a small town located about five kilometers north of downtown San Antonio.

"Look!" Rachel said.

Her voice was full of shocked surprise. Cody jerked around – frightened that something was wrong.

Rachel was pointing up at the sky.

There was a loud whooshing noise over their heads.

Cody looked up and saw a large flock of birds flying overhead. They raced past the travelers, a swarm of of black specks soaring effortlessly under a black canvas. Cody guessed they were looking at either crows or ravens. From a distance, they looked like a tribe of giant bats making a hasty getaway out of the city.

"Holy shit!" Nick said. "That's incredible."

Cody watched them fly overhead.

"How do they know where they're going?" he asked. "I thought they used the sun, sort of like a compass?"

Richards and Crazy Diamond had by now caught up with the others.

"They're probably using landmarks to guide them," Richards said, without taking his eyes off the display overhead. "It's also possible that they might be using the Earth's magnetic field. I guess we can't ever know for sure."

"So many of them," Rachel said, looking up in awe.

She skipped away from the group, climbing over the short concrete wall that separated both sides of the freeway. Rachel ran into the northbound lane and reached both arms up to the sky.

The birds seemed to linger for a few seconds, as if they were checking out the little girl standing on the road below. The massive cloud dipped in mid-air. Some of the crows flew in short, swooping circles overhead.

Rachel was laughing and pointing, almost as if she was sharing a private joke with the birds. It was a strangely intimate encounter, and Rachel was having the time of her life.

Soon, the misty ghost-like shape continued northwards. It faded out of sight.

Rachel watched them go until there was no trace left of the birds in the sky. She started walking back towards the southbound lane when she spun around quickly, as if she'd heard something.

She stood in silence for a moment. Staring towards the edge of the road.

"Dad," she said.

"What?"

"Do you see them?"

Cody looked towards the edge of the freeway.

"See what?" he said.

"Over there," Rachel said.

Cody peered towards the northbound side. He heard something – a faint trotting sound in the distance. Seconds later, he saw a hint of movement close to a row of trees lining the edge of the road.

Dark shapes hurried along the road in a northerly direction.

Nick walked over for a closer look. "Are those horses?"

"Zebras," Rachel said. "Check out their stripes Nick."

"Oh wow," Crazy Diamond said, tiptoeing over to the concrete wall. "She's right."

Cody saw them clearly now. There were about nine or ten zebras making their way up the road in a swift but orderly procession. The travelers were allowed only a brief glimpse. Maybe the zebras saw five humans and got spooked – whatever it was, they disappeared back into the dense foliage again.

"Did I just see a pack of zebras on the highway?" he said. "Have I finally gone crazy?"

"A zeal," Richards said. "A group of zebras is called a zeal. Or a dazzle."

"I'm dazzled alright," Nick said.

Crazy Diamond jumped the wall and stood beside Rachel on the northbound side.

"Where did they come from?" Rachel asked.

"Natural Bridge Wildlife Ranch," Crazy Diamond said. "That'd be my guess. It's not far from here. Or I don't know — maybe they came up from the zoo. Things have sure changed around here though, right?"

"Will they be okay?" Rachel said.

"Sure they will," Crazy Diamond said. "Doing better than us that's for sure. They've got the pick of the grass in Olmos Basin and all those large parks scattered around the city. Don't worry about them. Worry about us."

Cody didn't feel comfortable standing still for too long. What else was creeping around the freeway in the dark?

"C'mon you guys," he said. "Let's keep moving."

They walked in silence for a while. Tall, dark shadows sprouted up in the distance — these were the buildings in downtown San Antonio. The travelers were getting close to something but there was still no further sign of the blue signal in the sky.

They approached a smaller overpass on the city outskirts

Cody felt something land on his head and he jumped in fright. A drop of cool liquid trickled down the back of his head, running onto his neck. He felt his body stiffen with fear.

"Hold it!" he called out.

Nick stopped and turned around. "What is it?"

A drop landed on Nick's forehead. "Black rain" he yelled.

Richards hurried forwards, his face pointing at the sky. "It's those things," he said. "They're coming after us."

Cody scooped Rachel up off the ground. He staggered backwards under the weight of the two backpacks and his daughter.

"Under the overpass," Cody yelled. "Move!"

They ran in the glare of Nick's flashlight towards the overpass.

Cody and Rachel took cover first. Crazy Diamond and Richards were close behind them. They wiped themselves down in a panic, if the black rain was burning a hole through their flesh and sizzling its way down to the bone.

Cody turned around. Nick was slowing down. He was still out in the open, not yet under the overpass like the others.

"C'mon Nick!" Cody said. "Get your ass moving man."

But Nick had stopped dead. He was standing about ten feet from the shelter. With a look of pure concentration on his face, he was studying the raindrops running down the back of his fingers.

"Wait a minute," he said.

Nick shook his head and laughed. For a split second, Cody thought his best friend had gone mad with Black Fever.

"It's just rain," he said. "It's normal rain."

Crazy Diamond stepped cautiously out of the shelter.

"Are you sure?" she said. "You mean those things aren't coming?"

Nick's eyes were wide and childlike with wonder. Slowly he tilted his head back and let the raindrops trickle down his face.

"Been a long time since I felt that," he said.

Cody put Rachel down. Dropping the bags on the road, he took Rachel's hand and crept outside. Sure enough, the water that fell was clear. It was rain – natural rain, which had been scarce since the early days of the Black Storm.

Rachel and Richards joined the others standing under the light rainfall. They stood there in silence, allowing the cool water to wash over them, to soak their heads and hands. They drank the drops that met their lips. They rubbed the water over their faces and felt clean for the first time in a long time.

It was a rare blissful moment. It ended when Cody heard a noise further down the highway.

He spun around. The road was trembling under his feet.

It was the sound of a car engine. Coming closer.

"Now what?" Crazy Diamond said.

Cody pulled the Glock out of his pants. He nudged Rachel towards Crazy Diamond. "You, Richards and Rachel," he said.

"Grab the bags and cross the freeway. Hide in the trees. Hide anywhere. Nick!"

Nick had already taken up position at Cody's side. His AR-15 was pointing towards the sound of the incoming vehicle.

"Dad," Rachel said, pulling on his arm. "I don't want to go..."

A pair of dazzling white headlights pierced the darkness up ahead. Cody saw a small van, a few seconds from reaching the overpass.

"Go!" Cody yelled to the others. "Get out of here."

"It's too late," Crazy Diamond said.

She was right and Cody knew it. The van was too close. It had bolted up the highway and caught up with them easily. There was little chance of anyone getting away on foot, especially with the old man in tow.

A white Ford Transit van with a low roof skidded to a stop about fifty feet ahead of the group. Cody and the others stood still, caught in the trap of the blinding headlights.

Nick's rifle was locked onto the growling van.

Cody pointed the Glock at the windshield.

There was a loud click as the driver's door was pushed open. A second click followed coming from the passenger side.

"You won't be needing those guns," a man's voice called out from the driver's side. "We come in peace."

"Thanks for the advice," Nick said. "But I think we'll be keeping them all the same."

The driver's door slammed shut. Cody saw the dim outline of a man with a baseball cap standing behind the headlights. A woman with brightly colored hair stood on the passenger's side.

"We're not looking for a fight," the man said.

"Isn't that what everyone says before a fight?" Nick said.

"Yeah," the man said, laughing. "That's a good one. Let me guess, you're traveling downtown, right?"

"So what?" Cody said.

213

"Did you see a signal?" the man said. "A flashing blue light in the sky? And now you're looking for the people who sent that signal?"

Cody and Nick exchanged a brief glance.

"Maybe," Nick said, turning back to the speaker.

"Then maybe it's your lucky day," the man said. "Congratulations, you've found us. Or maybe we've found you. Either way, looks like we've saved you good folks a bit of walking. And if by any chance you want to thank me for that, you can start by putting those guns away."

CHAPTER SIX

The man and woman took a couple of steps towards the travelers.

As they came closer, Cody could see in the glare of the van's headlights that they weren't carrying guns. Or at least if they were, their weapons were concealed.

"That was you?" Cody said. "You sent the signal?"

"Sure did," the man said.

"So it wasn't the army then?" Nick said, looking disappointed.

The man shook his head. Cody guessed he was in his early to mid sixties at most. There was something fragile about the man's appearance – he had a wiry build and a gaunt face with cheekbones that could cut through glass. A flamboyant green Hawaiian shirt was half-unbuttoned, revealing a hint of a white vest top underneath clinging to his skinny frame. Greasy strands of brown hair poked out from the edges of his cap, spilling over his cauliflower ears.

In contrast, the young woman looked very much alive. She was wearing dark green camouflage pants and a tight-fitting black t-shirt over her robust build. Her shoulder-length hair was violent purple and her eyes were coated in black eyeliner, which made for a distinct Emo look.

"Sorry," the man said. "I don't think there is an army anymore."

"We're here to help," the woman said. "So take your damn guns off us. Do you know how risky it is for us to be here?"

"No we don't," Nick said. "We don't know jack shit. That's why we're pointing our guns at you."

The man coughed and hacked something up that landed in the back of his hand. Tilting his body to the left, he spat something onto the road – something that sounded more solid than liquid by the thud it made when it hit the ground.

"I'm Harry and this is my daughter Layla," he said. "There you go – now you know something. Who are you? Where are you coming from?"

"The airport," Cody said.

"Airport?" Harry said, slowly reaching a hand into his shirt pocket.

Cody's trigger finger stiffened. "Hold it."

"Just getting a cigarette?" Harry said. "That okay?"

"Slowly," Nick said. "I see anything other than a cigarette coming out of that shirt pocket and it's goodnight from you. Dangerous habit you got there."

"Sure thing boss."

Harry reached a forefinger and thumb into his shirt pocket. He pulled out a crumpled pack of Marlboro Reds and a matchbox. With a wink, he held them aloft as if to show Cody and the others that was all he was bringing out. Popping a cigarette in between his lips, he struck a match and raised the tiny flame to his face. He inhaled and blew a thick cloud of smoke into the air. Harry smiled, turning his face into a canvas of deep grooves and scars.

"Good," he said. "That's better. You know, these things are like gold dust. Marlboro Lights? You'll find them all over the city. Not even the end of the world makes me want to smoke Marlboro Lights. But Reds? That's a different story. Shit, if you're going to smoke, why not do it right?"

"How did you know we were here?" Cody said.

"We didn't," Harry said. "We always do a quick patrol after we signal. It doesn't bring much in the way of results nowadays but old habits die hard I guess."

"You're looking for survivors?" Cody said.

"Sure thing."

"Why?" Nick said.

"Lots of reasons dummy," Layla said, scowling at Nick.

Nick's jaw dropped.

"Easy Layla," Harry said. "That's rude. It's only natural to be curious."

"I'd like to hear those reasons," Cody said, looking at Layla.

The young woman turned her scowl on Cody.

"Alright then," she said. "First up, we give a damn about other people. Gettit? Remember good old-fashioned human decency? Love thy neighbor? Nobody who's still alive in San Antonio is having a good time believe it or not."

"Second reason," Harry said, cutting in. "Recruitment purposes. We're always looking for survivors to join us. I know we probably don't look like much but along with a few friends, we're the last of the resistance movement in San Antonio."

"Resistance?" It was Crazy Diamond who spoke. "What are you resisting against?"

Harry took a long, labored drag on the cigarette. He inhaled all the way down to the pit of his lungs.

"The Black Storm," he said, shooting out a fine spray of smoke from in between his lips. "Well sort of. To say we're fighting the Black Storm – that's like saying in World War Two we fought against German guns and tanks – against the machinery itself. You know what I mean?"

Cody shook his head.

"What are you talking about?"

"I'm talking about the Black Storm," Harry said. "What else? The fires went out in this city months ago. Humankind was almost wiped out and I presume it's the same all over the country, all over the world for all I know. But it's still here – the Storm – finding new ways to get rid of the leftovers. That's us by the way – any human being still drawing breath can consider themselves a leftover."

Cody lowered his gun. He felt like somebody had just punched him in the stomach.

"Back up a minute," he said, taking a step towards Harry and Layla. "Did you just say that the fires went out months ago? *Months?*"

Harry nodded. "At least six or seven months. Wouldn't you say?"

Cody and Nick exchanged confused glances. There was a hint of panic in Nick's eyes.

"But the city was still burning when we took off," Cody said to Nick. "That *was* today, wasn't it?"

Nick shook his head. "I knew something wasn't right," he said. "Listen Cody, I figured we might have lost some time up there but I didn't want to say anything in case I sounded crazy. Think about it man. Look at how the airport was trashed when we got back. That didn't happen in an hour."

"You guys aren't making much sense right now," Layla said. "Were you in a plane crash or something? Bump your heads?"

"No crash," Cody said. "But yeah we were in a plane today. The Black Widow brought us back."

Harry shook his head. "The Black Widow doesn't bring planes back. She crashes them."

"We know," Cody said. "Doesn't change the fact that we're still alive."

Nick swallowed hard.

"We tried to get away," he said. "It was always going to be a long shot and sure enough, she caught up with us. We ended up back at the airport where we started. Then we went outside and these things – ghosts or something – shot out of the ground. Hundreds of them. Killed the other passengers in seconds, drove them mad with the Fever and well..."

"Sliders," Harry said. "Yeah that's a nasty way to go."

Cody pressed a hand up against the gunshot wound on his side. He felt nothing.

"Maybe that's why I healed so fast," he said. "When we skipped forward, something must have happened."

"Like what?" Nick said.

Cody shrugged his shoulders. "Beats me man," he said. "If I ever read up on the effects of time travel on gunshot wounds I'll let you know."

Harry smiled at the five survivors. "Sounds like you've had quite the adventure," he said. "Must be quite a jolt to the system, knowing that you've missed six months of your life."

At last, Nick lowered his rifle.

"What do you know about the Black Storm?" he said, looking at Harry and Layla. There was a desperate look in his eye. "What the hell's going on down here? What did we miss?"

"I know some things," Harry said. "The Black Storm isn't a freak of nature like some people wanted to believe. And it's not a North Korean or Russian military weapon that leaked a shitload of chemicals into our brains and caused a mass hallucination. It's not ghosts either."

"So what is it?" Cody said.

Harry dropped the cigarette on the road and stamped it out.

"Technology," he said. "Plain and simple. That and other-worldly."

"Otherworldly?" Nick said. "You mean...?"

Before Nick could say anything else, Harry looked over at Rachel and smiled.

"Cute kid," he said, looking at Cody. "Looks like you. She's yours?"

"Yeah," Cody said. "She's mine."

Harry nodded, a thoughtful expression lighting up his leathery face.

"You know," he said. "Before the storm, if anybody had come up to me and started talking about time travel I would have called them crazy. I'd have turned around and walked away before they started drooling all over me. But nothing surprises me anymore. So I hope you'll extend the same courtesy to me and won't think me crazy when I use words like otherworldly."

Cody shrugged.

"I can accept otherworldly," he said. "I can even accept the fact that we skipped time when the Black Widow took us back to the airport. It's weird but I guess I can live with it. But there's still one thing I don't understand. One thing that's really bugging me. Why? Why did the Black Widow bring us back? Why us?"

Harry and Layla looked at one another. Cody couldn't decipher the meaning on their faces.

"Might be we can help you with that," Harry said, turning back to Cody. "All those big questions you got swirling around in your brain – we might have the answers."

Harry stole a quick glance at Rachel. Then he pointed a thumb over his shoulder towards the growling van at his back.

"Why don't you all come back downtown?" he said. "Get yourselves under a roof. Eat some food. We'll talk – what do you say?"

CHAPTER SEVEN

Cody and the others were driven downtown in the back of the Ford Transit. There were no lights or windows. They sat in darkness.

The engine hummed and its gentle rattle was soothing.

Cody was sitting on the hard floor next to Rachel. Although he couldn't see her face, he held her hand. They talked little throughout the journey. Everyone was grateful for a little quiet time, so it seemed. It was a chance to catch their breath.

It wasn't a long trip. When the van slowed to a stop, Cody heard Harry and Layla getting out at the front. There was a brief muffled exchange of words with a third voice – a gruff male voice.

Footsteps approached the back of the van.

Cody secured his grip on the handle of the pistol. He was almost certain that Nick, sitting directly across from him, would be ready with the AR-15 just in case there was a trap waiting for them outside.

When the door opened, they saw Harry standing on the street, a fresh cigarette dangling from his lips. The glowing ember of the white stick in his mouth was the only light in the city.

"Hope it wasn't too bumpy?" Harry said. "Damn potholes everywhere these days. We drive slow as a rule but they still have a way of sneaking up on you."

"Can we get out now?" Crazy Diamond asked. "My butt is killing me."

"Sure thing," Harry said. He stood aside, gesturing for them to step outside. "Stretch your legs folks. We're at the base. As soon as you're out, my man Donnie here is going to drive the van to another location."

"Another location?" Cody said, getting to his feet. He reached a hand down and helped Rachel up. In turn, she grabbed Bootsy by the arm and scooped the teddy bear off the floor of the van.

Harry nodded. "Another rule of ours," he said. "We never keep ourselves too close to the transportation, not if we can help it. We park the vans on the street with all the other dead cars – a lot of those lying around the city. Nobody pays any attention to them."

Cody jumped onto the street. His stiff legs wobbled on something that felt like cobblestones. He helped Rachel out the van. As he did so, Cody saw the dim outline of a row of storefronts in the distance. It looked like a gang of haunted houses all bunched up close together, waiting patiently to swallow up the next passerby.

He wouldn't be going anywhere near that.

Once Rachel was safely out the van, Cody turned his attention to the building they'd parked outside – the Resistance base. It was too dark to see much of anything. Upon first glance, Cody noticed a familiar hump shape located at the tip of the isolated structure. It took a few more seconds but at last, he finally realized where they were. In the dark, the outline of San Antonio's most famous building did indeed look like, as someone had once described it, the headboard of a massive bedstead.

"You're kidding me," Cody said. He couldn't help but smile. "Are you for real Harry?"

"Sure am," Harry said.

222

Richards walked up beside Cody. He took a long look at the Resistance base. "My eyes aren't so good in the dark," he said. "But is that...?"

"Yep," Cody said.

"Welcome to Base Seven," Harry said, nodding towards the building. "Or the Alamo as it's otherwise known. C'mon, let's get off the street."

Harry and Layla led their guests inside. As they walked in, the van's engine sputtered into life behind them. Donnie drove it away, taking it into hiding.

As they walked to the door, Cody glanced beyond the old wall, towards the modern buildings on the city horizon. Dead places. It would take the sunlight to fully expose the damage that had been inflicted on San Antonio. If the blackout was good for one thing, it was for blocking out the horrific aftermath of what had happened there.

Walking into the Alamo was like walking into an old, empty church. Cody knew enough to know that the Alamo had started out that way – as a Spanish mission, the San Antonio de Valero.

He looked around in quiet awe.

It was like stepping back in time, like walking inside an old candlelit church in Europe. Stone walls, cool air, and pale light were abundant in the main room. It was a large hall with a number of carved benches lining the edges of the interior. About fifteen to twenty people were sitting on the benches as they walked in – a mixture of men and women, mostly between the ages of twenty and forty years old. There were a few children there and a couple of elderly members. They were all dressed in ragged clothes that had seen better days – withered shirts, torn pants and tattered shoes.

The people inside the hall were eating as the guests were led into the hall. Breakfast, lunch or dinner – who could tell anymore? Their heads were down as they shoveled food into their mouths with a sense of urgency, like they hadn't eaten in days.

Harry pointed a finger to those gathered on the stone benches.

"That right there is the last stand of mankind," he said, loud enough so that everyone could hear him. "Isn't it a pitiful sight?"

"Go fuck yourself Harry," one of the older women said, speaking through a mouthful of food. She fixed a contemptuous look at the newcomers. Then with a snort of disgust, she lowered her head and went back to her meal.

"Love you too Maggie," Harry said, tipping his cap to the woman.

Richards walked ahead of the group. He was looking up, studying every intricate aspect of the Alamo's interior design as if he was taking photographs with his mind.

"It's quite fitting isn't it?" he said, looking back at Harry. "The last stand of humankind hiding out in the Alamo."

"Today we're hiding out in the Alamo," Harry said. "We move around a lot – that's the nature of the game. We've got a lot of places that we call home but for some reason we always end up coming back here, at least for a while. I guess it's good for moral."

"I'm sure it does," Richards said.

"So which one are you?" Cody said, looking at Harry. "Davy Crockett? Jim Bowie?"

Harry smiled. "What's your name son? You never did tell me back there."

"Cody.

"Where do I know you from Cody?" Harry said, tilting his head. "Your face looks familiar."

Layla walked over from one of the tables, a plate of food balancing in one hand. With the other hand, she pointed a fork at Cody.

"He's that washed up actor," Layla said. "You know the one. He's the stutter kid from *The Forever Boys*." She looked at Cody with a gleeful expression. "Didn't you go on to become a famous tabloid junkie or something like that? Man, you sure blew it."

Some of the other Resistance crew looked up from their dinner plates. Cody felt their eyes linger on his face. Although he'd been in that situation before, he was certain that none of these people were about to come over and ask him for an autograph.

At least he hoped not.

"*The Forever Boys*," Harry said, his eyes lighting up. "Good movie. Shame what happened to you after that, real shame. You had talent son."

Nick stepped forward. "I was an actor too," he said.

Layla looked at Nick with a blank expression. With a wry smile, she poked her fork around the pile of food on her plate.

"Oh yeah?" she said. "Don't recognize your face big guy. Sorry."

Nick shook his head in disgust and turned away.

Harry looked at Richards.

"You want to know why we're really here?" he said. "The Alamo is just another building. It's a broken down church and if you don't know the history, it doesn't look like much from the outside. It's inconspicuous. It's also still standing and the roof is intact - that makes any building around these parts appealing."

Harry pointed to a vacant stone bench in the corner.

"Sit down and we'll talk," he said. "You must be hungry, right?"

Nick glanced over at the food table. He pulled a face.

"What's on the menu?" he said. "Anything good?"

"Lots of stuff," Harry said. "And it's all good. Doesn't taste as bad as it looks either, I swear. We got tinned food – lots of tinned food. We got oatmeal and dried fruit. We can get you hot drinks – coffee, tea, hot chocolate. And we got plenty of water, straight from San Antonio Springs – the source of life. We boil it, we even got water purification tablets. You don't want to get sick these days, you know what I mean?"

Richards pulled gently at the tip of his white beard. "Remarkable," he said. "You've adapted well to these circumstances."

"We're alive," Harry said in a matter of fact voice. "Planet Earth is still spinning. It's not like the soil has been poisoned. There's no radiation out there. Food grows if you plant it, just as if sunlight was still there. The animals are thriving – you'll see more of them than ever before. The Black Storm – it came for us. People. Once you figure that out, it all makes sense. Sort of."

Harry led them over to a long wooden table covered in pots and a small pile of plates. With a large spoon, he scooped something out of a steaming pot, something white and lumpy that looked like oatmeal. He dumped it unceremoniously onto a plate and then reached a hand into a smaller bowl and sprinkled some blueberries on top of the oatmeal.

Harry pointed towards the pot of oatmeal and some other bowls, containing salad, crackers, and assorted fruit dishes.

"Help yourselves," he said. "I recommend the oatmeal and blueberries. Keeps you full for a long time. Wish I'd known about this stuff before you know? All that fried greasy crap that most people eat – I used to live off that. Bad fuel. That ain't no use when you need to run all the time."

Cody and the others helped themselves to a bowl of oatmeal. When everyone had something to eat, they followed Harry over to the vacant bench and tucked into the food. Nobody spoke while they ate. The food was warm and it felt good going down into their bellies. Cody didn't realize how hungry he was until he started shoveling it in. It felt like he was filling a deep hole.

When he was done eating, Cody drank several glasses of water. He made sure that Rachel did likewise.

Harry waited till everyone was done eating before sliding another Marlboro in between his lips. He lit up and as he blew out the first cloud of smoke, he leaned his back against the wall and sighed.

"Oatmeal is nice," he said. "But a man still needs a wicked vice or two."

He looked at the others and smiled before taking another drag.

Cody looked at Harry.

"What can you tell us?" he said.

Harry exhaled and wafted the smoke trail out of the others' path. He looked at Cody and nodded.

"There was an encounter," he said. "A few months ago maybe. It let us know more about what we're up against."

Richards leaned forwards, shifting onto the edge of the bench. His expression was one of deep concentration.

"What sort of encounter?" he said.

Harry looked at the old man. He lowered his voice.

"Something came down here," he said.

Cody felt a shudder run down his spine. "Something?" he said. "What sort of something?"

Harry hesitated. "It was..."

Layla called over from one of the other benches where she was sitting down and eating. "Let Dani tell the story Dad," she said. "She's the one who saw it."

Harry looked relieved by his daughter's suggestion. His eyes lit up.

"Yeah that's a good idea," he said. "You'll want to hear this one first hand."

Layla placed her plate on the floor and stood up.

"Dani," she said, calling over to one of the benches on the opposite side of the hall. "Hey Dani. Come here a second."

A young girl of about sixteen or seventeen got to her feet. She waved at Layla and walked over to her. With her long blonde hair and blue eyes, Cody thought the girl was a good indicator of what Rachel would look like when she reached her mid-teens.

Layla and Dani had a brief, muted conversation.

With a slightly anxious look, Dani walked over to where Cody and the others were sitting down. Harry scooted over, making room for her on the bench beside him. She sat down and pulled the collar of her green army style jacket up, as if her neck had caught a sudden chill.

"This is Dani," Harry said, pointing a thumb at the girl. "She's one of our best scavengers. Brings a lot of good stuff back." Harry pointed to his green Hawaiian style shirt and smiled. "She brought me this."

The girl looked at the newcomers. Her eyes lingered on Rachel.

Rachel was pressed up tight at Cody's side. Cody looked at his daughter and noticed her staring back at Dani; it was like they were having a first-to-blink contest. There was a frown on Rachel's face – a frown that Cody couldn't quite understand.

"Tell 'em what you saw," Harry said, giving Dani a gentle nudge on the arm.

Dani looked shyly around.

"Go on girl," Harry said. "You think it sounds ridiculous? These people are time travelers, didn't you know that? They took a plane ride that lasted six months today. They ain't calling anyone crazy."

Dani took a deep breath.

"I saw a spaceship," she said.

Up until that point, Nick's back had been pressed up against the wall. The AR-15 was at his side, the barrel pointing at the roof. When Dani spoke, he jerked forward in his seat. His eyebrows stood up.

"Did you just say...?"

"Spaceship," Dani said. She said it louder this time. "Here in San Antonio."

"An unidentified flying object," Harry said. "Does that sound better? Is that a little less Star Wars for you big guy?" He dropped his half-smoked cigarette onto the floor and stamped it out. Then he rubbed his wrinkled hands together, like he was starting to feel the cold.

"I know what I saw," Dani said.

"She knows enough about fighter jets, helicopters, that kind of thing," Harry said. "Whatever this thing was that landed, it wasn't one of Uncle Sam's."

"For real?" Nick said, looking unconvinced. "I'm a pilot and at some point or another in my life I've flown pretty much everything that there is to fly."

"Not everything," Harry said. "Go on Dani, tell the story."

The girl nodded.

"I was out scavenging," she said. "Going through apartment buildings, shops – that kind of thing. Looking for some supplies, I'm good at that kind of thing aren't I Harry?"

Harry winked at her. "Sure thing."

Dani grinned. There was a notable gap in between the girl's two front teeth that emphasized her youthfulness. Her eyes were much older; it was like they didn't belong to the rest of her face.

"I was coming out of a store on Broadway Street," Dani said. "That's when I saw it coming down. It was so quiet – not a sound. There was white light at the front and back, sort of like head and taillights. It wasn't round like the UFOs you see in books and movies – it was like a flat metal bird, with sharp silver wings, jagged edges – bright silver, the brightest silver I've ever seen. Almost hard to look at."

"That must have been pretty scary," Cody said.

"Not really," Dani said. "Sure I thought it was people. Told myself that maybe it was an army jet or something, even if it did look like nothing I'd ever seen before. I hoped so bad that it was all those people who were supposed to help us. Government, army, whatever. Thought they'd come back for us at last so I stayed close and hid behind an old car and watched."

"Then what?" Nick asked.

Dani hesitated.

"It sat there for a long time," she said. "Nothing happened for while. Eventually a door opened. Sliding doors. Something like a ramp extended out of the doorway from the ship to the ground. Again nothing happened. Everything seemed to be taking so long. Then..."

She swallowed.

"Machines came out," she said. "These weird looking little machines, robots, or whatever you want to call them. They were bright silver, just like the ship. Fat cubes with wheels underneath – that's what they looked like. They came out in a line, rolling down the ramp and onto the street. They split up fast, going their separate ways. I got the feeling they were looking for something. Survivors, I guess. By now I wished I ran off."

"Did they find anything?" Richards asked.

Dani looked at the old man and nodded. "They found me."

"Good Lord," Richards said, his jaw dropping. "What happened?"

"I followed them around the city," Dani said. "I knew it was dangerous but this was the first thing we'd seen in months. First sign of anything, of any life beyond the survivors that I knew."

Cody held up a hand, like he was back in school.

"But there was no trace of anything up there," he said. "I remember hearing it on the news at the time, back when the Black Storm first showed up. NASA, all those people in the know, they checked to see if anything was..."

"Just because we can't find something on our screens," Harry said, "doesn't mean it's not there. Not if it doesn't want to be seen."

"What happened next?" Crazy Diamond asked.

"They spotted me hiding," Dani said. "One of the machines

released some sort of hook from its body and I was locked in its grip. I was trapped and it was real strong. Next thing I remember, I was standing underneath those jagged wings looking up and thinking how much bigger that ship looked up close."

"My goodness," Richards said.

Dani nodded.

"It brought me up the ramp," she said. "The doors slid open. And there was someone there inside the ship. Somebody was waiting for me."

"Who?" Richards said. "What did you see?"

"I can't remember much," Dani said. "It's fuzzy. Just blurry images – the outline of a tall man or something like a man. He was bigger than a basketball player, that's for sure. I was strapped down on this countertop thing and he stood over me. Cold – I was so cold. The man – the thing's features were hidden in the white lights that came down from the ceiling. I felt like I was an animal in a zoo. Felt scared."

"This person," Richards said. "This thing. Did they speak?"

"It spoke to me in English," Dani said.

"What did it say?" Cody said.

Dani looked at Rachel briefly.

"You are not the girl."

Nick jumped forward in his seat again. "Say what?"

Dani nodded. "It said that I wasn't the girl."

"She got lucky," Harry said. His face was deadly serious. "Real lucky. We've had to fill in the blanks but the way I see it, they weren't on killing duty that day. These things she saw. They were looking for something. Someone."

"A girl?" Crazy Diamond said.

Harry looked over at Rachel and nodded. There was a hint of concern in his eyes.

"A girl like you sweetie," he said.

Cody felt like someone had just pulled a rug out from under his feet.

"What are you talking about?" he said.

"If you folks ask me," Harry said, "that's the reason why your plane didn't crash. The Black Widow brought you back because you had a special piece of cargo on board."

"Are you serious?" Crazy Diamond said.

It was Layla who cut in from afar. "You're alive aren't you?" she said. "You should have died when she hijacked your plane. Just like all those other poor bastards who tried to fly out of here. I doubt it's because of your movie star buddies sweetheart. It's because of that girl right there."

Richards leaned forwards onto the edge of the bench. He was looking intently at Harry.

"What is the Black Storm?" Richards said.

"Our best guess?" Harry said. "It's like a computer program, designed by something far beyond our technological comprehension. The Black Widow is one part of that program. Same with the Sliders and everything else that took us by surprise."

"And the technology has matured," Layla said, looking over in their direction. "The Sliders are here to finish what the Black Widow started. They kill faster. Whoever's doing this to us, it looks like they're in a hurry to knock off work."

Cody was staring into blank space.

"Yeah," he said. "It all makes sense."

Nick looked at him with a puzzled expression. "What makes sense?

"It *is* intelligent," Cody said. "I just remembered something that happened when we were driving to the airport."

"What are you talking about?" Nick said.

"The Black Widow appeared in my car," Cody said, looking at Nick. "In the passenger seat. And she was pretending to be Kate, trying to talk me into crashing the car – into killing myself and

Rachel. But the first time she came to me, she didn't mention Rachel, not one time. That triggered me. I told her – what sort of mother doesn't give a shit about her daughter? Well that got rid of her for a while. Then she came back. And second time around? She couldn't stop saying Rachel's name. Do you understand what I'm saying? It was like it had learned. Evolved. It was trying to get better at killing me."

Nick grimaced. "That's creepy," he said. He looked at Harry. "What are we fighting here? And what chance do we have?"

"Of winning?" Harry said.

"Yeah."

"None."

Nick nodded, like it was the answer he'd been expecting to hear.

"Why us?" he asked.

Harry pulled out another cigarette and tapped it off the pack.

"You ever stood on an ant?" he said, looking at Nick. "Did you feel the need to justify yourself to it?"

Cody locked an arm around Rachel's shoulders. There was a cold, uncomfortable sensation gnawing away at his insides.

"You're the Resistance," he said to Harry. "How do you resist?"

There was a look of resignation in Harry's eyes.

"This isn't a fight my friends," he said. "It's not a war either. What are we doing? We're just avoiding the extinction of the human race for as long as we can. What is the Resistance? It's our stubborn refusal to die. Pissing them off for a while – that's the best we can hope for."

Harry stood up and dusted himself down for crumbs.

"Now with those sparkling prospects in mind," he said. "How about it comrades? Will you join the Resistance? That's why we brought you here after all. And if whoever's behind all this *is* looking for Rachel, we'll do everything we can to protect her. Trust me on that one Cody. You've got a better chance if you stick with us."

Cody looked at Rachel. She was sitting on the bench finishing up the last of her oatmeal. She hadn't reacted to anything. He wondered if she'd been listening closely to everything Harry had said.

"Well?" Harry said, looking at his guests. "What do you think?"

Cody was about to respond when the roar of an angry car engine shattered the silence.

Everyone inside the hall jumped to their feet. Plates were dropped. Worried faces looked towards the front door.

"What's that?" Cody said, spinning towards the door. "Your people?"

Harry's skin was pale. His eyes were like two giant saucers staring into the abyss.

"All my people are inside this building," he said.

CHAPTER EIGHT

"Get out of here!" Harry yelled.

Lines of people quickly got busy passing out the weapons they'd stashed in dozens of wooden crates at the back of the Alamo. Rifles and pistols were handed out. Those who didn't take a weapon dealt with crucial items of baggage that had to be moved during the evacuation. Others dealt with food salvaging. It was rushed but orderly. Everybody seemed to know what to do except Cody and the others who stood in shocked silence. Their bags were taken off them with a promise that they would be put in a safe place and collected later.

A fierce-looking man with a shaved head rushed past Cody with a black and brown AK-47 strapped around his shoulders. A young woman with flaming red hair was close on his heels, carrying the same weapon in her arms. They moved towards the front door. Cody guessed they were scouts, tasked with taking a look outside.

"Okay everyone," Harry said. He spun around doing a 360, taking a look as if to make sure everyone was listening. "You know the drill. Out the back door. You know where we're going – the next hideout. Just a brisk run. Good exercise folks."

"Who the hell is out there?" Layla asked, looking towards the front door. Her eyes were spilling over with rage. "Who the hell followed us?"

"Don't know," Harry said. "Let's not stick around to find out."

Layla slammed her rifle butt off the ground. "Bastards."

Harry pointed to Cody and the others.

"Don't look so worried," he said. "We have a bunker located nearby. We're going to Denny's folks! Once we get there, we're going to be invisible for a while. It's just a short run so old-timers and slowpokes – do your best to stick with the pack. We'll be underground before anyone knows it."

Harry looked around the Alamo one last time.

"Everyone ready?" he said.

The reply was unanimous. "Ready!"

"Let's go!" a stocky Latino-looking woman called out. She had a ferocious voice that commanded respect. Clapping her hands together, she moved with the focus of a highly skilled sheepdog, steering the sheep towards the back of the building.

Everyone moved as quickly as they could. Cody, Rachel, Nick, Crazy Diamond and Richards did likewise. They filed through the back door into the garden area.

The sound of screeching brakes nearby was earsplitting. Doors opening. Doors slamming shut.

The two scouts emerged from the side of the building. They caught up with Harry and the fleeing Resistance crew.

"Two vans," the shaven-headed man said to Harry, keeping his eyes straight ahead. "Big ones."

"Keep moving," Harry said. "Don't slow down."

They ran through the overgrown gardens behind the building. The flowerbeds were empty or cluttered with trash that had been swept along by the wind. Long grass and weeds spilled over the edge onto the pathways.

From the Alamo, the Resistance ran onto East Crockett Street. They moved forward in one long line, a single procession with their feet tapping lightly off the concrete. The strongest and fittest, and those with weapons kept to the back of the procession as a last line of defense. The Resistance kept to the sidewalk, tucked up next to a burned out multistory building that might once have been an apartment block.

They ran past the landmark six-story Crockett Hotel.

Richards was slowing down. Cody could hear him at his back, breathing heavy and struggling with the pace of the group. Turning around, Cody saw that both Crazy Diamond and Nick had slowed down to help Richards. Crazy Diamond wrapped her arm around the old man's shoulders and encouraged him to push harder.

"Go!" Nick said, when he saw that Cody was slowing down to check on their progress. "Get Rachel to the hideout."

Nick slowed down further, allowing Crazy Diamond and Richards to run ahead of him. He covered their backs, his rifle pointing off into the darkness.

The Resistance took a right onto Bowie Street. Cody's heart leapt with joy when he saw the large Denny's sign up ahead. It was indeed a well-placed bunker, located just a few minutes run from the Alamo. Cody wondered how many other emergency locations the Resistance had scattered around the city.

Cody saw the Latino woman lead the procession through the empty Denny's car park. She reached the door first and wrapped her fingers around the handle. Looking over her shoulder, she waited for the others to catch up.

A set of squealing tires skidded around a sharp corner up ahead. Three sets of blinding headlights came racing down Bowie

Street at high speed, heading straight for the stunned crowd gathered outside Denny's.

"Shit!" Harry said, stopping dead. "They're trying to surround us."

Layla pulled up beside him.

"Three vans?" she said. "Where are they coming from?"

"Looks like Denny's is off the menu," Harry said. He ran up to the edge of the car park and stared in horror as the three vans sped down the street towards them.

When Harry turned around, his eyes were wild with fright. He clasped his hands over his head, crushing his baseball cap in the process.

"What have I done?" he said.

Layla was pacing back and forth at her father's side like a caged animal.

"What do we do now?" she said. "Dad, we've got like two seconds to come up with a plan."

Harry's face had dulled to a sickly gray color. He hadn't exactly been the picture of health before but now he looked like death warmed up. Still there was a defiant look in his eyes as he turned to his daughter.

He wasn't beaten yet.

"We'll be alright," he said, touching her shoulder.

Harry ran back over to the crowd. The Resistance crew were still standing outside Denny's, like a colony of rabbits trapped in the oncoming headlights of the three vans. Everyone appeared to be in shock. Cody was surprised to see that even though some of them had weapons in their hands, it didn't look like they were willing to use them. There didn't seem to be any fight in the Resistance.

"Keep moving," Harry yelled. "Follow me. Into the mall!"

Harry and Layla ran across Bowie Street and the rest of the Resistance followed. Cody ran alongside them, keeping Rachel hidden amongst the huddle of fast-moving bodies. There were various pieces of rubble on the road that they had to skip over. Bricks mostly, but Cody noticed amongst other things, a set of large padded headphones and a plastic doll's head.

Richards sounded like a man on the brink of exhaustion. Crazy Diamond was by now literally dragging him across the street. His body was broken. Nick was still at their back, pointing his rifle at the vans that had almost caught up with them. Cody wished that some of the other Resistance soldiers – those with weapons – would stand with Nick and start firing at the vans. At least that would buy them time. But nobody wanted to fight – they were only interested in running away.

It wasn't just Richards slowing them down. The older Resistance members were struggling to keep up. They were lagging behind, forcing others to turn back, retrace their steps and help.

The headlights shone brighter at their backs. The vans were getting closer.

"Forget the mall," a woman cried out. "'Make for the river instead. Force them off the road."

"No," a man replied. "We're not going to win a footrace against anyone."

"To the mall," Harry said.

The Resistance closed in on the Shops at Rivercenter mall. Just as they did, two other vans appeared in the distance up ahead. They were speeding towards the mall, one van on either side of the road like they were racing against one another. Now the Resistance was trapped on both sides – they had three vans at their backs and two in front.

There were cries of despair from within the Resistance line.

Harry and Layla slowed down to a jog. Eventually they stopped and held their hands up in surrender. Most of the others did likewise.

It was over.

Five Mercedes Sprinter vans rolled up outside the Shops at Rivercenter mall. There were two silver vans and three black – they were long and fast and bulky vehicles. Big and reliable. Cody could see the outline of dark shapes sitting inside all five of the Sprinter cabins. None of the people sitting there got out immediately. There were double cabs located at the front of all five vans, which meant two rows of people. More people. That wasn't good.

The vans' diesel engines growled in unison.

"Oh shit," Harry said, walking away from the mall entrance. He kept his hands up. "Now we're in trouble."

Layla pointed her rifle at the nearest van. "Last option available," she said. "We shoot the bastards."

Harry pushed the barrel of Layla's rifle down.

"Take it easy," he said. "You want to get everyone killed?"

Nick stepped forward.

"What the hell are you talking about Harry?" he said. "It's time to resist for God's sake. Look – that's just people sitting in those vans. I don't see no spaceships or little green men coming after us with laser pistols, do you? Grow a pair old man. We've got guns. We've got the numbers to fight them."

Before Harry could respond, there was a sharp clicking noise. One of the van doors was pushed open and several people stepped out onto the street. Three men and two women, all approximately in their mid-thirties, made their way towards the side of the vehicle's bonnet. To Cody's surprise, those who had been pursuing them were dressed like everyday office workers, albeit a bit on the black side. Both the men and women wore dark, tight-fitting suits with black ties hanging down the front. It was a smart and deadly uniform – all five of them carried a pistol at their sides. The gun was low, but ready.

More van doors opened. More people stepped onto the road. They were dressed in the same manner as the others – the office funeral look. Grim and tidy. They had guns too, either pistols or rifles that hung at their sides. Cody wasn't sure why they weren't pointing their weapons at the Resistance. They looked a little too relaxed.

The last man to step outside wasn't armed. The other suits immediately stepped to the side, opening up a path for him to cut through the middle.

This man walked amidst the tunnels of light cast by the headlights. He was a strikingly handsome man with a chiseled jawline and slicked back, blondish-brown hair that ran down to the back of his neck. He was probably in his late forties or early fifties and with his sharp silver-gray suit, he stood in contrast to the darker clothes of his companions.

Cody noticed a crescent-shaped scar underneath his bottom lip.

"Hello," the man said. His voice was like a sharp blade that cut through the air. "That was a good chase – a worthy effort on your part. I enjoyed that."

Nick pushed his way through the Resistance lines. He pointed his rifle at the man. Cody expected the suits to respond but they didn't – Nick might as well have been shoving a water pistol in their face.

"You ain't no little green man," Nick said. "I bet if I pulled this trigger you'd bleed red all over that expensive suit, am I right?"

The man didn't answer. His cold eyes scanned the Resistance lines, taking in each and every face along the way. When he saw Cody and Rachel standing near the front, the man's stare lingered for a while longer. The interest was obvious.

Cody knew what he had to do. He nudged Rachel towards Crazy Diamond. Rachel's arms reached back for him, but Cody shook his head.

Crazy Diamond took Rachel by the hand and stepped back.

Cody reached for the pistol tucked in at his waist. Drawing the weapon, he walked up beside Nick and pointed it at the silver suit's handsome head. He didn't care about the rest of the suits. Let them shoot it if they wanted to – Cody was all for that. He was ready to die. Anything was better than letting them get their hands on Rachel. And already he had little doubt – that's exactly what these people wanted.

If only the Resistance would fight alongside them. They would have a chance.

Nick and Cody exchanged a curt nod. They looked over at Layla, who'd reluctantly lowered her weapon on her father's orders. Layla's eyes lingered on Cody. Her expression was ruthless. With a grunt, she turned back to the suits, lifted her rifle and took aim.

"Fuck it," she said.

Layla's actions encouraged some of the others who were armed to come forward. Cody's heart rejoiced. They would take a stand against these people, whoever they were. There were about nine Resistance soldiers lined up alongside Cody, Nick and Layla. All had their weapons locked onto the suits.

Harry groaned, so loudly that it could be heard for miles. He dragged his feet forward, like he was wading through quicksand. Without saying a word, he tucked himself into the line of soldiers, front and center.

He looked down at the others and smiled.

"I don't know who you are mister," Harry said, turning back to the silver suit. "And I don't want to know. But if it's a straight shootout you want, we'll give you one. If you're here to get what I think you are, you're plain out of luck."

Harry pointed his revolver – an old-school Colt python – at the man's head.

The handsome man shook his head. "You can't win."

Nick snorted in disgust. His AR-15, like most Resistance weapons, was pointing directly at the silver suit. "Maybe not," he said. "But I can at least blow your head off before one of yours does the same to me. I got you in my sights pretty boy. You ready to die?"

The man's lips curved into a half-smile.

"I've been ready for a long time. How about you?"

"Are you sure you want to do it like this?" Harry called out. "Lot of people going to die in a gunfight like this. There's other ways you know. Nobody has to die."

The man nodded. "Yes they do."

Harry shook his head in disappointment. "Have it your own way shithead."

The Resistance leader lifted up a hand. With the other, he pointed the Colt at the suits.

"One..."

Cody's finger caressed the trigger. But something wasn't right and he knew it. The suits didn't look in the least bit perturbed that Harry was in the midst of counting down to a shootout. They didn't look stupid either – surely they weren't going to just stand there and let the Resistance open fire on them.

"Two..."

Cody exchanged a worried glance with Nick. The pilot's face said it all. Something definitely wasn't right...

"Three," the handsome man said.

The Resistance soldiers swung their bodies to the side. It was a swift and sudden maneuver and now their weapons were pointing at Cody and Nick. Harry rushed over and pressed his Colt against the back of Cody's skull. The cold steel pushed Cody's head forward so that he was forced to look down at the road.

"Nothing personal," Harry said.

"Son of a bitch!" Nick hissed.

Cody looked to his left. The Resistance had quickly encircled Crazy Diamond, Rachel and Richards. Three rifles closed in on the shocked looking trio.

Crazy Diamond pulled Rachel in tight by her side. She

243

clamped her hands on the little girl's shoulders and scowled at the treacherous captors who surrounded them.

"You bastards," Cody said. "How could you?"

Layla came forward, pushing the barrel of her rifle into Cody's chest. At the same time, Harry took his gun off Cody's head and took a backwards step.

"Careful what you say stutter kid," Layla said. "I'd gladly shoot you right here, right now. And by the way MacLeod, your movies suck big time. You're a shitty actor."

"Back off Layla," the man in the silver suit said. He looked at the fiery young woman with an unflinching stare. His tone was flat, almost uninterested.

Layla looked at the suit, unable to contain the hatred in her eyes. To Cody, it seemed like she hated everyone with the exception of her father. She probably hated him sometimes. With a sharp snort, she turned around and nodded to the other soldiers. The armed men and women of the Resistance hurried over and formed a tight circle around Cody and Nick. A moment later, Crazy Diamond, Rachel and Richards were led over and pushed into the circle.

"I mean it," Harry said, standing outside the circle. He'd lit up a cigarette and was talking through a cloud of smoke. "Nothing personal."

Cody glared at the emaciated-looking man. "It was all bullshit wasn't it Harry?" he said. "Everything you said back at the Alamo – a crock of shit."

Harry shook his head. "Not all of it."

"What about Dani's story?" Cody said. "What about the Black Storm?"

"Dani's story was bullshit," Harry said. "She's never scavenged anything in her life. But what I said about the Black Storm – that was true. You'll find that out for yourself soon enough."

Cody was disgusted with himself at falling for their tricks. They'd walked into the lion's den, thinking it was a refuge.

"And to think you brought us to the Alamo," he said. "Of all the places in San Antonio you took us there. For God's sake, I should have seen right through you. How'd you ever keep a straight face?"

"Drop your weapons," the handsome man said. "There's not going to be any gunfight here today."

Cody cursed quietly to himself as he laid the Glock on the ground. Nick gave up his rifle and with a glint of defiance in his eyes, took out the Beretta he'd tucked in at the waist and set it down on the road.

They were thoroughly searched for other weapons. Crazy Diamond, Rachel and Richards were patted down too.

When it was done, the leader of the suits took a step closer to the captives.

"I've been waiting a long time to meet you," he said.

The other suits stood at the man's back like a pack of scarecrows, basking in the glow of the van headlights. Not one had moved or spoken since stepping outside the van.

"Who are you?" Cody said.

"That's not important," the man said. "But you can call me Mackenzie if it helps."

"Mackenzie?" Nick said, nodding slowly. "Is that your first or last name? I like to know these things."

Mackenzie smiled, but said nothing. The man oozed a slimy calmness that was unnerving.

"What's going on?" Crazy Diamond said. "The signal, the Resistance, you guys – it's all connected isn't it?"

"You have a lot of questions," Mackenzie said. "Well the good news is I have the answers you're looking for. Me, and only me. I'm your best friend in the world right now. I can plug a lot of those holes in your mind."

Mackenzie tilted his head back and inhaled the cool air. For a second, it looked like he'd fallen asleep standing up.

"Didn't it all seem a trifle too convenient?" he said, opening his eyes again. There was a trace of disdain in his voice. Maybe it was pity. "You woke up on the plane, you saw a signal. The signal brought you to the city. The Resistance found you on the highway. They took you in and offered you answers about the Black Storm and most important of all – maybe they could protect Rachel."

"Fuck you," Cody said. He stood in between the man's cold eyes and his daughter. They'd have to go past him – they'd have to go through him. The objective hadn't changed since leaving Spring Branch – he was going to keep Rachel alive. Cody would protect her at any cost.

"It's like I told you," Harry said, looking at the captives. "Not everything we said was bullshit. They really are looking for a girl."

Richards took a step closer to the edge of the circle. When he spoke it was clear that he was still out of breath after the run from the Alamo.

"My wife died after getting off that plane," he said, looking at Mackenzie. "What do you know about it?"

"I know everything about it," Mackenzie said.

Richards' voice cracked with emotion. Both hands were curled into tightly clenched fists. "Tell me what you..."

"Later," Mackenzie said, cutting in. "We'll talk later."

"Now," Richards hissed.

Crazy Diamond put a hand on Richards' shoulder. At the same time, she looked at Harry and shook her head.

"So there never was a Resistance in San Antonio?" she said. "You just rolled over and died, is that right?"

"Of course there was a Resistance," Harry said. His face turned red with anger. With a hand over his mouth, he hacked up a vicious cough and wiped something dark off his bottom lip.

"We fought our damnedest to stay alive," Harry said. "But

back then we didn't know what we were fighting. Sooner or later young lady you realize that some fights you just can't win."

Harry turned to Mackenzie. There was a nervous look on his face.

"Alright Mackenzie," he said. "We've kept our end of the deal. Now give me back my wife. Give Layla her mother back for Christ's sake."

Harry looked over at the five vans.

"Where is she?" he said. "Where's Francine? Is she in the van?"

Mackenzie bowed his head. "Thank you Harry," he said in a cool voice. "You did a great job."

"Give me back my wife," Harry said. "Please."

Mackenzie nodded. "Of course."

Harry's face lit up.

"There's just one problem," Mackenzie said.

"What?"

"The captives get so bored," Mackenzie said. "It was the same with Francine. So we played a game with your wife to pass the time. You know what I mean don't you?"

Harry's face turned white. He staggered backwards. His eyes were bulging while his mouth slowly twisted into a macabre, disbelieving grin.

"No," he said. "Please, no."

Layla grabbed a hold of her father just in time, barely managing to keep him upright.

"You bastard!" she yelled to Mackenzie. Her eyes flashed with anger. "You killed her didn't you? You killed my Mom."

But Mackenzie didn't seem to be listening anymore. He'd closed his eyes, bowed his head and taken a backwards step. It looked like he was praying on his feet.

"You killed her!" Layla said, screwing up her face in rage. "We did exactly what you said and you killed her anyway." She clung to her father and they swayed together, like two limp stalks in a wheat field.

Mackenzie tapped a finger off his temple. It looked like he was turning on a button in in his head. His shoulders were taut and raised. His face was solemn.

A moment later, he opened his eyes. He looked at Harry with a sober expression.

"Forgive me Harry," he said.

Layla let go of her father and marched forwards. Her rifle was pointing directly at Mackenzie's head.

"What the fuck...?"

She was interrupted by a burst of sudden noise. Everyone in the Resistance slammed their hands against their ears at once. The noise came from everywhere. It was a high-pitched, slow shredding sound – as if the dark sky was being torn in two like a giant sheet of paper.

Cody's heart was pounding. He looked around, staggering backwards. He grabbed Rachel, scooping her up off the ground as if a stream of hot lava was gushing towards her. He buried her head in his chest and tried to cover her ears.

"Nick," he yelled over the terrible noise. "Crazy Diamond. Richards. Stay close to each other!"

The five survivors bunched tightly together.

The Sliders sprouted out of the ground like demonic flowers. The shredding noise of their entrance was now intermingled in a chilling unison with the childlike screams of the Resistance. There were about twenty Sliders surrounding Harry and his companions. The phantoms were tall and lifeless – humanoid statues built of black mist that shone like marble. No features, just an empty form.

The Sliders took the bodies of the Resistance soldiers.

"Don't look!" Nick said. "Everyone cover your eyes."

Cody buried his face in Rachel's hair. But before he did that, he saw a massive Slider pierce straight through Harry's gaunt frame. The Resistance leader barely had time for one last scream. Cody thought he heard a name in that mangled shriek – *Francine*. Harry's hands grasped outwards, reaching for something that wasn't there. Blackness seeped into his eyes. He dropped to his knees and convulsed violently on the road. The last thing Cody saw was Harry slamming his head off the road.

Cody shut his eyes. It sounded like he was standing blindfolded in the corridors of Hell. There were screams on all sides. Hard thudding noises, fast crawling sounds and the frantic scraping of fingernails against the road.

He clung onto Rachel with all his strength.

It was a long time before absolute silence fell over the city. When it did, Cody opened his eyes and gasped at the pile of mangled bodies sprawled at his feet.

The Sliders were gone.

His stomach lurched as he caught a whiff of that musty metallic odor he'd smelled at the airport.

"God," he said. Surely this time he would be sick.

Mackenzie walked over – as close as he could get without stepping in the numerous puddles of blood forming on the road. Cody thought he saw a hint of anguish in the man's eyes – regret perhaps.

"Put the bodies in the river," Mackenzie said, turning to his companions. "Quickly."

The suits leapt into action, hurrying over to pick up the bloody corpses of the San Antonio Resistance. They dragged the dead away one by one, and threw them into the back of the silver van like they were trash bags.

Harry was one of the last to be moved.

To Cody's surprise, Mackenzie saluted the old man. It was a clinical gesture – palm facing forwards, fingers almost touching the head – there was something effortless and authentic about it.

"Nothing personal Harry," Mackenzie said.

CHAPTER NINE

Cody and the others were led into the back of one of the vans.

Fortunately it wasn't the same van that contained the fresh, blood-soaked corpses of the San Antonio Resistance soldiers. That van was already on its way to the river.

A pale light trickled down from the roof of the van. Cody sat on the floor next to a silent Rachel.

Exhaustion and shock were intermingled in the eyes of everyone.

It was only a five-minute journey from the mall to their destination. When the back door opened, they were dragged out of the van. Cody was slow to rise as one of the suits tugged at his arms. His body was numb with fatigue but he struggled back to his feet and took Rachel's hand. They hurried outside and a cool breeze welcomed them with a caress. Cody looked around and saw that the convoy of Sprinter vans had pulled up outside a gloomy six-story building, a towering black shadow that looked untouched, unlike so many other buildings.

Cody saw a sign on the lower floor exterior:

· · ·

Public Safety Headquarters
  City of San Antonio

The five prisoners were taken to a large office on the sixth floor. The office space had been rearranged into an interrogation room. Several small tables had been pushed together in the center of the room to make one big table.

There were five plastic chairs sitting on one side and one on the other – the interrogator's chair.

Three glass water jugs sat in the center of the table. There was one other jug that contained a reddish-purple liquid, thick and pulpy, like something out of a juice bar. It didn't look appetizing, even to Cody's thirsty mind.

Five tall glasses had been placed next to the jugs. One glass sat on the interrogator's side.

Cody noticed a lumpy mound of well-worn sleeping bags and pillows that had piled up in the corner, underneath a small rectangular window that offered a view of the black sky outside and little else.

They weren't in the room for more than a minute before Mackenzie walked in.

Two stern looking women dressed in dark suits followed Mackenzie like shadows. Their black hair was tied back into long ponytails that fell down to their backs. Cody wondered if these fierce-eyed women were Mackenzie's personal bodyguards. They carried rifles at their sides and walked stiff and clumsy, like mechanical dolls.

"Make yourselves comfortable," Mackenzie said, gesturing towards the makeshift table in the center of the room. "Sit down, have a drink and refresh yourselves. I can arrange for some food if you're hungry."

Nobody moved or said anything.

Mackenzie sat down on the interrogator's side. He ran a hand through his slicked back hair, then gestured once again for the others to sit down.

"Please," he said. "We have a lot to talk about."

It was Cody who made the first move. He put a hand on Rachel's back and guided her towards the table. She dragged Bootsy along at her side.

Cody and Rachel sat down. Nick, Crazy Diamond and Richards came next. They pulled back the cheap plastic chairs and sat down.

Mackenzie waited patiently for everyone to settle.

"Have some water," he said, spreading out the five glasses and pushing one in front of everyone. "That was quite the workout you had back there."

He pointed to the jug of purple juice.

"You're more than welcome to have some of this," Mackenzie said.

"What the hell is that stuff?" Crazy Diamond said.

"This is a miracle in a jug," Mackenzie said. "This juice fulfills almost all of our nutritional needs. Vitamins and minerals – anything that we might have been lacking is taken care of right here. The recipe was what you might call a gift, given to us when we were struggling to survive. It tastes pretty good – once you get used to it that is. This along with the food that we grow ourselves means we've never been healthier."

He smiled, showing off his dazzling white teeth.

"But if that doesn't appeal," Mackenzie said. "I can get you coffee or tea."

Mackenzie looked at Rachel and smiled. "What about a little chocolate?"

Rachel shook her head and looked at Bootsy.

"I'm sorry you had to see that today Rachel," Mackenzie said, leaning forward in his seat. "By now you've seen more than a life-time's worth of horror."

"Are we prisoners here?" Cody said. "Is this an office or a prison cell?"

"We're getting to that," Mackenzie said, with a hint of annoy-ance on his face. "This is your room. You're going to be here for a while so try and make yourselves comfortable. You'll want for nothing."

"Except freedom," Cody said.

Mackenzie clasped his hands together and laid them on the table. He looked at the five faces across from him one by one, as if waiting for someone to ask him something.

Cody reached for a jug of water. Screw it, he *was* thirsty. He poured a glass for Rachel and then everyone else. Finally he filled his own glass. Both Crazy Diamond and Richards drank the water down in one. Nick took a tentative sip, his eyes locked onto the jug with the purple juice.

"Tell me something Mackenzie," Nick said, putting his glass on the table. "Now I ain't got no love for Harry and his people after what they did to us – but man, that's some cold shit you slung at the Resistance back there. Looks like you made a deal and then stabbed a lot of people in the back. Wouldn't you say?"

Mackenzie nodded without hesitation.

"Yes I agree," he said. "Harry and I have been fighting each other non-stop for the past five months. He was a noble man and he only tricked you because we captured his wife after a recent skirmish on the outskirts of the city. I'm not sure if he ever trusted me but he was desperate. So what choice did he have? He delivered you to the exact place we agreed upon. Unfortunately for them, once I had all the Resistance soldiers gathered in one place it was deemed too good an opportunity to miss. It wasn't my decision. Anyway, to hell with the deal we made. It's about winning."

Nick threw his head back and laughed out loud. Cody felt the ground shake under his feet.

"Nothing changes," Nick said. "Does it? Everybody still screws everyone else over. Not even the end of the world can get us on the same side. Man, I saw the Black Fever. I saw people running around this city, crazed out of their minds and doing sick twisted shit to each other. But at least they had an excuse – they'd been infected. Look at us now. Harry screwing us over, you screwing Harry over and I'm sure there's somebody else waiting in line to screw you over when the time comes. Ain't nobody infected with anything and the Black Fever is still here, it's still inside us. It always was."

Mackenzie clapped slowly.

"A wonderful speech Nick," he said. "Did you just come up with that? Or were you rehearsing it in the back of the van on your way over here?"

"Kiss my ass," Nick said, flipping Mackenzie the middle finger. He fell back in his seat and shook his head in disgust.

Richards leaned towards the table.

"You knew those Sliders were coming," he said, fixing Mackenzie with a hard stare. "Back at the mall. You knew didn't you? How?"

Mackenzie looked at Richards with a bored expression on his face.

"I have connections," he said. "In high places."

"Great answer," Nick said. "You know I'm really glad you found us. I'm starting to like it here."

"And what about that girl's story?" Crazy Diamond said. "Dani – the little storyteller. Spaceships landing in San Antonio – what was the point of all that?"

Mackenzie shrugged.

"The Resistance were given two pieces of information to

convey to you," he said. "They were to pass on information about the Black Storm and to let you know that somebody was looking for Rachel. The rest of it was entirely of their own making. Blame Harry or the girl for an overactive imagination. Their job was to draw you in. To make you trust them. To make you feel that you couldn't possibly protect Rachel without them. That way you wouldn't hesitate when it was time to run alongside them. But what Harry told you about the Black Storm is true – it's not the wrath of God or Mother Nature. It's a piece of brilliant, ruthless technology. It's a killing machine – like a thinking pesticide. Which makes us the bugs."

"And who's behind this technology?" Cody said.

"I don't know where they come from," Mackenzie said. "I don't really know what they are either."

"That's helpful," Cody said.

Mackenzie stared past them all for a moment. His gaze wandered to the back of the room.

"I used to read books about the possibility of extra dimensions in the universe," he said. "Beyond those that we know. Parallel universes, do they exist? And if so, what lives at these higher levels of existence? If there are such realms out there, then perhaps anything is possible."

"Thanks for clearing that up man," Nick said, raising his glass of water in a mock toast. "Now I understand."

Mackenzie reached over and poured himself half a glass of the pulpy juice. He took a sip and sighed. Meanwhile the two bodyguards stood behind Mackenzie, positioned on either side of his chair like statues. They were staring into empty space, distant and yet ready.

"Maybe if I tell you what happened on the plane," Mackenzie said. "It'll give you a better idea of what you're dealing with."

He looked at them with a stern gaze.

"Everything still feels a little bit strange doesn't it?" Mackenzie said.

"The Black Widow brought us back," Cody said. "We know that. And if Harry was telling the truth, it's because of Rachel. She brought us back because you or whoever's behind all of this wants Rachel. But why?"

"She pulled us out of the air like we were nothing," Nick said. "Dragged us back to this shithole of a city."

Mackenzie looked at Nick and shook his head.

"No she didn't."

The five survivors exchanged confused glances.

"What?" Nick said. "What are you talking about?"

Mackenzie leaned forward, like he was about to whisper.

"Your plane never took off," he said.

Cody fell backwards in his seat. For a moment or two, the room swirled around like he was riding on a merry-go round.

"Are you crazy?" Nick said. "I'm a pilot for God's sake. You think I don't know what it feels like to lift a goddamn sixty-five ton airplane off the ground? We took off and she brought us back. We didn't know why at the time – now we know it's because of Rachel."

"So you're a time traveler?" Mackenzie said. "Does that sound right to you Nick? Anyone?"

"What happened?" Cody said.

"Your plane never took off," Mackenzie said. "There was no magic or sorcery at work, only a form of technology light years ahead of our wildest dreams. The Black Widow was never on your plane."

Cody shook his head. "No."

"Six months passed," Mackenzie said. "You were on the plane but you didn't move. You didn't fly anywhere. You were put in a form of stasis – something like a cryogenic sleep state. Every single person on that plane."

"Bullshit," Crazy Diamond said. "I remember seeing the Black Widow too – that was real. Take off sure as hell felt real."

"Of course you remember take off," Mackenzie said. "And you all remember the Black Widow too. Because that's what you're supposed to remember. To us, it sounds far-fetched. For them, it was like keeping hamsters in a cage. The fuselage became a hibernation chamber. Your body temperatures were reduced and you entered a deep resting state. You were provided with all the sustenance you needed – water, oxygen and whatever nourishment was required to maintain your bodies."

Mackenzie pointed a finger to the jug with the purple juice. "It's incredible what they can do. What they know."

"Why make us dream about the Black Widow?" Crazy Diamond said.

"Because that was something that would make sense to you when you woke up," Mackenzie said. "It was feasible in your minds that the Black Widow would interfere with your escape plans. If you hadn't shared that dream you would have been badly disorientated upon waking up. You needed something to fill the gaps. Of course, you were left wondering why she hadn't crashed the plane. Nothing's perfect."

Mackenzie smiled.

"You know it's true don't you Cody?" he said. "How else could your gunshot wound have healed like that?"

Cody put a hand to his wound.

"Tell me something," he said, looking at Mackenzie. "Why did they keep us there like that? What's this all about?"

Mackenzie pointed a finger at Rachel. "But you know that already," he said.

Cody was almost up off his chair and across the table. A voice in his head told him to break the nearest glass off the table and go for Mackenzie's jugular. How far would he get before the two bodyguards sprayed him with bullets?

He sat back in his seat, stiff and upright.

"What the hell do you want from us?" Cody said. "What is this obsession with Rachel?"

"Think about it," Mackenzie said. "What Rachel did at the airport was incredible. She possesses something – an extraordinary power that she's too young to fully understand. I don't know what is – mind control, telekinesis, perhaps more. She stood up to the Black Widow. The Black Storm dropped out for at least a few seconds like somebody had pulled out the plug. They're fascinated and curious about your daughter here Cody. It's understandable that they want to find out what sort of power she possesses, especially if it can be used against them."

Crazy Diamond looked at Cody.

"What's he talking about?" she said.

Mackenzie took another sip of the purple juice. He wiped his mouth with the back of his hand and laughed.

"This little girl shooed the Black Widow away like a fly," he said.

Rachel looked at Cody. Her face was scrunched up in confusion.

"Is he talking about me?"

Cody squeezed her hand gently and smiled.

"You can thank Rachel for your lives," Mackenzie said. "The only reason that any of you are still alive is because you happened to be on that plane with her."

Richards slammed a fist off the table. All the glasses rattled and Cody felt Rachel jump in her seat. He got a fright himself.

"Damn it!" Richards said. "You evil monster. My wife died a gruesome death at the airport today. If these things – whatever they are – wanted Rachel so bad why didn't they just take her?"

Mackenzie nodded, like it was a good question.

"They were protecting her," he said. "I'll tell you something old man – San Antonio was like a war zone while the Black Fever raged. It was chaos and trust me, you don't know what chaos really means until you've seen something like that up close. They didn't want to risk Rachel's life – she was too valuable to risk exposing to our human madness situation. The plane was a perfect chamber in which to set their subject aside for a while. They put the bug in a jar. Like I said, everyone else – including your wife – just happened to be there."

Richards' eyes bulged with rage. Cody thought the old man was on the brink of having a stroke.

"And they deemed us expendable," Richards said "As soon as the rest of us stepped off that plane..."

Richards was edging up off his chair. The educated old gentleman was on the brink of turning into a wild man. The two bodyguards were staring at the old man with cold, focused eyes. Crazy Diamond placed an arm on Richards's chest and pulled him back onto his seat. Richards sat down but he was visibly trembling, his manic eyes leering at the handsome man sitting across the table.

"Easy Richards," Crazy Diamond said. "Don't give them an excuse."

Mackenzie turned his attention back to Cody.

"Perhaps now you have a better understanding of what sort of power you're dealing with," he said. "Don't try to wrap your mind around it. You can't."

"Assholes," Nick said. "We're dealing with assholes. You included."

Mackenzie wiped down a minor crease on the sleeve of his suit jacket.

"It's a terrifying prospect at first," he said. "But then it becomes liberating. It's incredibly comforting to find out how small and powerless you really are. You must stop fighting it by pretending to be something grand."

Richards's face was burning red.

"Enough of this nonsense," he yelled. "I don't care how great your masters are or how pathetic you think we are Mackenzie. My wife was killed by those things – these..."

"Exterminators," Mackenzie said. "That's what I like to call them."

"They killed her," Richards said. "Your Exterminators killed my Marianne. They kept us alive only to butcher us as soon as we set foot off the plane."

"They're not interested in your wife old man," Mackenzie said. "They never were. And to be frank, neither am I."

"How dare you?" Richards said.

Cody looked at the old man. Richards was a ticking bomb waiting to go off.

"How do you know all this stuff?" Cody said to Mackenzie, trying to steer the conversation away from Richards' wife.

"I know because they know," Mackenzie said. "And there are other gifts too. They're capable of great generosity to those who serve them."

"You're a monster," Richards said. "You sold out your own people."

A repulsive grin appeared on Mackenzie's face. Cody got the feeling he was trying to push the old man's buttons. So far, Richards was falling for it.

"Where are they?" Cody asked. "These Exterminators."

"Everywhere," Mackenzie said. "Nowhere."

Nick rolled his eyes. "Jesus."

An uncomfortable silence crept across the room. It felt like forever before it was broken.

"Why you?" Crazy Diamond said. "Why are they working with you?"

Mackenzie shook his head. "I don't have an answer for that," he said. "I hated the Black Storm like everyone else when it came.

It took everything that I ever loved. I despised them before I even knew they existed. But then one day, they spoke to me. I saw things from their perspective. That's all it is – a matter of perspective. Hard for a species like ours, full of self-obsession, to understand."

Mackenzie's hands were still clasped on the table. His knuckles whitened as he tightened his grip.

Cody edged forward on his seat. He clung to Rachel's hand.

"What exactly is going to happen here?" he said.

"I take Rachel to a specific location," Mackenzie said.

"And your Exterminator buddies show up and take her?" Cody said.

"They're not *here*," Mackenzie said. "Not physically at least. They don't have to be on this world to take care of the likes of us. But yes, a gate will be opened and Rachel will be taken through it. A simple transfer. They get what they want."

Cody's hands clenched into tight fists.

"After that," Mackenzie said, fixing his eyes on Cody, "she'll be the equivalent of a lab rat for the rest of her life. Whatever natural power she has will be taken from her and used for research purposes."

Cody snapped. He jerked forwards and reached for the glass in front of him. But Nick leapt to his feet at the same time and wrapped his arms around Cody's waist. While Cody struggled, Nick held him back.

"Don't do it man," Nick said, whispering in his ear. "Don't give this asshole the satisfaction."

Nick was right. Cody knew that. He also knew that he wouldn't be able to help Rachel if he didn't calm down. Although it was hard, he forced himself to take in a deep lungful of air and when he felt his heart slowing up, he sat down again.

At the same time, Mackenzie pushed back his chair and stood

up. He looked across the line of people – first at Richards, then Crazy Diamond and Nick. Last but not least, his gaze landed on Cody and Rachel.

"Okay," he said, with a twisted smile. "Now that we've got all that stuff out of the way – who wants to play a game?"

CHAPTER TEN

"A game?" Nick said.

Mackenzie's eyes were like blocks of stone as he took in the worried reaction on each and every face across the table. His perverse smile endured. He walked around the table a little. The two bodyguards kept close, making suitable adjustments to maintain their position as his shadow.

"We used to play games in this room all the time," Mackenzie said. "When the late Harry, his wife and lovely daughter still believed they could win the fight, we kept prisoners in here. They were brave people, some of them."

"So it is a prison cell," Cody said.

Mackenzie dismissed the remark with a lazy shrug.

"These are our headquarters," he said. "We live here, we work here. When my superiors decided that it would be helpful to employ a human presence to help manage the situation in San Antonio, we needed a base. I found this building and went to work."

"Went to work?" Nick said.

"I built a good team of people around me," Mackenzie said. "We fought hard to put a major dent in the Resistance. It's a waste of time fighting against the inevitable. Work *with* them and they'll reward you. We captured many prisoners and brought them here to gather information. They all believed they could escape, every last one of them. It was a problem. And so they took great personal risks to try and get back to the fight."

Mackenzie's expression darkened.

"I lost some good people during those escape attempts," he said. "One very good friend of mine in particular died at the hand of reckless fools trying to escape through that window."

Mackenzie pointed to something that looked like a red wine stain on the cream carpet. The circular-shaped blemish had formed a few feet from the window ledge.

"In my experience," Mackenzie said, walking slowly towards the window, "it's fear that makes a model prisoner. They have to be afraid of you, of what you'll do. We learned that the hard way. Nonetheless we learned."

"We'll be quiet," Crazy Diamond said. Her voice trembled. "We're not going to try and escape. There's nowhere to go anyway, you've made it clear."

Mackenzie looked out of the window for while. Beyond his reflection in the glass, a fog of darkness had swallowed the San Antonio skyline. There was nothing but a black desert to look at.

"That's what the Resistance said," Mackenzie said. He turned around and walked slowly back to the table, the bodyguards following his every move. "Almost word for word. All the prisoners say it."

"We promise," Crazy Diamond said. "We..."

"I don't believe you," Mackenzie said, cutting the young woman off. "I've seen what desperation does to people in here. I can see it in your eyes now. You'd be fools not to try something. Cowards even – and I don't think you are cowards. You'll charge at the guards, try the window, steal a weapon – the point is you'll try something. Only fear can stop you. On top of that, you're the most valuable guests I've ever had. I can't risk losing Rachel. That means I have to scare you."

Mackenzie turned back to his 'guests'.

"And so back to the game."

"To hell with your game," Nick said. "We won't play."

'The girl doesn't play,' Mackenzie said, pointing at Rachel. Then he looked at Cody and smiled. "Daddy's out too, at least for now. The rest of you are in."

Mackenzie walked around the table, bringing the bodyguards with him. They stopped behind Nick, Crazy Diamond and Richards.

"Stand up players," he said.

They didn't move. Mackenzie clicked his fingers and the bodyguards stepped forward with their rifles pointing at the trio.

"It's easier if you just stand up," Mackenzie said. "Less messy."

Crazy Diamond and Nick looked at one another, both seemingly unsure. There weren't many options left unless they wanted to find out what Mackenzie meant by messy. It was Nick who gave the nod, signaling to the others to get to their feet. Crazy Diamond stood up alongside him. Richards hesitated, but upon seeing Nick and Crazy Diamond get up, he did likewise.

There was a manic glint in Mackenzie's eyes as he looked at them. Cody could feel a sinister excitement bubbling up underneath the cool surface.

Mackenzie glanced at the bodyguards.

"Is Michael outside?" he said.

"Yes he is," one of the women said. Her voice was booming, like a warning bark.

Mackenzie turned back to the three captives. "Good," he said. "Tell him to bring the boxes in."

The bodyguard nodded and walked towards the door.

"It's not much of a game," Mackenzie said. He sounded genuinely apologetic. "But it's a surefire way of making a point."

Cody looked at his three companions. There was a tight knot forming in his stomach and his palms felt sweaty. He couldn't think of any way to help them. But he had to do something – he didn't know what Mackenzie had in mind but he shuddered at the possibilities.

"Look," Cody said. "You don't want us to try anything. I get it. Why don't you just handcuff us to the table or something? How about that?"

"You don't think we tried that?" Mackenzie said. "That's not pleasant for anyone involved. Some of the prisoners used to deliberately piss and shit themselves just to spite us. No thanks. The game is much more effective."

The bodyguard opened the office door. With a curt nod, she gestured to someone outside and seconds later, a clean-shaven man in a dark suit walked through the open doorway. He carried three cardboard boxes in his arms, all piled on top of one another.

The man set the boxes down on the floor. He lifted the top two off and spread them out evenly so that they formed a straight line. Bending over, he ran a hand over the surface of each box, as if to check they were thoroughly sealed. When that was done he gave a thumbs up sign to Mackenzie.

"Good," Mackenzie said. "You can go Michael."

Michael nodded and took off in a hurry.

Mackenzie turned back to the captives.

"The rules are simple," Mackenzie said. "Three boxes. Three people. Two of the boxes are empty – you'll find nothing but air in those boxes. One box however, isn't empty. If you find yourself sitting in front of an empty box, congratulations – you're a winner. But if your box isn't empty, well I'm sorry. You lose the game."

"And if you lose?" Nick said.

"You die," Mackenzie said.

266

There were loud gasps across the room.

"That's the shittiest game I've ever heard of," Nick said. "Don't you have Monopoly or something else? Operation? Snakes and Ladders?"

Cody let go of Rachel's hand and jumped to his feet. "Are you crazy man?" he said to Mackenzie. "You're going to kill one of us?"

"You're not involved," Mackenzie said. With a curled finger, he beckoned for Nick, Crazy Diamond and Richards to move towards the boxes. "I think I've explained everything clearly," he said.

"Don't do this," Crazy Diamond said. "Enough people have died already today."

"Almost," Mackenzie said. "One more to go."

He pointed to the three boxes lying on the floor.

"Sit down over there please," he said. "Cross-legged, in front of whatever box you feel most drawn to."

Still, nobody moved.

Mackenzie sighed. "Walk over there, sit down beside a box or my guards will shoot all three of you. Remember this, you're not necessary to my plans. Not one of you. What I'm offering here is the chance for two of you to live through this. You should be thanking me."

Cody felt helpless sitting on the sidelines. His arms were wrapped around Rachel who in turn, had her arms wrapped around Bootsy.

"Dad," Rachel said, looking back at him. "What's going to...?"

"Shhh," Cody said, pressing a finger onto her lips.

Nick was the first to walk over to the row of cardboard boxes on the floor. He glared at Mackenzie every step of the way.

Crazy Diamond and Richards followed him.

They stood in front of the boxes, like divers standing on a cliff edge.

"Don't overthink it," Mackenzie said. "That'll drive you mad.

You've reached the starting point – well down. Now just sit down. Trust your instinct."

"Easy for you to say," Cody said.

They took their places. Nick sat down in front of the box on the far left. Crazy Diamond took the one on the far right, while Richards lowered his ageing body next to the one in the middle.

"That's good," Mackenzie said. "This is starting to bring back so many happy memories."

Nick threw Mackenzie a hateful look. "So what now Bob Barker?" he said. "Do we just open the damn thing?"

Mackenzie clapped his hands together in mock praise. "Bravo Nick," he said. "I knew you'd be the one to start us off. And to answer your question, yes that's all you have to do. And when you've done it, show everyone else in the room what's inside your box. It really is a simple game."

"Yeah," Nick said.

"Can you at least take Rachel out of the room?" Cody said, calling over to Mackenzie. "She doesn't need to see this."

"I'm not going anywhere," Rachel said. She turned around and he was shocked at the stubborn look on her face.

"You'll go if I tell you to go," Cody said.

"There's no time for that," Mackenzie said. He was still looking at his players sitting on the floor. They looked like death row inmates waiting for their turn on the electric chair. "Besides Cody," he said. "Don't underestimate a child's capacity to endure the horrors of this world. In my experience, it's the adults who crumble first."

Mackenzie walked up behind Nick. He gave the pilot a pat on the shoulders and Nick flinched at the sudden contact.

"Get it over with Nick," Mackenzie said. "You go first."

"I hope you're enjoying this," Nick said.

He looked at the box in front of him. Tentatively, he began to pick at the layer of Scotch tape that clung to the side of the box, peeling back a long thin strip of the transparent material. When that was done, he scrunched the tape up and threw it to the side.

Nick took a deep breath. Slowly, he lifted up the flaps of the box and looked inside. The following seconds lasted forever. Cody's heart was racing and he could feel a pool of sweat forming at his brow.

Nick's shoulders visibly sagged. His hands were shaking.

Cody feared the worst.

But when Nick lifted up the box, it was empty.

"Congratulations," Mackenzie said.

"Fuck you," Nick said. His voice was trembling slightly. "You sick, twisted son of a bitch – I hope you're getting your rocks off."

"Next," Mackenzie called out.

It was Richards' turn. The old man gave Nick a sad smile as he pulled back the Scotch tape on the cardboard box.

Richards swallowed hard. He tilted his head forward and looked inside.

His expression was blank

"It's empty," he said.

"Show me," Mackenzie said.

But Richards didn't lift the box to show anyone. He was looking at Crazy Diamond, who was sitting to his right. He reached over and took the young woman's hand in his own.

Mackenzie leaned over Richards and stole a glance inside the box.

"Congratulations old man," he said. "Looks like that reunion with your wife will have to wait."

Richards didn't react. He was still looking at Crazy Diamond. There was a calm expression on her face and Cody wondered if she was still in shock. To look at Richards' face, anyone would have thought he'd just lost the game.

"The final box is a formality," Mackenzie said. "Ah what the hell, we'll open it up anyway."

Richards squeezed Crazy Diamond's hand. "You don't have to," he said.

"Open it," Mackenzie said, taking a step towards Crazy Diamond. "Remember what happens if you don't comply."

Crazy Diamond released her hand from Richards' grip. She opened up the last box, digging into the cardboard with her fingernails. Her stoic mask crumbled. There were tears in her eyes as she pulled back the tattered flaps.

She looked inside the box.

"You know the rules," Mackenzie said. "Show the room."

"Fuck you," Crazy Diamond said. But she lifted the box anyway, tilting it in mid-air so that Cody and everyone else in the room could see a small flower sitting at the bottom of it.

"It's a white stargazer lily," Mackenzie said. He turned around, as if he was giving a presentation to the rest of the onlookers. "That's one of several stargazers I laid over my wife and daughter's grave. It means the soul of the departed has had its innocence restored."

Mackenzie looked at Crazy Diamond. "I'm sorry," he said.

Crazy Diamond dropped the box. She sat on the floor with her face buried in her trembling hands.

"Jesus Christ," Cody said, standing up. "She's just a kid Mackenzie. She's twenty years old!"

Mackenzie clicked his fingers. The two bodyguards walked over and stood at Crazy Diamond's back. They looked over at their boss, waiting for the next command.

"Hold on a minute," Nick said. He stood up with his hands in the air like he was surrendering. "Let's talk about this man. We can..."

"Don't waste your time Nick," Mackenzie said. "Or mine. It'll only make things worse. She won't feel a thing."

Cody saw Nick's massive hands clench into tightly coiled fists.

"You motherfucker," Nick said. "I won't let you do it. I'm not going to just stand here and let you kill her."

"Pick her up," Mackenzie said.

The two guards pulled Crazy Diamond up to her feet and dragged her towards the door.

Nick jerked forwards, as if to run after them. The guards saw it and one of them turned her gun on the pilot.

"Don't Nick," Crazy Diamond said. Her face was damp and tearstained. "It's going to be okay."

Rachel was still sitting down, watching events unfold with a horrified look on her face. She looked back and forth between Cody and what was happening with Crazy Diamond.

"Mackenzie!" Cody yelled. "Don't do this. For God's sake."

"What's everyone complaining about?" Mackenzie said. "They played the game, knowing full well what was going to happen."

He turned back to the guards. "Put her up against the wall."

The bodyguards led Crazy Diamond over to the door. Crazy Diamond didn't resist. They pinned her up against the wall and took a step back, their rifles pointing at her.

Nick was pacing back and forth like a caged lion. He was shaking his head furiously.

"You're going to kill a girl?" he said. "You need to make a point about escaping right? Okay, shoot me instead. I'll swap boxes. I'll do whatever it takes."

Mackenzie smiled and shook his head.

"It's a bit late to start playing the tough guy Nick," Mackenzie said. "And just in case you hadn't noticed, this isn't one of your B-movies. Spare us the heroics."

Crazy Diamond stood with her back up against the wall, looking through a gap in between the two guards. "Nick," she said. "Just leave it."

"No I won't leave it," Nick said. Cody had never seen his friend so close to tears before. As a child actor, Nick Norton had been notorious with casting agents for his inability to cry on cue. It had cost him jobs but Nick had always taken a strange macho pride in this particular trait. He didn't cry when he got divorced many times over. He didn't cry when his Mom died.

But he was close now.

Cody looked at Rachel. She was up and standing beside him now. He reached down and wiped a tear off her cheek.

"I can make it right," Nick said, pleading with Mackenzie. "Shoot me for God's sake. Make an example out of me. That girl's got a life ahead of her."

Mackenzie slow clapped his hands.

"That was beautiful Nick," he said. "You're full of great speeches today. And do you know what? I believe you. I believe you'd die for her, right here, right now. But we've played the game already. Believe it or not, you won."

Mackenzie turned back to the guards.

"Do it."

One of the guards pushed Crazy Diamond, forcing her back up tight against the wall. Crazy Diamond looked the guards in the eye, defiant to the end. Her hands were trembling. Sweat was pouring down her forehead. But she wouldn't look away or close her eyes.

The bodyguards raised their weapons. They took aim.

Mackenzie's hand was held aloft. He was about to give the final order when Richards, who was still sitting on the carpet, spun around and grabbed Mackenzie's legs, tipping him off balance and sending him crashing to the floor.

Richards scrambled with remarkable speed and jumped on top of Mackenzie. He wrapped both of his gnarled hands around Mackenzie's neck and squeezed as tight as he could.

"You bastard," Richards hissed. "This is for Marianne. This is for all the people you've betrayed and killed. You turned against us, you treacherous bastard!"

The two guards hurried over with a shocked look on their faces. It was the first time Cody had seen any hint of emotion from either one of them. So they were human after all. They pointed their rifles at Richards and were just seconds away from blowing the old man's head off when Mackenzie lifted a hand in the air.

"No!" he said. "Don't shoot him."

Richards wasn't paying attention to anything else. He'd given up on trying to choke Mackenzie into unconsciousness. Now he was throwing a barrage of flimsy punches at the younger man's face. His eyes were spilling over with hate. He was breathing heavy.

"Bastard, bastard, bastard!"

Mackenzie was laughing.

Richards stopped when he saw this. He straightened up and looked at the man with horror in his eyes. He shook his head.

"You crazy..."

But Richards didn't get to finish the sentence. Mackenzie pulled his knees towards his chest. Then, launching both feet at the old man's stomach, Mackenzie kicked out and the old man was hurled backwards across the office.

It looked like he'd been launched straight out of a cannon.

Cody's jaw dropped. He'd never seen anyone kick another person so far. He thought that Richards, who'd been kicked almost the entire length of the room, was going to crash through the wall and land in the next office amidst a pile of smoking rubble.

"Holy shit," Nick said.

Richards hit the wall with a howl. He crumpled to the floor in a ragged heap but he wasn't unconscious. To Cody's surprise, a fire still burned in the old man's eyes and he tried to claw his way back to his feet.

"Richards!" Crazy Diamond yelled.

On the other side of the room, Mackenzie stood up and dusted his suit down. He looked over at Cody and grinned.

Cody looked back at the man and his blood ran cold.

The irises of Mackenzie's eyes were jet black. He looked demonic, like a supervillain out of a comic book – albeit a supervillain dressed like a lawyer.

He walked across the office towards Richards.

"No!" Crazy Diamond yelled.

Richards had by now struggled back to his feet. But the fight – if it had ever been one, was already decided.

Mackenzie seized the old man by the throat. Then he spun around and with one flick of the wrist, hurled Richards back over to the other side of the room. He might as well have been throwing a kid's doll around.

Richards crashed into the opposite wall and dropped to the floor. It felt like the building shook as the old man was tossed around. Richards' howl had faded to a dull, prolonged groan. He wasn't getting back up this time.

"Stop!" Crazy Diamond said. She ran over to Richards but the guards turned their guns on her and she stopped dead. Nick and Cody made a move to help the old man but the guns were all over them.

Mackenzie walked over and picked the battered old man up off the ground. He gripped onto the wrinkled skin at the back of Richards' neck and held him aloft, like he was scruffing a naughty kitten.

Richards opened his eyes and gritted his teeth. His eyes were alert and although the fire had dimmed, it hadn't gone out.

"*You're* the coward," he said. "Your wife and daughter would be ashamed of you. Coward!"

He spat the last word out with contempt.

Mackenzie's black eyes flickered with rage. He punched the

old man square in the face and there was a loud cracking noise as Richards' head snapped back.

The old man's body went limp and he dangled in Mackenzie's grip.

"Stop!" Cody yelled. He made another move to run over.

The guards turned their rifles on him.

"Back," one of them said in a cold, metallic voice.

Cody and Nick looked at the guards, then over to the other side of the room.

Mackenzie lifted Richards' head up and studied the old man's face. Richards' eyes were open but they saw nothing. Mackenzie then lowered the body gently onto the ground. Kneeling down, he placed his index and middle finger against the side of Richards' neck. He probed the soft hollow area below the windpipe and shook his head.

"Dead," he said.

Crazy Diamond let out a high-pitched shriek of horror. She ran over and Mackenzie, whose eye color had returned to its normal green, signaled to the bodyguards not to stop her.

"What have you done?" Crazy Diamond said.

She kneeled down and cradled Richards' limp body in her arms. With a pitiful wail, she buried her face in his tweed blazer while Richards' lifeless eyes continued to stare up towards the ceiling.

Cody felt dizzy, like the room was spinning.

Mackenzie wiped his suit down and walked away from the body.

"It was self-defense," he said.

Crazy Diamond lifted her head off Richards' chest. She turned her head towards Mackenzie.

"I'm going to kill you," she said. "I don't know how. But I will, I swear to God."

Mackenzie stopped and turned to face her. He pushed back a cluster of blondish-brown hair that was hanging loose over his forehead. He wiped a few specks of Richards' blood off the tips of his knuckles.

"Congratulations," he said. "You get to live."

CHAPTER ELEVEN

Mackenzie called Michael back into the office.

When the man who'd delivered the boxes returned, he walked over to where Richards was lying on the far side of the room in Crazy Diamond's arms. With a poker face, Michael gripped the frail body under the arms and dragged it away from the young woman. He then moved back towards the door.

Nick stepped over and put a comforting hand on Crazy Diamond's shoulder. She protested the removal of Richards' body with her eyes. Cody wondered if Nick was standing beside her, not just for comfort, but to prevent her from doing anything reckless.

"Wait," Rachel said, watching as Richards was being taken away. She wriggled free of Cody's arms and ran across the room.

Michael looked alarmed as Rachel ran towards him. It might as well have been a mountain cat charging his way judging by the look on his face. Even the two bodyguards looked uncomfortable as the little girl, who'd been quiet up to that point, approached them.

Rachel looked up at Mackenzie. She held Bootsy aloft.

"Can I give this to him?" she asked. "It's my bear."

Mackenzie looked at the teddy bear dangling in mid-air. His lips moved, as if he was about to say something but no words came out. He could only manage a feeble nod.

"Rachel," Cody said. "What are you doing?"

She spun around.

"I want Richards to have Bootsy," she said.

"But Mom gave Bootsy to you," Cody said. "Isn't that why we brought him with us?"

Rachel nodded. "Yeah but Richards needs him more than I do now," she said. "The Sliders got his wife and she's still back at the airport. He doesn't have anyone. He doesn't even have us anymore."

She turned back to Mackenzie.

"So can he have it?" she said. "My bear?"

Mackenzie was still cautious. "Well..."

"You're going to bury him aren't you?" Rachel said. "Isn't that what you're supposed to do now?"

"Yes, I suppose it is," Mackenzie said.

She offered Bootsy over to Mackenzie for a second time.

"Will you put this in with him?"

Mackenzie glanced at Cody. There was a dazed look on the man's face. It was as if he couldn't believe that Rachel would act so normal, so calmly, after what had just happened. A man had died – a brutal death. A child would be shaking, crying or screaming by now. But Cody knew what Mackenzie didn't. Rachel had seen so much brutality since they'd left Spring Branch together. She was a creature of this ugly new world and the truth was that she'd adapted to it better than a lot of grown ups. It broke Cody's heart to admit it but that's what she was. Maybe Mackenzie had been right about one thing – it *was* the adults who crumbled first.

Cody didn't know if Richards was going to receive a proper burial. For all he knew, the old man was going to be tossed in the nearest dumpster. Still, Mackenzie took the bear off Rachel. He looked at it for a long time. Finally he handed it to one of the bodyguards standing behind him. The woman took it, a look of disgust on her face like she'd been handed a warm bag of dog shit.

Richards' body was removed from the room.

"A noble death," Mackenzie said, watching the body being taken away. "He died to save a life. There was more to that old man than I thought."

Rachel walked back over to Cody and they stood beside the table. Cody looked to his right and saw the last glimpse of Richards' legs sliding along the corridor.

"We'll bury the body," Mackenzie said, edging towards the door where the bodyguards stood waiting. "You have my word on that Rachel. And now I hope you all understand the situation you find yourselves in. Stay quiet, stay put and this doesn't have to be painful. If you try anything, we'll play another game. There are two guards posted outside this room. Knock on the door if you need anything. Food, more water, to use the bathroom – anything. You're free to eat, drink and get some rest. But remember – there's no way out of this building."

Mackenzie turned around and walked into the corridor. The two bodyguards followed and the door was locked.

Cody sure as hell didn't have any words after everything that had just happened. Nobody else did too.

Crazy Diamond walked over to the mound of sleeping bags piled up in the corner. She pulled a faded blue bag out the pile, spread it out on the carpet and lay down. She turned her back to the others.

"You okay?" Cody said. It was a stupid question but he felt the need to ask.

"Tired," she whispered.

"Sure," Cody said. He looked at Rachel.

"Why don't we try to grab some sleep?" he said. "I think we need it."

"Okay," Rachel said.

Cody walked over, grabbed a couple of bags and pillows from the pile, and spread them out on the floor. They climbed into their bags and lay down on their backs, staring at the ceiling. Rachel's soft breathing was a comforting sound.

Across the room, Nick sat at the table. His fingers tapped off the wooden surface, like he was typing on an invisible keyboard.

Rachel fell asleep quickly. Cody turned onto his side and wrapped an arm around her tiny waist. She was warm and fragile.

His eyelids grew heavy.

The last thing Cody saw before falling asleep was Richards' head snapping back. He saw it over and over in his mind. And it was always followed by a glimpse of Mackenzie's black eyes looking across the room at Cody. Mackenzie would speak:

"And there are other gifts too," he would say. "They're capable of great generosity to those who serve them."

Cody woke up later, feeling surprisingly fresh. If he'd dreamed, he couldn't remember. He was unsure of how long he'd been asleep – it could have been ten minutes or ten hours for all he knew.

He sat up in the sleeping bag. His body cracked and popped, like a bowl of cereal.

Nick was still sitting at the table, staring out the window.

When he heard Cody sitting up, Nick jolted forwards. It was as if he'd forgotten there was anyone else in the room with him.

"Thought you were asleep," Nick said.

"I was," Cody said. "How long was I out for?"

"Couple of hours maybe," Nick said.

Cody looked down at Rachel. She was moving, groaning softly as her mind crawled back to the world. No point in talking to her now – Rachel was a slow starter, like her mother had been.

Crazy Diamond still had her back to the room. Cody couldn't tell if she was sleeping or not.

"Did you sleep?" Cody asked, turning back to Nick. He kept his voice down.

Nick shrugged. "Dozed a little," he said. "Dreamed a lot. I was back on that damn plane, taking off and landing all over again. Hey, what was the name of that guy in the Greek myth? The one who had to roll the giant boulder up a hill, only for it to roll back down again every time he reached the top."

Cody shook his head. "I don't know."

"Sisyphus."

It was Crazy Diamond who spoke. She turned over in her sleeping bag and faced them. Her brown eyes glistened under the pale light.

"It was King Sisyphus," she said.

"That's the one," Nick said. "Well I was King Sisyphus, sitting in the cockpit of my plane. I took her up every time – a perfect takeoff. San Antonio was on fire down below. I got those people away just like I said I would. Then I see a pair of silver eyes up ahead, like two moons in the sky. They're blinding me so I can't see a damn thing. I close my eyes. When I open them again we're sitting in the airport about to take off. It's like Groundhog Day man."

"Except we didn't take off," Cody said. "Not according to that sadistic prick."

"Damnedest thing." Nick said.

Crazy Diamond sat up. She ran her fingers through her jet-black hair, pushing it over her forehead. With the back of her hand, she wiped away the damp tearstains that lingered around her eyes.

"Maybe your dream's telling you something Nick," she said.

"Oh yeah?" Nick said. "Like what?"

"That you're trapped," Crazy Diamond said. "That there's no way out of here."

"Screw that," Nick said. "We've got no choice but to try. You heard what's going to happen to Rachel. As for the rest of us, we're expendable. That means we're dead sooner or later anyway. Richards was just the first."

Nick shook his head.

"What the hell happened to Mackenzie?" he said. "Did you see his eyes? Did you see how far he kicked Richards across the room? That shit ain't real."

"He said something about gifts," Cody said. "Remember? He sold his soul to the devil. Or something worse."

Crazy Diamond got up and walked over to the table. She picked up one of the jugs and lined up four glasses to fill with water. She stopped pouring before she'd filled the first glass. She put the jug down. Cody saw her staring into empty space. Was she thinking about Richards?

"I've got an idea," Crazy Diamond said.

She turned towards the others.

"I think there's a way out of here," she said. "It's a long shot but it's worth a try."

"I'm all ears," Nick said, sitting up straight. Despite a lack of sleep, Nick Norton looked fresh.

"Careful," Cody said. His eyes roamed across the ceiling. He checked for signs of anything unusual poking out of the walls. "What if this place is bugged?"

Nick shook his head. "Negative," he said. "While you guys were sleeping I was combing every inch of this room. Top to bottom, side to side – it's clean. They don't have the technology to install fancy equipment like that anymore. I'm surprised they've even got electricity running in this place."

"Alright," Cody said. "But what about those things – the Exterminators or whatever they're called. What if they can hear us? What if they're...what's the word? Omnipotent – what if they're omnipotent?"

Nick shrugged. "Fuck the Exterminators. The girl's got a plan."

Cody gave Nick a sarcastic thumbs up. "Okay," he said. "Glad we had that discussion big guy."

He looked over at Crazy Diamond.

"So what's the plan?" he said.

Crazy Diamond pointed to the large jug with the purple juice. It was still mostly untouched.

"This," she said.

"The juice?" Nick said.

"Yeah," she said.

"What the hell are we supposed to do with that?" Nick said, looking disappointed. "Throw it at the guards? I don't think there's any hydrochloric acid in it."

"Not quite what I had in mind," Crazy Diamond said.

"Then I don't follow," Nick said.

"First things first," Crazy Diamond said. "Did Mackenzie see any of us drink that stuff?" Her eyes darted back and forth between Cody and Nick. "Think fast guys."

"We didn't drink it," Cody said. "Nobody did, apart from Mackenzie."

Crazy Diamond's eyes lit up. "That's what I thought," she said. "Now tell me this boys. What's of value in here? Right here, in this room."

Nick and Cody looked around the office. Their eyes probed the furniture – the tables, the chairs, and then around the edges of the room, looking for anything remotely expensive looking."

"Nothing," Nick said. "The tables are cheap, the chairs are plastic and..."

Crazy Diamond turned sideways and pointed to Rachel, who was still buried deep inside her sleeping bag.

"Guess again."

"Rachel?" Nick said.

"What's the one thing *they* care about?" Crazy Diamond said. "Why are we here? It's Rachel."

"Where are you going with this Crazy Diamond?" Cody said.

Crazy Diamond held up a finger, as if to say *wait a minute*. She picked up a glass of water off the table and took it over to Rachel.

Rachel took the glass and sipped at the water. "Are you talking about me?"

"We sure are gorgeous girl," Crazy Diamond said with a grin. "Think we might have a way out of here and guess what? You're going to be our secret weapon."

Rachel smiled, enthused at the idea.

Cody wasn't happy that Crazy Diamond had brushed off his question. He had a right to know what the hell was going on – especially if Rachel was involved.

"What's going on?" he said.

Crazy Diamond took a deep breath and nodded.

"Okay," she said. "What if right now I'd just handed Rachel a glass of that juice instead of water? Mackenzie didn't tell us what was in that stuff, right? It looks gross, it smells gross and I'm sure it tastes worse. What if Rachel was allergic to something in there?"

Cody and Nick exchanged confused glances.

"What if she got sick?" Crazy Diamond said. "How much would that scare the shit out of Mackenzie?"

Crazy Diamond sat down cross-legged in front of Rachel. "What do you think sweetheart? Think you could pretend to be sick? Fool those people out there into believing it was real? That's all you'd have to do."

Rachel smiled shyly. "Dad was an actor," she said. "So was my Mom. But I've never done it before."

Cody looked at her and frowned. "Oh really?" he said. "What

about all those mornings when you didn't want to go to school? Remember? You tried to play sick even though I knew there was nothing wrong with you. Can't kid a kidder honey."

Rachel giggled.

"You think you could do it?" Crazy Diamond asked.

Cody held both hands up in the air. "I don't know about this Crazy Diamond," he said. "She's just a kid."

Rachel threw a furious look in Cody's direction.

"Hey!" Cody said. "I'm looking out for you. It's my job."

"I'm not just a kid," Rachel said. "How can you say that?"

"I didn't mean it like that honey," Cody said. "It's dangerous, that's all."

Crazy Diamond nodded. "Your dad's right Rachel," she said. "It is dangerous. But it's also our only chance of getting out of here."

She looked at Cody.

"Mackenzie's terrified of the Exterminators," Crazy Diamond said. "He wants to put us off the idea of escape so much that he killed one of us, hoping it would scare us into submission."

Cody let out a long breath he didn't even know he'd been holding onto.

"I don't know," he said.

"Lots of people tried to escape here CD," Nick said. "I don't think anyone ever did."

"You heard Mackenzie," Crazy Diamond said. "The Resistance were predictable – they tried all the usual methods – charging at the guards, trying to get out through the window. But we have something they didn't have – we've got Rachel. She's the grand prize. Right? If Rachel gets sick he's going to have to take her out of here and get some treatment. They must have some sort of medical room in a building this big with all these people. Rachel gets out of here. And she insists that you go with her Cody."

Cody's eyebrows stood up. "Great," he said. "You know Mackenzie won't allow it."

"Rachel needs her Dad," Crazy Diamond said. "Rachel insists. You go out, you've got a chance to make something happen. You've got time to think. Get a gun – seems like you know how to handle one of those. Then come back and bust us out. We grab Rachel and run for our lives. Look I know it's a lot to ask Cody but it's all I've got. It's either that or we just sit here and wait for them to take Rachel."

Nick nodded in agreement. "What do you think Cody?"

Cody looked at Rachel and sighed. He dropped into a sitting position beside her sleeping bag.

"Looks like this is your big break kid," he said. "Showbusiness. It's in your blood. Think you can do it?"

Rachel looked excited at the prospect, like it was game and nothing more.

"Yeah," she said.

"Don't overact like your old man used to," Nick said, winking at Rachel.

Cody looked at Nick and raised an eyebrow. "Remind me of something Norton. How many times did you get nominated for an Oscar?"

Nick shook his head. "It always comes back to that doesn't it? A friggin' statue. Who gives a shit about the Oscars anymore?"

"Yeah," Cody said. "That's what I'd expect somebody who was never nominated to say."

"Didn't win though did you?" Nick said.

"Boys," Crazy Diamond said. "Are we ready? Looks like we're all about to do some acting today."

Cody looked at Rachel. "You sure *you're* ready?"

"Stop fussing Dad," Rachel said. "We need to get out of here."

"Now remember," Crazy Diamond said to Rachel. "You've got to scream for your Dad when they take you out. He has to go with you. You do what you have to do – you raise hell and tell them how much you need him. Got it?"

"Got it," Rachel said.

"Atta girl."

Crazy Diamond got up and walked over to the table. She took an empty glass and filled it to the brim with the reddish-purple juice. Then she brought the jug over to Rachel, glancing at Nick on the way.

"This smells worse than your feet Nick."

"Very funny," Nick said.

Crazy Diamond dipped her index finger into the slushy liquid. Dropping onto her knees, she wiped some of the juice around both sides of Rachel's mouth and then on her chin.

"Make up done," she said. "Looking good."

Crazy Diamond backed up a little and dropped the glass on the floor. It fell onto its side, the pulpy juice leaking out slowly onto the carpet.

"Now we're ready," she said. "Everyone good to go?"

"Let's do it," Cody said.

Rachel looked a little more apprehensive this time. "Yeah."

Cody nodded. "3-2-1, action!'

Rachel dropped down onto the floor, clutching her stomach in agony.

"Scream," Crazy Diamond said. "Make some noise Rachel."

The little girl screamed. It sounded like her toes were being dipped into a vat of burning acid. Her hands clutched at her stomach, as if she was pushing back some monstrous growth that was swelling up inside her body.

"She's good," Nick said, looking at Cody. He was nodding along in appreciation. "She's really good."

Cody nodded, slightly in a daze.

"They'll be coming in," he said to Nick. "I'll take the lead."

"Gotcha."

Cody ran over to the door and pounded his fists against the slim glass panels. Through the glass, he could see a couple of dark-suited guards sitting down in chairs playing cards. They looked up and ran down the corridor. Panic spread across their faces.

They unlocked the door and rushed inside.

"What the hell's going on?" the taller of the two guards said.

"What the fuck took you so long?" Cody yelled. His face was contorted with rage. "Didn't you hear her screaming?"

The tall guard looked stunned. Clearly he hadn't been expecting that sort of response from the prisoner. Without saying anything, he looked past Cody towards Rachel who was writhing around inside her sleeping bag, next to the toppled glass and the juice stain on the carpet.

Crazy Diamond and Nick were kneeling at Rachel's side. Both had a look of anxious concern on their faces.

"What happened to her?" the guard asked.

"You're trying to poison us?" Cody said. "Aren't you? You're trying to poison my daughter with that juice."

The guard turned a sickly pale color. "Oh shit," he said. He looked at the other guard standing beside him. "Go get him," he said. "Quick!"

The second guard nodded. He turned and ran out the room.

The remaining guard nudged Cody back to the other side of the office, using the pistol in his hand as a prod.

"Get over there," the guard said. "And get those hands up."

Cody walked backwards, his hands in the air.

Mackenzie came storming into the room about two minutes later. The second guard trailed behind him.

When Mackenzie saw Rachel on the floor, his eyes nearly popped out of their sockets.

"What is this?" he said. "Is this a trick? After what happened earlier, you're trying to trick me?"

Cody knew he was going to have to put in the performance of

his life to make this work. He charged forward and swung a fist at Mackenzie's chin. Mackenzie ducked his head and dodged the blow.

"You're trying to kill my daughter!" Cody hissed. "After what you said? You're the one that's trying to trick us you bastard! Telling us how important she is and then trying to poison her."

Mackenzie's eyes were bleak and stunned. "What are you talking about?" he said. "I need her alive you idiot."

Crazy Diamond was by now cradling Rachel, rocking her gently in her arms and whispering comforting words in her ear.

"She took one sip of that purple poison," Cody said. "One goddamn sip and now look at her."

Cody was secretly pleased at how horrified Mackenzie looked.

Mackenzie gritted his teeth.

"There's a doctor in the building," he said. "We'll take her downstairs and have a look at her. Guard, pick her up."

The tall guard rushed over to Rachel and scooped her up in his arms, pulling her away from Crazy Diamond. He hurried back across the room towards the door where Mackenzie was waiting.

Rachel pounded her fists off the guard's barrel-like chest.

"Dad! I want my Dad! I want my Dad!"

"Let me go with her," Cody said. His voice cracked. It sounded like he was on the brink of tears. And if Cody MacLeod needed to cry on cue, he could do it. "She needs me," he said. "She doesn't know anyone down there."

Mackenzie shook his head. "No chance. Nobody else leaves the room."

"What the hell am I going to do man?" Cody said. A tear spilled down his cheek. "Don't you want her to recover?" he said. "How's she going to do that in a roomful of strangers, all of them standing around her with guns? She'll be scared out of her mind. Watch me, don't let me out of your sight – but let me go."

The guard lingered at the door with Rachel howling for her dad in his arms. He was waiting for Mackenzie to make the call.

"Dad!" Rachel screamed.

"Please," Cody said, not taking his eyes off Mackenzie for a second. "She needs me."

Mackenzie glared at Cody.

"You're a clever man," he said. "You're trying to fool me, aren't you?"

"No," Cody said. He was acting as intensely as he'd ever done before. "I'm just a father who's petrified. I'm angry too – I'm very angry Mackenzie. Your lifesaving drink has poisoned my little girl. I don't want her to die in this prison and if you're being straight with me about how important she is then neither do you."

Mackenzie signaled to the man standing at the door. "Go," he said. "Get her downstairs."

He turned back to Cody.

"Just you," he said, pointing a finger at Cody's chest.

Cody nodded. "Alright."

"Let's go," Mackenzie said. "You'll be watched every second you're outside this room. If I find out this is a trick..."

"It's not a trick," Cody said. "We're wasting time talking about it."

He followed Mackenzie to the door.

CHAPTER TWELVE

Mackenzie and Cody followed the guard and Rachel downstairs. They walked along a labyrinth of cold corridors until they approached a door near the front entrance of the Public Safety Headquarters building.

"The doctor will be here in a minute," Mackenzie said to Cody.

The guard walked ahead of the others, pushing the door open with his back and entering the room. Cody watched through the open doorway as the man placed Rachel onto a single bed.

The medical room was a small, plain-looking space. White walls surrounded the single bed, which was tucked into the side of the room. There was some equipment sitting on a countertop – a stethoscope, a variety of medications – but it was hardly a high-tech affair. Most of the higher end medical equipment in San Antonio had probably been lost amidst the chaos of the last days.

About a minute later, a dumpy little man and a woman with tied back reddish-orange hair came hurrying down the corridor. They were both approximately in their fifties. Cody looked at the doctor, who wasn't dressed to impress. The flustered-looking man was wearing an open dressing gown and Cody could see his crumpled, striped blue pajamas underneath. The woman, who Cody assumed was the nurse, was wearing a dark suit and tie, not unlike what the rest of Mackenzie's posse wore.

The chubby doctor glanced at Cody through narrow slit-like eyes.

"This is our doctor," Mackenzie said.

Cody extended a hand towards the man.

Mackenzie coughed. "No that's the nurse," he said to Cody. Mackenzie then gestured towards the woman. "Helen, she's our resident doctor."

Cody cursed himself silently. Had Kate, his ex-wife heard that, she would have clipped him over the head.

"Sorry," he said looking at the doctor. "I..."

The doctor looked at Cody like he was a clump of dog dirt stuck to her heel. When she turned to Mackenzie however, her blue eyes lit up. They walked over to the medical room together and the nurse followed like a worn-out lackey.

Cody walked at the back of the procession.

"I think it's best if you wait outside," the doctor said, turning back to Cody.

"That's my daughter in there," Cody said.

"I understand that," the doctor said. "But it's a small room and we don't have a lot of space. We'll have a better chance of finding out what's wrong with your daughter if you're not in our way. Thank you."

She smiled but her eyes were like daggers.

"There are seats in the corridor," the doctor said. "I'll update you as soon as I have more information."

Cody's jaw dropped "Now wait a goddamn minute..."

Mackenzie pointed at two plastic chairs tucked up against the corridor wall.

"You're lucky to be here," he said. "Sit your ass down or go back upstairs."

Cody backed off. He looked towards where Rachel was lying on the bed. She'd toned down the noise a little but her hands were still tightly clasped over her stomach. The occasional groan floated out into the corridor.

"I'll be right outside," Cody called out. "Hang in there honey. These people are going to help you."

Mackenzie and the medical staff walked into the room. Brief words were exchanged between Mackenzie and the barrel-chested guard who'd brought Rachel downstairs. The guard listened to every word, nodding intently. A moment later, he stepped back out into the corridor and closed the door behind him. Cody saw the black pistol tucked into the man's waist.

"Take a seat," the guard said.

Cody sat down. It was cold in the corridor and he rubbed his hands together. The guard took up position beside the door, his back pressed up against the wall.

There were noises spilling out of the medical room – muffled voices, the dull clunking of equipment being moved. Cody heard Rachel groaning and didn't know if it was real or fake anymore. He couldn't stand the thought of her being alone in that room with those people.

Especially Mackenzie.

Cody leaned his head against the cold wall. His nerves were jangling and he couldn't help but think that it showed on his face. Did he look like a man with something to hide? What was he supposed to do now? According to Crazy Diamond, he was supposed to take it to the next level. Get a gun, she'd said. He racked his brains, trying to think of a way to lure the guard in, maybe try and coax him away from the medical room. It was a big ask.

Mackenzie opened the door and stepped back out into the corridor.

Cody leapt to his feet.

"Well?" he said. "How is she?"

"Sit down," Mackenzie said, pointing at Cody's seat. "They're still checking her over. She's complaining about a dull pain in her stomach. Might be there's something going on. Mild food poisoning perhaps."

Cody wiped a layer of sweat off his brow. "She's not dying?"

Mackenzie looked at Cody like he was crazy. "I doubt it."

"Thank God for that," Cody said, sitting back down.

Mackenzie gestured to the guard standing by the door. "You can go," he said. "I'll wait here for a while."

"You sure?" the guard said, looking surprised.

"I'm sure," Mackenzie said. "Go back upstairs. Finish the rest of your shift."

"Yes boss."

The guard hurried down the corridor, like he couldn't get away fast enough.

Cody was left alone with Mackenzie in the corridor.

Mackenzie walked over and sat down in the vacant seat beside Cody. He let his head fall back against the wall and yawned. There was only a few inches gap in between the two chairs. Cody squirmed in silence.

They didn't talk for a couple of minutes. Mackenzie appeared content to keep it like that but Cody wasn't sure he could suffer such an unnerving silence for too long. He sat up in his seat, his body stiff like a wooden board.

He had to say something. Anything.

"Where'd you get the recipe for that juice?"

Mackenzie's eyes were fixed upon the corridor wall directly opposite.

"It was inspired," he said. "A gift. They know more about nutrition than we do. About what our plants can provide us with."

"What's in it then?" Cody said. "Why did Rachel react so bad to it?"

Mackenzie looked uninterested at the prospect of going into details.

"There are lots of things in it," he said. "Nothing dangerous to the average human. Does she have allergies?"

Cody shook his head. "No," he said. "Not that I know of. How many kids have you given that stuff to?"

"Just Rachel."

"If anything happens to her..." Cody said.

"Then we're both dead," Mackenzie said. His chiseled jaw tilted outwards as he leaned his head back against the wall. Cody imagined that the man came from good breeding stock with his rugged good looks and refined manner. Good family, good school, and a good job. Who was he? Was Mackenzie still recognizable as the man he'd been before the Black Storm?

"You said you had a daughter," Cody said. "Is that true?"

Mackenzie smiled through pursed lips.

"Once it was true," he said.

"What happened?" Cody said.

"The Black Storm," Mackenzie said.

"That's what I don't understand," Cody said. "Now you're helping them."

"You're right Cody," Mackenzie said. "You don't understand. It's as pointless to fight them as it is to try and stop the tide coming in. Our time is up in this world. It's a hard concept to grasp I know. But individual lives are no longer relevant – that means my loved ones, your loved ones and everyone else's. Don't waste your time clinging onto a history that no one will remember. The universe has moved on and we - the human race aren't invited."

"We still matter," Cody said.

"If you keep thinking like that," Mackenzie said, "you'll have more pain to endure."

Cody sat up straight. His back muscles were stiff thanks to the cheap seats.

"So what happens to you?" Cody said. "When it's over. When the last man or woman is gone. When they have Rachel and everything else they want. You've served them well. What happens to you after that?"

"I'll be betrayed and killed," Mackenzie said. "Or perhaps they'll keep their promise and take me out of here with Rachel. That's as close to eternal life as I can hope for."

The door to the medical room swung open. The doctor walked out and approached Mackenzie with a toothy smile.

She didn't even look at Cody.

"She's still in pain," the doctor said. "But it's not quite as severe as it was. I'd like to keep her overnight for observation if I may. Usually I'd discharge, send her back upstairs to rest but considering who it is..."

"You're the doctor," Mackenzie said, getting slowly back to his feet.

"Can I see her?" Cody said, standing up.

The doctor shook her head. "Not yet."

"Why not?" Cody said.

But the doctor had already turned her attention back to Mackenzie. She reminded Cody of an overexcited schoolgirl, fawning over the local heartthrob who'd just pulled up outside the gate on a motorcycle. "You look tired," she said. Her arm twitched, like she was desperate to reach out and touch Mackenzie. "When did you last sleep?"

Mackenzie scratched at a dark shadow of stubble under his chin.

"It's been a while."

Now there was a stern look in the doctor's eye, like she'd

reverted to playing a mom role. "Doctor's orders," she said. "Get someone else to keep watch over him and you go get some shut-eye upstairs. You're no use to anyone if you're not firing on all cylinders. Okay?"

She winked at him.

"Okay," Mackenzie said. "Thanks Helen."

"No problem," she said. "I'll go grab a guard from upstairs. Back in a minute."

The doctor walked down the corridor, her heels clicking off the floor tiles.

"I think she likes you," Cody said.

Mackenzie dusted down his suit jacket with his hands. "You should go back up..."

"I'm staying here," Cody said. "I told Rachel I'd be here."

Mackenzie looked too tired to argue. Cody was counting on it.

"Suit yourself," Mackenzie said.

It wasn't long before the doctor came back down the corridor with a guard in tow. The guard was a young man in his late twenties. He was clean-shaven with a slim build, and dressed in a tight fitting black suit. There was a faintly exotic look about him, a hint of East Asian origins with his light brown skin and monolid eyes.

The guard looked eager to please. He walked up to Mackenzie with a spring in his step like he was going to ask for the man's autograph.

"Want me to put him in cuffs boss?" the guard said, looking over at Cody. The guard reached a hand inside his suit, as if to pull out the restraints.

Cody watched. At that moment, the seed of an idea sprouted in his mind.

Mackenzie looked at the guard and shook his head.

"No cuffs unless he misbehaves," he said. "Just stay on him like a rash. If he goes for a piss then you hold his dick. Stay close, understand?"

"Sure thing boss," the guard said.

Mackenzie turned around and trudged back down the corridor. The doctor watched him go, her ravenous eyes lingering on the man's firm butt.

When he was gone, she went back into the medical room and shut the door.

The young guard settled into his shift. He leaned his back up against the wall and let out a bored yawn. Cody sat down on the plastic seat again, watching the man out of the corner of his eye. He noticed the black pistol grip poking out of the guard's waist. Cody had a feeling the man was packing a Glock 19, similar to his own.

It was a waiting game now. He'd make his move when it felt right.

Cody was thankful that he'd gotten some sleep upstairs. His mind was alert. It had to be – they were relying on him.

There was little chance of Cody striking up a rapport with the guard. What must the young man have been thinking? Here he was, watching over a stranger in the corridors of a random office building in the ruins of San Antonio. It sure as hell wasn't what he'd dreamed of doing with his life. How many people had this young man lost? What had Mackenzie promised him in return for his service?

"I need to go," Cody said.

The young man looked over at Cody. He lazily scratched his chin with the tips of his knuckles, as if out of boredom more than need.

"Go?" he said.

"Take a leak."

The guard's eyes rolled over. "Can't it wait?"

"No," Cody said. "I'm happy to go by myself. Or I can piss right here all over the floor. But I don't think your boss would like either one of those options."

"Fine," the guard said. He drew the pistol out of his waist. Sure enough, it was a Glock. Cody peered at the weapon but he couldn't tell if it was the same one that had been taken from him earlier.

"C'mon let's go," the guard said. "On your feet."

Cody walked down the corridor with the guard at his back. The guard called out instructions, directing Cody to the nearest bathroom, a mere thirty seconds hike from the medical room.

They walked inside and Cody ventured over to the urinal trough. He reached for the zipper on his pants. The guard followed him up to the trough, stopping just a few inches behind Cody's back.

"Are you serious?" Cody said, glancing over his shoulder. "You're actually going to hold my dick?"

"Not quite," the guard said. "Don't get excited."

"Give me a break," Cody said, turning around and unzipping his pants. "I understand there's not a lot of women around San Antonio these days but still..."

"Shut up and piss," the guard snapped.

But Cody struggled to get the waterworks flowing. He wasn't used to someone standing so close behind him while he emptied his bladder. His mind raced back and forth. The guard would get suspicious if Cody didn't start peeing right away. Would that put him on red alert?

Cody needed the guard to stay bored. He needed him off guard.

With a grimace, Cody closed his eyes and envisioned waterfalls and heavy rainstorms. After a few seconds, he got going although it sounded more like a leaky tap than Niagara Falls going into the trough.

When he was done, Cody zipped up his pants. He walked over to the sink and the large mirror that stretched across the bathroom wall. Once again, the guard followed close behind. Fortunately the young man's face reflected a mood of profound boredom. He was operating on autopilot, like someone standing in a long queue at the bank.

Cody took a deep breath. His heart was racing. He stole a glimpse at the guard in the mirror as he ran the hot water tap.

The Glock was hanging at the man's side.

"Hurry up," the man said in a flat voice. He moved closer to Cody. He couldn't get any closer now without touching.

Cody cupped his hands and pooled the water. A cloud of hot steam rose out of the sink, floating towards the white ceiling. The water was growing increasingly painful as it gushed onto Cody's skin.

This is crazy.

The water spilled over in Cody's hands. This was it. He had to do it now or his skin would melt. A voice screamed in his head.

Think about Rachel.

Cody spun around fast. He threw a handful of scalding water at the guard's face. The guard was so close that he took a direct hit in the eyes. He yelped and staggered backwards, his arms flailing in the air. It wasn't much – it was a distraction but it would buy Cody a precious few seconds.

It was enough.

Cody threw himself at the man, clamping one hand around his neck. He pushed backward to disorientate the guard further while he couldn't see. With his other hand, Cody twisted the guards' wrist backwards, trying to force him to drop the gun.

The guard shrieked. The gun spilled from his hand and fell to the floor. With a howl of rage, he charged forward and threw a big left hand at Cody's chin. Cody saw it coming and slid underneath the punch. At the same time, he dove in and locked his hands around the guard's right leg, lifting it up and pushing him back to tip him off balance.

Both men fell fast and hard.

The guard took the worst of it. The back of his head cracked off the tiles with a sickening crunch and he went out like a light. His arms went limp.

Cody jumped back to his feet. The man's body had cushioned his fall and he was unharmed.

With his heart pounding, Cody rummaged through the guard's pockets until he found the handcuffs. He put them down on the floor, sliding them next to the Glock.

Cody stopped.

He looked up at the door. What was that? Footsteps in the corridor? For a second, Cody thought he'd heard the light tip-tap of someone walking towards the bathroom. He tried to listen over the sound of his heavy breathing.

Nobody came in. Cody put it down to his overactive imagination and went back to work, removing the man's dark suit jacket and pants from his body. The shirt and tie came off too. Cody dropped the pile of clothes on the floor and then dragged the unconscious guard over to the sink. He cuffed the young man to the drainpipe and thought about gagging him. In the absence of a decent gag, he let it go. With any luck, the guard wouldn't wake up for a while.

Cody undressed and put on the man's clothes. They were a decent fit. Looking in the mirror, he ran a hand through his dirty hair, pushing it off his face. He had to look presentable if he was going back out there. A throbbing pain was growing in the back of his head, perhaps from the fall. There were no cuts on his face or visible signs of damage.

He picked up the Glock. After checking the magazine, Cody tucked it into the waist of his pants. Then he walked over to the bathroom door and pulled it open.

Taking one last deep breath, he walked outside.

His first instinct was to go back for Rachel. Cody wanted to get her out of that medical room as quickly as he could. But he knew it didn't make sense to make that his first stop. That would mean he'd have to drag Rachel back upstairs to bust Nick and Crazy Diamond out of the office. That was putting Rachel at even more risk. It was best to leave her till the end. The medical room was close to the front door. Once they broke Rachel out, they'd be home free.

Cody walked back towards the stairs. The journey up to the sixth floor was long and there were a few wrong turns on the way. As he climbed the stairs, his ears pricked up at the slightest sound.

Fortunately he saw no one.

He wandered onto a familiar looking corridor at last. In the distance, Cody saw two guards sitting in plastic chairs, playing cards. Further down the corridor, he saw the wooden door with the slim glass panel – the office prison.

The guards were new. The man who'd carried Rachel downstairs was gone and so was his companion. These two men were probably just starting their shift.

With any luck they hadn't seen Cody before.

He pulled the pistol out of his waist and kept it tucked behind his back. Then he walked slowly down the corridor towards the two men.

Both guards looked up at the same time.

"Hey guys," Cody said. Nothing to worry about – he was dressed like they were. He was one of them. Still, Cody's voice came out a pitch higher than usual.

"Boss sent me up here to update the prisoners," he said. "That little girl – she's real sick."

Cody stopped a few feet back, keeping out of reach of the light bulb hanging off the ceiling.

One of the men nodded and dropped his cards on the chair. With a sigh, he got to his feet and rummaged around in his pockets, searching for the office key.

The other man didn't get up. Cody could feel the man's eyes burning a hole through him.

"Wait a minute," the guard who was sitting down said. He inched slowly off his seat and was about to stand up. "I know you..."

Cody pulled the Glock out from behind his back.

"Sit your ass down," he said to the guard. "No wait. Drop your weapons on the floor first – both of you, do it now."

The man who'd been searching for the office keys held his hands up. He looked at his companion for guidance. After a moment of hesitation, both guards reached for the pistols in their suit pocket. Slowly, they put the weapons on the floor.

Cody kept the gun on them. He kneeled down and picked up both pistols, slipping them into his jacket pocket, one on either side.

"Now open that door," Cody said, nodding towards the office. "Be quick and stay quiet or you're dead."

The man with the keys walked down the corridor without protest. The other guard lingered, scowling at Cody. Had he been outside the mall earlier? Cody wasn't sure how the guard knew him – he didn't care. It was too late for that.

"Move it," Cody said, pointing the gun at the guard.

The man turned around and followed the other guard to the door.

The first guard unlocked the door and pushed it open. When Cody walked in behind the guards with a pistol on their backs, Nick and Crazy Diamond, who'd been sitting at the main table, leapt to their feet.

"Holy shit!" Nick said, grinning from ear to ear. "Guess who's coming to dinner?"

Crazy Diamond ran over and gave Cody a hug. "You did it," she said. "I knew you would."

"It's not over yet," Cody said. "We've got to get Rachel. Nick – how about you put on one of those suits?"

Nick looked at the guards, both of who were significantly smaller and slighter in build than he was. There was a bemused expression on his face.

"You serious?" Nick said. "It'd be like dressing up in a doll's costume."

"Alright," Cody said. "Screw that. We'll just pretend I'm moving you guys downstairs or something."

Cody pulled out the guns in both pockets. He handed one to Nick, who took it and checked the magazine.

"What about me?" Crazy Diamond said.

"I thought you didn't know how to use a gun," Cody said.

"I don't like guns," Crazy Diamond said. "But that's not going to help us around here, is it?"

Cody handed the spare pistol over. "You sure?" he asked.

"Yeah," Crazy Diamond said, taking the gun. "Needs must. C'mon Cody, let's go get that girl of yours."

Cody nodded and walked over to the door. "You two hide your guns on the way downstairs," he said, looking at Nick and Crazy Diamond. "You're my prisoners remember?"

They locked the guards in the office and crept back downstairs.

Cody kept to the back of the line, whispering directions to the others while pointing a gun at them. When they reached the first floor, they crept down the long empty corridor that led towards the doctor's room.

"Almost home," Cody whispered.

"Thank Christ," Nick said. "I never want to see this place again."

They slowed down as they approached the medical room. Tense glances were exchanged in the corridor. Crazy Diamond and Nick pulled out their guns and braced themselves.

Cody's Glock was pointing at the door. He gave the others a nod, then reached for the metal handle.

The door swung open before Cody could touch it.

The doctor was standing in the doorway. A smug grin was wrapped around her face. It stayed there, even when she noticed the guns in their hands. Rolling her eyes, the doctor pulled the door open further.

Rachel was sitting up in bed. Mackenzie was standing beside her, along with his two bodyguards, plus a third male guard.

All the suits, except Mackenzie, were pointing their guns at Rachel.

"Oh shit," Nick said, lowering his pistol.

Crazy Diamond and Cody did likewise.

Mackenzie walked over to the door. His stride was casual.

"Welcome back," he said, a half-smile on his handsome face. "The good news is that Rachel is feeling much better. She's going to be fine. The bad news however, is that we don't need you three anymore."

Mackenzie snapped out a crisp salute. Then he stepped backwards.

"Nothing personal," he said.

CHAPTER THIRTEEN

"Hand over your weapons," Mackenzie said.

Cody ignored the command. He was looking at Rachel who had three rifles pointing at her head. She was looking back at him. She sat up straight in bed with a sheepish look on her face, like a kid who'd been caught stealing. Cody wasn't stupid – he knew that if they handed their guns over, Mackenzie was going to kill them anyway. Five minutes, ten minutes from now – it didn't matter. They were dead. And with nobody to look out for her, Rachel would suffer an even worse fate.

"Give me the guns," Mackenzie said. "I won't ask again."

There was a quiet voice in the back of Cody's head.

Kill him.

But he couldn't do it. If Cody started a shootout in the corridor, it was almost certain that Rachel would get caught in the crossfire.

He handed the Glock over.

Crazy Diamond and Nick followed Cody's lead.

"You're an asshole," Nick said to Mackenzie as he handed the pistol over. "You ain't nothing without your invisible buddies backing you up. Isn't that right?"

Mackenzie ignored Nick's jibes. He took the guns and looked at Cody.

"The guard will be fine," he said. "He's going to have a bad headache for a while but he'll live. You should have gagged him Cody."

"Thanks for the advice," Cody said.

Mackenzie handed the guns over to the male guard standing behind him. The guard took the three weapons and cleared a patch of space on the countertop, pushing a cluster of white-labeled pill bottles out the way.

Cody saw the flustered-looking nurse back himself into the far corner. He was staring wide-eyed at the three guns on the counter-top. They were only a few feet away from where he was standing. He looked like a pacifist who'd found himself trapped in a nuclear missile launching facility.

"I'm very disappointed at how things have turned out," Mackenzie said. He stepped out into the corridor and his guards followed. The doctor and nurse stayed behind in the medical room with Rachel. "I'd hoped that what happened to your elderly friend upstairs – what was his name again?"

"Richards," Crazy Diamond said.

"Richards," Mackenzie said. "I thought it would be enough to keep you in line. Apparently not. To tell you the truth, the game rarely worked with the Resistance either. I just like playing it."

Nick walked over to Mackenzie. At well over six feet and almost as wide as he was tall, Nick Norton was an imposing phys-ical presence. Mackenzie was quite a big man himself, but he was well outmatched by Nick.

The three guards readied their weapons.

"You're a traitor," Nick said.

Mackenzie stared back at Nick, not blinking.

"You're nothing," Nick said. He spat out the words like they were poison. "Nothing but a filthy, cowardly traitor. You turned your back on your own kind. You're pissing all over your wife and little girl's memory. You're in bed with their killers now. Hell I bet you killed them yourself, right? Is that what your masters told you to do."

Mackenzie's face broke out into a manic grin. He started laughing.

"You're right about one thing Nick," he said. "I am nothing. That's what I've been saying all along – *we* are nothing. Now you're starting to look at things the right way. You're getting close."

He turned around and looked into the medical room.

"Except Rachel," Mackenzie said. "She's something. Of that there can be little doubt."

When Mackenzie turned around, his eyes were black.

Cody's insides clenched in horror.

Nick's eyes grew wide with fear. "Son of a..."

Mackenzie threw a hard right uppercut that landed on Nick's stomach. Nick was lifted off the ground and flung back across the corridor by the force of the blow, crashing into the wall with a crunching thud.

The building shook under Cody's feet. It felt like King Kong was outside, trying to pick it up.

Nick's eyes were stunned. He sat up quickly, fighting for breath.

Mackenzie stormed across the corridor, his black eyes seething with rage. With those charcoal irises, he looked more like a robot than a man.

Cody tried to block Mackenzie's path to Nick by jumping in between the two men.

With a brief swat of the hand, Mackenzie pushed Cody out of the way. Cody toppled over backwards like he'd been tackled by a freight train. The lights went out. When they came back on, he was lying face down on the floor.

"Dad!" Rachel yelled from somewhere. "Are you okay?"

Cody looked up. The corridor was spinning. "Yeah," he said, not sure where to look for her.

Mackenzie's fingers were clamped tightly around Nick's throat. He lifted the pilot off the ground like Nick was no more than a kitten. Nick's legs kicked furiously, hitting nothing but air. His eyes were bulging out of their sockets. Large veins protruded from the side of his head and choking noises spilled out of his mouth.

Crazy Diamond charged at Mackenzie. She jumped on his back, sliding her arm around his neck and trying to pull him backwards. He paid no attention to her until she reached over and tried to claw at his eyes with her fingernails.

Mackenzie jerked backwards and Crazy Diamond crashed to the floor.

Cody struggled back to his feet. Crazy Diamond leapt up to hers like a panther. They ran at Mackenzie together but this time the three bodyguards hurried into the corridor and forced themselves in between Mackenzie and his would be attackers.

Three gleaming rifle barrels stared back at Cody and Crazy Diamond.

"Let him go!" Cody yelled, looking past the bodyguards.

Mackenzie's response was to tighten his grip around Nick's throat. He lifted the pilot further, reaching as high as his arm could stretch. Cody's jaw went slack. The great Nick Norton was being manhandled like a baby.

"Stop it!" Crazy Diamond yelled. She edged forwards but the guards met her halfway, blocking the route forward. "You're killing him."

Mackenzie looked over his shoulder at Cody and Crazy Diamond. His black eyes lingered in their direction. A second later, he released his grip and Nick crashed to the ground in a disheveled heap.

Mackenzie walked back across the corridor. He was breathing heavy. He looked like a man who still had a lot of steam to blow off.

The bodyguards stood aside, making space for their boss.

Cody and Crazy Diamond rushed over to Nick's side. Taking a shoulder each, they pulled him back up into sitting position. Cody was relieved to see that his friend's eyes were clear.

Nick signaled that he was okay.

"I almost had him," he said, his voice mangled and hoarse.

Cody and Crazy Diamond pulled Nick back to his feet. It wasn't easy given the size of the man, but Nick wrapped his arms around their shoulders for balance as he regained his legs.

Mackenzie and the three bodyguards stood on the opposite side of the corridor. Cody looked over that way and saw Rachel sitting up on the bed. She was peering out through the doorway, a shocked look on her face.

The doctor stood over Rachel like a personal guard. Making sure the little girl didn't try to make a run for it.

Mackenzie stepped forward. His head fell back like he'd suddenly lapsed into a standing unconsciousness. His eyes were closed, his face pointing towards the ceiling.

His finger touched his temple.

Cody pressed his back up tight against the wall. He knew what was coming. But despite that his thoughts turned to Rachel. His daughter was only a short distance away and yet there was no way for him to reach her. No way without getting shot. He might as well have been standing in front of a thousand foot wall.

Rachel edged forwards on the bed. The doctor saw it and shot out a firm hand and clutching her by the sweater, pulled Rachel backwards. The young girl threw the woman a furious look.

Cody wanted to call out to his daughter. If this was it, he

wanted to tell her that it was going to be alright. To say all the things he was supposed to say. But as he stood there, watching Mackenzie in a trancelike state, he knew deep down that it wasn't going to be okay. It was anything but and he didn't want his last words to Rachel to be a lie.

"I'm sorry," he said.

Mackenzie's eyes opened and they were green again.

A raucous din lit up the corridor. Cody had heard it before – a bloodcurdling noise that filled his soul with a sickening dread.

It sounded louder than ever before. Maybe because it was coming for him.

The three bodyguards exchanged worried glances.

Crazy Diamond looked back and forth between Nick and Cody. Her eyes were wide with fear. She reached out and pulled both men close. It seemed important to her. This was the only comfort they had left in the world – to know that they wouldn't die alone, without friendship.

The shredding noise got louder. It came from everywhere. It sounded like a giant tidal wave had burst through the walls of the building and was at that moment racing along the narrow corridors of the building.

Getting closer.

Cody put his hands over his ears.

"Rachel!" he yelled. But he couldn't see her now. She was hidden behind Mackenzie and the bodyguards. Cody had never felt more terrified in his life. More than anything, it was the realization that he wouldn't see her again. He couldn't accept it.

The Sliders shot up from the floor. Three of them this time - black demons on an elevator ride straight out of Hell. One for each of the adult prisoners.

They were no more than a few feet away from Cody and the others. The Sliders' blankness, their sheer lifelessness – it was chilling in its lack of detail. Even more so up close. And yet there *was* something in there, something at work inside that marble-like exterior – a program, a purpose, with a target in mind.

Cody's fingers clawed at the wall behind him. It was a deep-rooted survival mechanism at work. He wanted to get away but there was nowhere left to go. It was no use trying to run either. He'd seen how fast those things could move. There was no way any human being on Earth could ever hope to outrun them.

They were dead. And if this was the end, he couldn't make peace with it.

"Rachel," Cody said.

The Sliders bolted forward at a dizzying speed. Cody closed his eyes and tensed up – his muscles were taut like wire, and he braced himself for the end.

He kept his eyes closed, wondering if the Sliders had already infected him. Was he numb? Was this as bad as it got? Maybe he was dead already. Maybe his brain was in the process of shutting down.

Somebody gasped at Cody's side. It was Crazy Diamond.

He wasn't dead.

Cody opened his eyes.

The Sliders were frozen on the spot. They'd halted their vicious attack just inches away from their targets. They were so close that Cody could have stuck out his tongue and touched the one in front of him on its black, gleaming head.

Crazy Diamond and Nick were still in one piece beside him. The look on their faces – eyes bulging and mouths hanging open – said it all.

It had been that close.

Cody tilted his head and looked past the Sliders. On the other side of the corridor, Mackenzie looked every bit as shocked as Cody's companions. Even more so. It was the same with the three bodyguards standing by his side. They looked dumbstruck.

Mackenzie spun around. Frantically, he pushed the guards out the way whose stiff bodies were blocking the door to the medical room.

"Move!" he cried out.

A gap opened up. Cody looked inside the medical room.

He fell to his knees.

"Rachel," he said.

She was standing on the bed. Her eyes were locked onto the three Sliders. Both arms were outstretched, like she was pushing an invisible force away from her. Her face strained with the effort.

The doctor and nurse shrunk back into the medical room. Their feet couldn't carry them away from Rachel fast enough. The nurse dropped onto the floor in a clumsy sitting position, his satin dressing gown sprawled out underneath him like a crumpled cloak. The doctor pressed her back up against the wall, her eyes ablaze with terror.

They all flinched when Rachel jumped off the bed.

Rachel paid no attention to them. She walked through the vacant doorway, her arms still outstretched and reaching for the Sliders. Cody noticed her shoulders were trembling. Her breathing was labored.

"Rachel," Cody said. His voice was flimsy and hoarse – a shadow of its former self. "What...?"

But Rachel didn't look at Cody. Slowly, she lifted her arms over her head and both hands curled into tightly clenched fists. Her eyes closed and her knuckles whitened. She held this pose in place. Then with a fierce grunt, she pulled her arms sharply downwards, tucking her elbows tight into her side.

The Sliders were flung back across the corridor. They crashed into the three unsuspecting bodyguards, their black, misty forms swallowing up their hosts.

Rachel collapsed onto the floor.

Cody ran towards her but the three guards, their bodies now possessed by the Sliders, toppled to the floor and blocked his path.

They were like a moving roadblock – convulsing violently as the Fever took hold of their minds. Their twisted, wriggling bodies formed an impromptu barrier that kept Cody back.

The bodyguards destroyed themselves in a fit of madness. Cody could barely watch as they crawled onto all fours and slammed their heads against the floor, again and again, like they were human-sized electric drills.

Mackenzie backed towards the doorway. He looked at the bodyguards, not a trace of pity in his eyes. Reaching into his suit pocket, he pulled out a set of handcuffs. He kneeled down and locked the cuffs around the unconscious Rachel's wrists. Then he scooped her up off the ground and threw her over his shoulder in a fireman's lift.

He ran down the corridor towards the front door. Rachel's head lolled against his shoulder as he ran.

"No!" Cody yelled.

The bodyguards stopped moving on the blood-splattered floor.

Cody, Crazy Diamond and Nick went to run after Mackenzie. A volley of gunshots rang out in their ears. They ducked down, unsure of what was happening. When they looked to the far end of the corridor, they saw three men in dark suits charging towards them, their arms extended, their pistols locked onto their targets.

On the other end of the corridor, Mackenzie was running towards the door. Rachel was still unconscious in his arms.

Cody was about to take off after him but the gunfire kept coming, forcing them onto the floor.

"In there!" Nick said, pushing both Cody and Crazy Diamond towards the doctor's room. "Move!"

They crawled inside.

The nurse was still cowering at the back of the medical room. Tears were streaming down his red cheeks as Cody, Nick and Crazy Diamond wriggled along the bloody floor.

The doctor charged forward, a look of white-hot anger on her face.

"Get out of here!" she yelled. "You sick bastards."

Crazy Diamond jumped back to her feet. She walked up to the doctor and threw a hard right to the jaw. The doctor's legs gave out and she fell to the floor unconscious.

"Bitch," Crazy Diamond said, shaking out her hand.

Nick grabbed their guns off the countertop and handed them out.

"He's getting away with Rachel," Cody said. "I have to go."

Nick nodded. He edged over to the doorway and peered outside.

"Shit," he said.

"What is it?" Cody asked.

"I think they've holed up in one of those offices down the corridor. Looks like they want to keep us here for a long shootout."

Cody shook his head. "Screw that," he said. "I can't stay here. You know what he's going to do, don't you?"

Nick's face was grim. "Yeah."

Crazy Diamond crept towards the doorway. Her elbows were tucked in tight, as she readied the Glock in her hand.

"What's he going to do?" she asked.

"He's going to hand her over to those things," Cody said.

"Where?" Crazy Diamond said.

Cody shook his head. "I don't know. That's why I have to follow him. But if I stay in here much longer I'm going to lose the bastard."

"We'll stay here and cover you," Nick said. "You make a run for it. But it means you're going to have to face Mackenzie alone."

"I know," Cody said.

"I don't like it man," Nick said. "The odds are bad."

"What choice do we have?" Cody said.

He looked at the three bodyguards on the blood-splattered

floor outside.

"I need a van," Cody said. "Mackenzie's not going wherever he's going on foot. With any luck, one of those guards might have a set of keys in their pocket."

"Alright partner," Nick said. "Let's do this." He gave Cody a tap on the arm and then turned to Crazy Diamond.

"Cover me," he said.

She nodded. "Right."

Crazy Diamond stood at the edge of the doorway and let off a couple of rounds of fire. At the same time, Nick dropped belly first onto the bloody floor. Sliding further out, he reached over and pulled on the legs of the nearest bodyguard. It was one of the women who'd stuck to Mackenzie like glue upstairs. She was barely recognizable as the same person.

"Jesus," Nick said, pulling the mangled body back into the room. "Those Sliders really know how to make a mess."

Cody grimaced as he rifled through the woman's pockets. Everything was hot and sticky and covered in blood. He found a set of keys in the inside pocket but they were smaller keys attached to the chain – interior door keys and padlock-sized keys. Anything but a van key.

"No," he said.

"Crazy Diamond," Nick said. "Round two."

She fired down the corridor but this time the suits came back with shots in return. Nick dove onto the floor, crawling on his hands and knees. He had to go further to reach the next body this time – it was the heavyset male bodyguard.

With bullets zipping back and forth above his head, Nick dragged the man's body back into the doctor's room.

"Oh shit," he said, getting back to his feet and looking at the blood smeared all over his clothes. "I hope I don't have to do that again."

Cody searched through the man's pockets. A panicked voice in his head was screaming at him to hurry up. Every second lost was a potential disaster. He pulled out a small wallet and a loose black and white photograph of a young woman with a kind smile. He threw them to the side. Cody eventually found a set of keys inside the man's suit jacket and his heart leapt for joy when he saw a black flip key attached to the chain.

"Here we go," he said.

Cody jumped back to his feet. "Ready," he said.

Crazy Diamond and Nick both looked at him. There was an anxious expression on both their faces.

"Alright," Nick said. "We'll cover you man. But you're going to have to be fast. Like grease lightning fast."

"I'll be fast," Cody said. "You just keep them off me."

Nick pulled Cody in and gave him a brief hug.

"You bring her back," Nick said. "You hear me?"

Cody nodded. "I hear you man."

Crazy Diamond reached over and grabbed Cody by the shoulders.

"We'll see you again soon," she said. "Both of you."

"Yeah," Cody said. He picked the Glock up off the floor and tucked it into his pants.

"I'm ready."

Nick and Crazy Diamond exchanged a curt nod. Tucking themselves in at the edge of the doorway, they opened fire down the corridor.

Cody didn't hesitate. He ran as fast as he could down the corridor. Raucous gunfire rang out behind him. There was still a chance he could take a bullet in the back. And what of Nick and Crazy Diamond? What would happen to his friends if they couldn't fight off the suits?

He couldn't think about that now.

Rachel. She was all that mattered.

And she needed him.

CHAPTER FOURTEEN

Cody pushed the door open and ran outside.

A gust of foul-smelling wind hit him in the face. He could still hear the high-pitched crack of gunfire at his back, although it was fading out of earshot.

The headlights on one of the black Sprinter vans parked outside the building lit up. The engine growled and the wheels started to roll.

"Son of a bitch," Cody said.

He watched as the van drove off in a southerly direction.

Cody pointed the flip key at the four remaining Sprinter vans. The silver van parked at the back beeped and the lights blinked. Cody raced over to it while keeping his eyes on the bright headlights receding in the distance.

He jumped into the cabin and turned the engine on. After a frantic search for the headlights, he put his foot down on the gas and the van roared down the street.

Cody gripped the steering wheel. The van felt heavy and sluggish. He prayed to God there was nothing wrong with it – that was the last thing he needed, to lose his daughter to something as trite as mechanical failure.

"Okay we're moving," he said, keeping his eyes on the black Sprinter van up ahead. "Now where are you taking her?"

He followed Mackenzie towards the South Pan Am Expressway, heading north. The wreckage of downtown San Antonio passed by in a blur. There was debris lying on the roads and sidewalks. Some of it was human. That would account for the rotten smell blowing in the wind.

They traveled north on the McAllister Freeway. The black van took a right towards Brackenridge Park, about three hundred and fifty acres of public space that included the San Antonio Zoo, the Japanese Tea Gardens, and other local attractions.

Cody followed Mackenzie as they drove along North Saint Mary's Street – one of several roads that cut through a large section of the park. Mackenzie must have known he was being followed – he was an asshole for sure, but he wasn't stupid or blind. Judging by the leisurely driving speed he'd maintained, the man had shown little concern that someone was on his tail.

Cody leaned forward in the driver's seat. There was something up ahead – a strange reddish glow that lingered low in the sky like a solitary cloud.

"What the hell is that?" Cody said.

Deep down, he already knew.

Mackenzie rolled the black van to a stop at the edge of the road.

Cody took his foot off the gas, crawling forward at a snail's pace until the silver van stopped a short distance away from Mackenzie's stationary vehicle. He looked up at the small cluster of light forming above a section of the park.

It was getting brighter.

He pulled the key out of the ignition. In the silence, he felt small. Cody missed the presence of Nick and Crazy Diamond beside him.

The driver's door of the black van fell open. Mackenzie stepped out onto the road and looked towards the red cloud in the near distance. He then walked over to the back of the Sprinter, throwing a disapproving shake of the head in Cody's direction.

Mackenzie opened up the back of the van, went inside and came out with an unconscious Rachel in his arms. She was still handcuffed. He then cut across the road and walked onto a stretch of withered grass. Cody had kept an eye on the signs as they'd entered the park and if he was right, Mackenzie was taking Rachel towards the Tony 'Skipper' Martinez Softball Field.

Cody stepped out of the van and looked at the red cloud up ahead. Sure enough, it was descending over the softball field.

"Oh man," he said, closing the van door.

His muscles were taut and tense as he followed Mackenzie and Rachel. He pulled out the Glock 19 and it nearly slipped through his sweaty fingers. With a grimace, he secured his hand on the rubber grip.

The softball field was just a short walk from the road. Apart from the ball of light gathering overhead, it looked like any other softball field. The diamond infield consisted of patchy lumps of reddish-brown dirt while the grass on the outfield had worn down to a shadow of its former glory, although some wild flowers had shot through in its place.

Cody approached the open gate.

The gate was open. Mackenzie was standing inside the field, still cradling Rachel in his arms. There was a look of rapture on his face as he watched the mist forming above his head. It was swelling up in size. There were other colors now, intermingling with the initial red – blues and greens, the colors blending together in a dazzling collage that was in stark contrast to the black sky that surrounded it.

Mackenzie placed Rachel on the dry grass, her face pointing to the sky. He dropped to his knees and looked up at the cloud in anticipation.

Then he saw Cody standing at the gate.

"It was a good try," Mackenzie said. "But it's inevitable Cody. Give up – we all have to let go at some point."

Cody's gaze skipped back to the colors. It reminded him of photographs he'd seen of the Aurora Borealis – the dancing lights caused by collisions between electrically charged particles from the sun. Only this was a much smaller and more concentrated version.

"I want my daughter back," Cody said. He walked into the softball field and pointed the Glock at Mackenzie. "She doesn't belong to you. Or to them."

His trigger finger flinched as a sudden noise seeped out of the colored lights. It was like a chorus of dissonant cellos playing in the sky. And over the wailing cellos came something else –a low-pitched frequency sound, like a massive pod of whales all talking to each other at once.

Mackenzie dropped onto his knees. He looked up at the singing colors with a crazed look on his face. The colored mist descended, spreading itself out until it encircled both Mackenzie and Rachel.

Mackenzie reached for the light. He was like a greedy kid grasping at a bowl of candy but the light evaded his grasp.

"Yes!" he yelled. Mackenzie held his arms up in a victory pose and looked up at the sky. "I'm here."

The mist wrapped itself around them further. It was like a giant python, slowly seizing a hold of its prey.

"Rachel!" Cody yelled. "Rachel, can you hear me?"

She didn't move.

Cody dropped onto one knee, aiming the Glock at Mackenzie's forehead. There was no way he could miss from here.

"Give me back my daughter," he called out.

No answer.

Cody squeezed the trigger and fired. The bullet should have ripped through Mackenzie's head but instead there was a loud ping as it bounced off the mist.

"Oh fuck," Cody said. "That's not fair."

He shot again. No luck – the mist was shielding Mackenzie. Whatever it was, it was bulletproof.

Cody had never felt so helpless in all his life.

Now things were getting worse.

Rachel was fading away before his eyes. So was Mackenzie. They were both being absorbed by the colors that skipped and danced around them – every speck of which burned brighter than anything Cody had ever seen or dreamed of. Brighter than anything his imagination could conjure up. Whatever this light was, Rachel and Mackenzie were becoming at one with it.

They were being taken away.

Somebody was stealing his daughter.

Cody's heart was racing. He had to do something – anything to try and stop it happening. The trouble was he'd run out of ideas.

All except one.

Cody charged at the colored mist with a wild shout of rage. It didn't matter if it sounded more like a scream of terror in his ears. He was a berserker with a gun in his hands. He was going to get his daughter back or die trying.

Mackenzie saw him coming. He sprang out of the mist and intercepted Cody before he could get too close to the light. Both men fell backwards, away from the colors wrapped around Rachel.

Mackenzie leapt to his feet first. He reached over, wrapped a hand around Cody's throat and lifted him up off the ground.

Cody felt like a Tyrannosaurus Rex had its teeth locked around his neck. The lights were going out in his mind – black walls closed in from all sides. The pain receded into a blissful, numbing sensation. *Don't give up.* He choked and fought for breath. His legs kicked at Mackenzie, hitting nothing but air.

Mackenzie looked at him. His eyes were two dead, black orbs. Empty things.

He threw Cody across the softball field. Cody hurtled through the air and crashed into the chain link fence.

With a groan, he fell onto the diamond.

His fingers clawed at the dirt. He fought his way back to his feet but his head was still spinning. Something was wrong. The gun was missing – he'd lost it during his mid-air flight across the softball field. There was no time to look for it.

"I'm coming Rachel," he said.

Cody ran across the field towards the light. It was a blind charge, all heart. His body ached but his determination carried him forward.

Mackenzie blocked his way. Cody looked past the silver suit, past the black eyes, towards his daughter.

The light was dancing across Rachel's body; it was a multicolored display of electric sparks that skipped over her legs, chest, head and hair. She was covered from head to toe. The low-frequency noise had dulled. There was now a spitting noise coming from the light, like the pop and crackle of a wood fire.

The cloud was trying to lift Rachel up off the grass.

"No!" Cody said.

He raced towards his daughter. Mackenzie held his hands out like a soccer goalkeeper, grabbing Cody and throwing him backwards. Cody fell hard and his innards jolted.

"Stop fighting it Cody," Mackenzie said. "Remember what Harry said. Some fights you just can't win."

Cody looked up.

The light had elevated Rachel several feet off the ground. She was fading further into the misty depths that would swallow her whole. She would be gone soon – in a matter of seconds.

Cody leapt to his feet.

Mackenzie punched Cody in the stomach, forcing him to double over. Cody's hands clutched at the crippling sensation around his solar plexus. It felt like an elephant had kicked him.

Cody staggered and fell to the ground. He tried to get back up but his legs wouldn't obey the commands of his brain.

A steel-like hand shot out and seized his neck.

Mackenzie dragged Cody up to his feet with brutal force. Cody choked as his lungs fought desperately for air. He tried to swing several punches at Mackenzie's face. His blows were nothing – he might as well have been trying to swat a dragon with a rolled up newspaper.

"It'll be over soon," Mackenzie said. "Stop fighting me."

Cody felt the lights going out for a second time. There was no pain. If not for Rachel, he might have welcomed the end.

"No," he said.

And then he saw something – a flicker of movement over Mackenzie's shoulders.

Rachel was back on her feet. The colored lights still danced around her body like she was a living, breathing Christmas decoration. Red lights, blue lights, green lights. There was a sense of desperation about their attack now. They bounced off Rachel's skin like tiny mosquitoes. The light would scatter. Then they'd come back and try again.

She wasn't fading away anymore. Her body was back in Brackenridge Park.

Cody smiled, despite the fact he couldn't breathe. Mackenzie tilted his head in confusion. He looked over his shoulder and dropped Cody to the ground. Cody fell onto the grass in a crumpled heap; he was on the brink of unconsciousness but somehow he found the energy to get back to his feet.

"What's going on?" Mackenzie yelled. He was screaming at

the mist like it had wronged him. Like it was an unfaithful lover. "I brought her to you. Take her!"

The lights above the softball field had dulled. Those electric sparks were like the petals of a dying flower, still beautiful but not for much longer. An agonized groan bled out of the retreating mist – it sounded like a wounded animal, howling in pain.

"Take her!" Mackenzie yelled.

Rachel looked up at the mist. It was floating away, like a balloon rising towards the night sky.

When she turned back to Mackenzie, her eyes were as black as coal.

"Rachel!" Cody cried out. His voice was thin and raspy. He could barely hear it himself.

Mackenzie shook his head in disbelief. "What's happening?"

Rachel's arms were still bound by the handcuffs. She looked at the restraints and her lips moved, whispering something that no one else could hear. The cuffs clicked open and fell to the ground.

Mackenzie reached for the retreating lights above their heads. His hands clawed at the sky.

"Don't close the gate," he said. "You promised to take me with you."

The light continued to fade. The colored cloud over the softball field had become a pale shadow of itself. Soon there was only darkness.

"No!" Mackenzie cried out. "Come back."

Cody dropped onto the grass. His head was spinning and he expected to pass out at any moment.

Mackenzie looked over at Rachel. His eyes had reverted back to green. His body was as taut as tripwire. He turned around and with a frantic grunt, tried to reach for Cody's Glock, which was lying on the grass nearby.

The weapon flew out of range before he could touch it. It was as if somebody had pulled it away with hidden wires.

Mackenzie spun around to look at Rachel.

"What's going on?" he said. "What happened to you?"

Rachel's face was like a block of white stone. Slowly, she tilted her head back and looked towards the sky.

She pointed a finger at Mackenzie.

"I said what's going on?" Mackenzie shouted. His voice was screechy with fear. "I can help you Rachel. You've taken something from them, I can see that. Power. It feels like too much doesn't it? Well I can help you understand. I can help you control it. Nobody else can help you – only me."

There was a whooshing noise.

Cody looked up. He saw something in the sky – a sea of movement. An army of black shapes swooped down towards the softball field, their wings flapping in unison. The whooshing got louder – it sounded like a monster was galloping across the park towards them.

"Oh God," Cody said.

The crows dive-bombed Mackenzie. They were like hundreds of jet-black missiles aimed at his face. They flew low, thrashing around him, their glistening beaks pecking at Mackenzie's handsome features like a thousand woodpeckers drilling on a tree. They stabbed at his eyes, nose, mouth and pulled furiously on his ears with their beaks, twisting the flesh back and tearing it off at the edges.

Mackenzie screamed. He tried to cover his face with his hands but it was no use. The birds tore at the flesh on his fingers, some of them trying to peel the fingernails off with one sharp pull of their mouths.

Mackenzie's mangled hands muffled his cries for help. He tried to run from the softball field but fell several times. The birds weren't in the least shy of getting closer to the ground either – they went low, resuming their vicious attack on the fallen man. Not giving him a second to breathe.

Rachel continued to point at Mackenzie.

Cody crawled backwards, moving away from the carnage. But the birds weren't interested in him. Those who weren't pecking on Mackenzie were waiting on the sidelines, their wings flapping furiously as they searched for an opening.

Mackenzie climbed back to his feet after yet another fall. He spun around several times, running one way and then another, searching for a way out. The crows had shielded his escape route. In the end, Mackenzie charged in a straight line and vaulted the nearest fence. After that, he ran for his life with whatever strength he had left in his legs.

Cody watched him go. In a matter of seconds the darkness had swallowed both Mackenzie and the birds.

The screams lingered before silence filled the park.

"Rachel," Cody said. He climbed back up to his feet, ignoring the jolt of pain that shot up and down his body. He wobbled on unsteady legs. His arm reached out for something that wasn't there.

"Dad!"

Rachel ran over and grabbed a hold of him. She took his arm and Cody waited for the dizziness to pass.

He looked at Rachel and cupped her face in his hands. Her eyes were blue, thank God.

"What happened?" he said. His voice was still hoarse.

"They tried to take me with them," she said.

"I know," Cody said. "But Rachel, your eyes, that light on your body...what's going on?"

Rachel tapped a finger off her head. "It's like he said - I took something from them," she said.

"What do you mean?"

She shook her head. "They tried to steal me away. But I ended up stealing something from them. That's how I knew how to call the birds for help."

Rachel's expression darkened. "There's something else."

"What?" Cody said.

"I heard them talking," she said. "When they were leaving."

Cody cleared his throat. "You did?" he said.

"They're angry," Rachel said. "Angry with me because I wouldn't go with them. Because they couldn't make me go with them."

"Angry?"

Rachel nodded. "They can't beat us," she said. "They can't win. At least not from where they are."

Cody shook his head. "What does that mean?"

Rachel hesitated. "They're coming here," she said.

"The Exterminators?" Cody said. "Coming here?"

Rachel looked up at the ocean of darkness above their heads. Her eyes drifted off into the depths.

"Let's get out of here," Cody said. "Nick and Crazy Diamond are still back there. They might need us."

"Dad," Rachel said, putting a hand on Cody's arm to steady him.

"What is it honey?"

"I can fight them," she said. "When they come."

Cody looked at her. "Fight them?" he said. "Rachel, you're just a kid for God's sake. I don't care what powers you think you stole off them. I don't care if you're Supergirl. Now let's go."

"We have to fight them," Rachel said. "They're coming."

"Let's go Rachel."

They walked back to the van in silence.

Cody opened the driver's door and climbed behind the wheel.

There were two steering wheels in front of him.

"Damn it," he said. "I think my vision is a little wonky."

He concentrated and tried to slide the key into the ignition. After a short struggle, he couldn't find the slot. He tried again with no luck and punched the steering wheel in frustration.

"This isn't good," he said.

"What's wrong?" Rachel said.

Cody sat back in his seat. Both steering wheels looked back at him – challenging him to try again.

Everything else was a blur.

"Rachel," he said. "We might have to wait a while before we go anywhere. Think I took a bump to the head back there."

"Alright," she said. "But..."

He looked at her. Her face was a blur like everything else. "But what?"

"I think I can drive the van."

Cody managed to laugh, somehow. "You don't know how to drive."

"I sorta do," she said.

Through his skewed vision, Cody saw Rachel screwing up her face in concentration. A long silence lingered in the cabin. Cody was about to break the silence when he heard the choking sound of the Sprinter's engine.

It was trying to spurt into life.

Cody looked at his hand. The key was still there, locked in between his forefinger and thumb.

"Wait a minute," he said. "How...?"

The engine coughed and spluttered but it wouldn't start. Rachel's eyes were still closed as she tried to tempt the van into starting. Cody wasn't sure if he was seeing things, but he caught a brief glimpse of what looked like colored sparks dancing at the tips of his daughter's fingers.

After about a minute, Rachel fell back into her seat. She looked at her dad and smiled, like she'd almost mastered a new trick. She was breathing heavy.

"You gotta start somewhere," she said, sounding more West Texan than he'd ever heard her before. "But it's going to take a while."

"This isn't happening," Cody said. "Whatever it is, it's not happening."

"It is," Rachel said.

Cody's head fell back onto the seat. It felt good to stop for a moment. He closed his eyes and everything was peaceful.

"Let's just sit here for a while," he said. "I'll drive us back when my eyes are good. Then we'll go help Nick and Crazy Diamond. Okay?"

"Okay," Rachel said.

Father and daughter sat in silence together.

Above Brackenridge Park, a gentle rain began to fall. It made a soft pitter-patter noise as it landed on the roof of the van. The black sky grumbled from afar; it sounded like a dark premonition of bad weather.

In the distance, Cody heard the flapping of bird wings.

BLACK EARTH (#3)

'Out of the night that covers me,
Black as the pit from pole to pole,
I thank whatever gods may be
For my unconquerable soul.'

Extract from 'Invictus'
By William Ernest Henley

CHAPTER ONE

"Go ahead," Cody said. "Make a wish."

Rachel leaned over the tin of peaches on the wooden table. The lid of the tin had been peeled back slightly in an inviting gesture. A solitary green candle was poking out at the top, having been wedged in between the lid and the small opening. A dull orange flame flickered on the candle's head.

As Rachel blew out the flame, a clumsy rendition of Happy Birthday rang out across the room.

Cody watched with a pained smile as the small audience sang to his daughter. It had been almost six months since the incident at Brackenridge Park with the Exterminators. So much had happened since then. The most important thing was that Rachel was getting to grips with her newfound talents – and she was doing so at a remarkable speed.

It had all started with her attempts at lifting various pieces of furniture – in fact the first thing she'd tried to do was lift this same rectangular coffee table that was taking the weight of her birthday tin.

Cody smiled at the memory.

He recalled how Rachel had sat cross-legged for hours in front of the table during those early days of training, like a miniature blonde Buddha, shutting everyone and everything else out. Eyes closed, face screwed up in concentration. It hadn't come easy to her. The table had shook and swayed, as if some hidden puppeteer on the ceiling was jerking it back and forth on invisible strings. That's how it went for a while. It was several days before the breakthrough came and when it did it didn't last long. The table had levitated an inch or two off the ground, shaking violently as if an evil spirit was trapped inside, trying to fight its way out of the reddish brown, rustic wood.

Then it had crashed back to the ground.

Rachel had come a long way since then. And now she was eleven years old. In fact she'd been eleven for a while but nobody knew the exact date anymore so it was hard to gauge how late they were in throwing her a birthday party.

"Happy Birthday Rachel!" Crazy Diamond said. The young woman took her gloved hands off her ears now that the celebratory singing had stopped. She turned to the giant figure of Nick Norton sitting on the floor beside her.

Crazy Diamond scanned an imaginary piece of paper in her hands. "It says here on the program that you're up for entertainment duties Nick," she said. "What have you got in store for us big guy?"

Nick's body was wrapped up in a dark green winter coat. He threw down the massive hood, revealing the small afro that he'd been growing over the past few months. He scratched at his salt and pepper beard, throwing a bemused look at Crazy Diamond.

"Do I look like Coco the Clown to you?" Nick said. "My freezing cold ass is staying right here."

Rachel walked over to Nick and Crazy Diamond. She was carrying the tin of birthday peaches in her hand.

"You want to see me lift something?" Rachel said, looking at Crazy Diamond.

Crazy Diamond's eyes lit up with excitement. "Yeah," she said. "Can you lift Nick?"

Rachel looked at Nick.

"Easy," she said.

"Cool," Crazy Diamond said, rubbing her cold hands together. "He won't mind. He's a pilot and they love to fly. Ain't that right Nick?"

Nick looked up at Rachel who was standing over him. There was a look of pure mischief in her eyes.

"I've always been nice to you Rachel," he said, pointing a finger at the girl. "Now you remember that. Remember who it was that suggested we throw a birthday party for you. Me, that's who."

"Because you were bored," Crazy Diamond said.

Nick kept his eyes on Rachel.

"That's not true."

Cody reached over and locked an arm around Rachel's waist, pulling her back towards him.

"Alright smart ass," Cody said. "We get the picture – you're a genius. Now eat the rest of your birthday cake and stop showing off."

Rachel wriggled free of Cody's grip. She turned around and looked him dead in the eye.

"I could lift you instead," she said. "You'd be easier than lifting Nick."

Cody laughed. He was surprised at how nervous it sounded.

"Do it and see what happens," he said. "But alright if you really have to lift someone, go ahead and lift Nick."

"Thanks buddy," Nick said.

Cody reached out and pulled the zipper up on Rachel's silver North Face jacket so that it touched her chin. "Don't forget to keep this up," he said. "You're the last person around here we need catching a cold and then pneumonia."

Cody took the tin of peaches out of Rachel's hand and pulled the lid fully open. He reached a hand into his daughter's coat pocket and pulled out the small silver spoon that she always carried around with her for mealtimes.

"For you," he said, handing her the spoon. "Now eat up."

Rachel took the spoon and held the can aloft. "Does anyone want some?"

Everyone shook their heads.

"It's all yours," said a gruff man's voice on the other side of the room.

Three people sat bunched close together, a little further apart from Cody, Nick, Crazy Diamond and Rachel. They were dressed in thick winter clothing – parka jackets, zipped up to the chin, gloves covering their hands and beanie hats on their heads.

Marvin Hearns – known as Marv – was the leader of the trio. Marv was a grizzled war veteran – a taciturn, leather-skinned man of sixty-two who'd seen combat in Iraq and several other far-flung places that most people had only ever heard about in the news. Marv's face looked like it had lived a thousand lives – his pale blue eyes were full of untold stories, and the deep crags and grooves in his skin, along with several impressive scars, hinted of a life of hardship.

Rita and Lance were sitting beside Marv. They were both about thirty years old. Rita was a slim, black woman with a pretty face and dark, intuitive brown eyes that didn't miss much. Lance was tall and pale, with round boyish eyes that betrayed a sharp war veteran's mind. He'd fought with Marv in the armed forces and also in San Antonio after the Black Storm. A soft tangle of brown fluff hung from his youthful face, barely passing for a beard.

Marv, Rita and Lance were former Resistance soldiers. After the Black Storm hit hard, Marv and the others had fought alongside Harry and the San Antonio Resistance – right up until Harry had sold out and made a deal with the suits who were trying to get their hands on Rachel. Even though the suits had kidnapped Harry's wife, Marv had been disgusted with their decision to work with the enemy. He'd walked away at that point. Rita and Lance, like the loyal soldiers they were, went with him.

Rita smiled at Rachel. She pointed to the 'birthday cake'.

"That's all yours darling," Rita said. "That right there is a Happy Birthday present from the San Antonio Resistance." She looked at Lance and smiled. "The real Resistance that it is."

Lance laughed and threw his hood up over his head. A Browning automatic rifle lay on the floor at his side.

"Yeah," he said.

Nick looked over in that direction and shook his head.

"C'mon you guys," he said. "You know I don't like that name. We're not the San Antonio Resistance. Those assholes have been and gone. They're history. We gotta come up with something else – the New Resistance or Resistance 2.0 or Human Lives Matter or something like that. Anything but the SAR. Because unlike those cowardly bastards who sold us out, we're actually trying to resist something."

"Go easy Nick," Marv said. His breath was a fine mist that dispersed slowly across the room. "Not everyone in the Resistance sold you out. I don't remember anyone here trying to screw you guys over. Just the opposite in fact. Who was it that turned up to help you guys when you and Crazy Diamond were locked in that building, shooting it out with the suits?"

Nick held up a hand. "Alright," he said. "I wasn't talking about you guys. I'm talking about Harry and his band of treacherous assholes. Damn near got us killed."

"One of us did get killed," Crazy Diamond said. She looked at Nick with a blank expression. "Remember?"

Nick nodded.

There was a brief silence in the room. It was broken only by sound of Rachel's spoon clinking off the tin as she wolfed down the peaches.

Cody looked at Rachel's birthday treat. A tin of fruit with a candle stuck on top. But tins were nothing new in their lives. The 'New Resistance' had been living off them for a while and thank God for them or they'd probably have starved to death by now. Fortunately for Cody, Rachel, Nick and Crazy Diamond, Marv and the others had taken them to the old Resistance hideouts and bunkers scattered across San Antonio. There were plenty of supplies out there – food, clothing, flashlights and everything else they'd need to stay alive.

"We tried to find you a Coke or something," Cody said, looking at Rachel. "But there's nothing out there anymore. Sorry honey."

Rachel shoveled another spoonful of peaches into her mouth.

"I stopped craving Coke," she said, talking with her mouth full. "Can't even remember what it tastes like."

Nick nodded. "Tastes like pi..."

Crazy Diamond clipped him on the back of the head.

"Language," she said.

The room went back to silence.

Cody leaned his head against the wall. He looked around the room they'd called home for the past five months or so. The survivors had taken up residence in the eight-story Rand Building on East Houston Street, located on the western edge of downtown San Antonio. They were on the seventh floor of the red-brick building, which was a familiar sight around the city and had been since its first appearance in the early twentieth century.

Cody and the others had cleared out most of the furniture they'd found in the Rand and taken it downstairs, piling it up in the lobby. As the months passed, they'd worked through it slowly, building the occasional fire outside when the cold became intolerable.

Cody could barely remember what it was like to be warm. Like memories of blue skies and bright sunny mornings, the sensation of warmth was fading to the back of his mind. It had been hard on everyone at first, the gradual decline in temperature. They'd gotten used to it, but that didn't make it any easier.

A few items of furniture remained in the room – quirky desks, red sofas and fancy office seats – a testament to whatever hipster business venture had once thrived there. Now it was no more than a gathering space for possibly the last human inhabitants in San Antonio.

"Think I'll go out for a smoke," Marv said, getting up to his feet. "Any of you part-timers want to join me?"

"Yeah," Cody said. "I could do with the air."

"I'm in," Rita said.

"Screw it," Nick said, groaning as he climbed to his feet. "I'm coming too."

Part-timers – as Marv had called them, were people like Cody who didn't smoke but had become regular companions of Marv on his frequent smoking breaks. Even though they didn't smoke, the part-timer would always end up smoking anyway. In truth, there was little else to break up the long spells of boredom were such a huge feature of their lives. Cody hadn't smoked for years, not since the days of his Hollywood bad boy image when he'd appeared on countless magazine covers with a cigarette dangling from his lip. Even then he hadn't liked it much. The taste of a cigarette hadn't changed in all those years. He still didn't like it but he had to admit, smoking had a weird way of making him feel a little warmer. Maybe it was nothing more than a distraction from the cold.

Cody zipped up his black parka to the neck. Then he pulled a pair of gloves out of his coat pocket and slipped them over his hands.

They walked downstairs in silence.

Marv pointed a flashlight ahead and a tunnel of pale white light shone upon the remnants of things that no longer served much of a purpose. The first floor of the building had once contained a retail space with the second to eighth floors being used for office and commercial purposes. On the first floor they passed an abandoned bar and several coffee shops and breakfast joints. Cody always imagined the same thing when he walked past those places – all the workers filing in and out on weekday mornings – the smell of freshly brewed coffee in the air. And after work? Straight to the bar for a cold beer. Shoot the breeze and catch the eye of that cute girl in the office. Maybe even pluck up the courage to ask her out on a date.

They stepped outside into the cold darkness.

Cody looked up and saw the three gates in the sky. It was always a sobering reminder – the first thing anyone saw when they stepped outside.

The gates had appeared in the sky several months ago, not long after the incident at Brackenridge Park. They were the first signs of light that had appeared in the San Antonio skies for a long time, but they were far from reassuring. They were three giant suns hanging in a neat row on the black sky, their centers like an iris, bursting with a variety of brightly colored light. They were similar to the gate that had opened above the softball field in Brackenridge Park when the Exterminators had tried and failed to kidnap Rachel.

Except these were much bigger.

The weather had taken a turn for the worse not long after the gates had first arrived on the scene. The Black Storm has grown more intense. The sky was even darker than before, something that would have seemed impossible at one point. Darker and colder.

Heavy, icy winds blew across the land, coming from all directions. The wind tore at the survivors' skin like a slashing knife.

The black snow had followed soon afterwards. Since then it had fallen almost every day, mostly coming down in a light sprinkling but sometimes it was heavy too. The temperature in the city hadn't reached freezing yet but the snow continued to fall like it was below zero. It felt more like a warning of things to come than a reflection of the wintery temperatures. The city streets were covered in a thick black carpet, a perfect companion to the ebony sheet that had swallowed the sky.

They kept close to the door, trying to shield their bodies from the cold wind. Marv took off his gloves and pulled out a pack of Camel cigarettes. He offered the pack to Cody, Nick and Rita, who each took one. Reaching into the pocket of his thick coat, Marv pulled out a box of matches, lit one up and passed it down the line. There was a chorus of exhaling noises, sending a cloud of smoke over their heads.

Marv put his gloves back on, keeping the cigarette locked in between his lips.

"You know what this feels like to me?" Nick said, stamping on the black snow under his boots. "Know what it looks like? Like the Earth is changing. Know what I mean? Like it's becoming something else."

There was a look of concern in Rita's eyes.

"What are you talking about?" she said.

"I mean look at this shit," Nick said. "Black snow for God's sake. A black sky. The temperature is going to drop to freezing sooner or later and it's going to stay that way, right?"

"I guess," Cody said. His freezing lips squeezed down on the cigarette filter and he inhaled.

Nick pointed up at the three gates.

"Damnedest thing," he said. "Want to know what I think? I think this is what *their* world looks like."

"That's not as crazy as it sounds," Marv said.

"That's right Marv," Nick said. "What do we know after all? Might be they're coming here for good. Making themselves feel at home before they even get here."

Cody raised an eyebrow. "You've been thinking about this big guy?"

Nick shrugged. "What else is there to do?"

"It's not over Nick," Rita said. "You sound like you're giving up or something. This is our home. Not theirs."

Nick looked at her. For a moment, his bearded face was scrunched up in confusion. Then he nodded slowly.

"Right," he said. "Our home."

"Anyway we've got Rachel," Rita said. "And we've all seen what she can do."

"Poor Rachel," Nick said, shaking his head.

"I don't like it any more than you do Nick," Cody said. "But I saw her that day in the park. When she fought them off, it was incredible. We've got a chance."

Rita shivered and then pulled the collar of her coat closer together. Her teeth chattered, making a clicking noise.

"That must have been something," she said.

Cody nodded. "It was," he said. "And what's even better is that *she* took something from *them* that day. All that power. They were trying to steal her away and she beat them at their own game. That's my girl."

"She beat them from afar," Nick said. "But now they're coming here. They're doing that because they must know it's going to make a difference. Now I wouldn't say it in front of Rachel but I gotta tell you – that's been giving me a lot of sleepless nights."

"Yeah," Marv said. "Me too."

Rita took the cigarette out of her mouth. She looked at it with the expression of someone who loathed everything about smoking.

"Damn," she said. "Are we fooling ourselves into thinking we've got a chance?"

"I hope not," Cody said. "For Rachel's sake."

Rita let the cigarette drop out of her fingers. She stamped it out and rubbed her gloved hands together.

"I suppose we'd better get some sleep," she said, looking at Cody. "We're up bright and early as usual. Gotta take the kid to school. I sure hope she isn't going to have a birthday hangover after all those peaches."

There was a sad smile on Cody's face.

"She never was much of a morning person," he said.

He looked up at the three gates.

"You know," he said. "When all this started, I was supposed to be the one protecting her."

Marv dropped his cigarette onto the black snow and there was a faint sizzling noise at his feet.

"Hey Cody," he said. "I never asked you this but did Rachel ever, I mean was she special before this? Was she gifted in any way?"

Cody had spent nights lying awake thinking about that. Searching for something – anything that might have been a hint that Rachel was different or special in any way.

"I don't know," Cody said. "As far as I'm aware, there was nothing until the Black Widow."

"Right," Marv said. "Well she's a helluva brave kid."

"She is that," Cody said.

"What do you say we get back indoors?" Marv said, looking at the other three faces hidden underneath their hoods. "It's a little less cold in there than it is out here. And I'm pretty sure I can hear my sleeping bag calling."

CHAPTER TWO

Rita was waiting for Cody and Rachel in the morning. She was standing at the door on the first floor, pointing her flashlight in their direction as they walked towards her with a sluggish stride.

Cody's flashlight met Rita's halfway and the two light streams formed a cross shape.

"First up again?" he said.

"What can I say?" Rita said. "I'm an early riser."

Rita's energy levels in the morning never failed to amaze Cody. She looked fresh and raring to go, like she'd had a full eight hours sleep in a king sized bed. Her brown skin was glowing as if she'd been scrubbing it clean with a bristle brush. A green parka jacket was zipped up to her neck and with matching khaki pants, as well as her beloved Savage rifle slung over her shoulder, Rita looked like a G.I. Jane doll.

"Morning Rachel," Rita said.

Rachel trudged along at Cody's side in silence. Cody had a hand placed on her back, trying to encourage her legs to move faster.

She grunted in response to Rita's greeting.

"You think it's actually morning?" Rita said. She put a hand on Rachel's hair and gave it a playful shake – that was their regular morning greeting and it required little effort on Rachel's part.

Cody opened the door and peered onto the street. A gust of cold wind swarmed around his face. Apart from the distant glow of the three gates, it was pitch black out there.

"God knows," Cody said. "It could be midnight for all we know."

Rita laughed. "Let's get this kid to school."

Cody put Rachel's hood over her head and directed her towards the front door. She staggered forward.

"Gloves on," Cody said.

Rachel pulled the gloves out of her pocket. She slipped them over her fingers in slow motion like she was trying to solve a puzzle.

Cody and Rita put their hoods up and with Rachel tucked in between them, they walked through the door.

"My God," Rita said, pausing to take in the weather. "I swear man, it's getting colder every single day. Anyone else notice that?"

Cody nodded.

"The first steps are the hardest," he said. "Don't think about your sleeping bag. Don't think about being warm up there on the seventh floor with everyone else. Just remember that life sucks and here we are."

"Comforting words," Rita said. "You know Marv was awake when I got up. He wanted to come, said I should take the morning off. Wish I'd taken him up on it now."

"He's right," Cody said, looking at her. "You deserve a break for God's sake. It shouldn't always have to be you that comes with us."

Rita shook her head. "Nah it's alright," she said. "I kind of like tagging along with you guys. It's something do at least."

She glanced at Cody and smiled. He caught her eye, felt a jolt
of embarrassment and looked away quickly.

"Hey Rachel," Rita said, giving the little girl a gentle nudge
with her arm. "That was some party last night, huh?"

Rachel groaned.

"You alright?" Rita asked. "Feeling it today?"

Rachel shook her head. "I'm just tired."

Rita laughed. "I hear ya."

A light drizzle of black snow fell as they walked. There was a
pleasant crunching noise underfoot, as if they were walking on
regular freshly fallen snow. Cody closed his eyes for a second and
allowed his mind to wander. He envisioned the short winter days
of old – the holidays, snowball fights and the gleaming frost that
lingered on the windows of the buildings...

He opened his eyes and shook his head.

Those memories were a waste of energy.

It was a short walk to the Robert E. Lee apartment building on
West Travis Street. It was an unspectacular looking ten-story block
with easy access to the roof and which offered a solid view of the
three gates up above. There was a massive neon sign fixed to the
top of the building – *Hotel Robt. E. Lee*, a reminder of the building's early days as a hotel, not to mention of San Antonio's historical links to the Civil War. The sign's gaudy colored light had long
since extinguished. Underneath the main sign was a smaller one. It
simply read, *Air Conditioned*.

Cody, Rachel and Rita walked into the dark building with
their flashlights leading the way. They climbed the staircase to the
roof like they'd done many times before. Cody figured he could
probably get up there without a flashlight, not that he wanted to
try it anytime soon.

This was usually the point where the cobwebs in Rachel's
mind were swept away. Perhaps it was the reality of getting closer

to the three gates that did it. Cody wondered if she felt like a soldier, approaching the field of battle.

Whatever it was, a switch was turned on.

They stepped onto the roof and walked to the far edge of the building. The three gates towered above them – distant sun-like orbs that were always getting closer, bringing not heat but the promise of a bitter, unbearable cold.

Rachel's expression was calm as she looked up at the gates. Cody didn't know if that was because she was still half-asleep or if she'd become hardened to the task at hand. Maybe she was just good at hiding it. If so, then she'd truly surpassed Cody's abilities to put the terror aside.

"They're getting bigger," Rita said. "Closer."

She glanced at Cody. There was a look of defeat in her eyes. "Don't you think?"

Cody didn't disagree but he wasn't going to say it in front of Rachel. So he shrugged his shoulders and looked away.

They turned towards the city – to the buildings that populated the downtown San Antonio region. Most were hidden, lurking in the long shadow of the Black Storm. While the three gates were radiant and drowning in a wealth of light and color, the poverty of the dark Earth below stood in stark contrast.

"We ain't the alpha species anymore," Rita said. "Guess we never were, huh?"

Rita aimed her rifle at the gates. She made an explosive sound with her mouth, imitating the crack of gunfire.

"If only," Cody said.

Rita lowered her rifle and sighed. "If only."

She kept her eye on the gates and took a step back from the edge. At the same time, she shook her head.

"Have we lost our minds?" Rita said. "What are we thinking? How the hell is a ten-year-old kid supposed to stop this?"

Rachel turned around and peeled the hood back from her head. Black snowflakes landed softly on her long blonde hair.

"I'm eleven," she said.

"Sorry," Rita said. "That makes all the difference."

"I can do it," Rachel said, turning back to the gates. "I did it before, right Dad?"

Cody grimaced at the memory of Brackenridge Park. The cuts and bruises he'd suffered that day had long since healed but the terror he'd felt at the thought of losing Rachel to the Exterminators still stung.

"Yeah," he said. "You did."

Rita held a hand up in the air like she was calling a sudden timeout. There was an apologetic look on her face. Or maybe it was embarrassment.

"Damn I'm sorry you guys," she said. "Don't listen to me. I don't know why I'm being such a wuss this morning. It's just that sometimes when we come up here it's like I'm reliving my holy shit moment. Like I'm seeing those gates for the first time. Other days, I don't bat an eyelid."

"I know," Cody said. "It's alright."

Rachel had her back turned to the adults. She was standing at the edge of the building, something that always gave Cody the chills considering how slippery it was on the roof. But that's where she needed to be, so she'd said – as near to the gates as physically possible.

She took off her gloves.

Meanwhile Rita patrolled the edges of the rooftop. The Savage rifle was locked onto the streets below, primed to respond to the first sign of movement.

Rachel held both arms out at the sides, so that she was forming the position of a cross. Above her, the three gates towered in the black sky, their insides like giant eyeballs swirling with vibrant colors. With her arms raised like that, it looked like Rachel was challenging the Exterminators to come and get her.

There was a sudden sound – the sharp crackling hiss of electricity. Cody watched as the first spark of colored light appeared on the tip of Rachel's fingers, just like magic. The colors were vivid – red, green and blue – but so much more. Cody could see these same colors inside the three gates. The light skipped and danced down Rachel's hand, working its way along her forearms, spreading out from head to toe like it was drawing an outline of her body.

Cody felt a combination of awe and wanting to throw up. She was his little girl for Christ's sake.

The light formed a shield around Rachel.

She pointed towards the abandoned buildings, stretching over the horizon like relics of another era.

A few moments passed.

Something blinked in the distance.

Tiny pockets of yellow and white light appeared in several of the far-off buildings. Distant light bulbs flickered on and off in various rhythms, like a tangle of Morse code signals coming back across the city. Cody had seen Rachel do this many times before but it still wowed him every time.

He couldn't help but smile.

Cody watched as the tallest, most distinguished buildings were at his daughter's command. He could see the Weston Centre, one of San Antonio's tallest skyscrapers, blinking on and off like a faulty toy.

"I wish I could do that," Rita said. "I remember when you could only do one building at a time Rachel."

Cody nodded. "You've done well kid."

Rachel turned around.

Her eyes were as black as the sky.

Cody shivered, but not from the cold.

"Dad," she said. "I asked you not to call me kid anymore."

Rachel's eyes, combined with the city still blinking behind her, made Cody feel like he was looking at a creepy work of three-dimensional art. His little girl looked like a demon child who'd stepped out of the shadows, her ghoulish features caught in a split second of fleeting light.

"Uh sorry," Cody said. "I forgot. Old habits die hard and all that."

Rachel turned back to the front. The lights blinked faster now, more urgently. Watching Rachel whip the city into a frenzy was like watching a highly skilled conductor leading the orchestra towards a thrilling and heart-stopping climax.

"Looks like you're about ready to take off your training wheels," Cody said. He glanced up at the gates. "Just in time too."

"I sure hope it's going to be enough," Rita said.

Cody looked over at her.

"She's getting there," Cody said. "Whatever this thing is – whatever the power is, it's in Rachel's mind. She has to exercise it just like any other muscle."

Doubt lingered in Rita's eyes.

"Not feeling too good about things today are we?" Cody asked.

Rita looked up at the gates. She peered through narrow eyes, as if the sight was too much for her.

"Can't we just close them now?" she asked. "Might save a whole lot of trouble down the line don't you think? When the Exterminators get here they'll find that Rachel has already slammed the door shut in their faces. Who knows? Maybe they lose heart, turn off the Black Storm and bingo – it's over. Party time on Earth all over again. What do you think?"

"I don't think it works like that," Cody said.

"Me neither," Rita said, resuming her rooftop patrol. "Tell me something Cody. Why does everything in life have to be done the hard way?"

"Beats me," Cody said.

Rachel was still standing at the edge of the rooftop. She lowered her arms back to her sides slowly and the dazzling shield began to fade out. There was a brief electric hiss that dulled to a whisper.

The flickering lights across the city went out.

Rachel spun around quickly. She was looking at Cody with a mischievous smile on her face.

Her eyes were still black.

The shield reappeared in a flash, wrapping itself around her body. Rachel clenched a fist and pulled her arm back like she was tugging on a stiff lever.

There was a crashing noise. It came from the street below.

Cody drew his pistol from the holster at his hip. He ran over to the edge of the building and Rita was right behind him, her finger locked onto the trigger of the Savage rifle. They looked down onto the road, scanning left and right. At first they saw nothing, but when Cody looked further to the right he saw an abandoned car had flipped onto its back in the middle of the road. The car was swaying back and forth like it had crashed just seconds ago.

Rachel stood at the edge of the roof, watching her handiwork. She giggled into the back of her hand.

The shield was gone again. Her eyes had reverted back to their normal blue.

"Don't show off," Cody said. He could hear the irritation in his voice. "You're not here to play around."

"I'm practicing," Rachel said with a smile.

"Sure you are," Cody said.

"That's me warmed up now," Rachel said. She took a look at the gates and the smile faded from her face.

"Can you sense anything?" Cody said.

She nodded.

"They're close," Rachel said. "Real close."

Cody rubbed his hands together. It was anything but gleeful anticipation. The cold breeze on the rooftop felt like a sharp stinger on his skin.

"How long?" he asked.

"I don't know," Rachel said. "Not long."

Cody nodded. "Do you know how far they've...?"

He was cut off by a noise coming from the street.

Footsteps. They were light, a gentle pitter-patter skipping over the snow. It sounded like someone who was trying to sneak through the city undetected, but doing a terrible job at keeping quiet.

Rita hurried along the rooftop, trying to catch a glimpse of the runner. She leaned her head over the side. The rifle was pointing streetside.

"You see anything?" Cody asked.

Rita dropped to her knees, her fingertips grabbing a hold of the edge for support. She leaned over a little further.

Her jaw dropped.

"What?" Cody said, noticing the shocked expression on her face. "What is it?"

"I think it's a kid."

"A kid?" Cody said.

"Yeah," Rita said. "I think so."

Cody turned to Rachel. He felt a surge of anger swelling up inside.

"You see what you did with your stupid stunt?" he said. "You scared the crap out of some street kid who was hiding out down there. Maybe he was sleeping in one of the other cars when you flipped that one over for kicks."

Rachel glared at Cody. She had the same penetrating scowl as her mother.

"We need to go after that kid," Rita said.

"I don't know if that's such a good idea," Cody said. "We've got work to do here."

Rita stood up and dusted a layer of black snow off her coat.

"And what if it was Rachel wandering the streets by herself?" she said, looking at Cody. "What if she had no one to look out for her? Wouldn't you want someone like us to help her if they could?"

Cody looked towards the street. He shook his head.

"It might not be what it seems," he said. "It probably isn't."

"And what if it is?" Rita said. "C'mon man, I won't be able to sleep tonight. Will you? Knowing that we might have left a child out here to freeze to death? That shit's not good for my mind. Whoever that is down there, they won't make it alone. Not for long."

Cody sighed. She was right and yet a loud voice at the back of his mind told him it was a bad idea. Besides that, it was an unwanted distraction – they were supposed to be overseeing Rachel's training. That was still the most important thing.

Wasn't it?

But Rita didn't let up. After the words had stopped, she kept pleading with her eyes.

Cody sighed and slid the Glock back into the holster. Then he gave Rita the smile she was looking for.

"Alright," he said. "Let's go."

CHAPTER THREE

Cody and the others ran downstairs as fast as they could.

There was nothing outside. No sound. No kid. Only a wall of silence that stretched across San Antonio for miles. The only thing that had changed since they'd first gone into the Robert E. Lee building that morning was the car that was now lying upside down in the middle of the road.

It wasn't swaying anymore.

Cody glared at Rachel. She didn't seem to notice.

They stood on the sidewalk, listening for a moment. Rita's face was a mask of concentration, her eyes and ears alert as she sought some trace of the runner. She turned to the left and looked along the street, holding a finger up so that nobody interrupted her concentration.

The sound of crunching snow. It was faint but it was there in the distance.

"Up there," Rita said, pointing towards the sound. "C'mon."

They followed the footsteps, taking a sharp turn east onto North Main Avenue. Looking around, they were surrounded by a huddle of ugly tower blocks and square buildings – a huddle of haunted houses to occupy a city full of ghosts. Everything was dark and out of focus. Let it stay that way, Cody thought. He felt no desire to linger here any longer than they needed to.

The footsteps stopped up ahead and left a gaping silence. A moment later something else – a different noise, came drifting down the street towards them.

A child was crying.

Rita, who'd been leading the pack in its pursuit of the runner, slowed down when she heard it. With a finger pressed to her lips she crept further up the street while Cody and Rachel stayed close behind her. It was obvious by the careful manner of her step that Rita didn't want to spook the kid.

Cody drew his pistol. Kid or not, he wasn't taking any chances.

Rachel walked at Cody's side. Her stride was the most carefree out of all of them, like she wasn't really paying attention to what was happening. Cody had the feeling that some part of her was back on the roof of the Robert E. Lee building, still tinkering with the city lights.

"Sounds close," Cody said, listening to the sobbing.

"I see him," Rita said, pointing straight ahead. "End of the street. In the grass."

"Got it," Cody said. "Just one?"

"I only see one," Rita said.

They found the child cowering in a small patch of dead grass. It was a little boy, about twelve-years-old, with dirty brown hair who looked at the approaching strangers with wide and frightened eyes. He was tucked up next to several coffin-shaped flowerbeds, which spewed out a mass of dead, strangled weeds that had at some point succumbed to lack of sunlight. There was a scattering of wooden picnic benches close to the flowerbeds. Cody thought that the area might have been a small public garden, an oasis of green in contrast to all the concrete and metal.

They walked towards the boy. Rita was still on her tiptoes, like she feared the presence of a hidden crevasse underneath the black snow.

It was Rachel who walked ahead of the adults. Cody saw her take the lead and wanted to reel her in. But it was too late.

"Are you okay?" Rachel asked the boy.

Cody and Rita scanned the area, looking for anything out of the ordinary. Any sign that they were being tricked. Visibility was dire. They could only see so far into the distance, even with two strong flashlights at their disposal.

The boy took one look at the rifle in Rita's hands. His eyes nearly burst out their sockets and he tried to claw his way back through the snow in reverse. He bumped into one of the flowerbeds and had nowhere else to go. This only frightened him further. His fingers dug deep into the soft black snow, holding on for dear life.

"Don't kill me," he said. His voice was a whimper.

Rita lowered the rifle slowly.

"We're not going to hurt you," she said. "Look, I'm putting the weapon away. Okay?"

Rita brought the rifle further down so that the barrel was pointing at the street.

Cody lowered the Glock to his side. He didn't feel great about doing that but as soon as Rita had lowered her Savage rifle, the boy's petrified face turned towards Cody.

"We're here to help," Cody said. "That thing with the car back there, it spooked you right? Well that was our fault. It was an accident. Right Rachel?"

"Sorry," Rachel said.

The boy said nothing.

"Are you alone?" Rita asked.

"Why do you want to know?" the boy asked.

Rita shrugged. "Just want to know. Okay if I come a little closer?"

The boy didn't answer. Rita tiptoed forward anyway, keeping the rifle by her side. Cody walked beside her and he almost bumped into Rachel who'd stopped dead in front of him.

"Dad," she said, looking over her shoulder.

"What is it?"

"Something's wrong."

Cody heard a rustling sound nearby.

The noise came from somewhere behind the young boy. Cody's heart sank right away. A voice screamed in his head, yelling at him to raise the Glock, to spin around and shoot at anything that moved. Either that or run.

They'd been stupid. Now it was too late.

Four men leapt out from behind the flowerbeds. Street urchins. They were dressed in grimy, dirt-stained winter coats that looked like they'd been lifted off the streets. All four of the heavily bearded men were wearing black beanie hats, which were pulled low over their foreheads. There was a slightly unhinged look in their eyes as they came forward, each one carrying a pistol in their hands and pointing it at Cody, Rachel and Rita.

One of the men smiled. His front teeth were missing, which added to an already gruesome appearance. Cody couldn't help but think that this gang belonged in a Dickens novel, alongside the likes of Bill Sykes and Fagan in nineteenth century London.

"Good work Jack," one of the gunmen said, speaking in a thick West Texan drawl.

The boy's gap-toothed grin almost reached his ears. Standing up and shuffling backwards, he took his place behind the four adults.

"Don't try anything smart now," the same gunman said, pointing a finger at the rifle in Rita's hand. "We got more guns than you."

He looked at Rachel and gave her a twisted grin.

"You too missy," the gunman said. "I know all about you and

you'd best behave sweetheart. I got this gun right here pointed at your daddy's brain. You so much as blink in a way that displeases me and I'm going to splatter his bits and pieces all over the snow. You understand me?"

Rachel looked at Cody. He nodded, hoping that she understood.

Cody heard a clutter of footsteps off to his right. He looked that way and saw five other people walking towards them in a hurry. They were dressed in the same disheveled winter clothing: well-worn coats, hats and hoods pulled over their heads. Thick beards and dirty faces. A couple of them were carrying flashlights. They had guns too – pistols mostly, but one of them carried what looked like a shotgun.

They were tramps with attitude. A real ragtag army for sure.

"Oh shit," Rita said. She looked at Cody and didn't have to say anything for him to understand what she was thinking.

"I'm sorry. I'm..."

She was cut off by a solitary set of footsteps at their back.

"Jesus," Cody said.

How big was the ragtag army?

Somebody was standing directly at Cody's back. Cody could hear this person, whoever they were, breathing. Not only that, he could feel it blowing onto his skin. A gust of warm breath touched his neck and although Cody was curious, something stopped him from turning around. Rita and Rachel kept their eyes to the front too.

A gloved hand tore the Glock out of Cody's grip.

The person at their backs walked down the line in what seemed like slow motion. Rita's rifle was likewise snatched out her hands.

Seconds later, a cloaked figure walked in front of the three captives. The person, whose head was buried underneath a large hood, was carrying their guns – one in each hand. He walked over towards the emaciated looking boy that the toothless ragtag had called Jack.

The jet-black cloak swayed in the icy breeze.

Jack looked up at the cloak's hidden face. The boy smiled and his rotten teeth looked like broken stones in his mouth while his eyes spilled over with adoration. The kid reminded Cody of a little dog, his mouth drooling in anticipation of praise and reward.

Cody felt the cold barrel of a pistol pressing up against the back of his head. A second gunman had also snuck up behind Rita and pushed a gun against her skull.

Rachel turned around, looking at the two gunmen. Cody knew she was thinking about doing something. Her eyes had already narrowed in concentration, but then she must have thought otherwise because she turned back to the front and kept quiet. Cody breathed a sigh of relief. With a gun on the back of her dad's head, Rachel was smart enough to know that her gifts weren't fast enough to make a difference.

The cloaked figure dropped Cody's Glock on the grass. He kept the Savage rifle in his hands however and leaned forward to examine the weapon more closely. One of his black-gloved hands wrapped itself around the barrel while the other gripped the stock on the opposite end. With a single thrust, the cloak pushed down and bent the rifle, bringing the two ends together. The weapon groaned as it was disfigured into the shape of a horseshoe.

The cloak dropped the rifle like it was a piece of trash.

"Thanks," Rita said. "Thanks a lot mister."

The gunman standing behind Rita struck the barrel of his gun off her head. Rita yelped and tilted her head forward to try and put some distance between the pistol and her skull.

"What the hell's going on?" Cody said. He was looking at the cloak. "What do you want with us?"

The cloaked man – Cody was fairly certain it *was* a man by the broad shoulders – stood in silence with the most of the ragtags gathered at his back. About ten seconds of uncomfortable silence followed Cody's question. Then the cloaked stranger pulled at the fingers of the black glove on his right hand. He peeled the glove off slowly, one finger at a time.

Cody's blood ran cold. The man's hand was covered in scars. The fingers looked slightly crooked, as if they didn't work properly anymore. Then the second glove came off and it was the same thing.

The mangled hands reached towards the head. Slowly they pushed back the hood to reveal the cloak's face.

Cody heard Rachel let out a quiet shriek.

"Hello again," Mackenzie said. He looked back and forth between Cody and Rachel. There was a half-smile on his face.

"Oh Jesus," Cody said. He felt like he'd been punched in the stomach.

Mackenzie was barely recognizable as the sharp-suited, handsome man who'd caused them so much trouble several months ago. Like his hands, Mackenzie's face was horribly scarred. It was a mess, like he'd tried to shave with a lawnmower. A maze of deep grooves and lines smothered his features against a backdrop of painful and tender-looking red skin. There was a black patch fastened over Mackenzie's left eye. Mackenzie's remaining good eye, the right one, was barely open and the lid badly scarred around the edges. His hair was still long but whereas it had been well groomed before, now it was wild and ragged. There were scattered bald spots on the top of his head where the crows had pulled the hair out in chunks.

It was a miracle he was even alive. Cody recalled how hard the birds had gone after Mackenzie in Brackenridge Park that day. It wasn't something Cody was ever going to forget and in fact, he'd seen the action replayed in his dreams in the first few weeks that had followed their return from the park.

"You look surprised," Mackenzie said.

"That's one word for it," Cody said.

Rita looked at Mackenzie. Her jaw had almost dropped to the ground.

"Is that really you?" she asked.

Mackenzie nodded.

"It's been a long time," he said, looking at Rita. "If memory serves me well, you were one of the Resistance soldiers who refused to cooperate. I never forget a face. That was a smart decision you made, all things considered."

"Yeah it was," Rita said. "I heard what you did to Harry and the others."

Mackenzie smirked slightly.

"What do you want?" Cody said.

"Oh I don't know Cody," Mackenzie said. "Take a wild guess."

Cody nodded. "Okay," he said. "Well I guess you're pissed off about what happened to your face. Real sorry about that. Tell me something, does that lady doctor still have the hots for you?"

"She's dead," Mackenzie said in a matter-of-fact voice. "Your good friends Nick and Crazy Diamond saw to that. As they did with all of my former colleagues."

"What a pity," Cody said. "She was a charmer that one."

Mackenzie raised a delicate hand to his face. He touched the red skin, as if to soothe something that was burning.

He was staring at Rachel.

"Don't look so worried," he said to her. "It's just my flesh that burns. This sort of thing isn't important. It doesn't matter to the likes of us – not for much longer anyway."

"Well that's very decent of you," Rita said. "Now if you'll just let us go we'll be on our way and..."

"We've been watching you," Mackenzie said. "Up there on the Robert E. Lee building. You're getting ready aren't you? I understand your optimism, especially after what happened last time. But you know that when they get here you don't have a chance against

363

them Rachel. They're more powerful than you can imagine. Look around you for God's sake. They did all of this from a great distance. Now they're coming *here*."

"What do you want Mackenzie?" Cody said.

"Nothing's changed since we last met," Mackenzie said. "When they come I'll be waiting with the girl as my welcome gift to them. I underestimated you last time Rachel. And do you know what? So did *they*."

Rachel glared at Mackenzie. Her fingers curled into a tight fist.

"Don't do anything stupid Rachel," Mackenzie said. "Think before you act."

Mackenzie pointed a gnarled finger to the gunman at Cody's back. The pistol barrel felt like a tube of ice pushing up against Cody's skull.

"You're powerful Rachel," Mackenzie said. "No doubt about that. I've seen it with my own eyes and it's incredible. I can only imagine what you've become over these past few months with regular practice."

"Let us go," Rachel said. "Or you'll find out what I've become."

Mackenzie shook his head.

"You're too confident," he said. "Let me bring you back down to Earth for a second Rachel – you're not that fast. There's a bullet just inches from your father's head. But go on, little girl. Call the birds again why don't you? See if your dad isn't lying dead in a pool of blood by the time they get here."

Cody glanced at his Glock. It was still lying at Mackenzie's feet.

"Here's what's going to happen," Mackenzie said, looking at Cody. "They'll be here soon. Until then we're going to keep you with us at all times. You and Rachel. It'll be fun. Some daddy and daughter time – I remember what that was like back when I had my own little girl."

Mackenzie's face darkened.

"I'll have a gun on Cody at all times," he said. "If either one of you tries anything then Daddy dies first. What do you think about that Rachel?"

"I think it's bullshit," Cody said, jumping in. "There are bigger things going on here than the price of my life. Don't think she doesn't know it."

Mackenzie touched his face again. Cody saw him wince as the fingers made contact with the angry red skin.

"I don't doubt she knows it," he said in a quiet voice. "And it's a most practical philosophy in theory. But you and I both know Cody that it's a lot harder for a little girl to put something like that into practice. Rachel isn't just going to stand by and let her beloved father die like that – not if she can help it. Isn't that right Rachel?"

Rachel shook her head. "Leave us alone."

"You caught me by surprise last time you little bitch," Mackenzie said. Now the hate shone through in his good eye. "It won't happen again."

Cody could feel a surge of anger bubbling up.

"What do you think's going to happen when they get here Mackenzie?" he said. "You think you're going to get a gold star for this or something? A pat on the back for your service."

Mackenzie took a step forward.

"Same thing that was supposed to happen last time," he said. "My companions and I – we'll become a part of them. We'll be absorbed by a power that's beyond human comprehension. This broken suit of flesh that I'm wearing won't matter anymore – I'll be free of it. A suitable reward, don't you think?"

Cody looked at the others gathered behind Mackenzie, including the boy Jack.

"Gee Mackenzie," he said. "These guys might not dress as well as your last fan club but they don't look stupid to me. Do they really think you're going to take them with you? That's if you're even going anywhere in the first place. You assume the Exterminators will keep their promise and that's..."

Cody felt the gun barrel clip him on the back of the head. A sharp pain bounced around his skull.

"Don't be so negative Cody," Mackenzie said. "Didn't I tell you once before that they were a generous species?"

A trickle of black snow began to fall. Mackenzie looked up to the sky and held a hand out, gathering the dark snowflakes on his fingertips.

"So beautiful," he said with a smile.

Rita looked at Cody and raised her eyebrows. "Man I heard this guy was crazy," she said. "They weren't lying."

Mackenzie glanced at Rita.

"They're not monsters you know," he said. "That's our job. The few down here who serve them will be saved."

"Whatever you say pal," Rita said.

Cody felt an increasing sense of hopelessness wash over him.

"You're going to keep a gun on me until they get here?" he said. "Just to keep Rachel in line? That's your master plan?"

"Yes," Mackenzie said. "It is."

Rita let out a snort of disgust.

"And what about me Mackenzie?" she said. "I'll be damned if I'm going to go along with any of this. You're not keeping a gun on my head."

Mackenzie looked at Rita and he gave a curt nod.

"Truth is," he said. "I don't really need you."

There was deafening crack in Cody's left ear. He jumped as if a massive explosion had taken place behind him.

Rachel screamed.

Rita dropped like a bag of stones onto the black snow. She didn't move or make a sound after she'd hit the ground. She was already gone. The gunman who'd shot her stepped forward and gave her a probing kick, making sure that she was dead.

"Rita!" Cody yelled.

Rachel shrieked and tried to grab Cody's hand. Cody moved towards her but the gunman standing at his back swatted Rachel's outstretched hand away like it was a mosquito in his face.

Rachel threw the man a hateful look.

Cody stared at the body of Rita. His mouth was hanging open and although he wanted to go to her, he knew what would happen if he tried. Not that it would do any good.

"You bastard!" he said, turning towards Mackenzie. His head was spinning like he'd just stepped off a high-speed merry-go-round. "You sick fucking bastard. Why'd you have to do that?"

"This is no time to be sentimental Cody," Mackenzie said. There was that slightly bored look in his eye again, like he was talking to someone beneath him. "To tell you the truth, your lovely Rita is lucky to be out of it. Be happy for her – this city is going to get much worse in the days to come."

Rachel took a step closer to Mackenzie.

Mackenzie's good eye was gleaming. There was a hint of a smile on his cracked face.

"Now now Rachel," he said, wagging a finger back and forth. "Be a good girl. Think about your next move very carefully. There's only one other person left amongst us that I'm willing to shoot today. It's not you and it's not any of my friends. Can you guess who it is?"

Cody looked at Rachel. He saw the hint of a smile creeping onto his daughter's face. She was staring at Mackenzie, not blinking.

"Well?" Mackenzie said. He'd seen the smile too and now he looked pissed off. "Who will I shoot next Rachel?"

Before Rachel could answer there was a blast of gunfire. It came from behind them. Cody's heart jumped. At first, he thought that Mackenzie had given the man at his back the order to shoot him in the head.

But it was the gunman who went down.

Cody felt the cold steel barrel slide off his head. There was a crashing sound in his ears as the gunman fell face first onto the snow in a bloody heap.

Cody spun around and saw a small group of dark human shapes hurrying down the street. They ran forward for a while, getting closer, and then ducked for cover behind the cars on the road. A head peered out from behind the near-skeletal remains of a burned out SUV. Cody saw movement elsewhere – someone was leaning out of a storefront window nearby. A rifle barrel was pointing at Mackenzie and the ragtag army.

"Take this you ugly motherfucker!"

Nick Norton pulled the trigger.

Crack-crack-crack!

Mackenzie's crew scattered as bullets sprayed everywhere. Shots were fired from behind the cars on the street too. It made for a tremendous racket. The ragtags raised their pistols and started shooting back. A blast of shotgun fire rang out. There were panicked cries from the ragtags as they tried to make sense of this sudden attack. Cody saw one of Mackenzie's crew take a bullet in the gut and collapse onto the snow.

Mackenzie looked towards the shooters. There was a manic, furious look in his eyes. He looked like a man who'd just been grossly insulted.

Cody pushed Rachel onto the ground and lay on top of her.

He covered her ears as gunfire went back and forth above their heads.

Another one of the ragtags went down. It was now obvious that they were too exposed to defend themselves.

Mackenzie turned around, giving the order for his soldiers to retreat. Cody looked up and saw the gunmen take off in a hurry.

But Mackenzie didn't run.

Unlike his troops he wasn't in a rush to retreat into the darkness. Cody looked up and noticed that Mackenzie's one good eye had turned black. Cold hatred spewed out of that lifeless socket, gazing in the direction of gunfire. Cody saw a couple of bullets literally bounce off the man and he realized that whatever power the Exterminators had bestowed upon Mackenzie all those months ago, it was still there.

Mackenzie walked towards Cody and Rachel with a purposeful stride. His black eye burned as he reached down for father and daughter who were still lying on the ground dodging bullets. The gunfire slowed down at that moment, as if Nick and the others realized they were in danger of hitting Cody and Rachel.

"You're coming with me," Mackenzie said, his arms outstretched. The scarred hands came closer.

Cody felt Rachel pushing him from underneath. At first, he tried to keep her pinned down and out of reach. But Rachel wriggled her way free of his grip with surprising ease.

She jumped to her feet. As she got up, she glanced over her shoulder, searching for the source of friendly fire.

Cody saw her eyes. They were as black as Mackenzie's – maybe even blacker. A spark of light crackled around her lean frame, spreading out, getting faster by the second. The shield was on its way. Cody felt like he was watching his daughter puff out like an angry bird, swelling up, becoming something bigger.

Mackenzie took a backwards step.

Cody looked over at Rita. She was just a couple of meters away and he groaned at the sight of his fallen companion. Her body was a twisted mess – arms flailing backwards, knees bent at awkward angle. Her eyes were open and a small trickle of blood ran down her chin.

"Rita," Cody said.

Rachel and Mackenzie stood facing one another.

"C'mon Rachel," Mackenzie said. "You can't win this time. No matter what it takes, I'll hand you over to them."

Rachel didn't say anything. Instead she lifted her arms in a crucifix position. Mackenzie must have known what was coming because he took one look, turned around and ran off, following the ragtags. Mackenzie ran so fast that it was a miracle he didn't slip or trip over his long cloak.

Rachel started to run after him. But Cody was already up on his feet and as she took off, he wrapped an arm around her waist to stop her.

"Leave him," he said, pulling her back.

Rachel's head turned towards Cody. She scowled at him with her black eyes and Cody shuddered. It was like looking at someone else. *Something* else.

"Let me go," she said. "He killed Rita!"

"You're not going after him," Cody said, although he did release his grip. "For all we know that's exactly what he wants you to do."

Rachel's shield dimmed around her. As her eyes returned to their natural color, she stared into the direction in which Mackenzie had taken off.

Cody heard a noise behind them.

He spun around and saw Marv and Lance running up the street towards the little garden area. There was a look of horror on both men's faces and it only got worse as they raced towards the body of Rita.

"Oh God!" Marv said. Both he and Lance dropped onto their knees beside her. Marv lifted Rita's head and checked for any vital signs. But it was obvious to Cody that she was dead

Nick and Crazy Diamond weren't far behind. Nick's trusty AR-15 was pointing in the direction that Mackenzie and the ragtags had made their getaway. Crazy Diamond had her pistol in hand, her eyes roaming across the surroundings for signs of anything suspicious.

"Oh shit," Nick said, looking at Rita. He stopped running close to where Marv and Lance were kneeling beside the body. Both of Rita's Resistance comrades were tough, grizzled men who'd seen horrific things in their lives, both before and after the Black Storm. Now they were on the brink of tears, their hearts broken by this latest loss.

"We saw somebody go down," Nick said. "But I didn't want to believe it was one of ours."

Crazy Diamond looked at Cody and Rachel.

"Are you guys okay?" she said.

Cody's face was grim. "We're alive I guess."

Nick turned to Cody. His rifle was still primed in his arms, ready for action.

"That piece of shit ain't dead?" he said. "Are you kidding me?"

"Apparently not," Cody said.

"I thought the birds tore him apart." Crazy Diamond.

Cody shrugged. "They did."

"Well what did he want?" Nick said. "What did he say?"

"Nothing he hasn't said before," Cody said. "He still wants to hand over Rachel to the Exterminators. Still thinks that's his ticket to Paradise."

"I swear to God," Crazy Diamond said, looking at Rita. "I'm going to kill that bastard."

Cody looked at Rita's body, sandwiched in between Marv and Lance. They were both holding her up, taking a side each. Her eyes had been closed.

"Hey," Cody said, turning back to Crazy Diamond.

"What?" she said.

"How did you know?" he said.

Crazy Diamond shrugged. "What do you mean?"

"How did you know we were in trouble?" Cody said. "And how did you know where we were?"

Crazy Diamond nodded. "Oh that."

"Yeah that," Cody said. "Well?"

Crazy Diamond pointed a thumb at Rachel, who was looking back at the young woman with a calm expression on her face.

"Your little girl here," Crazy Diamond said. "That's how."

"What do you mean?" Cody asked. He looked at Rachel, but it didn't look like she was giving anything away.

He turned back to Crazy Diamond.

"What's going on?" Cody said. "What did she do?"

Crazy Diamond tapped the side of her head.

"She told me everything."

CHAPTER FOUR

They took Rita's body to the San Antonio National Cemetery.

It was about a ten minute drive from their base at the Rand to the cemetery, which was located on Paso Hondo, a couple of miles due east of the downtown area. It was Marv's idea to take Rita there. The National Cemetery in ordinary times had been reserved for members of the armed forces. In Marv's own words however, they were all soldiers now.

On their way they'd stopped off at the La Paz funeral home. The building had remained untouched during the last days and still looked as if it was open for business. Cody and the others had crept inside, keeping the noise down as if they were walking through a church in the middle of service. While there they'd tended to Rita, cleaning her wound and washing her down. Marv selected an oak casket from a display room and when it was time she was placed inside.

After that, they said their goodbyes.

Marv, Lance, Nick and Cody carried Rita's casket into the cemetery on their shoulders. Crazy Diamond and Rachel walked a few paces behind. Crazy Diamond had one arm wrapped around

Rachel's shoulders. With her spare hand, she pointed a flashlight into the cemetery to guide the pallbearers.

Cody noticed a tall flagpole standing in the middle of the grounds. At the top of the flagpole, a large Stars and Stripes was blowing stubbornly in the breeze.

The cemetery was packed with headstones. Cody wondered if there was room for even one more person in that place. But Marv knew what he was doing – he led the way to a section that he'd used months back to bury a couple of close friends who'd died during the Resistance war with Mackenzie and the suits.

The mourners walked for several minutes. With Crazy Diamond shining a light in front of them, Marv guided the procession towards a strip of snow-covered grass tucked in beside a weather-beaten stone wall. The wall ran parallel to the main road.

They laid the casket down on the black snow. Marv and Lance went back to the van to collect three shovels that they'd brought with them. When they came back, Marv, Nick and Lance went to work digging the grave and the plan was to do it as quickly as possible.

Cody and Crazy Diamond stood nearby, staying close to Rachel.

Digging was hard work. As temperatures in San Antonio dipped further, the soil was on the brink of becoming impenetrable. The three men used their shovels to remove the snow from the chosen gravesite and they had to stab hard into the dirt in order to make any sort of progress.

Cody kept lookout while the other men were digging. His attention was focused on the road behind the wall, but he also kept his eyes within the cemetery grounds. He was looking for any sign of movement. The next attack could come from anywhere.

As he looked around he noticed two simple wooden crosses marking the spot where Marv had buried his other friends. Both crosses sat at the head of a small mound of rectangular soil, which was almost completely buried in black snow. If Cody had been more literary minded he might have thought that was symbolic. Like the new world was swallowing them up, swallowing up the entirety of human history.

Rachel was looking at the wooden crosses too. She led Cody over to the modest headstones and made her way around the upturned dirt. Then she did a half-squat, leaning towards the nearest cross. Crazy Diamond shone the flashlight on the marker to help her get a closer look.

There was some writing on the horizontal strip of wood.

"What does it say?" Cody asked.

"It's a name," Rachel said, wiping down the marker with her sleeve. She pointed to the cross on the left. "That one says Johnny Boy." Then she looked at the second cross. "That one says Elaine, I think."

"We called her Laney," Marv said, putting his shovel down and looking over. He lit up a cigarette and blew a cloud of smoke into the air. "She was crazier than a soup sandwich. Johnny Boy was much the same – he was high on life that kid. They were just young people – good people caught up in the madness. Neither one of them was older than thirty when they died."

Marv's gaze drifted beyond the wall.

"Rita was good friends with Laney and Johnny Boy," he said. "She'd be happy lying next to them both, I have no doubt about that. Bit pressed for space mind you but well that's alright."

Lance nodded. "It's a good call Marv," he said.

"We do the best we can right?" Marv said.

"Right," Lance said.

Marv sighed and went back to digging. The cigarette was still dangling in between his lips.

"You alright Cody?" Crazy Diamond said, shining the flashlight on his face. "You look a bit pale if you don't mind my saying. Are you going to puke or something?"

"Must be all that back-breaking digging," Nick said with a laugh.

Cody shook his head. He waved the flashlight off his face and Crazy Diamond took it away.

"I've never liked graveyards that's all," he said.

"What's not to like?" Crazy Diamond said.

"I know some people find peace in these places," Cody said. "Or perspective or whatever you want to call it. But they just make me uneasy." He looked up at the black sky and the gates that watched over them. "Especially when it's so damn dark everywhere."

"The dead gotta go somewhere," Marv said, stabbing the cutting edge of the shovel into the ground.

"Yeah I know that," Cody said. "But that's what cremation is for. Right? Burn the bodies and scatter the ashes. Doesn't take up any space either. I don't know, there's something about just leaving a body in the ground to rot and letting it turn into worm food over the years. No thanks."

Nick stopped digging and looked over at Cody. "You scared of waking up in the box or something?" he asked.

Cody shrugged. "I don't know. Maybe."

"Yeah well I don't care what happens to me," Nick said, resuming the task of digging Rita's grave. "Put me here. Put me anywhere. I'll be dead. Who cares?"

Nick stopped digging again.

"On second thoughts, maybe a little sunshine overhead," he said. "That's all I ask. After all this neverending darkness, I'd like a few rays shining over my last resting place."

Cody looked at Rachel. "Don't ever put me in the ground kid," he said.

"Don't call me kid!" Rachel said.

"Alright, alright," Cody said. "*Rachel.* When my time comes, you can leave me on the side of the road for the birds to gobble up for all I care. Just don't put me in the ground. Yeah?"

Rachel looked at Cody with a frown. "I don't want to think about that."

Crazy Diamond kneeled down in front of Johnny Boy and Laney's graves.

"If the Exterminators are as good as we think they are then you don't have to worry about it Cody," she said. "There won't be anything left of you to bury or scatter."

"Right," Cody said. "I feel so much better now."

There was a noise behind them.

Cody spun around and looked over the wall towards the street. Although he couldn't see anything he heard the sound of an engine humming in the distance.

Everyone else stopped what they were doing.

"What the hell?" Lance said. "What is that?"

Cody spotted a pair of narrow headlights edging down the street. The vehicle rolled down the road in slow motion before coming to a stop.

Nick dropped the shovel and grabbed his rifle off the ground. Then he ran over to the wall as fast as he could without slipping on the snow. Lance did likewise, his fingers wrapped around the handle of a Smith & Wesson.

"That's a school bus," Nick said, looking over the wall. The vehicle was by now lingering about a hundred meters from where Nick and Lance were perched. Its engine was still chugging away at low volume.

Nick looked at Lance. "Don't you think?"

"You're not wrong big guy," Lance said. "It's a school bus alright."

Cody walked over to the wall and peered over the edge. His Glock was pointing towards the long bus, which had to be at least twenty-five feet in length, if not more. The headlights lit up the front grill and dark fender at the head of the vehicle.

"Looks like our old pal Mackenzie has come to pay his respects," Nick said.

"What an asshole," Crazy Diamond said. "He's stalking us now?"

Nick snorted in disgust. "That's just plain old disrespectful," he said. "This is Rita's funeral for God's sake. He won't even let us bury our dead in peace now? Well that settles it. This guy's going down and the only burial he's getting is the one that takes place underneath my goddamn foot."

"Not now Nick."

It was Marv who spoke. He'd stayed by the half-dug gravesite while the others had gone over to check out the bus. Beside him, Rita's casket was a solemn ornament, reminding them of why they were there.

"We're here for Rita," Marv said in a quiet voice. "Remember?"

'You know I think I've seen that school bus before," Crazy Diamond said. "Or I've seen *a* school bus, one just like that. Parked near the Rand. Might be a different one but I don't know."

"He knows where we're staying?" Cody said.

"Maybe," Crazy Diamond said.

"We're going to have to start putting two people on watch," Lance said. "Either that or we think about moving someplace else."

"All our supplies are stored in the Rand," Cody said. "Moving is kind of a big deal."

"Not being safe in our home is also kind of a big deal," Lance said, scratching at his fluffy beard. "If Mackenzie's watching us, we gotta do it. He could go after us, after our supplies – I don't like it."

"Better if we dust this asshole now," Nick said. "And all his little ragtag groupies. Then we don't have to move anywhere."

As Nick dropped back down off the wall, Cody watched him pacing back and forth like a caged lion.

"What do you say guys?" Nick said. "Do we finish it? Right here, right now."

Before anyone could answer there was a noise on the road.

The school bus was reversing slowly down the street. Nick held both hands in the air as the glaring headlights began to shrink from view.

"Hey shithead!" he called out. "Leaving so soon? Don't you want to come over here and admire your handiwork?"

Nick turned to the others. There was a look of desperation on his face.

"He's getting away," he said. "Listen to me guys. That son of a bitch isn't going to stop – not until we're all dead and he's handing Rachel giftwrapped over to those Exterminator sons of bitches."

Nick looked at Cody. Then at Crazy Diamond.

"For God's sake people!" he said. "Let's finish it. We'll regret it if we don't."

"Nick," Marv said, leaning on the shovel. "Nobody wants to see that bastard dead more than I do. Look around you. Three of my friends are here because of Mackenzie and the things he's done. Countless others lie in unmarked graves all over the city."

The narrow headlights were by now a faint glow in the distance.

"There's a lot of blood on that man's hands," Marv said. "And I promise you, we're going to make him pay for every last drop. But this isn't the time. More than anything, I don't want to turn Rita's funeral into another shootout. She deserves better than that."

The fire in Nick's eyes cooled a little as Marv spoke. With a grunt, he lowered his rifle to the side and watched the school bus disappear into the thick web of darkness that surrounded San Antonio. Then he walked back over to the gravesite and picked his shovel up off the snow. For the next five minutes, Nick cut through

379

the solid ground as if his life depended on it. With such enthusiasm, it didn't take them long to dig Rita's grave and lay her to rest. But once or twice during the job, Nick would stop digging and his eyes would stare off into the distance.

Cody knew that look.

Nick was still chasing the school bus, at least in his mind.

———————

That night they awoke to something like thunder.

It was a deep bellowing sound and it felt like King Kong and Godzilla were fighting on the roof of the building. It was close too – like the thunder coming from other places besides the heavens. Almost like it was coming from below, from somewhere underneath the Earth.

There would be no sleep after that. They were all sitting up in their sleeping bags, lost in their private thoughts. Candles had been lit. Worried faces glanced across the room at one another while the thunder escalated outside. Eyes drifted towards the windows, inevitably drawn towards the distant light of the gates.

Cody glanced at Rachel who was sitting up in bed. She'd gone to sleep with her winter coat on, forced to do so by yet another drop in temperature. The hood was pulled over her head and her blonde hair poked out at the sides, spilling down to her shoulders. She was blowing into her hands to warm them up. Her eyes looked tired and far away – the eyes of a much older person stitched onto a young face.

"Rachel," Cody said.

"What?"

"You okay?" Cody asked.

"Yeah" she said.

He nodded. "You sure?"

She looked at him. "Won't be long now."

Cody felt a tight knot forming in his stomach. "Better go to sleep if we're going to get up for practice tomorrow," he said.

Rachel nodded slowly.

"It won't be the same without Rita," she said. "I miss her."

"I know," Cody said. He glanced over to the far corner of the room where Rita used to sleep. It was just an empty space now. "I miss her too. We all do."

Rachel put her head back down on the pillow. She let out a long sigh and pulled the sleeping bag over her head.

"Night Dad."

"Night Rachel."

Cody knew he wouldn't get any sleep that night. Instead he sat up, thinking about Rita and listening to the raucous sounds shaking the night outside. At the same time, he tried not to think about what the future might bring.

On more than one occasion he looked at Rachel beside him.

She was shivering as she slept.

CHAPTER FIVE

The next day they were back on the roof of the Robert E. Lee building.

Black snow had been falling all night and it was still going strong. The snowflakes were almost invisible in the darkness but Cody could feel them landing on his hood as they walked from the Rand to the building where Rachel did her daily training.

Everyone was there as an armed guard for Rachel. They weren't taking any chances after what had happened with Rita yesterday.

Rachel was standing near the edge of the roof. She turned towards the city and turned on the lights. As she practiced, Cody stood by her side, as quiet and as constant as her shadow. He was thinking about Rita and feeling her absence, especially so in this place where they'd spent so much time together. Behind Cody and Rachel, the armed guard, which consisted of Nick, Crazy Diamond, Marv and Lance, patrolled the rooftop with guns and flashlights, looking out for movement on the street and on the tops of nearby buildings.

The gates were getting bigger. There was little doubt about

that now. It was a hard thing to admit – like watching a wound that was progressively getting worse. Cody spotted countless shafts of light spilling out of the circular suns. It was expanding and pushing outwards. It was as if there was something behind the gates, trying to force its way through.

"That's a helluva sight," Marv said, looking up with a blank expression. "All this to get their hands on that little girl, huh?"

"And to finish the rest of us off," Cody said.

Nick was staring at the gates, a look of disbelief on his bearded face.

"I don't know what I'm supposed to be pointing my rifle at," he said. "Down at the ground or at those things up there."

"I don't think a bullet is going to be much use up there," Crazy Diamond said, calling over from the opposite side of the roof. "Save your bullets for the ragtags. For the guaranteed mortals. Leave those things up there to Rachel."

As they spoke amongst themselves, Rachel continued with her exercises. Cody turned back to the front, watching the city blink on and off at her command. He'd gradually come to notice some of the subtle things she was doing during these practice sessions. It wasn't just an automatic orchestration – she truly had the concert fully under control. He watched as Rachel's left-hand index finger stretched a little to the left. At the same time, the buildings in that direction would shut off entirely while everything on the right would continue to blink in the same steady rhythm. She'd then switch hands and turn it around and back again. If her finger jerked restlessly, the light show in San Antonio would speed up and slow down. Both of Rachel's fingers would occasionally push down like she was tapping two buttons on an imaginary keyboard. The light would then go on and off, mimicking her plodding beat, and when she stopped the city was plunged into darkness. Then she'd start tapping again and the entire city would light up, as if coming back onto the stage for an encore.

Cody couldn't help but smile. She'd come a long way from the girl in the airport who'd charged at the Black Widow. But no matter how good she was, he couldn't stop thinking – would it be enough?

Lance called out from behind.

"Holy shit!" he said. "Look up there. You guys see that?"

Cody spun around and pulled his Glock out the holster.

Lance was pointing to something in the sky.

Marv – who was usually the epitome of calm – gasped out loud. He was pointing at the same thing as Lance, his face a picture of shock and excitement.

"Good God," he said, lowering his gun. "What is that?"

Cody walked over and stood beside them. It took a moment, but eventually he managed to focus on what they were looking at.

Something was traveling towards them.

Hundreds, perhaps thousands of tiny circles of white light were floating through the air. Down they came, drifting towards the Robert E. Lee building and leaving a thin trail of white dust at their backs. Cody might have been looking at some type of underwater creature floating in the sky – a giant swarm of jellyfish, transparent and jewel-like.

They floated towards the rooftop, both gentle and menacing. Even though it looked like they were moving slowly, they were covering an incredible amount of distance at great speed.

The lights came down and converged around Rachel, like moths to a light bulb. They circled her at a safe distance, almost as if they were cautious of the girl. After a couple of minutes the lights moved across the rooftop and glided past the five adults, all of who were watching this spectacle with their mouths hanging open.

Nick was pointing his rifle at the circles as they took a close look at him before drifting off towards Crazy Diamond.

The adults were deemed worthy of the briefest of glimpses. As the swarm of lights lingered around Cody he could sense their lack of interest.

When it was over, the lights glided upwards again. They moved away from the roof, drifting back towards the gates and in a matter of minutes they began to disperse, as if sliding through an unseen door in the sky.

"What the hell was that?" Lance said, as the white circles slowly disappeared from view. "I mean, what just happened there?"

Marv rubbed the back of his hand off the jagged stubble on his chin.

"Don't know," he said.

"They're taking a closer look at us," Cody said. "What do you think Rachel?"

Rachel's shield slowly fizzled out. She turned to look at Cody and the others. Behind her, the city lights gave way to a thick wall of blackness.

"Scouts," she said.

Cody looked at the darkness behind them.

"You know," he said. "You shouldn't have stopped what you were doing. Doesn't matter what's coming at you, you can't let yourself be distracted by anything. It's important that you keep your concentration at all times. You understand?"

Cody felt like a prize shit for scolding her. Easy for him to say, right? He'd been distracted by the lights like everyone else – why would his eleven year old daughter be any different? And yet she had to be. She had to be better, stronger and more focused than any of the adults. It wasn't fair – it was anything but fair. It was downright shitty. But that's how it was. Rachel was their only chance and who else was going to discipline her if not her father?

Rachel looked embarrassed by Cody's rebuke.

She turned her attention back to the city. With a nod, the shield crackled open. The lights switched on in almost every building as far as the eye could see. It reminded Cody of looking out of an airplane window at night while flying over a major city. How the plane would glide over a sea of electric light – a reminder of mankind's presence and its refusal to stay in the dark.

Rachel turned to her right and pointed a finger towards the nearby car park. There were about twenty or thirty vehicles in the car park, some parked neatly in the allotted spaces while others had been dumped at random, as if the owners had been in a hurry to ditch them. At Rachel's signal, all of the cars began to rock back and forth in a clumsy puppet-like dance. Their headlights flickered on and off while their horns blared in loud protest of this violation.

Lance and Nick laughed at this unexpected source of entertainment.

But Cody wasn't amused. He had a feeling that Rachel was straying from the task at hand – that she was perhaps trying to outdo the white circles, almost as if they'd triggered her competitive streak. Either that or she was deliberately trying to piss Cody off, to get back at him for embarrassing her in front of everyone.

The wind was blowing harder now.

Cody pulled the collar of his coat together at the neck even though it was already zipped up as tight as he could get it. He glanced up at the gates, feeling like an ant that was staring up at a giant foot. More than ever their task felt like a hopeless one. What the hell was he thinking about putting Rachel in front of all this? What sort of man would throw his daughter to the lions? Mackenzie had been right about one thing yesterday – when the Exterminators arrived it would be a lot different than it had been at Brackenridge Park.

Cody looked at Rachel. She was still making the cars tremble and she was clearly having fun while doing it. Rachel was laughing as the vehicles rocked back and forth like they were caught up in a major earthquake.

"Stop," Cody said.

Nothing happened.

"Rachel," he said, raising his voice. "I said stop it. Now!"

The cars stopped. Silence.

Rachel looked over her shoulder at Cody. The shield fizzled out again like he'd poured cold water all over her fire.

Cody walked over to Rachel and put a hand on her shoulder. A surge of heat was gushing out from underneath her coat.

He took his hand away and stepped back.

"This is too much," Cody said. "We can't do it."

He looked around at the others, hoping for some sign of agreement on their faces. Some indication that yes, they'd tried their best but the reality was they were screwed if they hung around San Antonio for much longer. Up until then, their only hope had been to stand and fight. But as noble as that was, Cody saw now that it was a false hope. The fog had cleared. This was too much for Rachel, too much for all of them.

"We've got to get out," Cody said. "We've got enough fuel left to get as far away from San Antonio as we need to. I mean, look at those gates for God's sake. What the hell is going to come through there? We don't know anything about what we're up against here. What are we thinking? What was I thinking? I'm not putting Rachel in front of that – no way. It was a stupid idea. Rita's dead for Christ's sake."

"No."

It was Rachel who spoke.

"There's nowhere else to go Dad," she said. "They'll find us no matter how far we run. They'll find me."

Cody shook his head. He didn't want to believe that.

They looked at each other in silence. Before anyone could say anything else on the matter, they heard the sound of a growling engine down on the street.

Marv rushed over to the edge of the rooftop. He looked down

and sighed. "Guess who?" he said.

Cody peered down to the street.

The yellow bus was creeping slowly down the road.

"Can we still get a restraining order against this guy?" Lance said.

"It's that goddamn school bus," Nick said. He glanced at Cody and there was a flicker of anger his eyes. "I told you man. I told all of you. If we'd taken care of him yesterday then this threat wouldn't be hanging over us all the time. Listen, I hear what you're saying about running Cody. But no matter where we go, this asshole's going to be on our tail, never mind the Exterminators. We've got something they want."

Nick dropped to his knees. The rifle barrel pointed towards the street.

"How good are you with a rifle Marv?" he asked. "You've got the most experience out of all us. Think you could shoot out the tires from up here?"

Marv looked at Nick with a puzzled expression.

"You don't ask much do you Nick?"

"We gotta stop that bus man," Nick said. "If we can take out the tires then they're on foot. If they're on foot, we can go down and finish it."

Marv leaned over the edge and took a good look at the bus. Cody and Rachel stood further back, but with their eyes glued to the street like everyone else. The bus had rolled to a stop directly outside the Robert E. Lee building. Mackenzie clearly didn't care that they knew he was there. He had to be sending them a message – letting them know that he was going to keep following them until he got what he wanted.

Without a word, Marv took the AR-15 out of Nick's hands. He looked down the barrel and shook his head.

"It's dark as hell," he said. "But I'll give it a go."

"Don't bother," Rachel said.

She came over and stood beside Marv, Lance and Nick at the edge. Cody followed and they both had a good look. The school bus was pointing east on West Travis Street. But as Rachel leaned further over, the bus began to crawl forward a few meters. From afar it looked like somebody who was driving around a new neighborhood in slow motion, looking for the right address.

The bus continued forward. Now it picked up a little speed, like it was on its way out of there and in a hurry. Cody could hear the distant crunching noise from below as the wheels rolled over the freshly fallen black snow.

"He's teasing us," Cody said.

"He's getting away," Nick said. "That's what he's doing."

Rachel reached a hand towards the street. The bright colors of the shield returned, dancing along the edge of her forearms. Her eyes dulled to charcoal black.

She clenched a fist and tugged on something that wasn't there.

The bus jerked backwards on the road. The engine made a harsh choking noise and the wheels sprayed black snow everywhere.

"Holy shit," Nick said, jumping up to his feet. He burst out laughing and clapped his hands like he'd just won the lottery jackpot. "Now that's what I'm talking about. Let's do some asshole fishing. Go on Rachel! You bring him to us girl."

Rachel continued to pull her arm back into her body. It looked like she was tugging on a piece of heavy rope, reeling it in slowly. Her teeth were clenched. Her black eyes focused. Cody knew that look – he'd seen it on her face many times before. The first time he'd seen it was in Brackenridge Park when she'd called on the crows to annihilate Mackenzie. It was a look of absolute concentration.

The bus's engine continued to scream in protest. It sounded like a wounded, frightened animal begging for release.

Nick, Marv, Crazy Diamond and Lance had their guns trained

on the bus. They were waiting to open fire. Any second now, somebody was going to jump out the door and make a run for it. And when they did, the shooters would be ready.

With any luck, Mackenzie would be the first to jump ship.

But then the truck staggered forwards a few meters. There was a thudding noise as the chassis bounced on the road and then the engine howled with relief.

The bus raced down the street, picking up speed.

"Damn it!" Nick said, staggering back from the edge.

Rachel spun around to look at Cody. He saw the confusion all over her face and he shrugged as if to tell her it didn't matter. At the same time, the colors of the shield disappeared while her black eyes cooled to blue.

"Sorry," Rachel said, looking at Nick. "I thought I had it."

"Forget it babe," Crazy Diamond said, throwing the girl a smile. "We'll see him again soon enough."

Nick pursed his lips together and gazed at the empty street.

"That lucky son of a bitch," he said.

Cody walked over to Rachel. He put his arm around her shoulder and looked at the others.

"You see?" he said. "Do you get it now? We're not ready for this. Rachel's not ready for this. How's she supposed to control the Exterminators when she can't control a bus?"

Rachel wriggled free of Cody's grip. She looked up at her father and her eyes were ablaze with a barely controlled anger.

"*I'm* ready," she said. "What would you know about it? You're just standing there on the sidelines like a stupid coach telling me what to do all the time."

Cody was shocked. He looked at Rachel and felt a terrible sensation – almost like he was looking at a total stranger.

"I'm just telling the truth Rachel," he said. "You're still my daughter and I'm still your dad. I'm not trying to be an asshole – I'm trying to protect you."

Rachel shook her head. "I don't need your protection anymore."

She walked over to the other side of the building. A moment later, Cody heard the violent rattling of the cars dancing on the street again.

"We need to get back," Crazy Diamond said, stepping forward. She spoke in a calm and quiet voice, perhaps in an attempt to diffuse the familial tension. "We're all tired and stressed and let's face it, a little bit cranky. And besides, it's damn cold out here."

But Rachel made them wait a little while longer. She forced the cars to dance and there was nothing anyone could say to make her stop. It was practice after all, even if it wasn't the most delicate kind. She stood alone for at least another ten minutes. Eventually it was Crazy Diamond who persuaded her to call it a day.

Back at the Rand, the temperature inside the building continued to drop. Nobody on the seventh floor took off their coats, hats and gloves after getting back from the Robert E. Lee apartments.

They ate sparingly. Nobody had much of an appetite but they shoved a little food into their mouths. It was a chore that had to be done.

After dinner, Lance and Nick went downstairs to stand guard.

Cody and Rachel sat next to one another on the floor. But even though they were close, Rachel still hadn't said a single word to Cody since they'd come back from the Robert E. Lee building. She hadn't said much to anyone. For his part, Cody regretted voicing his doubts so publicly. He could have waited. He could have been a bit more tactful perhaps. By speaking his mind, he'd instilled his fears in Rachel and she had enough of her own to deal with.

They sat in silence, like death row prisoners waiting for the call.

CHAPTER SIX

Cody did fall asleep eventually.

He must have because the sound of gunfire woke him up.

Loud, frantic footsteps pounded on the floor. They might as well have been trampling over his head.

Cody heard Marv's voice yelling something about being under attack. He sat up and tried to wriggle his way free of the sleeping bag, all the while trying to clear the fog in his mind.

Rachel was sitting up beside him. She unzipped her bag and got to her feet.

Crack-crack-crack!

This second round of gunfire spurred Cody's freezing cold hands into life. His fingers found the zipper and he pulled so hard that he almost yanked the damn thing off, which would have left him trapped inside the bag.

"What the hell's going on?" he said, jumping to his feet. He took off his gloves, grabbed the gun belt beside the sleeping bag and wrapped it around his waist as fast as he could.

Crazy Diamond hurried over to his side. Cody's first thought was that she looked fresh – her long jet-black hair was combed to perfection and it poked out both sides of her hood. There was a sharp look in her eyes. Unlike Cody, she was ready for this. Whatever this was.

Her gloved fingers gripped the handle of her pistol.

"Give you one guess," Crazy Diamond said.

"Mackenzie?" Cody said. "He's here?"

She nodded. "He's paying us a midnight visit."

Cody groaned. "I hate that guy so much."

"Well let's go and tell him," Crazy Diamond said with a wink. "Sounds like Nick and Lance could use the help."

Cody had almost forgotten that Nick and Lance were downstairs on watch duty. He looked over his shoulder at Rachel who was standing a few feet behind the adults. She was looking at Cody but she hadn't ventured over to his side.

"What about Rachel?" he said.

"She stays here," Crazy Diamond said. She turned to the girl. "You hear that Rachel? You stay in this room and don't do anything or go anywhere until we get rid of these guys. No magic tricks. You keep out of sight."

Rachel nodded. She looked at Cody, then went back to her sleeping bag and sat down cross-legged on top of it.

"It'll be okay," Cody said to her.

She nodded but didn't look at him.

"Let's go," Marv said, checking the magazine on his Glock 17.

Cody and Crazy Diamond followed Marv out of the room and shut the door behind them. They hurried towards the stairs while listening to a burst of rapid gunfire coming from further down the narrow stairwell.

They rushed down a couple of flights towards the fighting. Cody's heart was racing, his finger glued to the pistol trigger.

It wasn't long before they ran into Nick who was retreating backwards up the staircase. They met somewhere around the third floor. Nick had his back to the others – he was facing downstairs, his AR-15 pointing towards the lower floors.

Marv bolted downstairs when he saw that Nick was alone.

"Nick!" he said. "Where's Lance?"

Nick's body jerked backwards at the sound of Marv rushing towards him. He breathed a sigh of relief when he saw the others standing at the top of the stairs. Then he looked at Marv and shook his head. "Sorry Marv," he said. "He took one in the chest when they stormed the building. The bastards jumped us out there – they threw some sort of smoke bomb at us in the street. Forced us back inside the building. It was chaos man. They got in and threw another bomb on the first floor, pushing us back further to the stairs. That's when they started shooting."

"Oh Jesus Christ!" Marv said, doubling over. He looked like he was about to be sick on the landing but almost immediately he straightened back up again. Cody saw the old war veteran trying to put his game face back on. As far as Cody could tell, it was getting harder for Marv to do that.

"How many?" Crazy Diamond said.

Nick shook his head. "Hard to tell," he said. "Gotta be at least fifteen to twenty ragtags down there. Mackenzie too. I saw that bastard walk through the smoke like he was Darth Vader. I don't even know if I hit any of them. I've just been shooting at smoke all this time."

"Oh shit," Cody said. "We're all that's left between Mackenzie and Rachel – just the four of us."

"Lance," Marv said, running a hand through his hair. "Rita, Laney, Johnny Boy, Harry – all of them, they're gone. Those bastards have killed them all."

"It's not over yet Marv," Crazy Diamond said. "We're still here. Right? It ain't much but it's gotta count for something."

Marv looked at Crazy Diamond and nodded. But Cody could see

in Marv's dazed expression that the old soldier was struggling to process these latest deaths. It wasn't surprising – Lance and Rita might as well have been his own kids, such was the close bond they shared.

They heard a rattling noise further down the stairs.

Nick leaped down a couple of steps and fired a volley of angry shots down the staircase. Cody did likewise. They had to at least let Mackenzie know that they were still there and with any luck, drop a few of the ragtags too. If nothing else, it would buy Cody and the others time to think.

The ragtags weren't slow in returning fire. A barrage of bullets came back upstairs. At the same time, a faint cloud of smoke drifted slowly upwards, as if it was making its way towards the roof.

"Did I just hear a machine gun down there?" Cody said, when the shooting had stopped. "Where the hell did they find a machine gun?"

Nick shrugged. "Looks like they've let off another smoke bomb too," he said. "They're trying to work their way upstairs. They know she's up here."

"How the hell are we getting out?" Cody said.

"What about the back door?" Crazy Diamond asked.

"Mackenzie might be ugly but he's not stupid," Nick said. "He's bound to have covered the back."

"Yeah I know that smart ass," Crazy Diamond said. "But if he's put anyone out back on guard it'll be the bare minimum. Two or three ragtags at most. You said maybe about twenty followers down front? Mackenzie can't have many more soldiers than that. That's about the same number we saw with him yesterday. And besides, you know what that cocky bastard's like – he doesn't think we've got a chance of getting to the back door. That's gotta be our best chance."

There was a stamping noise from below. Loud footsteps came

charging up the stairs and it sounded like a SWAT team had stormed the building.

"Here they come again," Nick called out.

Marv leaped down a few steps, pushing his way past Nick and Cody. Then he opened fire and started shooting down the staircase.

"C'mon!" Marv yelled. "Come and get us."

This challenge was met by a vicious onslaught of return fire. Cody could see the ragtags leaning over the handrail a couple of flights down and shooting up at random. They weren't aiming at much in particular, but Mackenzie's troops were getting closer. And they were still on the move.

The shooting stopped. The stairwell echoed with the sound of feet pounding off the hard floor.

Cody, Nick and Marv were forced back upstairs to where Crazy Diamond was waiting.

The ragtags halted their approach.

A sudden silence swept over the staircase.

"There's no way we can push them back," Crazy Diamond said, whispering to the others. "They're going to keep coming at us until we've got no room left to run."

"We have to push them back," Cody said.

"It *has* to be the back door," Nick said. "We've got to get Rachel out of here."

A single pair of footsteps marched towards them.

"You're brave soldiers," Mackenzie called up the stairs. "No one can say otherwise. But I've got news for you my friends – the Exterminators are upon us. I'm here for Cody and the girl – nobody else has to die today at my hand. What do you say Cody? What would the hero do in one of those movies of yours?"

"Go fuck yourself!" Nick yelled. "You want them, come and get them."

"I will Nick," Mackenzie said. "You're outnumbered. I can kill you at anytime I want."

Nick looked at Cody and grinned like a crazy man. Cody glanced back up the staircase towards the seventh floor where Rachel was alone.

They could at least give her a fighting chance.

"We push them back," Cody said in a hushed voice to the others. "No matter what. As long as Rachel has a clear path to the roof of the Robert E. Lee apartments, that's all we can hope for. Right? It doesn't matter what happens to us – there are bigger things at stake. We haven't been working our asses off these past few months for nothing. Neither has Rachel."

Marv nodded. "Right," he said. "We make a path. One full of dead ragtags."

"Ready?" Cody said.

"Ready," Crazy Diamond said.

"3-2-1..." Marv said.

Cody took a deep breath.

"Go!" Nick said.

They charged downstairs, dropping down to the next floor in a matter of seconds. There was no subtlety in their attack – it was all or nothing now. They reached the landing and turned to the right. The ragtag soldiers were standing at the foot of the stairs.

Both groups looked at one another. No more barriers in between them.

There was a split second of silence that seemed to last forever.

The ragtags aimed their weapons upstairs.

Cody's finger squeezed the Glock's trigger and then...

An explosion.

It was a noise so loud that Cody didn't hear it so much as he felt it rattling his bones. For a second he thought he was dead – that the ragtags had shot him and this violent jarring sensation was the experience of his soul falling into the abyss.

The building shook under their feet.

Cody must have blacked out at the moment of the explosion because when he opened his eyes he was on the floor lying on his back. He could see a streak of ferocious white light beaming through the window, temporarily blinding everyone on the staircase as it passed the building.

Confusion spilled through both groups of soldiers. People began scrambling back to their feet, eager to resume the battle.

The sound of gunfire came from below.

Cody pulled himself upright to see who was doing the shooting. There didn't seem to be any bullets coming his way. Marv, Crazy Diamond and Nick were unharmed too. Cody looked downstairs and saw that Mackenzie's troops were in disarray. But it wasn't just the explosion that had knocked them off their stride. There was something else going on. Now they'd turned their backs on Cody and the others to focus on yet another disturbance from further down the staircase.

Cody leaned his head closer to the stairs for a better look at what was going on down there. Looking towards the lower landing, he saw some of the ragtags lying dead on the stairs.

Crack!

Another one dropped on the stairs.

Someone came running through the smoke.

Lance charged at the huddle of ragtags from behind. His face was ghostly pale and his hair and soft beard were drenched in sweat and blood. There was more blood on his chin, trickling down from his mouth. Despite his injuries, Lance's eyes were alert and he rushed forwards with reckless abandon, shooting into the gang of ragtags and sending them into a panic.

But the element of surprise didn't last.

The ragtag soldiers opened fire and Lance was flung back under a hail of bullets. Blood sprayed from his body. He collapsed on the lower landing, his arms stretched out on both sides, lying flat on his back on the floor.

"Lance!" Marv yelled. His eyes were wide with horror.

Marv didn't hesitate after that. He charged downstairs and fired at the ragtags with no thought of personal safety. Nick was right behind him and once again the ragtags were caught off guard as they dealt with an attack coming from upstairs.

Crazy Diamond turned back to Cody. She grabbed his arm and stopped him charging downstairs with Marv and Nick.

"This is the only chance we'll get," Crazy Diamond said. "Go upstairs and get Rachel. We'll push the ragtags down to the first floor, no matter what it takes. Get her to the rooftop and tell her to send those Exterminators back to wherever they came from. They're here Cody."

Cody glanced through the window. The city was ablaze with a swarm of light sweeping across the sky. There was something else too. Cody heard a familiar noise out there – the dissonant whale noises that he'd heard in Brackenridge Park.

It was much louder this time.

"Don't think about it Cody," Crazy Diamond said, slapping him hard across the face. Gunshots rang out at their back. He heard Nick and Marv yelling at the top of their voices, hurling insults at the ragtags.

"Get Rachel," Crazy Diamond said. "Now!"

Crazy Diamond pushed Cody away and ran downstairs to join Nick and Marv.

Cody turned and ran upstairs. He tried to ignore all the noise at his back. There were muffled cries of pain from the stairs, intermingled with the sound of the Exterminators' arrival in San Antonio.

He reached the seventh floor and found Rachel sitting inside her sleeping bag. Despite the chaos unfolding elsewhere, she looked fairly relaxed about the situation.

"They're here aren't they?" she said.

Cody nodded.

"Are you ready?" he asked.

"Yeah."

"It's time to go to work," Cody said. "The others are making a path for us."

Rachel climbed out of the sleeping bag and looked around the room. "What about our things?"

"It doesn't matter," Cody said. He ran over to his sleeping bag and gathered a couple of items together. "You got your coat and gloves, right? Your hat?"

"I'm wearing them," Rachel said.

"That's all you need."

They ran towards the door. Cody offered his hand but Rachel didn't take it. He wasn't sure if she'd deliberately snubbed him or whether she hadn't noticed the offer. Either way, it stung.

They hurried downstairs, edging closer to the sound of gunfire.

Fortunately, Marv, Nick and Crazy Diamond were on a roll. They'd forced the ragtags back to the first floor and that's where the action was taking place. It allowed just enough of a gap for Cody and Rachel to bypass the shooting and sneak through the dark towards the back exit. As they approached the door, Cody checked the magazine in the Glock. He was carrying extra rounds in the inside pocket of his parka. It was the only thing he'd brought with him from upstairs.

They reached the back door, located next to the Rand's car park. Cody took a deep breath and opened the door slowly. Rachel was tucked in close at his back.

Cody peered outside and couldn't see anything at first. Seconds later, he was met by the high-pitched crack of a pistol shot, which pushed his head back inside the building.

Rachel was standing at his back, a look of curiosity on her face.

Cody shook his head.

"How many?" she said.

"Two I think," Cody said. "Maybe three."

As quietly as he could, he opened the door again.

Cody looked outside and saw two dark shapes standing in the middle of North Main Avenue. Two ragtags keeping watch. They must have been pretty sure of themselves because they were standing out in the open with only the darkness for cover.

No wonder they were so confident, Cody thought. They'd seen Mackenzie's gifts and had become hypnotized by the man's otherworldly power and promises of immortality. They must have believed they were every bit as special as Mackenzie was if they too were going to be saved by their masters.

But of course the ragtags wouldn't listen if anyone told them the truth. The truth, the hopelessness of it, would drive them mad.

Cody looked around for a way out. He noticed a constant stream of colored light floating up through cracks in the road and drifting towards the sky. It looked like the invasion was also seeping up from the bowels of the Earth.

"We see you!" one of the ragtags shouted to Cody. "You ain't going nowhere mister. End of the line for you."

They fired at the door, forcing Cody back inside.

"We don't have time for this crap," Cody said. "We should have been on the roof ages ago."

He looked at Rachel.

"Is there anyway you can distract them?" Cody said. "Make a noise or create a disturbance at their back, just long enough for them to look the other way. I only need a couple of seconds."

Rachel took a step back and closed her eyes. She hung her head low in concentration.

Cody turned back to the door and teased it open again. He felt the cold air of black winter scraping at his skin like a claw. His muscles were taut. His finger was like a block of ice hovering over the Glock's trigger.

There was a sudden crashing noise nearby. It sounded like a door being kicked open from somewhere across the street.

The ragtags jumped back with fright. They looked over their shoulder at the same time, pointing their weapons into the darkness.

"Who's there?" one of them said.

Cody rushed outside. He took aim and fired, hitting both men square in the back. Two shots and they dropped like stones. One didn't move but the other – a fat bearded man who couldn't have been much older than twenty – crawled along the ground on his elbows for a few seconds before dropping face first onto the snow.

"C'mon," Cody said, turning back to Rachel. He grabbed her by the arm and they ran outside.

They heard gunfire from the other side of the building. Cody had a feeling that Crazy Diamond, Nick, and Marv were in for a long standoff with the ragtags. But that could only be a good thing as long as his friends didn't get killed. Let Mackenzie think that Rachel was still hiding out upstairs on the seventh floor. That would allow Cody to get Rachel to the Robert E. Lee building.

Cody looked up and saw the enemy everywhere.

Streaks of free-floating light and striking color danced across the city. Were these the monsters? Cody had half expected the Exterminators to look like Godzilla or some other bulked up prehistoric creature, clawing their way through the gates with brute force before jumping down to Earth to run rampage across the city.

That might have been better.

CHAPTER SEVEN

Cody and Rachel hurried along North Main Avenue.

They lost their footing several times as they walked over the soft snow. The sound of gunshots faded in their ears, and the colorful display of the Exterminators was a constant reminder of the terrible urgency of their situation.

Cody could hear the low-pitched whale noise of the Exterminators. It was everywhere, creeping up through the cracks in the city streets, through the drains, bouncing off the walls and up there in the sky too. But that wasn't all. The loudest thing was the crashing and rumbling of the city as it was being torn apart. Cody could hear large chunks of stone and metal falling from great heights onto the streets.

The ground was swelling up under their feet. In several places, the surface of the road would push up like a giant hematoma forming on the skin. Then it would go back down again. Then it would come back up. It was like something was alive underground, poking its massive head up in a probing manner, looking for a way to break out of its den. The hard surface of the road looked soft, almost like liquid as it rose up and down at regular intervals.

The three gates watched from afar like medieval kings observing the battle from a distant hillside. They spilled over with color, which seeped out like blood from a wound, trickling down towards San Antonio.

At last, Cody and Rachel reached the Robert E. Lee building. Their tired legs climbed up to the roof faster than they'd ever done before.

As they ran towards the edge of the building, a thin streak of red and gray light swam through the air towards them. It lingered in front of Cody, floating just inches from his face.

Cody looked directly into the light and saw Kate's face staring back at him.

She was lying on the floor of a filthy apartment, one covered in broken glass and half-empty takeout boxes. There were rats on the floor, scurrying back and forth in slow motion. Kate was screaming in terror, her face twisted and unrecognizable. She looked at Cody and crawled backwards. *Wriggled*. Her naked body was revealed as she made her retreat. There were at least a dozen needles stuck in the crooks of her arms – dirty, giant syringes spilling over with a brownish liquid that Cody knew was heroin. At the point where each needle pierced her skin, Kate's ghoulish white flesh had mutated into a horde of hungry mouths, all of them opening and closing, sucking on the point of the needle like a baby on a pacifier.

Kate's eyes were bloodshot. She reached across the sheet of red and gray mist, begging Cody to come to her.

"Please," she said. "I need you Cody."

Cody walked forwards. Something – a faint whimper at the back of his mind – protested. It said no. But his legs decided to ignore the command and take charge of the situation. They pushed Cody towards her. Kate needed him, didn't she? This was his chance to be there for her. It was a second chance because he'd failed her once before and that sure as hell wasn't going to happen again.

Cody reached through the mist. Kate nodded, assuring him with her doll-like eyes that it was the right thing to do. She was smiling now. Her hand, with dried blood encrusted on her finger-nails, reached for his face.

Cody took a step towards the edge of the building.

They were almost touching.

"Kate," he said.

One more step and...

Something pulled at Cody from behind. The sudden jolting sensation forced him to let out of a yelp of protest. The mist retreated quickly, taking Kate's disappointed face with it.

Rachel was standing at Cody's back. She had a firm grip on his coat pocket.

A grim expression was etched on her face.

"Don't let them in," Rachel said. She tapped a finger off the side of her head.

Cody's head was spinning, like it was trapped in between being blind drunk and the hangover from hell.

The swirling fog of red and gray had vanished.

"Kate," Cody said. He looked at Rachel and felt his head clearing. "I saw your..."

"It wasn't real," Rachel said. "They'll show you whatever you want to see. Make you do things you don't want to do. Don't look into the light Dad – never look into the light."

Cody nodded. He ran a hand through his dirty blond hair while a gust of cold air scraped against his face.

He looked up at the gates. A vicious frothing sound snarled in his ears. Cody didn't know if it was coming from the gates or inside his head.

Rachel stepped towards the edge of the building, just like she'd done during her training. The three gates towered above her, bleeding an endless river of light and color.

"Close the gates Rachel," Cody said. "You can do it."

Rachel held her arms out at both sides. The shield crackled into life, spreading quickly over her forearms and covering the rest of her body.

There was little he could do to help her now. But he could at least be there, standing beside her for whatever it was worth.

Cody took his place at her side.

Rachel's eyes were tightly closed. Her face was screwed up in a mask of deep concentration. Cody wanted to say something to his daughter, to find the right words of encouragement and most of all, to let her know that she wasn't alone.

But it was a lie. As far as this fight went, she *was* alone.

She let out a muffled grunt and her arms stiffened. Cody watched her footing – she was so close to the edge of the ten-story building that he thought he was going to have a heart attack.

He heard a noise from the sky. It sounded like distant cannon fire.

Cody looked up at the gates and his heart bounced with joy. Something was happening up there. The gate on the left was fading – it was noticeably duller than the other two, which were still spitting out a fresh barrage of color. But the left gate was barren. That door had been shut. It was like Cody was looking up at a wilting rose sitting next to two others in full bloom.

"It's working," Cody said. He could barely contain the excitement in his voice. "Keep going Rachel."

He looked at her.

Rachel was straining badly. Cody could see the rope-like veins sticking out on her neck and head. It reminded him of weightlifters that he'd seen on TV at the Olympics, lifting heavier and heavier. It was only after they were squatting down with the weight of the world on their shoulders that they realized what they were up against.

"Dad," Rachel said. Her voice was shaking. "It's too heavy."

Cody didn't know what to say to her. Was he supposed to tell her to stop and try again? Take a deep breath and reset? But he knew that even if she did that, it wasn't going to get any easier.

She was their only hope of closing the gates. Of turning this thing off.

Cody watched as the invading army floated across the city. They were translucent marauders from another dimension. Long strips of multicolored light cut through massive buildings like a sword slicing through a pile of bamboo sticks. Large blocks of stone, wood and metal crashed to the ground. There was a permanent clattering noise in San Antonio. Elsewhere the light continued to drift out of the ground like steam.

The marine-like call of the Exterminators was constant. They were the hidden conductors of all this, orchestrating the destruction from the shadows.

"Rachel," Cody said, watching his daughter's body tremble under the pressure. He'd never felt so helpless in his life. He didn't know whether to grab her and run or to stand firm and encourage her further.

"Fight them," Cody said through gritted teeth. "Hang in there baby. You're stronger than they are. You've worked hard for this and..."

Something hard slammed into Cody's chest. It felt like a monster truck going straight through him and he was knocked backwards across the rooftop.

"Dad!"

Rachel's voice sounded far away.

Cody rolled like a soccer ball along the roof. Seconds later, he felt the solid base underneath slip away. His body hung in midair for a second and it felt like time had stopped altogether. It was during that brief moment that his fingers, which must have been running on automatic pilot, grasped for something – anything to keep him from plummeting down ten stories to the street.

He grabbed a hold of the ledge.

With a cry of terror, Cody held on for dear life to the side of the building. The ledge, icy and narrow, felt unwelcoming. His legs dangled in midair like clothes hung out to dry in a stiff breeze. The giant hotel sign, with its promise of air-conditioned rooms, towered over him.

Cody tried to pull himself back up. Looking across the rooftop, he saw that Rachel had stopped fighting the Exterminators and now she'd turned around and was staring at him with look of panic on her face.

"Dad!" she cried out. "Get back on the roof!"

"Keep going!" Cody yelled. His voice was hidden beneath the sound of the city being pulled apart. "Don't stop Rachel. I'm alright. You have to close the..."

One hand slipped off the ledge. Cody's body jerked downwards. He gasped and clawed for the side of the building again.

He saw Rachel running across the roof towards him. The shield fizzled out around her and Cody saw the left gate, the one that had been wilting moments earlier, surge back to life. It swelled up like a peacock stretching out its magnificent tail. A flood of heat and color surged back into its gray center.

Rachel kept running towards her dad. Cody could hear her breathing heavy as if she was on the brink of collapse. She thrust out an arm, reaching for the ledge. Reaching for Cody.

"Take my hand," she called out.

Rachel was almost at the edge of the rooftop when she let out a sudden shriek. Cody watched in horror as a cloud-shaped dart of blue mist shot towards her and scooped Rachel off the ground, making her look like a feather caught in the wind.

Rachel hovered in the air, caught within the Exterminators' grip.

The blue mist slowly wrapped itself around her.

"Rachel!"

Cody gritted his teeth and fought to get back onto the roof. But his arms were sluggish and heavy. Despite the urgency, he had to be careful or his fingers would slip on the icy ledge and then he'd be no help to anyone.

"Rachel!" he yelled. "Hang on. I'm coming."

Cody pushed the upper half of his body over the ledge. He was almost there when he heard a high-pitched scream. He looked up and saw the blue mist shoot Rachel through the air like she was an arrow from a bow. She flew over Cody's head and he looked over his shoulder only to see his daughter plummeting over the side of the Robert E. Lee building.

"RACHEL!"

Cody's body fell backwards. But somehow his fingers maintained their grip on the ledge.

Rachel dropped to the street at a frightening speed. Everything else in the world stopped for Cody in that moment.

"No!" he yelled.

Cody watched as the shield lit up around his daughter's body, just seconds before impact. She crashed into the black snow with a soft thud. To Cody's immense relief, Rachel bounced back to her feet as if she'd done no more than jump off a doorstep.

"Thank God," Cody said.

From his vantage point, Cody saw a sea of light drifting towards Rachel. It was coming from all sides, slowly working its way towards her. There were a few scattered streaks of white mist buzzing around Cody's head too. He refused to look at them, concentrating only on Rachel, as well as maintaining his grip on the roof.

Had the Exterminators tried to kill Rachel? Cody didn't understand. He thought they wanted to take her back alive. Maybe they did. Maybe the Exterminators knew she'd come to no harm and what just happened was their way of showing her who was boss this time around.

"Bastards," Cody said.

From below, Rachel looked up at her dad. Their eyes met but from such a distance, Cody couldn't understand what message she was trying to communicate, if any. He saw Rachel glancing at the pack of light drifting towards her. She looked up at Cody again and then ran towards the car park.

"Rachel!" Cody yelled. "Where are you going?"

But whether she heard him or not, she didn't stop.

Cody's arms were getting heavier by the second. He knew he had to get back on the roof while he still could. The white light that had hovered around him was now floating towards the car park.

The roar of a car engine caught Cody's ears.

He looked to his right just in time to see a black SUV skidding out of the car park and onto the road. The car jerked back and forth as the tires struggled to grip the surface. With the colored mist closing in fast, the SUV took off at a ferocious speed.

"Rachel," Cody said. "What are you doing?"

With a grunt, he pulled himself back onto the roof. One slip and Cody was a goner. Fortunately his gloved fingers had a solid grip this time and he hauled himself over the edge.

His body landed on the rooftop with a crashing thud. Cody lifted his head and looked around to see if there was any malicious light on his tail. There wasn't. He picked himself up and ran full speed towards the door that led to the stairs. But he was barely halfway there when his worn down boots lost their grip on the snow. This time his hands couldn't help him. Cody's body flipped backwards. It was a clumsy, brutal somersault and when he crashed to the ground it was his head that took the brunt of the fall.

Cody lay on his back and stared up at the gates. Now he was the one that was floating – floating towards the three suns in the black sky. There was no noise, almost. But Cody could still hear one thing as the lights went out in his mind – it was the faint mechanical hum of a car in the distance.

CHAPTER EIGHT

Rachel barely had enough strength left to control the car.

The shield was fizzling out around her. It was hissing and spitting like an angry snake, almost as if it was crying out in distress.

Her mind, which should have been focused on controlling the car, was still thinking about her dad. She'd left him back there clinging onto the edge of the building. How could she have done that? She'd driven off and after everything he'd done for Rachel, what must he have thought of her?

Still, she'd done the right thing.

She hadn't run off for her own sake. When she'd noticed that small cloud of white mist drifting towards her dad, she knew he was in trouble. Deep trouble. Rachel also knew that there was only one way to help him. The light would follow her if she took off in a hurry. All the light. If she hadn't done it the mist would have planted another hallucination in her dad's mind. And that would have been his last.

As long as they were chasing her, it would buy him time. Time to get back on the roof. Time to run downstairs and find the others.

Besides, she was no good to them. All those early morning

training sessions, the long months of preparation – it had been for nothing in the end. Whatever power she had taken from the Exterminators, it was nothing compared to what they still had left over. She couldn't compete with them, not in a million years.

She wasn't strong enough.

The car skidded to the right.

Rachel felt herself losing control of the SUV. It felt like she was playing a video game with a faulty controller – a game in which the rules were quickly getting lost in the fog of her mind. Her reactions were sluggish. The battle with the Exterminators had taken everything out of her and even as the car raced through the darkness she could feel the drowsiness taking over her body.

Sleep. More than anything, she wanted to close her eyes and sleep.

But she fought through it. Rachel pulled the car to the left, skidding onto West Martin Street. It continued straight and then cut another left onto North Zarzamora Street. The car swerved back and forth. No matter how hard she fought, it was slipping away from her.

Must sleep.

Rachel decided to switch to manual even though she didn't really know how to drive a car properly. She grabbed the wheel and jerked it, while reaching for the brake with her foot. Thank God she was tall for her age.

But manual wasn't much better than her own unique form of automatic. Either way, she had to concentrate and she didn't have it left in her.

The car was out of control.

Rachel slammed the brake down as best she could, pulling the wheel left and forcing the SUV off road.

It sped into the car park of a small hair salon.

As Rachel slammed the brakes hard, the SUV did a spinning dance across the icy car park. Rachel shrieked as one side of the vehicle lifted up off the ground, tipping over so that it came crashing down on the driver's side. The SUV kept sliding across the car park and there was a crunching noise as it hit the front of the hair salon. An airbag exploded out of the steering wheel and almost smothered Rachel.

Everything went quiet after that.

Rachel was still conscious in the driver's seat. Her body felt stiff and a little sore from the impact but apart from that she was fine. There was a strange smell in her nostrils – it was as if she could smell the burning heat of the metal that had been ground away by the surface of the road.

She started thinking about the car crashes that she'd seen in the movies. About how those cars always exploded not long after the crash.

Get up. Get out.

Rachel tried to sit up. A jolt of hot pain shot up and down her body but she ignored it and kept moving. She was lucky that her dad had drilled the importance of fastening her seatbelt into her at an early age. He'd played those crash test dummy safety videos to her where the dummies went flying through the windshield. With that in mind, it could have been much worse. She didn't feel like anything was broken but what did she know?

Rachel grabbed the handle of the passenger side door. It was the only way she was getting out of the car now that the driver's side was flat to the ground. After a brief struggle with the metal handle, she pushed the door open and climbed out through the passenger side. Then she jumped down onto the snowy surface and immediately felt the cold wrap its claws around her throat.

She staggered off, putting some distance between herself and the SUV. It hadn't exploded yet so maybe it wasn't going to.

Rachel ran onto the middle of the road and glanced towards downtown. The city was drowning in a deep sea of smoke and noise and light. Whatever had chased her to the car park was nowhere to be seen now. From what she could tell, it looked like the Exterminators were destroying the city first, not to mention everything human that still lived and breathed there.

Rachel doubted they'd forget about her. She'd be next.

But what about her dad? Had they forgotten about him? Or had they gone back to find him on that rooftop ledge?

She would have to go back and find out. Even though she couldn't beat the Exterminators, she wouldn't leave the only family she had to suffer alone. She had to try. She had to do something. And her dad – why had she been so horrible to him before about the things he'd said to her on the roof that day? Turns out he was only saying what everyone else, including Rachel, had been too afraid to say.

She couldn't win. And he'd been right.

Rachel walked forward and her legs turned to jelly. She dropped onto the road, landing on her knees. After a brief dizzy spell, she fell onto her chest and felt herself sinking into a deep sleep. She knew that it was dangerous in cold temperatures like these, but nonetheless it was such an inviting thought.

Stop. Go to sleep.

Black snow clung to her lips. It tasted cold and salty.

She lay there for a while, staring into space and waiting for sleep to come. Wondering if she was dying. Wondering what would happen to her dad and the others.

It wasn't supposed to be like this.

She looked straight ahead and there was something on the road. It was moving. Coming closer.

Rachel lifted her head off the ground.

A large vehicle rolled to a stop about twenty feet away. A pair of bright, narrow headlights pointed at Rachel – it was a fierce glow that came towards her, like being caught in the path of two giant spotlights.

The school bus.

Rachel dropped her head back onto the black snow. She didn't have the energy to run from Mackenzie or to fight him. But she didn't have to look at him. She had that at least. Rachel kept her eyes closed, listening to the bus door hiss as it opened. Her ears followed the sound of footsteps crunching over the snow towards her. She kept her face buried in the snow. No matter what, Rachel wouldn't give Mackenzie the satisfaction of seeing the defeat in her eyes.

The last thing she felt before blacking out was the sensation of being carried. It felt like falling.

Rachel opened her eyes.

The sound of distant thunder had awoken her.

The first thing she remembered was the school bus and it made her sit up straight. Where was she? She was in a sleeping bag but it wasn't hers. Looking around, she saw a massive hall lit by hundreds of candles. Her mind scrambled to make sense of her surroundings.

She was in a church – a big one.

Rachel glanced towards the roof and realized she was lying under a dome-like structure, located at the head of the church. This was the altar and it was easily the prettiest altar she'd ever seen in her life. The walls were made up of a simple grayish-white stone. There was a lavish looking shrine to her left with a cluster of meticulously crafted angels all looking up at Jesus.

To her right was a huge archway that separated the altar from the rest of the church. Behind that was a long aisle that led to the back of the building – or the front for all Rachel knew – with a stack of wooden pews located on either side. There were more statues and a vast array of breathtaking stained glass windows down there. The woodwork and the stonework displays scattered throughout were equally as beautiful.

She heard hushed voices at the back.

Looking over that way, Rachel saw a group of about twenty children gathered around the last two rows of pews. Their heads were leaning close to one another, as if they were in the middle of a serious discussion. She saw some of their lips moving but the voices were muted and the words out of reach. The children were dressed in a variety of plain winter clothing – thick padded jackets, parkas, scarves and beanie hats – all of which looked several sizes too big for them.

Rachel blinked hard several times and her brow furrowed in concentration. Who were they? Had Mackenzie rounded up more innocent kids to hand over to the Exterminators?

She pressed a hand against her temple. It felt tender.

The children noticed that Rachel was sitting up straight on the altar. Their hushed meeting stopped and they shifted in their seats, looking over at her with wide-eyed, curious expressions. A few of the shorter kids got to their feet, as if to try and get a better view. Their breath was a fine mist as they stared at Rachel. They looked at one another. There were some muffled whispers and then one of the children – a lanky boy of about fourteen, stood up and hurried through a large door behind them.

None of the remaining kids spoke or tried to approach Rachel.

Rachel sat in silence, listening to a plethora of crashing, shaking and shattering noises from downtown. How long had she been sleeping anyway?

Her thoughts inevitably returned to her dad. Was he still alive? She couldn't bear the thought that something bad had happened to him.

Panic spilled back into her thoughts. She should never have run off like that.

The door swung open at the back of the hall. The lanky boy

stepped through the doorway and using his back to keep the door open, stepped aside as if someone else was coming up behind him.

A set of slow footsteps approached.

Rachel's heart was racing. She sat up straight, fearing the worst.

But it wasn't Mackenzie who walked into the church. It was an old lady that stepped through the open doorway, shuffling past the lanky boy without a word and moving slowly into the main hall.

There was a tray of food in her hands.

Rachel looked on, both curious and fearful. She couldn't tell how old the woman was. She could never tell that sort of thing with old people because well, they all looked the same age to her – they looked old. Maybe the woman was about seventy. Not much older than that probably. She was a heavyset figure with dark wrinkled skin. Might have been Mexican or something like that. She walked towards Rachel slowly, wincing with every other step. A bright red coat, which was buttoned up tightly, was wrapped around her ample frame. She looked at Rachel and her eyes were kind, tucked in behind a pair of cat eye, thick-rimmed glasses. Her hair was white and curly, the sort of haircut that Rachel knew only as a 'granny perm.'

The lanky boy helped the woman step onto the altar. The boy didn't go with her though. He looked curious enough, but there was a hesitancy about him that suggested he was a little afraid to get too close to Rachel.

"Hello Rachel," the old woman said, approaching with the tray in her hands. "My name is Anna. The children call me Grandma Anna."

She offered the tray to Rachel. Rachel got up and took it off the old woman to save her having to bend down. She sat back down on the sleeping bag. There was a bowl of soggy looking fruit in the center of the tray and next to that, a tall glass of water and a plate of shortbread biscuits.

"We don't have much to offer I'm afraid," Grandma Anna said. "But it'll do you good. Make you strong again."

She encouraged Rachel with a smile.

"Eat," she said. "It's very important that you do."

Rachel lifted up the bowl of fruit and dipped the plastic spoon inside. Tinned peaches – what else? She took in a mouthful and then dropped the spoon back into the bowl. The familiar sweet sugary taste revived her. She picked up the spoon and ate some more, wiping a dribble of peach juice off her chin.

The old woman looked pleased.

"That's good," Grandma Anna said. "You're quite alright with us my dear. Don't you worry about a thing."

The other children had quietly crept forward down the aisle. Now they were sitting in the pews nearest the altar, like eager worshippers who'd arrived in church early to grab the best seats.

"Where am I?" Rachel said.

"You're in a safe place," Grandma Anna said. "The safest place of all one might say. This is the Basilica of the National Shrine of the Little Flower. Have you ever been here before?"

Rachel shook her head. "Are we still in San Antonio?"

Grandma Anna nodded.

"Thank God this place was unspoiled," she said, looking up at the statue of Jesus and the angels on the altar. "You know, I like to think it's no coincidence that the few children left in this city can take shelter under this roof. Including you my dear. God isn't done with us yet Rachel MacLeod. I truly believe that and with any luck, so will you."

The children watched Rachel with riveted, unblinking expressions. With so many eyes on her, Rachel tried not to dribble any more fruit juice down the front of her mouth while she ate.

Grandma Anna pointed to the glass of water on the tray.

"Drink too," she said. "I'm afraid we don't have much time.

You have to recover from this quickly Rachel and I believe, thanks to your gifts and youth, that you will. The city can't bear this assault for much longer. We have to act."

Rachel shook her head. "I'm so tired."

"I'm not surprised you're tired dear child," Grandma Anna said. "Nobody has given more than you in this fight Rachel. None of us here can even begin to imagine what you've been going through these past few months. What it's like to be you. To have what you have."

"It doesn't matter," Rachel said. "It wasn't enough."

The old woman kept smiling.

"How do you know my name?" Rachel asked.

"We've been watching you for quite some time," Grandma Anna said. "Watching what you've been doing every morning."

Rachel looked at the audience sitting on the pews.

"All these children survived the Black Storm?" she asked.

"Of course they did," Grandma Anna said. "Let me tell you something Rachel – if anyone was going to survive this hell on earth, it would be the children."

Rachel's face took on a puzzled expression.

"What do you mean?"

"We've got a lot to talk about," Grandma Anna said. "And I'm afraid, so little time left to do it."

Rachel took a sip of water. It was freezing cold, like it had ice in it. Then she looked at Grandma Anna and frowned.

"How do you know me?"

"Everybody knows about you," Grandma Anna said. She spoke in a soft whisper that Rachel could barely hear. "You're the girl who took on the Black Widow and won. It was the talk of this city during the last days. In such a time of despair, it was the only bright thing we had left. It was precious – it was hope."

"How did you find out about that?" Rachel asked. "About the Black Widow?"

Grandma Anna looked over her shoulder. There was a serene expression on her face as she gazed at the children sitting on the pews.

"I don't know how the news got out sweetheart," she said. "Maybe you and your friends weren't the only ones in the airport that day. Someone must have seen you I suppose. But word did get out and thank goodness for that. Most people didn't believe or understand at first. I didn't understand either – not until I saw for myself."

"Saw what?" Rachel said.

"The children," Grandma Anna said. "Until I saw the children."

Rachel shrugged. She wasn't following the old woman's train of thought. "What about them?"

Grandma Anna's gaze fell to the floor. She nodded slowly, smiling to herself.

"The Black Storm came here to punish mankind," she said. "Now I don't know much for sure sweetie but I believe that this storm was intended as a form of justice, not divine justice, but something almost as grand as the Lord. Something bigger than us."

Grandma Anna pointed a wrinkled finger to the ceiling.

"Something decided we had to go," she said. "Perhaps they assumed that the world would be better off without humans in it. Can't blame them I suppose, not after the things we've done. The Black Storm was brutal and brilliant in its efficiency. But it wasn't perfect. You see in all their wisdom, our judge, jury and executioners thought all humankind equally guilty. They either didn't consider or understand that the children were innocent of whatever crimes they'd decided to punish us for."

Rachel reached for a biscuit on the tray. She picked one up and took a small bite, all the while listening closely to the woman as she talked.

"The Black Storm came to punish the guilty," Grandma Anna

said. "But the children were innocent. And it's that innocence that made them immune to the Black Fever. It was easy to miss at the time of course – I should know, it took me long enough to see for myself. When the Black Storm hit San Antonio, I ran as far as I could with my daughter-in-law and two grandchildren. We got in the car and drove off to a safe place. The Black Widow followed us of course."

"She followed my dad and me too," Rachel said. "When we ran."

Grandma Anna's lips curled into a smile.

"You saw her?" she asked. "The Black Widow spoke to you?"

"Yes," Rachel said.

"But she couldn't infect you with the Fever," Grandma Anna said. "I saw it for myself with my grandchildren. Then I saw it with others too and that's when I started to notice a pattern. The adults were easily infected when the Black Widow spoke to them but I never saw a child that succumbed to the Fever. Not one. Of course the reason that nobody noticed was that most children died anyway – but they died at the hands of the adults who'd been driven mad, not by the Fever itself."

Grandma Anna paused. She fidgeted with a loose button on her coat.

"And then there's you Rachel MacLeod," she said. "You're the only one who attacked *her*. You turned the tables on the Black Widow. Incredible. They say the sky went blue, just for a second. What I wouldn't give to have been there and to have seen it with my own eyes."

Rachel took another biscuit off the plate. Her third or fourth. Now that she'd started eating she realized how hungry she was.

"What about the Sliders?" Rachel said, talking in between bites. She could feel the kids gawping at her while she ate and was starting to wish they'd give it a rest. "The Sliders attacked us at the airport. There were lots of children there and they all died."

"It wasn't the Sliders that killed those children Rachel," Grandma Anna said. "It was the adults – their parents, their families who did the terrible deed. Yes it's a terrible thing and of course you didn't notice at the time because it was so awful."

"I stopped the Sliders," Rachel said, putting a half-eaten biscuit back on the plate. She took a brief sip of water. "I was able to control them. Before the thing at Brackenridge Park, before I took the Exterminators' power away. I'm not sure how I did it."

"What were you doing when you charged at the Black Widow in the airport?" Grandma Anna said.

"Helping my Dad."

"And with the Sliders?"

"The same."

Grandma Anna nodded. "All children have it in them," she said. "But you're the only one I know of that took them on."

Rachel looked at the lanky boy who'd helped Grandma Anna onto the altar. His hair was short and spiky, his features long and angular.

"How old are you?" Rachel said.

"I'm t-twelve," he said, sitting up straight on the bench as if he'd been called to attention. "Most people think I'm older b-but I'm just tall for my age."

Some of the other kids giggled behind him.

"Me too," Rachel said, looking at the boy. "Well I'm eleven but I'm tall for my age too."

The boy's face turned bright red. Even his ears were blushing.

"These things," Grandma Anna said. "They might be technologically superior. They might be superior to us in every way imaginable. But we know something they don't. These things..."

"Exterminators," Rachel said. "We call them Exterminators."

Grandma Anna's face lit up. Oddly enough, she seemed to like that.

"These Exterminators," she said, "they have a weakness. They

423

don't know that children are immune to their powers of mind trickery. It's *you* they want Rachel. They think that it's something in you – something special about you that they don't understand. Tell me something child, did you have gifts before the Black Storm? Any sort of psychic gifts?"

Rachel shook her head. "I don't think so."

"Your gift is the natural immunity of a child," Grandma Anna said. "Your other gift however, was courage. You stood up to the Black Widow in the airport and that was the beginning of your journey. You showed us that tanks and guns and bombs were of no use in this war. It's the children – the children are the ones who can beat the Exterminators."

Grandma Anna sat there, giggling quietly.

"And now you *are* gifted Rachel," she said. "In a supernatural sense I mean. They tried to steal you from us and instead you stole from them. Like I said, we've been watching you for a while. Your mind is incredible. *Their* power – it runs inside you. That means – it *has* to mean – that whatever they can do, you can do."

"How long have you been watching us?" Rachel asked.

"For some time now my dear," the old woman said. "Of course we meant to introduce ourselves and in fact, we were on the brink of doing so when they came a little earlier than we'd hoped for."

Rachel looked at the plate of food sitting in front of her.

"What am I supposed to do now?" she said.

"Fight them," Grandma Anna said. "You're supposed to fight them Rachel."

Rachel pushed the plate away. "I already tried fighting them," she said. "And it's no good. I can't win."

There was a sympathetic smile on the old woman's face.

"Dear Rachel," she said. "My poor girl. It's not fair to put so much pressure on the shoulders of one so young and yet all the pressure *is* on you. But not just you – you and all the children in this church. You can still be the future if you want to be."

"How can there be a future anymore?" Rachel said. "Almost everyone's dead."

Grandma Anna was about to say something but she was cut off by a loud blast in the distance. It sounded like an explosion or maybe it was another of San Antonio's finest skyscrapers hitting the ground.

"You need a little more rest," Grandma Anna said, looking closely at Rachel. "Another hour I'd say."

"My dad needs me," Rachel said. She stood up and brushed the crumbs off her coat. Quiet gasps floated across from the benches.

Grandma Anna hobbled over to Rachel. She put a hand on the girl's shoulder and guided her back down to the sleeping bag.

"Sleep now child," Grandma Anna said. "An hour – we can spare no more than that. When you wake up we'll talk some more. Oh my dear girl, there's so much to talk about tonight. So many secrets still to be revealed."

CHAPTER NINE

Rachel slept for a while in the sleeping bag on the altar.

When she awoke for a second time, a fresh plate of food was sitting beside her, alongside another glass of water.

She sat up in the bag and stretched her arms over her head. Her body was stiff and creaky like she'd been asleep for days, but to her surprise most of the aches and pains of the car crash were gone. Whether that was down to youth or her gifts she didn't know.

Rachel pulled at the collar of her coat, bringing it together to ward off the cold from her neck. She tugged at the hood, bringing it over her forehead. It was freezing inside the church even if the candlelight atmosphere did make it look cozy. Rachel hated the cold – it had been so long since she'd felt the sun on her face that she'd almost forgotten what the rays felt like. Sometimes she dreamed about the sun and about walking barefoot on a beach of golden sand. There were always lots of other people in her dream too, sunbathing, playing beach volleyball or swimming in the ocean. It felt so real she could almost taste the salt in the Pacific.

She reached for the glass of water. As she drank it all down, there was a flurry of movement to her right. The other kids were still sitting on the wooden benches, watching her. Had they been there all the time while she slept? Now that she was awake they didn't seem to be mindful or embarrassed about the fact that they were still staring at her.

Rachel took a sip of water. There was no sign of the old woman.

The kids muttered under their breath to one another. There were all sorts of ages down there on the benches – the lanky boy with the spiky hair was the oldest looking, although he'd said he was only twelve. The others might have been anywhere between the ages of five and thirteen.

The spiky-haired boy whispered something into the ear of a pretty black girl sitting beside him. The girl nodded and said something back. Then she shoved the boy off the bench with a surprising amount of brute force. The boy was thrust forward, an anxious look on his face as he crept towards the altar. Towards Rachel. He was wearing a long black winter coat, several sizes too big, that went all the way down to his feet. A matching pair of fingerless gloves clung to his long, pale fingers.

"Are you okay?" Rachel asked the boy.

He jumped back, albeit briefly. The other children giggled at his back.

The boy nodded his head.

"Yeah f-f-fine," he said. "It's just..."

"Where's the old lady?" Rachel said, cutting in. "What did she say her name was? Grandma Anna?"

The boy swallowed hard. He opened his mouth but no words came out.

"Sleeping," the black girl said. She got to her feet and walked over to the edge of the altar.

"Don't mind Stutter here," the girl said, pointing a thumb at the boy. "He's the oldest so he takes it on himself to be our spokesperson. Trouble is he can't speak too good and that's not much use is it? Not if you want to be a spokesperson and all."

Rachel looked at Stutter. She thought briefly about her dad whose breakthrough role as an actor had come in the 1980s in *The Forever Boys* where he'd played a kid with an even worse stutter than the tall boy. He'd done such a good job in the movie that later on in life, much to his annoyance, people still referred to Rachel's dad as the stutter kid.

"What's your name?" Rachel asked the girl.

"Tegan," the girl said.

An uncomfortable silence followed.

"Are you guys okay?" Rachel asked. "You're not scared of me are you?"

Stutter shook his head and tried to say something. When the words stalled at the tip of his tongue, he turned around to the others for support. But the other kids weren't exactly jumping in to save him. Rachel gave Stutter and the kids an encouraging smile. They looked like a bunch of abandoned children whose parents had forgotten about them. Like items of lost luggage that hadn't been claimed.

Tegan looked at Rachel and shrugged. There was mildly embarrassed look on her face.

"Yeah I guess we're acting kind of weird," she said. "Thing is Rachel, you're like a legend around these parts. We've been hearing stories about you from Grandma Anna for a long time now. Then she took us out in the bus and we saw for ourselves what you could do. Wow, all that cool stuff with turning the lights on and off – it's awesome. And then you tried to grab our bus – that was insane! Let's face it – you're the girl who stood up to the Black Widow. That makes you a legend in my book. When I saw that ghost woman for the first time I damn near pissed my pants."

There was more giggling at their backs.

Rachel smiled. "Me too," she said.

"Yeah?" Tegan said. "Man, she was so creepy with those eyes. And yet according to Grandma Anna, I could have kicked her ass just like you did. But I guess I didn't have your guts, huh? How were we supposed to know she couldn't hurt us with her mind voodoo?"

A couple of the other kids crept closer to the altar, as if reassured by the progress of the conversation so far. Stutter was standing at the front of the group, grinning at Rachel. It was clear by the way he was shifting back and forth that he wanted to say something.

Tegan looked at the boy and frowned.

"Spit it out Stutter," she said. "You might look like the village idiot but you don't need to act like one."

Stutter nodded.

"How do you d-do that thing?" he asked Rachel. He took a deep breath before tackling the second sentence. "That th-thing when all the light comes up on your body. It's so cool."

More giggling from the benches.

Rachel thought she heard somebody whisper 'Stutter loves Rachel'.

"The shield?" Rachel said, ignoring the rest of the kids. "I think about it and it just happens."

"Make your eyes go black!" a little kid with red hair said. He edged closer to the altar, but stayed behind Tegan and Stutter. The boy was tiny, barely reaching up to Stutter's waist.

"Maybe later," Rachel said. "It kind of freaks me out to be honest."

Rachel hadn't been around any kids her own age for a long time. Now they were acting like she was the most popular kid in school. Rachel guessed that this was what it had been like for her dad back in his Hollywood heyday. He'd been a big star a long time ago, way back in the eighties. All that attention, it was easy to see how people could get addicted to it.

The little red haired kid stepped ahead of the others.

"They call me Benji," he said.

"Hi Benji," Rachel said.

"Your dad's Cody MacLeod isn't he?" Benji said. The boy's eyes shone with excitement.

"Yeah," Rachel said.

She was used to people asking about her famous dad. It had been going on for most of her life, whether they were talking about his films or like some of the meaner kids at school, the drink and drugs years and how he'd wasted his talent. That was their parents talking through them – usually the dads who were jealous of Cody MacLeod.

"I just want to tell you that I love *The Forever Boys*," Benji said. "Your old man is awesome in it. It's so cool – it was my mom's favorite movie ever. Hey if he's still alive when this is all over do you think he'll give me his autograph?"

Tegan looked at Benji.

"Her dad may be cool but he's not as cool as Rachel," she said. "Her dad can't make his eyes go black can he? He can't put a big wall of funky light around his body and make the cars dance. Right Rachel?"

Rachel opened her mouth to say something but Benji cut in.

"Shut up Tegan!" he said.

Rachel didn't know if Benji had something wrong with him or he was just naturally short but the kid was tiny. Munchkin tiny. It didn't stop him standing up for himself though. "Rachel is super cool of course but don't diss *The Forever Boys*."

Benji looked at Rachel and smiled.

"Will he give me his autograph?" he said. "You think he will?"

"Sure," Rachel said. "Just don't call him the stutter kid."

Benji was grinning from ear to ear. He reached an arm out and slapped the lanky boy standing beside him on the arm.

"No way," he said. "We've got our own stutter kid right here."

"That we have," Tegan said, smiling.

Rachel took another biscuit off the plate. It tasted good, if a little too sugary. Or maybe she'd just eaten too many of them.

"Where do you all come from?" she asked. Most of the children were by now gathered at the edge of the altar, like a flock of groupies lingering near the stage after a rock concert. Hoping to get a word with their idols.

"Right here in San Antonio," Tegan said. "Every last one of us."

"We've stayed outside the city for a while," Benji said. The boy spoke in a mad rush of words. Rachel imagined his little heart drumming at six hundred beats a minute like a hummingbird. "Been watching those gates," Benji said. "Grandma Anna said we have to bide our time before we could make contact with you. Show patience, that sort of thing. But the Exterminators – is that what you called them?"

"Yeah," Rachel said.

"Well I guess they beat us to the punch," Benji said. "They came early or we waited too long. Either way, we're screwed."

Tegan and Stutter exchanged worried glances.

"You'll fix it won't you Rachel?" Tegan said. "You'll send them back?"

Rachel dropped the biscuit back onto the plate and pushed it away. She looked up and a sea of desperate eyes stared back at her.

"I can't," she said. "Sorry."

"But your p-powers," Stutter said.

Rachel saw the disappointment on their faces. "It's not enough," she said.

"What are we going to do then?" Tegan said. "Is there anywhere else left in America with people? Anywhere we can go to get away from these things?"

"There's gotta be somewhere," Benji said.

"We don't know that for sure," Tegan said. "This might be all that's left."

"We can run," Rachel said. "When I find my dad and friends, we'll hit the road and go north. You guys can follow us in the bus if you want."

The door at the back of the church swung open.

Grandma Anna walked slowly up the aisle. She had a strange walk – the gait was almost mechanical as if her legs couldn't quite bend properly with each stride. As painful as it looked however, the old woman was smiling.

Stutter went over to help her but Grandma Anna waved him away and approached the edge of the altar.

"How is everyone feeling?" she asked.

The glum faces on display answered her question.

"That bad is it?" she said, laughing softly.

It was Tegan who spoke up.

"Rachel can't fight the Exterminators," she said. "It ain't gonna happen the way we planned it Grandma Anna. They're too strong."

Grandma Anna looked at Rachel and winked.

"You children should be resting or eating," she said, turning back to the others with a stern expression. "You should be building up your energy reserves."

"What's the point Grandma Anna?" Benji said, turning away from the altar. There was a flicker of anger in the small boy's eyes that matched the color of his hair. "I thought you said she was going to fix it."

Grandma Anna gently slapped Benji on the back of the head.

"I told you to eat something," she said. "No wonder you're so small. You need your strength as much as anyone if we're going to win this fight."

Benji looked stunned by the rebuke.

Grandma Anna addressed the crowd of children.

432

"Nothing has changed," she said. "The plan remains the same as it's always been. Now do what I tell you – go eat and get some rest. Remember that your bodies are weapons and must be strong at all times."

The children grumbled amongst themselves. But they turned around and walked down the aisle like they were told to. Some of them turned around and gave Rachel a wary glance.

"Hurry up," Grandma Anna said, shooing them away. "Dios mío! You'd think you lot were the ones pushing seventy-five!"

Grandma Anna turned back to Rachel. The sweet smile was back on her face.

"Are you cold sweetheart?"

Rachel nodded. "Yeah a bit."

"And apart from that?" Grandma Anna said, approaching the altar again. "How do you feel otherwise? Have you eaten anything?"

"I've eaten a little," Rachel said. "And I feel a bit better I guess. Stronger."

Grandma Anna looked at the half-empty plate of food. She scratched at her chin and laughed softly.

"Good," she said. "Very good. In that case Rachel, let's go outside. We have work to do."

CHAPTER TEN

Grandma Anna and Rachel walked down the aisle together.

They stepped through the wood paneled double doors, walking outside into what would have once been a pretty little garden area. It was now a small stretch of dried grass, mostly buried under the black snow and surrounded by small trees at the front of the church. There was a statue of a saintly looking woman further along that would have greeted visitors, both worshippers and tourists, as they made their way to the basilica door.

Rachel shivered in the cold. She thrust her gloved hands into her pockets as they walked in the garden.

This was her first glimpse of the building that Grandma Anna had brought her to after the crash. There were two towers at the front of the church, standing out above all else. Grandma Anna – who seemed to know a lot about the basilica – pointed to the north tower telling Rachel that a seven-foot tall statue of St Thérèse was fixed up there. But it was too dark to see the statue from the ground. The southern tower, which was a little taller than the north one, was the bell tower and it had a wrought iron Roman cross on top.

"It's pretty," Rachel said, looking around.

"Yes it is," Grandma Anna said. "I used to come here a lot before the Black Storm. It's a nice spot for an old lady to do some uninterrupted thinking."

Rachel saw a permanent haze of bright colors hanging in the air over San Antonio. Directly above the city, the three gates watched over the chaos.

"They're turning San Antonio into a junkyard," Grandma Anna said. Her soft features hardened into a frown.

"I can't fight them," Rachel said, turning to the old woman. "You weren't there. You didn't see how bad it was. How bad I was."

Grandma Anna looked at Rachel. Her back was hunched over slightly as she stood in the cold.

"You lost the first round," she said. "Nothing more, nothing less."

Rachel shook her head. "You don't understand," she said. "Nobody does."

"You're gifted child," Grandma Anna said. "Of that there's no doubt. But it's you who doesn't understand."

"What do you mean?" Rachel said. The weight of other people's expectations was starting to get on her nerves. Ever since she'd woken up in the church, Grandma Anna and the kids had been leaning on her, going on and on about how she was going to go back and fight the Exterminators. But she'd done that already and look how that turned out. She'd tried to explain to these people that she wasn't their savior. But still they looked at her with that awful, gut-wrenching hope in their eyes.

"You don't fully understand your gifts yet," Grandma Anna said. "At least, not all of them."

Rachel shrugged and shivered yet again.

"I thought I was doing well," she said. "All those early mornings on the roof with my dad and Rita in the freezing cold. I never said this to Dad or anyone, but there was a moment when I thought it was going to be easy. Like it was in the park the first time around. That's how stupid I am."

"Rachel," Grandma Anna said.

"What?"

"You have their power in your mind," Grandma Anna said. "Now I have no idea how it happened except that when they tried to kidnap you they failed and you absorbed something of them. That something has flourished inside you ever since. Now I can't know for sure but if those things can tap into our minds, then I'd be willing to bet that you can too."

"What?" Rachel said.

Grandma Anna tapped the side of her head. "Have you ever communicated with anyone? With this?"

Rachel almost shook her head. Then she remembered.

"Yeah," she said. "I spoke to Crazy Diamond. I called her to come and help us when Mackenzie attacked us on the street. When Rita died."

Grandma Anna stroked her chin in a slow, thoughtful manner. "I'd say that's just the tip of the iceberg when it comes to what you can do."

"I don't understand," Rachel said.

"Telekinesis," Grandma Anna said. "Electrokinesis. Are you familiar with any of these terms child?"

"No."

"No," Grandma Anna said. "Well both these things are part of your extraterrestrial inheritance. To put it simply, telekinesis is the ability to move things with your mind. Electrokinesis is the psychic ability to control electric charges, electrical currents and so on. I suppose that's how you're able to switch on the lights in all those buildings."

"I don't really think about what it's called," Rachel said. "I just do it."

"Of course," Grandma Anna said. "And that's the best thing about it. You don't need to know what it's called. Who cares what it's called? There have been many great musicians throughout history who haven't been able to read a single note of music or understand the first thing about theory. Like you, they go by instinct. Having said that, it's still good to expand your knowledge base. Especially if you're underachieving – as I believe you are."

The old woman squinted her eyes.

"You must realize your true potential," Grandma Anna said. "This is what I hoped to tell you before they arrived. I'm not trying to criticize your father or your friends, God knows I'm not, but you haven't been coached properly. If you can do what the Exterminators can do, there's no limit to the power that's swimming around in your mind right now. Forget turning lights on and off – that's nothing!"

Grandma Anna took a step closer to Rachel. She moved slowly, taking care not to slip on the snow.

"Let's try something out," she said. "A test. Is that okay?"

"Okay," Rachel said, taking a deep breath.

"I want you to close your eyes," Grandma Anna said.

Rachel did as she was told.

"Now I want you to concentrate," Grandma Anna said. "Concentrate on my thoughts. Don't force it and don't strain yourself. Let it come. Playing with cars on the street is all very well, but let's see what else you've got in there Rachel MacLeod. Just relax, empty your thoughts and reach out to me."

Rachel tried but the destructive noises coming from the city knocked her off stride. She opened her eyes and saw Grandma Anna standing in front of her. The old woman's eyes were shut. Rachel shook her head and then closed her eyes again. Her muscles were as taut as piano wire.

The first thing she pictured was her dad hanging off the edge of the Robert E. Lee building.

Where was he now?

"Nothing else exists," Grandma Anna said. Her voice was flat and emotionless. "Just you and I. Reach out to me child."

A strange sensation came over Rachel. It happened suddenly and she felt like she was sinking inside herself. Like she was sliding down a long, narrow chute at a hundred miles per hour and although she could see nothing but darkness, she was certain that she was traveling towards something.

The movement stopped. It felt like Rachel had launched off the edge of the chute and now she was floating in midair. She stayed there for a while, hanging in limbo.

Then she fell hard and fast.

That's it.

Grandma Anna's voice was loud and clear. Rachel had landed in the old woman's head – she knew that for sure. She barely resisted the urge to open her eyes and check to see if Grandma Anna was moving her lips.

Rachel waited for the woman to say something else, to instruct her. But there was only the silence of standing in a dark, vast wilderness alone. It was like Grandma Anna had gone on vacation and left Rachel in charge of her mind.

She was surprised at how natural it felt to trek through someone else's headspace, like she was doing no more than wandering through an extension of her own mind.

At last she gave into temptation. Rachel opened her eyes.

Grandma Anna was standing in front of her. The old woman's eyes were tightly closed and her thick arms hung limp at her side. Nonetheless her posture was alert, even if she did look like she was fast asleep standing up.

Rachel lifted her left arm. Grandma Anna's left arm mirrored the gesture perfectly. Rachel wasn't surprised – it felt natural somehow. She held her arm in that same position for a few seconds as if it was a yoga pose. Grandma Anna did the same. When

Rachel finally dropped her arm to the side in a fast snapping motion, the old woman did likewise.

Rachel smiled. She felt like a puppet master, pulling strings only with people instead of wood. A renewed sense of wonder shone through, as if she was discovering her power for the first time. Had she become complacent? Why hadn't she uncovered these skills before? She'd been doing the same thing over and over again in practice, hoping it would be enough.

What else was she capable of?

Rachel looked at her left forearm. She clenched her teeth and willed the shield to come alive. Did she still have the strength to summon it? Nothing happened at first and Rachel felt a shred of panic in her guts. For a moment, she was terrified that she'd lost the ability to do it. But then she heard the familiar crackling noise. A spark of red and blue light appeared, dancing along Rachel's fingers and working its way up her arm.

It was the same with Grandma Anna's left forearm. The shield was working its way up towards her shoulder.

Rachel gasped. She put the shield out right away and let her arm fall to the side. Grandma Anna mimicked the gesture.

"Wow," Rachel said.

She had to talk to Grandma Anna. There were so many questions.

First she had to get out of the woman's head.

Rachel closed her eyes and resisted that initial urge to tense up again. How to best evacuate another person's mind? She'd slid down a chute first time around so now it only made sense that she'd have to go back up. She envisioned climbing out of a deep, dark pit with zero visibility. She couldn't see the light but like before, when she knew she was sliding towards something, she knew the exit door was up there. Soon it was effortless, almost like a pair of helping hands had reached down to help Rachel out the void.

There was a brief swooshing noise.

Rachel opened her eyes.

Grandma Anna was blinking hard, as if snapping out of daydream. Although she looked a little disorientated, there was a huge smile on the wrinkled face.

"You did it," Grandma Anna said. "You were in my head, weren't you?"

"You don't know?" Rachel said.

"How could I?" Grandma Anna said. "Now let me ask you something Rachel. Was it easy? It was, wasn't it? Instinct took over and you knew exactly what you were doing in there. Isn't that right?"

"Yeah," Rachel said. "I guess."

Grandma Anna was glowing with excitement.

"Do you see the potential now?" Grandma Anna said. "What-ever they can do, you can do. You could even create a Black Storm of your own if you wanted to. You could do what the Black Widow did and plant hallucinations in human minds that would drive them to despair. Are you starting to understand why I brought you here?"

Rachel nodded. "I saw other things in your head," she said. "It was in the background but since I've come out the pictures are becoming clearer."

"Oh really? Grandma Anna said.

"I saw what happened to you," Rachel said. "To your family."

Grandma Anna was ashen-faced.

"Yes I thought you might."

"I'm sorry," Rachel said, not knowing what else to say to the old woman. She'd never understood why grown ups always insisted on apologizing for things that weren't their fault. They did it all the time when bad stuff happened.

The black snow was falling hard as they stood outside the basilica.

"My daughter's name was Samantha," Grandma Anna said. "She was named after my mother. She looked like my mother too with her black hair, Latina good looks, and she had the feisty nature to go with them."

"How long were you on the run for?" Rachel asked.

"We left not long after the Black Storm first hit," Grandma Anna said. "Samantha, my two grandsons and myself. We went up to Canyon Lake where we'd vacationed in the log cabins many times before with the entire family. Took enough supplies to last us for months but the Black Widow was never far away. It was maybe a week or so before the Fever caught up with Samantha. That changed everything. We had to run again but this time it was from my daughter."

Rachel already knew how the story ended. She'd seen it and didn't want to hear the rest but Grandma Anna kept talking.

"Samantha chased after us," she said. "Her own mother and two children. We had to leave her behind in Canyon Lake and take our chances."

Grandma Anna dabbed at the side of her eye. Black snowflakes clung to her glistening cheeks.

"We didn't get far," she said. "She caught up with us pretty quickly. And then, well, a mother doing that to her children – it's something that no one should ever have to see or hear. I hit her over the back of her head with a piece of lead pipe but it was too late to save the boys."

"I'm sorry," Rachel said. She figured now that people said this because there was nothing else to say. Nothing that would help.

"I was still alive," Grandma Anna said. "Just me, someone who could have died years ago and still claimed to have lived a long life. I was a mess when I came back to San Antonio. But I wasn't ready to die. I was so angry with the Black Storm and I wanted to do something, to fight against it – to defy it. So I started helping the children around the city. There were so many of them Rachel –

441

they were like stray dogs on the streets with nowhere to go. I began rounding them up one by one. Thank God, I found that school bus abandoned in the middle of the road. That's when it began to feel like fate. I drove a school bus back in the sixties and seventies."

"Do you still miss them?" Rachel asked.

Grandma Anna scraped a frozen teardrop off her cheek.

"I'd give anything to have them back," she said. "Anything to see those boys' beautiful faces again. Oscar and Sam. And of course, Samantha – *my* Samantha."

"Did you ever fight?" Rachel said. "With your family I mean."

"All the time," Grandma Anna said, wiping her eyes dry. "Like I said, my Samantha was a feisty girl and she was damn stubborn too. Yes we fought, tooth and nail sometimes. That's what families do Rachel. Most of the time it doesn't mean anything. You don't stop loving someone or being loved because of a little squabble. Don't you fight with your dad?"

Rachel nodded. "Sometimes."

Grandma Anna came over beside Rachel. She put an arm on the girl's shoulder and gave it a gentle squeeze.

"Will you fight them?" Grandma Anna said.

Rachel wanted to say yes. But she couldn't forget how badly things had gone during her first encounter with the Exterminators. Wasn't she being naïve in thinking that she could go back and take them on? Sure, there was more to her powers than she'd first thought. Grandma Anna had opened her eyes to many possibilities but still, would it be enough?

"I can fight," Rachel said. "But I don't think I can win."

Grandma Anna and Rachel were standing close to the statue of St Thérèse, which was drowning in a hail of black snow. There was something calming about its presence; it was a divine comrade watching over the children.

"My dear girl," Grandma Anna said. "Who can blame you for being frightened? This burden should never have been placed on the shoulders of one so young. And yet this particular burden, it *has* to be a child. Only a child can do it."

Rachel glanced at the old woman's face. She tried to smile.

"We'll fight them together," Grandma Anna said, taking Rachel's hand in her own. "And we'll win. We have weapons inside the basilica that will help you crush them."

Rachel screwed up her face. "What weapons?" she said, looking towards the church. "I didn't see any weapons in there."

"Oh but you did," Grandma Anna said.

Her eyes sparkled with a strange, steady light.

The old woman laughed heartily and with a firm hand on Rachel's shoulder, she led the way back towards the door of the basilica.

CHAPTER ELEVEN

Cody opened his eyes.

His head was pounding. It felt like he was lying in a deep freezer.

He lifted his head off the ground and saw the colored light everywhere. There was more of it than ever. It looked like it had multiplied tenfold while he'd been out and that was putting it mildly. Streams of light floated across the city skyline in various guises – low-hanging clouds, tube-like beams, pockets of slow-moving mist and much more. It was still pouring out of the gates and seeping up from below, as if emerging from the center of the Earth.

Cody's hand probed under his hood and he found a large bump on the crown of his head. Man, that was big. It was going to throb for a while. How long had he been out anyway? Ten minutes? Twenty? As he struggled to his feet, a carousel of recollections flashed through his mind. He was clinging onto the edge of the roof. He'd climbed back up and ran towards the door that led to the stairs. That was when he'd slipped and banged his head.

Why had he been running?

"Oh shit," Cody said. "Rachel."

He saw it happening again in his mind – his daughter being thrown over the side of the building like a baseball. Cody's stomach lurched at the vivid memory and for a second he thought he was going to be sick. Luckily the feeling passed. He pushed himself up, ignoring the sensation of something cracking in his skull. Then he hurried over to the edge of the roof, his heart pounding.

Cody saw the car park opposite the Robert E. Lee building. It was coming back now. A large SUV had driven out of there, going too fast on the slippery roads and traveling in a northerly direction.

"Where are you?" Cody said, straining his eyes to catch a glimpse of the SUV's tracks on the snow. But it was too dark to see anything.

He had to find her. She couldn't have gone that far in twenty minutes and with any luck she'd pulled over to the side of the road to lay low for a while. All Cody had to go on was the type of car she'd taken. It was better than nothing, as long as he found himself a set of wheels in quick time.

He knew exactly where to find transport.

Cody ran for the stairs. As he did, he looked towards the horizon and saw one of the tallest buildings in San Antonio crashing to the ground like it would under a controlled demolition. A snake-like streak of golden yellow light was wrapped around the space where the building had been seconds earlier.

Cody didn't stop to watch the aftermath He pulled the door open and ran down ten stories to the street as fast as his legs would carry him.

As soon as he stepped outside, Cody jumped back. A flotilla of rainbow-colored mist was coming down the street towards him. Cody made the mistake of looking directly at the light and as he did so, an army of Sliders shot out of the mist and came straight for him at a ferocious speed.

Cody ducked back inside the entrance of the apartment building. He dropped to his knees and buried his face in his hands.

"It's not real," he said, shaking his head back and forth. Rachel's words swam around in his groggy, aching head – *don't let them in*.

He stayed there for a while, stealing the occasional glance outside and waiting for the mist to pass. As it moved slowly down the street, Cody heard that familiar whale-like noise, deep and moaning. It was a cold, impersonal sound.

When it was gone, Cody stepped back outside.

The plan was simple. He had to go back to the Rand to get the van and hopefully he'd find Nick, Crazy Diamond and Marv still in one piece.

And after that? Find Rachel. Then once they'd found her they'd point the van north, get the hell out of San Antonio and keep driving until they ran out of gas. When that happened, they'd walk. There had to be somewhere left in this goddamn mess where people didn't have to fight all the time.

Or was he just trying to fool himself?

Cody started running towards the Rand. He didn't get far before he saw a small cluster of dark shapes running up North Main Street towards him.

His fingers tightened around the handle of the Glock. Cody was about to duck behind one of the trees beside the sidewalk when he heard a familiar voice.

It was Nick Norton.

Cody stepped out from his hiding place, waving his hands in the air. When the others saw him they stopped.

"It's me," Cody said. "Don't shoot for God's sake."

"Cody?" It was Crazy Diamond. "Is that you?"

"Yeah."

They rushed forward to greet him.

Crazy Diamond threw her arms around Cody and when she

didn't let go at first, the two men gave him a warm pat on the shoulder.

"What's going on?" Crazy Diamond said, releasing her grip on Cody at last. There was a worried look on her face as she looked over Cody's shoulder. "Where's Rachel? Is she still up there on the roof?"

Cody shook his throbbing head. "She took off," he said. "Jesus, it was a disaster up there. She was overwhelmed. They're too strong for her. How could I have done that to her? Put her up against those things."

The others didn't look surprised.

"We all did it," Nick said. "Shit. Where'd she go man?"

"I don't know," Cody said. "I had a bit of trouble on the roof. I slipped and blacked out for a while. When I woke up, Rachel was gone and that's when I came back here to get the van and go after her. She can't be too far away."

"You can't go back to the Rand," Marv said, pointing a thumb over his shoulder. "We held our ground as long as we could. Ended up having to slip out the back door ourselves."

"Yeah," Nick said. "We're lucky it lasted as long as it did. Stupid assholes must have thought Rachel was in there the whole time."

"How long?" Cody said, looking past his friends towards the Rand. "How long since I ran out of there with Rachel?"

Marv shrugged.

"Don't know for sure Cody," he said. "We held them off in there for at least five hours. Maybe six."

Cody felt like he'd been slapped in the face.

"Are you serious?" he said.

"As a heart attack," Marv said. "It was a long fight."

Cody clamped a hand over his mouth. "Oh shit."

"Good thing you're wrapped up like an Eskimo," Crazy

Diamond said. "You're lucky you didn't freeze to death up on that roof."

"To hell with that," Cody said, looking at her. "Rachel's been gone for hours? I thought I was out for ten minutes. Twenty max. Well that settles it then. I need the van. I've got to go after her."

He moved towards the Rand.

"You can't go back there," Nick said, blocking Cody's path with his muscular frame. "Mackenzie and the ragtags will be coming up behind us any second now."

Cody shook his head. "I don't care," he said. "Nick – she's scared and alone out there. God knows what sort of state she's in. Everything she worked so hard for all those months, all those early morning starts, it was wiped out in seconds."

There was a frenzy of noise further down the street. A door was kicked open. Loud voices piled on top of one another. Heavy footsteps, like a pack of soldiers marching on the snow.

"Well that didn't take long," Crazy Diamond said. "Here they come."

"You can't go back Cody," Marv said in a calm, quiet voice. "You're right, we need to find Rachel. But we'll find a car out there somewhere and hit the road. We're not going to leave her, I promise."

Cody felt Nick's hand on his shoulder, gently steering him away. There was a knot in Cody's stomach at the thought of leaving the only transportation he knew of behind.

"The van..."

"Not this time," Nick said.

Cody saw the ragtags coming through the darkness. A cloaked figure stood at the front, leading the way.

There was little doubt where they were going now. They were going to the Robert E. Lee building to find Rachel.

Cody and the others turned and ran.

They heard a chorus of gunfire behind them.

"I guess they've seen us," Nick said, glancing over his shoulder as they ran up the street. As he spoke a swirling white light, shaped like a shuriken – a star shaped throwing weapon from Japan – came rolling down the street towards them like a runaway tire.

"You've got to be kidding," Marv said.

"Don't look at the light," Cody said. "Over here. Move!"

They hurried to the side of the road and put their backs up against the wall. At Cody's command, they hid their faces in their hands. When the rolling star went past it disappeared into thin air. Cody looked down that way and now there was only Mackenzie and the ragtags, still following them up the street. Still shooting.

Mackenzie was at the head of the group, his long cloak flowing behind him. Cody thought he could see a burning black hole where the man's good eye was supposed to be.

"Let's get out of here," Crazy Diamond said.

The ragtags kept shooting, forcing the four survivors back towards the Robert E. Lee building.

"We need to take cover," Nick said. "We're too exposed out here in the open."

"The car park," Cody said, pointing a finger up ahead.

They ran over the black snow, pumping their arms and legs as hard as they could. Nick and Marv fired back at Mackenzie and the ragtags who seemingly had no interest in taking cover. They were only interested in coming forward like a pack of robotic hunters who sensed that a kill was imminent.

Crazy Diamond led the others across a small square of grass bordered by naked trees on all sides. There were a few abandoned cars parked on the grassy oasis, one of which was lying upturned like it had been involved in a crash. The survivors cut across the grass towards North Flores Street, running past the Robert E. Lee building and into the small car park where Rachel had made her exit from earlier.

449

They ran to the back of the car park, taking cover behind the bed of a dirty maroon pickup truck.

Cody realized to his horror that Marv wasn't with them. Peering over the edge of the truck, he saw the veteran solider standing at the entrance of the car park. His head was tilted back as if he was transfixed by something up in the sky.

A small cloud of mist descended towards him. It was reddish-pink and it looked like a large piece of floating cotton candy.

"Marv!" Nick said. "What the hell are you doing man? Don't look at it."

Further back, Mackenzie and the ragtags walked over the grassy square that led towards the car park.

Marv took a step towards the mist.

"Rita?" he said. "Is that you darling?"

"No," Cody said. "Marv, snap out of it!"

Nick jerked forwards. "I'm gonna get him," he said.

By now, Marv was reaching for the mist with one hand. The other, carrying his gun, was lowered at his side. "Oh God Rita," he said. "I'm so sorry. I should have..."

He staggered forwards like a drunk, grasping for the mist.

As Marv chased his vision, the cloud vanished. Where the cotton candy mist had been, now there was only Mackenzie and the ragtags, standing on the road just a few feet from Marv.

"Oh shit," Nick said. He was still edging forwards but it was suicide to go out there now.

Marv's arms were still up in the air.

"Rita?"

The sound of gunfire cut through Cody's head like an electric drill. He and the others watched in horror as Marv was shot to pieces by the ragtags. His tough old body stood up to the assault for a few seconds and he shook violently like he was being electro-cuted. The gunmen stepped in front of Mackenzie, a cruel look on their faces as they kept shooting. Even when Marv went down, they still sprayed bullets at him for another five or ten seconds. Just to be sure.

The shooting stopped.

"You bastards!" Nick cried out. He took aim with his AR-15 rifle and started shooting into the crowd. One of the ragtags fell immediately.

Cody and Crazy Diamond fired back too. This sudden attack was enough to force Mackenzie's men back towards the grassy oasis. They took cover behind the trees, waiting out the assault.

But Mackenzie didn't move. While his soldiers hid, he stood alone on the corner or North Flores and West Travis Street.

Behind Mackenzie, a comet-like streak of white light shot across the sky. It crashed into a building and the explosion carried across the city. The noise made Cody's Glock sound like a peashooter.

A thick cloud of black smoke rose up on the horizon.

Cody and the others stopped shooting and kept their cover behind the pickup. They peered out once or twice, staring across the road. Mackenzie was standing there in plain sight while the ragtags kept to the trees.

"Where is she?" Mackenzie called out. "I'm talking to you Cody."

"Go fuck yourself!" Nick yelled. He peered over the edge of the pickup. "Murdering bastard. You're so ugly nowadays Mackenzie I bet you have to sneak up on the mirror, am I right?"

Crazy Diamond scowled at Nick. "How is that helping the situation?"

"It makes me feel better," Nick said. "I'm done with this guy. Marv was a good man, Lance and Rita and Richards – they were all good people and this asshole took them out. I'm going to shoot out his good eye. Blind the motherfucker. Dying's too good for the likes of him."

"We need a car," Cody said. "Remember the plan Nick. We've got to find Rachel."

Nick shook his head. "I'm done running from this asshole."

"You can't kill him Nick," Cody said. "Bullets won't stop this guy, no matter how many you shoot. And look around you man. The Exterminators are tearing this city apart and when they're done they're going to go after Rachel. My daughter! Meanwhile we're boxed in here and if it's a straight shootout we're screwed. We've got to get out of here now. We need to go back to the Rand and get the van."

Crazy Diamond nodded. "Yeah," she said. "You're right Cody. We're going to have to make a run for it again."

Nick slammed the butt of his rifle against the pickup.

"We can't all go back for God's sake," Nick said "If the three of us make a run for it at once they'll pick us off."

"What are you saying?" Crazy Diamond said. "One of us should go?"

"Right," Nick said, taking a look around as if to assess their prospects. "One of us goes back for the van. Going to have take the long way back to the Rand. No straight lines. Whoever it is, they'll have to cut over at least two blocks to avoid getting picked off by these guys."

"I'll go," Cody said. "I'm probably the fastest runner."

"We don't have time to argue," Nick said. "I'm going. I've got the keys to the van anyway."

Cody shook his head. "Nick..."

Nick held up a hand. "Look no offence Cody," he said. "But you're a lousy driver man. I wouldn't trust you to bring a golf cart back here in one piece."

Cody screwed up his face. "What the hell are you talking about?"

"Whoever goes back is going to have to be on their A-game," Nick said. He was shaking his arms, loosening his muscles as he spoke. "Get the van here, drive past Mackenzie and the ragtags, and pick the other two up. And the driver's gotta do all that without getting shot. That requires a cool head. You're too messed up about Rachel man."

"Maybe I should go back," Crazy Diamond said. "I think I'm probably faster than either one of you guys. And I'm a smaller target."

"I'm going," Nick said.

"Alright then," Crazy Diamond said, holding her hands in the air like she was surrendering. "We don't have time to argue about this. You go."

Nick smiled.

"We're talking sense at last," he said. "Now listen up people. You two be ready to jump in that van because it's going to get ugly when I show up. They're going to do everything they can to stop us getting away."

"You gotta be quick," Cody said. "Mackenzie could say to hell with all this standoff bullshit and walk over here at any moment. He probably will sooner or later."

Nick nodded and looked across the car park. There was a small cluster of trees on the opposite side from where they were taking cover. Cody knew what Nick was planning – if he could cut over and disappear behind the trees he'd be out of sight.

"Run fast," Cody said.

Nick looked at him. "You guys just be ready."

"We will be," Crazy Diamond said.

Without another word, Nick sprang upwards and sprinted towards the trees.

The ragtags marched forwards, opening fire as soon as they heard the sound of Nick's boots pounding off the ground. A storm of bullets tore into the cars on the far side of the parking lot. Cody heard the sound of shattering glass and he feared the worst. Nick was a big target.

But although he was big, he was fast. Surprisingly fast.

With a final burst, Nick made it behind the last line of cars and leapt behind the trees like he was diving into a swimming pool.

"Stop shooting," Mackenzie called out, raising a hand in the air.

The firing ceased.

"I know you're still there Cody," Mackenzie said. "And that's what matters. You know where she is don't you? If anyone knows where Rachel MacLeod is then it's her daddy."

Cody didn't answer.

"I'm done talking," Mackenzie said. "I'm through playing games with you and all your friends. You're going to die here if you don't tell me where she is. And do you know what Cody? We'll find her anyway."

Cody looked at Crazy Diamond. She lifted her pistol, the barrel pointing at the sky. She gave him a quick nod.

"I hope Nick's a fast runner," she said.

"Me too," Cody said.

Footsteps crunched over the snow. Coming closer.

Cody took a deep breath. He clamped his fingers around the Glock's rubber grip and looked at Crazy Diamond. Then slowly, he mouthed the words:

"One. Two..."

They started shooting on two.

CHAPTER TWELVE

Cody and Crazy Diamond fired into the ragtags but their attack didn't last long.

Mackenzie walked through their shots, his black eye gleaming and a grotesque grin etched on his face. About twelve ragtag came up behind him, returning fire with reckless abandon.

"Shit!" Cody said.

He pulled Crazy Diamond back down and they took cover behind the vehicle.

"What are you doing?" Crazy Diamond said, looking at him in surprise.

Cody shook his head. "I can't die here. Rachel's out there and she needs me."

"That's why we're fighting back," Crazy Diamond said. There was a fierce look in her eyes. "We're dead if they catch up with us. Remember?"

Cody's head fell against the back of the pickup. Sometimes he was amazed at how mature Crazy Diamond came off, especially for a young woman barely in her twenties. He should have been the one telling her to get up and fight. And she was right – of course she was. Either way, the ragtags and their boss were going to kill them. Worst-case scenario – even if they couldn't take Mackenzie out they could at least take out some of his men.

"Ready?" Crazy Diamond said. "Take two."

Cody nodded.

They jumped back to their feet, firing a volley of bullets into the ragtags.

Mackenzie didn't flinch. His mangled features stared back at Cody with a look of calm loathing.

Crazy Diamond stepped out from behind the truck. Cody gave her a look that said she was crazy but he didn't hesitate to go out with her. There might as well have been a piece of rope tied around their waists, joining them together.

Cody concentrated on his aim. He took out two ragtags with two shots. Crazy Diamond hit one square in the forehead. As they walked forwards, moving past the other cars, Cody could hear the ragtags' bullets pinging off the stray vehicles, smashing through windshields.

After a few seconds, Cody dropped to his knee and kept shooting. He took out a skinny teenager who dropped to the ground, wriggling in agony with his long, bony hands pressed to his stomach.

Mackenzie realized that his men were dropping like flies. He looked at Cody and Crazy Diamond and came charging towards them.

Now Cody pointed his pistol at the man in the black cloak. But before he could squeeze the trigger he heard Crazy Diamond let out a high-pitched shriek beside him. Her pistol dropped out of her hands and as Cody looked to his left, he saw her reach for her right shoulder.

Mackenzie halted his approach. He smiled and there was a cruel glint in his eye – it looked like he wanted to relish the moment.

Crazy Diamond grasped for her fallen pistol at her feet. But it was Cody who kneeled down and grabbed it and with a barrage of gunshots whizzing past his ear, he dragged Crazy Diamond back behind the pickup.

They were both breathing heavy, like they'd just tackled the hundred-meter sprint. Crazy Diamond was screwing up her face in pain.

"Damn it," she hissed.

The ragtags' gunfire stopped. The car park was dead silent again.

"I gave you every chance I could," Mackenzie said. He sounded like he was still standing in the middle of the car park. "Time's up. We'll find the girl ourselves and I want you to know this Cody – when I hand her over to the Exterminators she'll be screaming your name. How does that make you feel?"

Cody looked at Crazy Diamond, doing his best to ignore the bait. She gritted her teeth, her hand still pressed tight up against the wound. He unzipped her parka and saw a bloody patch seeping through her sweater.

"Keep the pressure on it," Cody said. "It's not as bad as it looks."

"Give me my gun Cody," Crazy Diamond said. "We're not done with these bastards."

"I'll fight," Cody said. "You stay here. You're in no shape to..."

"We'll both fight," she said.

What choice did they have? At the very least they could die on their own terms.

Cody picked up Crazy Diamond's gun and put it in her hand. Crazy Diamond winced as she wrapped her bloody fingers around the handle.

They looked at one another and exchanged tense smiles.

"Been nice knowing you," Crazy Diamond said. The fierce

457

glint in her eye was still there. Cody had a feeling she was actually looking forward to getting back out there.

"You too," Cody said.

"Screw the count," Crazy Diamond said. "Let's just do it."

They jumped to their feet.

Mackenzie and the ragtags were barely ten feet from the pickup truck. The ragtags had their weapons trained on Cody and Crazy Diamond, who in turn had their pistols locked onto Mackenzie and his followers.

Cody's finger caressed the trigger but something made him stop squeezing.

It made everyone stop.

A noise.

It was the sound of the cavalry trumpet riding in from afar. Only in this context, the trumpet was replaced by the triumphant roar of a large Sprinter van engine being pushed to breaking point.

The silver van shrieked as the tires skidded around the corner. In the blink of an eye, it came racing down West Travis Street at a fierce speed. The bright headlights charged closer. The van was heading for the car park and in particular at Mackenzie and the ragtags, all of who'd moved back towards the road to see what the sudden noise was.

Nick Norton poked his head out of the driver's side window. There was a massive grin on his face as he extended his middle finger towards Mackenzie.

"DIE MOTHERFUCKER!"

The ragtags scattered when they realized the van was coming straight at them. Mackenzie did no such thing. He faced the Sprinter head on. He stood tall and spread his arms out wide, as if challenging Nick to go through him.

Nick was only too happy to oblige.

Cody and Crazy Diamond watched as the Sprinter crashed into Mackenzie. There was a brutal thud and the hood of Mackenzie's cloak was flung backwards behind his head. But Mackenzie didn't go down. His arms grabbed a hold of the van's hood and his boots clamped down onto the slippery surface of the road. The van pushed him backwards while a geyser of black snow sprayed up at his feet. For a moment, Nick had turned Mackenzie into a human snowplow.

The van bullied its way forward while Mackenzie resisted with his unnatural strength. It was a high-speed duel. Both men were staring at one another through the windshield, daring the other to crack first.

Neither man did. It was the van that gave way first.

Mackenzie, perhaps sensing that the tide was turning, dug his heels in deeper. His long cloak flew backwards and his face twisted in agony as he tried to force the van to slow down.

The tires shrieked and scraped off the road.

The van was losing speed fast.

Cody heard Nick pounding on the steering wheel like it was a tiring racehorse slowing near the finish line. But Mackenzie was too strong, even for the likes of a huge Sprinter van. It slowed to a painful stop and Mackenzie took his arms off the hood. He staggered back a couple of steps and Cody saw a trail of smoke rising up off his feet.

Mackenzie stood in front of the van. His eyes closed and his index finger touched his forehead. His face creased up in concentration.

Seconds later, there was a loud hissing noise.

Cody and Crazy Diamond looked to their left and saw a massive ball of white light, about the size of a house, rolling down the street at a hundred miles per hour. There was a whooshing noise as it stormed past the car park, closing in on the back of the Sprinter van that was sitting stationary in the middle of the road.

"Nick!" Cody yelled. "Get out of the..."

Too late. The ball of light crashed into the back of the van and went through it like a bowling ball slamming into a wooden pin. There was a sick, crunching noise and Cody and Crazy Diamond watched horrified as the Sprinter was lifted clean off the ground. It flew over Mackenzie's head in a somersault, hanging in the air for a few seconds before it crashed onto the road fifty feet from where it had started. The van flipped over upon impact, tipping onto its back and sliding forwards until it came to a stop.

Cody felt his heart pounding. He opened his mouth to yell but there was nothing. Shock had taken the words.

"Nick," Crazy Diamond said. Her hand was clamped over her mouth.

Mackenzie walked back towards the car park. His hood was still down, revealing his horrifically scarred face. He strode in silence, looking at the ground as if lost in deep thought.

The ragtags were regrouping in the middle of the street. Some of them were staring at their boss in awe with worshipping eyes. Others stared at the upturned van. Cody could barely see much of their faces since the hoods of their coats were always up. There was only the occasional glimpse of a young, eager pair of eyes poking out from behind the wall of a winter balaclava.

Mackenzie stopped at the edge of the car park. He touched the red skin on his cheek and pulled his fingers back quickly like there was electricity in his fingers. Cody saw a trickle of blood running from one of the long scars on his face.

"Tell me where I can find Rachel," Mackenzie said, turning to Cody. He pointed to Crazy Diamond's bloodstained coat. "That wound of yours, I doubt it's fatal. Tell me where Rachel is and I'll let the woman live."

Cody looked at Crazy Diamond. She didn't waste any time in letting him know what she thought.

"You'll *let* me live?" Crazy Diamond said, speaking loud enough for everyone to hear. Her cheeks were damp with fresh tears. Tears of grief, tears of rage. "Well that's mighty big of you

Mackenzie. Do you remember what I told you after you killed Richards? I said I was going to kill you. It's not in your best interest to *let* me live."

Mackenzie pulled his hood back over his head.

"As you wish," he said.

He turned around to face the ragtags.

"Kill them both," he said.

Mackenzie walked away from the car park. The ragtags on the other hand, walked over with their weapons raised and locked onto Cody and Crazy Diamond.

Cody glanced at the upturned van in the distance. He'd lost Rachel, probably for good. His best friend was lying dead or dying further up the street. Thinking about it, there was only one thing left to do.

He looked at Crazy Diamond. She was already nodding her answer to the silent question.

"Yeah," she said.

Cody dropped onto his stomach. In a flash, he pointed the Glock at the ragtags while Crazy Diamond dove down and did the same. She yelped with pain as she used her wounded shoulder to regain balance on the ground.

They fired their pistols into the crowd, dropping a couple of ragtags. But Mackenzie's troops didn't lose their cool – they marched forward with their guns pointing into the car park.

Cody knew that he was almost out of ammo. Wouldn't be long now. He heard Crazy Diamond scream with frustration when she realized that her gun was empty. There was no time to reload, not in the middle of this shitstorm. As a last act of defiance, she threw her pistol at the ragtags.

Cody's Glock clicked next.

Empty.

"Shit," he said.

The ragtags rushed forward and swarmed all over them.

Cody felt himself being lifted off the ground by several pairs of rough hands. Two men dragged him towards the road while several others pulled Crazy Diamond back into the car park. She was trying to fight them off but as well as being wounded, she was hopelessly outnumbered.

Cody caught a glimpse of Mackenzie, standing on the other side of the road. He was a solitary figure, staring into space. Perhaps this was how he'd planned to get the information out of Cody all along. Mackenzie must have known he was more likely to get them to spill the truth after a prolonged dose of torture.

"I thought you were going to kill us," Cody yelled across the street.

Mackenzie didn't look at him.

Cody's reward for opening his mouth was a fist in the stomach.

He wheezed and doubled over in pain. From nearby, he heard Crazy Diamond snarling and screaming as the men dragged her over to one of the cars. A clicking noise. The back door of a Honda was pulled open. Crazy Diamond's feet scraped along the ground as she went, fighting for a solid grip.

"She's real pretty this one," a muffled voice said, drooling with excitement from behind a balaclava. "Time for a little reward, right boys?"

"Jesus it's been so long," another ragtag said. "I'm so horny I could burst."

"Who are you kidding?" said another. "You're a virgin, don't pretend like it's been long when it's been forever."

"Fuck you Mike. I ain't no..."

"Just hold her down for God's sake. Everyone gets a turn."

"Hey!" Cody yelled. He was being held back by one of the big ragtags. The man was holding onto Cody's collar like he was restraining a dog on a leash.

"She's hurt," Cody said. "Can't you see that? Leave her alone you fucking bastards!"

One of the hooded men looked back at Cody. "She ain't hurt down there," he said, pointing to Crazy Diamond's groin. "That's all that matters to me."

They laughed. It was maniacal playground laughter.

"Hey that guy was a movie star!" one of the ragtags said, pointing a finger at Cody. "Why don't we have a go at him as well? It's something to brag about later ain't it? Fucking a celebrity and all."

"Yeah," another voice said. "He's still kinda pretty too. I'll do the honors first, huh? Break him in for y'all. Hey Curly, knock some of the fight out of that boy will ya? A bloody nose always put me in the right mood for a little romance."

The one called Curly threw a series of hard punches at Cody to soften him up. Most of the ragtags however, were gathering by the car where Crazy Diamond was being pinned down on the backseat. She was still fighting, kicking at her assailants, but she was slowing down, running out of steam fast.

"Get off her!" Cody yelled.

Curly responded with a swift kick to the groin.

Cody doubled over again, his head hanging down. Crazy Diamond's screams rang in his ear but they were far away now. Cody was swimming in the void – he saw brief glimpses of familiar faces in his mind, flashing by like it was another one of the Exterminators' hallucinations. He saw Rachel, Nick, Marv, Crazy Diamond, Rita and Lance. They were all smiling and waving at him. Without speaking, they were telling Cody to let go. To just roll over and die.

The pain began to dull. But Cody knew that Curly was still hitting him because of the dull jolt he felt with each fresh blow.

Whack.

He fell forward, dropping onto the black snow. His palms were flat against the ground, the only thing stopping him from tipping over. They'd stopped hitting him all of a sudden. But why?

Cody looked up, groaning in agony. The world was a grainy blur, spinning faster than it normally would. He sucked in a lungful of air. At least the pain had spread out, distracting him from the headache he'd acquired on the roof. Now everything hurt.

A few ragtags were still standing over him. The others were lined up at the car but they weren't paying any attention to Crazy Diamond anymore.

They were looking at something else.

Cody turned his head to see what had interrupted the attack. His neck made a clicking noise as he looked to the left.

There was something on the road. Two slit-shaped headlights were cruising up North Flores Street in slow motion.

Cody wiped a dribble of warm blood off his chin. He leaned forward slightly, ignoring an explosion of pain in his stomach.

His heart sank.

It was the school bus.

"No," he said, spitting out a puddle of blood.

It had to be reinforcements arriving on the scene. Not that Mackenzie needed any – the ragtags might have taken some losses but they were well in control of the situation now. The school bus was just another nail in the coffin of the Resistance, the New Resistance, or whatever Cody and his group were called.

What did it matter? Cody felt his last reserves of hope being trampled upon. Surely this was the end.

Except something strange was happening. The ragtags, rather than being overjoyed, looked troubled by the arrival of the school bus. Casting their eyes over in that direction, Cody thought they looked like they'd seen a ghost.

It was the same with Mackenzie. He was standing tall, tense and alert.

The bus was sitting stationary, its engine purring quietly. Cody noticed that a cloud of colored mist had come down and was now lingering near the vehicle. As he sat up on the snow, more light appeared, coming from all directions and drifting towards the bus at a steady, cautious pace.

Cody's Glock was lying nearby on the snow. It wasn't that far. If he could just get his hands on it...

He saw Crazy Diamond sitting up in the backseat of the car. Fortunately she looked intact if a little dazed – the ragtags hadn't gotten much further than pulling open the zip of her parka. There was a bewildered look on her face.

Mackenzie signaled to the ragtags by clicking his fingers.

"Over here," he said.

They hurried over to their boss's side like well-trained puppies. At the same time, Cody heard the swift whooshing of the bus doors opening from afar. He climbed back to his feet, reenergized by curiosity, wincing at the countless aches and pains all competing for attention around his body.

He kept his eyes on the bus.

Somebody stepped out of the vehicle and stood in the middle of the road.

A solitary figure.

Cody's heart nearly burst with joy. He strained his eyes for a better look, convinced that he was hallucinating again.

"Rachel," he said. "Oh thank God."

She was standing there in silence, staring at Mackenzie and the gang of ragtags who were walking slowly in her direction.

Despite the distraction, Cody knew this was his chance. He crept over and picked up the Glock lying on the snow. Then he went over to help Crazy Diamond but she was already out of the car and back on her feet. As she zipped up her coat, the shocked expression on her face said it all.

"Guess we don't have to go looking for her," Crazy Diamond said. "She's found us – that's some kid you've got there Cody."

A silent standoff between Rachel and Mackenzie was underway. Rachel stood beside the bus while Mackenzie and his men had taken up position at the opposite end of the road. It was like watching the climactic shootout of a western movie, two gunslingers facing off to decide who was fastest.

The colored lights lingered overhead.

Cody pulled the spare magazine out of his pocket. As quietly as he could, he released the empty one and put the fresh rounds into the Glock.

Crazy Diamond was looking over at her pistol, which was still lying at the entrance of the car park where she'd thrown it at the ragtags earlier. Cody saw the hungry, vengeful look in her eyes. It was obvious that she was desperate to go after it.

Further down the street, Mackenzie took a step forward.

"Excellent timing," he said to Rachel. "Where have you been Rachel?"

When she didn't reply, Mackenzie pulled off a chunk of torn skin from his chin. The ragtags had gathered behind their boss, but they kept a respectable distance. In their excitement to answer Mackenzie's call for backup, it looked like they'd forgotten about Cody and Crazy Diamond. Either that or they didn't consider them much of a threat anymore. The two captives had been softened up after all.

Had they turned around, they would have seen Crazy Diamond creeping towards her pistol. They might have seen the hellfire in her eyes too – that was for them. Revenge had been sworn for a vile deed not committed perhaps, but intended. She moved quietly, trying not to attract any attention.

"You're stronger than me Rachel." Mackenzie said. "You can beat me but you know very well that you can't beat them." He pointed to the floating lights above their heads. "Bow to your masters girl. Give up now before it's too late for your dad."

Rachel didn't blink. She didn't speak either.

Cody saw a flicker movement near Rachel – something or someone slipped out from behind the nearby trees.

It was a small black girl.

The girl stepped onto the road, taking up position a few feet behind Rachel. Her fierce eyes scowled at Mackenzie and the ragtags. If looks could kill, the battle would have been over.

More kids began to appear, slipping out from behind the trees. They came out of the darkness like young fairies that had been hiding in plain sight all along, waiting for the right moment to make their entrance. Others emerged from behind abandoned cars. Cody watched this sudden turn of events in fascination. The kids were all dressed in layers of winter clothes – jackets, hats and gloves, all of which were at least a couple of sizes too big for them. They looked like a gang who'd just raided their parents' closets.

Even more kids spilled out of the bus. They stood alongside the others on the street, forming a triangle shape that stretched out at Rachel's back. There had to be somewhere in between twenty to thirty children with Rachel at least.

Crazy Diamond gave Cody a puzzled look. Cody shook his head and shrugged. He didn't have a clue what to think about all this – he was just delighted to see Rachel back again and standing there in one piece.

There was low-pitched growling sound. Slowly, the bus began to reverse back down the street, moving away from the group of children. As it made space, the kids spread themselves out in the middle of the road, all the while keeping the triangle intact at Rachel's back.

The bright headlights of the bus receded. At the end of the street, it reversed around the corner and drove away.

Mackenzie held his hands aloft, signaling to the colored light that watched over them all.

"Here she is!" he called out, pointing a crooked finger at Rachel. "I deliver her into your hands. Please take her."

The light overhead had taken on a deep bluish-red tinge. It swooped towards Rachel. She looked up and at the same time, the shield lit up around her. Her blue eyes clouded over and turned black.

The colored light probed the girl like a key searching for a lock. A moment later, it drifted upwards again. Cody heard the Exterminators let out a loud bellowing noise that made the ground tremble under his feet.

"Yes," Mackenzie said, one hand pressed to his temple. "Open a gate. Take us home with you."

The light was spinning in a clockwise motion. The blue and red colors thrashed back and forth at a furious tempo, bouncing off one another, swelling and getting brighter all the time. Something began to emerge in its center. It was a circle. The circle got bigger. Cody recognized what he was seeing immediately – the Exterminators were opening up another gate just like they'd done in Brackenridge Park. This was the door that they'd try to pull Rachel through.

Rachel took a deep breath. Slowly, she closed her eyes. Her face wrinkled up in a look of deep concentration.

The gate swelled above her head on a background of bluish-red light. It stretched like a piece of loose fabric, spreading out far and wide. Drops of color leaked from the eye, trickling down to the children below. This gate was at least ten times the size of the one Cody had seen last time.

It looked like a hungry mouth, begging to be fed.

"Oh Jesus," Cody said.

Now the gate began to descend. The mouth-like hole gaped open, its jaws reaching for Rachel and the children standing underneath.

But Rachel kept her eyes closed.

She lifted her chin, exposing her neck to the gate. After what felt like a lifetime, Rachel clenched her fist and in a quick snapping motion, pulled on something invisible.

A wall of light surrounded the children. A massive shield.

Cody staggered forward, one hand over his mouth. Both he and Crazy Diamond stood there, lost for words. Every child standing at Rachel's back was under the protection of the shield. Their eyes were as black as coal, just like hers. Just like Mackenzie's one good eye. Looking on from afar, the children looked like brightly colored ornaments, festive decorations in the middle of the street.

"What the hell is going on?" Crazy Diamond said.

Mackenzie took a step back. He shook his head briefly and it was obvious the man was rattled.

Rachel didn't hesitate. She turned back to the gate. As she tilted her head to look up, all the kids mimicked her actions. It was as if they were connected. This strange choreography continued further when Rachel lifted her arm and pointed a finger at the swelling gate.

The children did likewise.

Rachel held her finger in the air, keeping it trained on the gate like it was a magic wand, warding off evil spirits.

All of a sudden the Exterminators made a noise that sounded like a human scream. The steady, churning rhythm of the gate was jolted out of its complacent momentum. It began to shrivel up. It was like somebody had pulled the plug on its life support. The light within its heart shook violently and began to fragment into hundreds and thousands of pieces of individual light, drifting separately away from one another.

Rachel and the children stood like mannequins. Their heads and fingers pointed upwards and while the gate thrashed angrily for its life, they didn't so much as blink.

Cody's heart was racing. *They* – the children were winning. He wasn't sure what was happening, what he was watching, especially considering how badly things had gone during Rachel's first tussle with the Exterminators. It had to be the children of course. Did they possess the same gifts as she did? Or was Rachel using them somehow, harnessing their energy and using it against the Exterminators?

Rachel lowered her arm to her side. So did the children.

Mackenzie was waving his arms in the air. He was gesturing towards the blue and red light that still lingered in the sky above their heads.

"Kill her!" Mackenzie yelled. "If you can't take her through the gate then just kill her."

Mackenzie stopped suddenly, like he'd frozen on the spot. Then slowly, he turned to the side and Cody saw the man's side profile poking out of his hood. There was still a hint of the handsome face of old in that rugged profile. Mackenzie closed his eyes and lifted a hand to his head. It looked like he was receiving some sudden inbound communication. An urgent message.

"Yes," he said, nodding his head. "Use me. Give me the strength and I'll kill her for you. Give me the power – give me everything you've got."

Crazy Diamond looked at Cody. "What's he talking about?"

Cody kept his eyes on Mackenzie.

"The Exterminators can't get past the children," he said. "I don't know why but it looks like they need another way in."

Mackenzie stood with his arms outstretched as the bluish-red light swirled around and then shot into his body like a giant laser beam. He was flailing wildly like he was being electrocuted. As the light continued to work its way inside the man, Mackenzie screamed hideously, like he was strapped to a medieval torture device.

The ragtags backed away. Whatever this was, it was beyond their level of expertise.

Rachel watched Mackenzie's transformation with wide eyes.

She was breathing heavily. Cody noticed that the children, still under her control, were breathing in a similar rhythm.

The screaming stopped.

Mackenzie ripped the cloak off his back. As his body swelled outwards the rest of his clothes were torn open and in a matter of seconds, the man was standing stark naked, exposing more jagged-looking scars. There was a loud thump. Seconds later, a white shield lit up around Mackenzie. It was such an intense glow that it swallowed up his features – his eyes, nose, ears, mouth – all the little details of the man were consumed.

The Exterminators were now inside him.

Mackenzie lifted his hands, bringing them closer to his featureless face. He examined them with the fascination of a child.

He turned to his left, lifted his arm and made a brief slicing motion that looked like a karate chop. A row of nearby trees crashed onto the black snow. They fell so cleanly and suddenly it was like they'd been caught out by a silent chainsaw.

Mackenzie looked at his hands again. There was a brief moment of noise that might have been laughter.

Then he turned back to the children.

CHAPTER THIRTEEN

Mackenzie pointed to the abandoned cars lying on the grass.

His arm was a blur as he pulled it back towards his body with the same snapping motion that Rachel used. The car – a burned out Prius – rolled across the grass at his command. It went towards the children, crashing over the huddle of fallen trees that Mackenzie had cut down just seconds earlier.

Rachel held up her right hand, like she was waving at the runaway vehicle. The children standing at her back did likewise.

The car altered course, switching its angle of attack so that it was rushing towards Mackenzie.

Mackenzie was ready. He pushed the car back towards the children and followed this by rolling yet another car off the grass – a beat-up tan Subaru, that charged towards Rachel and the children at an even faster speed.

Rachel and the children held both their arms aloft. They leaned back and then pushed at the air, diverting the vehicles, hurling both of them towards Mackenzie who in turn, threw them back again.

It made for a terrible racket. Metal scraped against the road, forcing Cody and Crazy Diamond to cover their ears.

They were still standing at the edge of the car park.

Crazy Diamond nudged Cody on the arm. Then she crept forwards, making a move for her gun, which was lying just a few feet away on the dark snow next to the road. She stayed on tiptoe so as not to alert the ragtags, who were absorbed in the tennis-like duel that was going on across the street.

Crazy Diamond kneeled down and picked up the pistol. She kept still for a second afterwards, as if expecting the ragtags to turn around and catch her out. They didn't. With the gun in hand, she ran over to Cody.

"Back in the game," she said.

Cody watched as she slid a spare magazine into the gun. There was an enthusiasm, an eagerness about her as she worked. Cody saw the bullet hole in the shoulder of her parka jacket and he wondered if she'd forgotten about getting shot already.

"Did you hear what I said?" Crazy Diamond said.

"What?" Cody said, snapping out of his daze. "No. What did you say?"

"The ragtags," she said. "We gotta hit them now. Look at them – it's like they've forgotten all about us."

"Can you blame them?" Cody said, his eyes turning back to the duel.

"Look I know it's hard for you," Crazy Diamond said. "But Rachel knows what she's doing over there. Her fight is with Mackenzie and the Exterminators. Our job right now is to take those ragtag bastards out of the picture. They're sitting ducks. And after what they were about to do to us..."

Cody remembered only too well. He squeezed the handle of the Glock.

Then he closed his eyes and nodded.

"Alright," he said.

Cody opened his eyes again. The ragtags were standing in the middle of the road – a captivated audience watching as Rachel and Mackenzie duked it out with a barrage of four wheeled missiles. Mackenzie was mixing it up now – he'd added a number of fallen tree trunks into the arsenal, throwing them at the children like javelins.

"Should we take cover?" Cody said, looking at Crazy Diamond. "Or are we just going in guns blazing?"

"Guns blazing," Crazy Diamond said. "They're too far away from cover. We jump them from behind and show no mercy – just like they would do to us."

Cody saw the seething hatred for the ragtags in her eyes. He'd never seen Crazy Diamond this angry before.

They crept onto the road.

The ragtags were standing in a tight gang, like they were watching a street fight.

Cody and Crazy Diamond pointed their pistols at their backs. Sitting ducks. There was no guilt in Cody's mind about shooting anyone in the back. Crazy Diamond was right – the ragtags wouldn't hesitate if the shoe was on the other foot.

"Now," Crazy Diamond whispered.

They opened fire.

There were cries of fright within the gang. Somebody screamed in agony.

Two of the ragtags fell, shot in the back.

The others recovered quickly, turned around and returned fire. There were only five ragtags left on their feet but they still outnumbered Cody and Crazy Diamond. Now it was the final shootout. The two sides both pressed forward – it was an open battle in the center of the road, with little thought of cover from either side.

"Bastards!" Crazy Diamond yelled.

Cody squeezed the trigger like a man possessed. He walked

forwards and felt invincible, like he was a bulletproof character out of a superhero movie. Crazy Diamond was right – they were bastards, all of them. He was going to take them out, the murdering would-be rapist sons of bitches. And he was going to enjoy it.

He yelled at the top of his voice as he sprayed bullets everywhere. It was a fierce warlike cry that fuelled his courage.

Cody's bubble of invincibility couldn't last forever.

As the bullets whizzed back and forth, he felt an excruciating burning sensation in his side. He gasped for air and dropped onto the ground.

Confusion flooded his mind.

Somebody screamed behind him.

Cody put a hand to his side and saw a hole in his parka. He pressed his hand to the area and winced. It was almost the exact same spot where he'd been shot before in the airport by the crazy fake cop.

Only this time it wasn't a graze.

"Damn it," he cried out, more in frustration than anything else.

His gun was lying on the road beside him. He didn't even remember dropping it. With the sound of bullets flying over his head, Cody's fingers clawed for the weapon, grasping at the cold black snow.

He couldn't reach it.

"Cody!"

Crazy Diamond appeared at his side, kneeling down in front of him. She kept shooting at the ragtags, shielding him from the assault. Her hood was down and Cody saw the back of her head. A strange passing thought went through Cody's mind about the beautiful shade of blue-black that Crazy Diamond's hair was. He'd never noticed it before.

There were four ragtags left and they were closing ground fast. There were plenty of others lying dead or dying on the ground.

Like most people under stress, the ragtags couldn't shoot for shit but that didn't dampen their spirits. They were playing a numbers game – shoot lots of bullets and you'll hit something eventually.

Cody reached again for his Glock. He had to help Crazy Diamond but although he tried, he couldn't reach it.

Gunfire exploded at Cody's back. Crazy Diamond heard it too and she turned around, a look of wild panic in her eyes.

Cody twisted his neck around to take a look.

Nick Norton was running down the street, his AR-15 pointing at the ragtags. His face was covered in a thick mask of blood. His long winter coat was torn in several places and his movement was heavy and staggered.

"Nick!" Cody said. He was both delighted to see his friend and shocked at how beat up he looked.

The ragtags turned their guns on the big man. But Nick stood his ground – he had to, he wasn't in any state to move or dive for cover. It seemed like the only thing that worked was his trigger finger. He dropped one of the ragtags before taking a bullet to the leg. Still he didn't go down.

"C'mon you bastards!" he yelled. The defiance was still intact at least. Nick smiled, showing a row of teeth that were drenched in blood. One eye was half-closed.

He fired again and a bullet went through one of the ragtags' skull.

The last two rushed at Nick.

Crazy Diamond shot at them, forcing them back a few steps. But seconds later she was out of bullets again and she screamed out of pure frustration and at her inability to stop the inevitable. Cody's fingers grasped at the snow, trying yet again to grab the Glock but the ragtags were quick and as he wriggled along the ground, reaching for the pistol, Mackenzie's men put two more bullets in Nick, who dropped onto his knees in silence.

The rifle slid out of his hands.

"Nick!" Crazy Diamond screamed.

The ragtags hurried forward, buoyed by this success. They'd put the big man down. One more bullet and they'd finish Nick Norton off. They moved fast, like young men in their prime, like hunters sure of the kill.

"Waste him," one of them shouted.

The ragtag with his pistol pointing at Nick took aim. Cody couldn't see his lips but he knew just by looking at the man's eyes that there was a cruel smile on his face.

But there was no shot fired. The ragtag lowered his pistol and spun around, as if he'd heard something.

"What the hell...?"

A pair of bright headlights charged towards them out of the darkness. The school bus was racing down the road, driving at high speed on the slippery surface.

The two ragtags screamed. So did the bus as it accelerated harder, leaving the gunmen no time to get out of the way. It went through the two bodies like a battering ram and sent them hurtling through the air. There would be no getting up after that. The driver then took a sharp right to avoid running over Nick, who'd fallen onto his back.

The bus went over the curb and skidded to a stop.

Crazy Diamond stood up and dragged Cody to his feet. Cody groaned in agony. The pain was starting to come through but worse than that, his heart sank when he saw Nick lying flat out on the snow. He wasn't moving.

To Cody's surprise, an old woman stepped slowly off the bus. She walked over to Nick and signaled Cody and Crazy Diamond to hurry over.

"Come," she said. "Let's get you people onto the bus."

Crazy Diamond and Cody reached Nick and grabbed an arm each. It didn't look good. Nick's face was buried under a mask of blood. Before they climbed onto the bus with him, Cody looked towards North Flores Street, where the battle between Mackenzie and Rachel was still in full swing.

"You can't help her," the old woman said, putting a hand on Cody's arm.

"I have to do something," Cody said. "She's my little girl."

The woman shook her head.

"It's up to the little girl to save us."

———

Rachel was vaguely aware that something was going on beside the car park. She'd heard the constant gunfire. But it was a minor background noise that she couldn't let interfere with what she was doing.

The children were inside her head and she was inside theirs. Rachel had access to everything; she could see their stories if she wanted to – terrible stories about the horrors of the Black Storm and the happy memories that had come before. Happy memories, always fading. But those thoughts, like the gunshots, couldn't interfere either. She was drawing on their strength, the natural immunity that Grandma Anna had told her about. It took a special kind of focus to hold it.

She saw Mackenzie step forward. He was starting to close the ground on her. Both his arms were stretched outwards, reaching for the children like he wanted to throttle their necks. He was barely recognizable as human but he *was* human. Mackenzie was still in there underneath that white glowing shield.

Rachel felt an increase in power as he came closer. For the first time since the duel began, a hint of doubt crept into her mind.

Could she keep this up?

With a grimace, Rachel sent the latest barrage of missiles back up the street, hurling them at Mackenzie with all the strength she could muster.

Mackenzie lifted a finger and stopped it dead.

One finger. It looked so easy.

Was he getting stronger?

This neverending rally of cars and other weapons that was being flung at her – the Exterminators were playing the long game. They couldn't destroy her mind but they could exhaust her body, especially now that they had one of their own to wear her down with. If Rachel's body broke, everything inside would break too. And what about the children? What would happen to them if she fell?

Rachel watched as Mackenzie took another step closer. His hands were upturned, palms facing the sky. He raised his arms slowly over his head like he was transitioning into a yoga pose. As he did so, everything on the street – three cars, a mass of dismembered tree parts, a wooden bench, and a multitude of rocks and bricks, were lifted off the ground.

Mackenzie leaned back. His body jerked forwards, both arms snapping forward in a whip-like throwing motion.

The barrage of missiles came at the children in a blur. The cars rolled over, the tree stumps flew like fat spears, and the stones and bricks were like bullets.

Rachel's mind sprang into action. Her body stiffened and the tendons and veins on her arms and legs stood up. She didn't stop the assault cleanly. All she could do was strike it away clumsily, like her mind was a bat reaching for a hundred baseballs at the same time. Rachel staggered backwards and lost her balance. She dropped onto her knees and her body trembled under the pressure of this latest assault. She heard the children fall onto their knees behind her.

"Rachel!" somebody yelled in the distance.

Was it her dad? It didn't matter, not now.

She climbed back to her feet.

Rachel stared at Mackenzie, who was still wrapped in a shield of white light. He was inching towards her slowly, daring her to try and stop him. But how could she? It was like she'd run into a dead-end. The Exterminators were too strong for her in mind. Mackenzie was stronger than her in matter. Together they had her beat. She had the children on her side of course, but still it wasn't enough.

Don't panic.

That's when Rachel heard Grandma Anna's voice in her head.

Whatever they can do you can do.

She looked at Mackenzie. He continued to approach the children at a casual pace. Even though his features were buried, she could sense he was smiling.

"Whatever they can do you can do," Rachel said.

The idea came to her so suddenly, so easily that she was convinced it wasn't a good one and that it couldn't possibly work. But could it? She realized there was only one thing left for her to target – Mackenzie's mind. If anything was going to be the Achilles' heel of the Exterminator-Mackenzie alliance it was that. And his mind had to be in there, somewhere.

What if she could reach it? Like she had with Grandma Anna and the children. Could she pull the switch once she was in there?

Now it was her turn to take a step forward.

The children walked behind, matching her stride for stride.

Rachel reached an arm towards Mackenzie. Her fingers stiffened and stretched as far as they could go.

She closed her eyes and searched for him. Her mind grasped furiously at the darkness, like fingers looking for a light switch. In that moment, Rachel was an explorer traveling through a dark underground cave alone and although it was crazy and undeniably dangerous, there was treasure nearby.

She could feel it.

The familiar sliding sensation – she felt it. It was the same thing she'd experienced back at the basilica with Grandma Anna –

a sensation of sliding down a black chute and falling into some-body's private abyss.

Yes.

She'd found him.

It was dark and cold. Mackenzie's mind was a twisted labyrinth that didn't want her there. Rachel, the unwelcome guest, felt a mob of unseen forces pushing her back and she had to bully her way through the thick, jagged tangle of thorns that led to the center. She could smell something rancid – a lingering odor of rot hanging in the air.

Rachel pushed forwards, ignoring the animal cries of the Exterminators that she could hear in the background. They knew she was in there but they couldn't stop her. She continued forwards, slowing down only when she saw a bright light in the distance beckoning her down the corridors of Mackenzie's mind.

It was an image. A moving picture.

Rachel went in closer.

A woman's face was looking back at her. The woman, who was probably in her late thirties, was beautiful, but her facial expression was one of pure terror. Her hair was blonde, hanging loose down her back. The hair bounced up and down as the woman ran as fast as she could, occasionally looking back over her shoulder at Rachel – or rather at Mackenzie, because this was his memory that Rachel was revisiting.

There was a child running beside the woman – a little girl who was probably about Rachel's age. She looked like a miniature version of the woman, who Rachel assumed was her mother. The woman's hand was locked around the little girl's hand, holding on for dear life as they ran together.

They went as fast as they could. The child was screaming while the mother was in tears.

Birdsong.

They were in a large park. Rachel looked straight ahead and

saw what they were running towards – it was a silver car parked on a looping concrete path that wound its way through the heart of the park. Rachel saw other people running back and forth too. There were loud screams everywhere. Hideous, high-pitched screams. People chasing other people with weapons in their hands – their eyes as black as the sky above.

The woman looked over her shoulder. Rachel – Mackenzie – did the same and now at last Rachel could see what the family was running from. A gang of six men was chasing them down, black-eyed and armed with metal bars, which they were wielding over their heads in a frothing rage. Rachel felt a surge of fear just looking at them – or was that Mackenzie's second-hand emotion she was experiencing?

Mackenzie was yelling at the woman and child. Telling them to get to the car. Begging them to run faster.

They were almost there. Then Mackenzie tripped and fell. He dropped onto the grass, spun around and Rachel felt a sense of terrible anticipation as she waited for the metal bars to land on Mackenzie's head. She was aware of Mackenzie's strange relief at this outcome – if the men concentrated on him it would at least buy his wife and daughter time to get to the car. There was a spare key in the glove compartment.

They'd be fine.

But nothing happened.

Mackenzie looked on in horror as the men with the metal bars raced past him and continued to chase after his wife and daughter.

He jumped back to his feet to go after them and that's when he felt a sharp crack on the back of the head. Everything went hazy after that. His legs went out from underneath him. Somebody else ran past him and Mackenzie watched as the pack closed in on the only two people he gave a damn about in the world. He tried to get up several times but his body wouldn't or couldn't obey the command. When he screamed, his voice wasn't there.

And yet he didn't black out.

He could see everything.

Rachel turned away quickly. This was the memory that had come to her first. That told her that it was foremost in Mackenzie's mind – that it was always there, eating away at him.

She focused on the woman and child's face. She built a picture of them and recalled their voices as they ran. The girl yelled at Mackenzie. She called him dad. The woman called him by his name – John.

John Mackenzie.

Rachel envisioned the hallucination she was trying to create. It was a terrible thing. When it was intact, she planted the seed in Mackenzie's mind.

They would appear to him, like Rachel's mom had appeared to her dad in the Dodge Challenger. They would talk to him.

Traitor.

That's what his wife and daughter, bloody and battered to a pulp, would call Mackenzie for turning his back on his people. For working with the same enemy who was responsible for their deaths that day in the park.

How could you?

The hallucination began to grow like a black flower with sharp thorns running along the stem. Rachel saw it floating away like a piece of driftwood and then suddenly it was pulled down, dragged deep into the darkness of Mackenzie's mind.

It was done.

Rachel slipped out of the black hole. In truth, she was glad to be out of there – Mackenzie's mind was like a dark, haunted forest with only rotten trees and stagnant water pools for company. She opened her eyes and her legs wobbled underneath her. The children were standing behind her. The giant shield had dropped and their eyes had reverted back to their natural colors. Rachel must have lost contact with them while she'd been in Mackenzie's mind.

It was lucky for them that they hadn't seen the things she had in there.

The children were looking at her with a mix of puzzled and hopeful expressions.

"Is it over?" Tegan asked Rachel.

Rachel shook her head. "Not yet."

She turned around and looked at Mackenzie, who was standing in the middle of the road. How long would it take? Was it even going to work at all?

Rachel began to get nervous when nothing happened.

A few seconds passed. Then Mackenzie jolted backwards all of a sudden like he'd been electrocuted. His feet were lifted about four feet off the ground and Rachel saw the white shield around him tremble and dim.

As the shield thinned further, Rachel saw Mackenzie's horrified expression appear through the fading light. His one good eye bulged in horror. Rachel knew exactly what he was looking at in that moment. She could almost hear their angry voices in his head – screaming at him, accusing him of treachery towards his family.

The shield powered up again, covering his tormented features.

But Mackenzie resisted. He shook his head and scraped at the light, like he was trying to claw it off. Like it was smothering him or burning his skin.

The shield disappeared for a second time. Now Mackenzie stood naked and scarred in the street – a man, just a normal man. His black eye was gone. The look of horror on his face returned and he reached for something. For someone who wasn't there.

"No," he said, his hand grasping in front of him. "It's not like that. I did it for..."

The shield came back and Mackenzie shook it off again. Now he was at war with the Exterminators, battling for control of body and mind. And no matter how strong the Exterminators were they couldn't hope to understand the powerful feelings that stirred in Mackenzie now.

But Rachel knew there wasn't much time. Either the Exterminators would reclaim Mackenzie's mind and body or they would leave it altogether and the fight would continue elsewhere. It was inevitable – the only question was how long did they have?

Rachel looked through the fallen tree foliage, over at the school bus parked in the distance. She closed her eyes again.

Quickly.

She opened her eyes.

Crazy Diamond was hurrying towards her, carrying Nick's rifle in hand. She walked through a gap in the fallen debris and stepped cautiously onto the road. She looked at Rachel and gave her a brief nod. Then Crazy Diamond walked over to where Mackenzie was standing in the middle of the street, still darting back and forth in between human and Exterminator mode.

"I'm sorry," Mackenzie said, after shaking the white shield off him yet again. He was breathing heavily, still reaching a hand to no one, trying to cup the faces of his wife and child.

The white shield smothered him. Mackenzie fought it off like someone was trying to put a plastic bag over his head and suffocate him. He was oblivious to Crazy Diamond standing beside him, pointing the AR-15 at his head.

The shield dropped.

Crazy Diamond's finger was sitting on the trigger.

"I told you," she said. "I told you what I'd do."

Mackenzie turned his head towards her. He looked at Crazy Diamond with a strange bug-eyed recognition. He opened his mouth to say something but Crazy Diamond didn't give him the chance. She squeezed the trigger. There was a loud bang before the bullet ripped through Mackenzie's skull, taking a large chunk of the man's head with it. He dropped like a stone onto his back, his arms spread out wide.

"Dead," Crazy Diamond said.

Rachel took a step forward. She was about to call over to Crazy Diamond when the ground shook violently under her feet. A loud, unbearable cracking noise forced her hands over her ears. Some of the children screamed behind her, calling out to one another in frightened voices that were drowned out by the noise.

The Earth shook back and forth like it was having a seizure. The children were flung off their feet and rolled around the ground in a chaotic horizontal dance. Rachel went down too and as she tried to scramble back to her feet, she saw the black snow melting all around them. Her eyes lit up. There was a dull sizzling sound that accompanied the snow's rapid demise.

The black sky made a crackling noise like a broken television.

Then everything stopped.

Silence.

A flood of light and heat shot down from the heavens like an avalanche. It happened so fast, like somebody had turned on a switch.

Rachel dropped to the ground and covered her eyes.

She heard footsteps running over beside her.

Rachel looked up, wincing at the fierce light behind Crazy Diamond who was standing beside her. She tilted her head in confusion and glanced briefly at a beautiful clear blue sky. But as beautiful as it was, it was hurting her eyes. She shrank from the sunlight like a vampire.

Crazy Diamond helped Rachel back to her feet. Rachel peered through her fingers and saw a flood of tears in the woman's eyes. She didn't know if they were happy tears or sad ones.

The other children, like Rachel, were trying to adapt to the sudden reappearance of sunlight. They stood there for a few moments, in muted celebration. Tears and laughter came a few moments later. The children looked to the sky, marveling at the sunlight on their skin.

Crazy Diamond turned to Rachel. The smile on her face was gone.

"Rachel," Crazy Diamond said. "Your dad's been shot."

Rachel's stomach lurched.

"What?"

Crazy Diamond nodded. "Yeah it's a bad one. And Nick..."

"What about him?" Rachel said.

Crazy Diamond shook her head. "C'mon let's get over there."

Crazy Diamond put an arm around Rachel's shoulder and led her back to the school bus. They passed Grandma Anna on their way. The old woman was waddling towards the children as fast as her old legs would carry her.

Grandma Anna stopped to embrace Rachel.

"I knew you could do it," Grandma Anna said.

The old woman's face was damp with tears. Like Crazy Diamond, she looked happy and sad at the same time. Wiping the tears away she pointed a thumb over her shoulder, gesturing for Crazy Diamond and Rachel to get back.

"Go," she said.

Grandma Anna walked towards the children. They were still standing in the middle of the road celebrating victory. Rachel glanced over that way, just in time to see some of the kids pulling their winter coats off, their gloves and scarves too, and throwing them down like heavy chains that had been locked for too long.

CHAPTER FOURTEEN

Cody had dragged Nick out of the bus to show him the blue sky. He wanted his friend to feel the sunlight on his skin and to know that their long fight against the Exterminators hadn't been in vain. Cody could feel it too, softly burning on his forehead – a tender kiss from a long lost friend. The blue sky was dazzling, crystal clear, and the sound of children laughing in the distance was a fitting accompaniment.

It should have been perfect.

Except it wasn't. His best friend was dead.

Nick's muscular body was stretched out next to a pile of freshly formed black slush. He was bloody and battered, still dressed in his winter garments. Cody had already closed Nick's eyes over and he'd never know for sure if his pal had caught a glimpse of the blue sky before he slipped away.

He could only hope.

Cody's own wound was in a bad way. He knew that. It wasn't that painful but it felt deep – significant. He figured it would hurt eventually, once the adrenaline and excitement and despair had worn off. He was still wrapped up in his winter clothes and he could feel his body starting to bake under the sunlight.

He heard footsteps approaching the bus. Looking up, he saw Rachel and Crazy Diamond hurrying towards them.

Cody reached up for Rachel and she dropped onto her knees, burying her head in his chest. He felt a stabbing pain in his side upon contact but tried not to show it. For almost a minute, neither one of them spoke. They just held onto one another.

Crazy Diamond sat down on the road. She reached over and stroked Nick's blood-soaked hair gently. Rachel lifted her head off Cody's chest and looked at Nick. She grabbed his hand and for a long time she stared at the dead man, as if trying to will him back to life.

Rachel noticed the bullet hole in Cody's parka.

"Yeah," Cody said, seeing the look of concern in her eyes. "Don't worry honey. It's not so bad."

He couldn't help it. Sometimes lying was the right thing – the kind thing.

Cody grabbed Rachel by the hand and squeezed tight.

"You did it," he said. "I'm so proud of you Rachel. We won."

A tear ran down Rachel's cheek.

"Doesn't feel like we won," she said.

They sat in silence for a few minutes. This was broken when Grandma Anna came back, surrounded by a flock of giddy children. Cody tried his best to smile at the kids whose faces sobered up when they saw Nick. Cody didn't exactly understand what part these children had played in the battle against the Exterminators – but he knew that whatever it was they'd played it well.

A little red-haired boy crept out in front of the crowd.

"You're Cody MacLeod," he said. "From *The Forever Boys*. Ain'tcha?"

"Benji," Grandma Anna said, grabbing the kid by the collar like she was scruffing a kitten. "Not now."

Benji stepped back in line with the other kids.

Grandma Anna kneeled down in front of Cody. Without a word, she opened up his parka and lifted his sweater so she could examine the wound. The sad expression on her face was all the confirmation Cody needed.

Grandma Anna glanced at Rachel. Then she turned back to Cody.

"We can go to the hospital," she said. "Find some equipment to take the bullet out."

Cody shook his head and sighed. "All the hospitals are gone," he said.

Crazy Diamond leaned in closer. She had a hand pressed over the wound on her shoulder. "Don't give up Cody," she said.

Cody looked at Rachel. She was pressed up tight next to him, not giving her dad an inch of space. Her arm was locked around his.

"I won't," he said.

"So what now?" Grandma Anna said. "What do we do next?"|

Cody looked at the old woman. Despite everything, he smiled.

"I saw a lot of jerry cans in the back of the bus," he said.

"We've got fuel," Grandma Anna said. "If that's what you're asking?"

Cody nodded. "How about we take a road trip?" he said. "I think it's time we were moving on from San Antonio, or what's left of it."

"A road trip?" Grandma Anna said. "Have you got anywhere particular in mind?"

Cody kept smiling.

"As a matter of fact I do," he said.

Before they left San Antonio, the survivors took Nick and Marv's bodies to the National Cemetery. At Cody's insistence they'd also stopped in at the Rand to recover Lance as well. Last of all, they took several crates of of tinned food and some other supplies and loaded them onto the bus for the journey.

Cody wanted to stop at the funeral home to pick up caskets for the men. He wanted to dig graves too but it was Crazy Diamond who explained that there wasn't enough room in the bus to transport three caskets to the cemetery. On top of that, they lacked the proper muscle to dig the graves.

In the end, they'd wrapped Nick, Marv and Lance up in their sleeping bags. They placed the remains next to the wall of the cemetery beside Rita, Laney and Johnny Boy, keeping the bodies in the shade. All except Nick. Cody remembered what Nick had said about wanting the sunshine to linger over his gravesite.

They left stone markers with the names of the men carved onto the front.

After the funeral, they hit the road. They took the Interstate Highway 10 heading west out of San Antonio.

Grandma Anna was at the wheel while the children sat scattered around the bus in various small groups. Crazy Diamond and Rachel were at the back, tending to Cody's gunshot wound with what little supplies they had. Crazy Diamond's own wound had turned out to be little more than a graze. Looking at her now, it was hard to tell she'd even been hurt at all.

Cody was lying in the backseat. He had a blanket over him and a couple of pillows propping up his head so he could look out the window and watch the natural progression of day to night. Such a simple thing, how he'd missed it. Crazy Diamond checked the wound regularly. It wasn't bleeding too badly but the bullet was still in there. Taking Grandma Anna's advice, Crazy Diamond cleaned out the site of the wound, administered a gauze bandage roll and wrapped it around Cody's waist. With any luck they'd find some facilities and equipment on the way to help them remove the bullet. Otherwise, infection remained a possibility.

Grandma Anna had a small flask of whiskey. She'd given it to Cody, told him to drink what he needed.

He did.

The trip from Texas to California took a little over twenty hours. They passed nothing but ghost towns along the way, including the remains of El Paso and Tucson. Now the bus approached Los Angeles on the San Bernardino Freeway, which was deserted except for a long parade of cars and other abandoned vehicles scattered across the freeway.

Cody forced himself to sit up as they neared LA. He wanted to see the city again, to catch the choking stench of the smog but of course that was absent now. The air was thriving, cleaner than he'd remembered.

In the distance, a dark red sun was shining over downtown LA.

"Where do you want to go Cody?" Grandma Anna said, calling from the driver's seat. "Anything in particular you want to see."

"Yeah," Cody said. "Let me come down there and I'll give you directions."

He threw the blanket off and got to his feet. His arms and legs were weak and he felt lightheaded. With the help of Rachel and Crazy Diamond, he walked down the aisle towards the driver's seat. He felt the eyes of the kids all over him as he passed, especially that little redheaded boy who thought he was the second coming.

Grandma Anna kept her eyes on the road.

"Just tell me where to go," she said.

Hollywood Reservoir, also known as Lake Hollywood, was just a short drive north of Los Angeles. The reservoir was located in the Hollywood Hills area, hiding amongst a small brushy valley.

Cody remembered the last time he'd been there. Ten years ago, not long after he'd moved out of California, he'd been forced to undertake a solo journey back from Texas to scatter Kate's ashes. He'd done the walk around the reservoir that day with the urn in his bag, taking in the dramatic views of the water, as well as the expensive looking houses that could be seen in the distance. Then he'd scattered the ashes in full view of the Hollywood sign. Kate would have liked that.

Now he was back.

The school bus stopped in the car park a little south of the hiking trail.

Cody had to be helped off the bus by Crazy Diamond. Rachel was glued to his side, her hand locked in his. Cody was dressed in a blue t-shirt and khaki pants – glorious summer clothes he thought he'd never put on again. Now with the California sun on his face, the dark and wintery nightmare of San Antonio was like a bad dream.

Cody nodded his appreciation to Grandma Anna, who was still sitting at the wheel.

"Thank you," Cody said. "For everything."

"Go on," she said with a smile. "Take your little walk. We'll be here waiting."

"Will you be okay?" Crazy Diamond said, standing beside Cody and Rachel outside the bus. There was a look of concern on her face. "I know this is a private thing between you two but I can tag along. I can hang back. You know, just in case you need me. You're in no condition to go on a friggin' hike Cody."

Cody gave her a gentle squeeze on the arm. "I'm alright Crazy Diamond," he said. "I've got enough left in the tank yet."

Crazy Diamond bit her lip nervously. "Alright," she said. "If you say so. Just make sure you come back in one piece. You hear?"

"Yeah. I hear you."

Cody and Rachel followed the path that led around the reservoir.

The silence of that place was its greatest asset. There was nothing to be heard except the constant chirp of birdsong and an occasional duck squawk. The Hollywood sign peered down at them from the hillside above. It was a piece of symbolism that Cody had never managed to escape in life, no matter how many miles he'd put between himself and the industry. But now that he was back, he was surprised at how happy he was to see the sign.

Cody and Rachel didn't talk much as they walked. They were content just to enjoy each other's company and Cody was careful to preserve his energy for the hike, which although mostly flat, was still more grueling than he'd thought it would be.

He'd forgotten how hot the sun was.

Eventually they arrived at the ornate Mulholland Dam, which for many people had been the highlight of the hiking route. They walked across to the middle and leaned over the edge. Cody pointed out the lavish arches and the sculpted bears that decorated the columns. He'd always liked those little details – he liked them even more so now. Rachel didn't seem interested. He noticed that her eyes were red and sore. Cody had lost count of the number of times he'd heard her crying on the bus during the journey.

The dam offered a clear view of the Hollywood sign. From the other side, Cody could see towards Hollywood and Los Angeles. He felt at home here.

A wave of lightheadedness came back. His body was running away from him.

Cody gripped onto the edge of the dam, not trusting his ability to stay upright for much longer. He felt weak and didn't know how he was going to make it back to the bus.

"Are you alright Dad?" Rachel said.

"I always said I'd take you here," Cody said, ignoring the question. "Well here we are at last. At least one of my plans worked out."

She took his hand and brushed up tight against him.

"Is this where you...?"

"Yeah," Cody said. "This is where I scattered your mom's ashes. Still don't know if I was allowed to but what the hell? I'm the bad boy of Hollywood, remember? This is my town."

He laughed and it hurt like hell.

Cody turned towards Rachel. He was about to say something else but before he knew it, he'd dropped onto his knees. Rachel shrieked with fright and grabbed onto him, seizing Cody by the shoulders to stop him tipping over further.

She was standing over him. He was on his knees looking up at her.

"You're safe now," he said. His voice was faint and scratchy. "You don't need me to be safe."

Rachel's lips were pursed tightly together.

"You're not going to die," she said. "Please don't Dad. I still need you."

He reached up and ran a hand over her cheek. Her skin was soft and warm.

"Remember what I told you?" Cody said. "No burial. I want you to put me here beside your mom. You understand? It's where I want to be."

She shook her head.

"No," she said.

"No grave," Cody said. "No marker either. I've earned the right to be anonymous, don't you think? And besides, I don't want that creepy little redheaded kid to write 'Here lies the stutter kid' on my headstone."

Rachel didn't laugh.

"You're safe," he said again. "That's all I wanted – all I could hope for. Damn, I tried my best Rachel."

Cody collapsed, slipping out of Rachel's grip and falling onto his back. If nothing else, this position offered him a great view of the summer sky and he bathed in its warm magnificence. Rachel sat down and lifted his head so that it was resting on her lap. The last sensation he felt was her stroking his hair. The last sound he heard was Rachel talking to him in a soft voice.

"Don't worry Dad," she said. "We'll be alright."

That night, Rachel was led down the trail and taken through the gap in the chain link fence. The path led towards the water's edge.

This was where the cremation would take place.

Crazy Diamond was right there beside her.

Rachel started walking down the trail to the water. Then she stopped. Her body went stiff when she saw her dad's sleeping bag lying on a standing platform of wood. The two jerry cans were sitting nearby on the ground. Rachel imagined they'd already soaked the funeral bed and all that was left now was to light it.

Would they ask her to do it?

She felt breathless. Her legs were rooted in the dirt.

"I don't want to go," she said, looking up at Crazy Diamond. "I can't watch this."

Crazy Diamond put an arm around Rachel's shoulder and pulled her close.

"Well how about we stay here?" she said. "On the path. Keep our distance from the water. That way we're still there for your dad but we've got a little breathing room. Does that sound okay?"

Rachel wanted to run back to the bus. But she didn't want to leave her dad with a bunch of people he didn't know with the exception of Crazy Diamond. Wouldn't he want her there?

That was easy. He'd want what was best for her.

And that's why she should be there.

Rachel nodded. "Okay. We'll stay."

They sat on the path while the cremation took place. The flames rose high above the reservoir, thick smoke plumes gushing out and floating up towards a sky that was covered with bright stars.

Rachel squeezed up close to Crazy Diamond. Their arms were wrapped around one another as they watched the fire and inhaled that thick, intoxicating smell of burning wood. The fire hissed and popped. Several times, Rachel buried her face in Crazy Diamond's long hair. But she always resurfaced quickly.

The fire burned all night and into the morning.

The next day the children presented Rachel with a plastic box containing Cody's ashes. The box, about the size of a shoebox, had been one of many storage containers in the bus. Today it was given the task of being an urn.

Rachel took the box. It was heavier than she'd thought.

"Want me to come with you?" Crazy Diamond said.

Rachel thought about it. But something inside told her she was supposed to make this trip alone.

"I'll be alright," she said.

"You sure?"

"Yeah."

Rachel walked the trail to the dam by herself. She had to make several stops along the way for a rest. But she didn't mind – there was no rush to either get there or go back to the bus. Sometimes while she was catching her breath she'd listen to the birds singing and talk to her dad like he was there beside her.

Which he was. Sort of.

Eventually she reached the dam. With the box in hand, Rachel walked to the same place that her dad had scattered her mom's ashes ten years ago.

Rachel took the lid off the box and looked at a mixture of light and dark grey ashes sitting at the bottom. She felt strangely unaffected by the sight. They were the last physical trace of the man – but *not* the man. She glanced over at the Hollywood sign in the distance and thought about her parents.

"Bye Dad," she said. "Bye Mom."

She tipped the ashes over the side and watched them scatter in the breeze.

Rachel stayed there for a long time afterwards. Staring out towards the water and the hills. She had no idea how much time had passed before she was ready to leave and get back to the bus. But the light was starting to fade and she decided to go, even though she would have been happy to stay there all night.

"I'll come back," she said, staring across at the Hollywood sign. "Wait for me, okay?"

She paused, as if waiting for a response.

The next morning they were all set to leave the reservoir. Grandma Anna and Crazy Diamond oversaw a number of supply checks, food and fuel mostly. Some of the children helped the adults out while others played amongst themselves on the hiking trail. There was a large roadmap in the bus but as far as anyone knew there was no particular destination in mind.

Crazy Diamond walked up to Rachel and grabbed her by the shoulders.

"Hey," Crazy Diamond said. "You okay?"

Rachel shrugged. "Suppose."

"I just wanted to ask you something," Crazy Diamond said. She looked around as if she didn't want anyone else to overhear. "Your powers. I mean your gifts...are they gone?"

Rachel looked away. A couple of kids were playing hide and seek near the entrance to the hiking path.

"Rachel?" Crazy Diamond said. "Are they...?"

"Yeah," Rachel said. "All gone."

Crazy Diamond nodded. She was looking at Rachel with a searching eye.

"Right," she said. "And you're okay with that?"

"I'm relieved," Rachel said. "I'm normal again. I've earned the right to be normal, don't you think?"

"You sure have."

There was a loud tooting noise. Grandma Anna was leaning over the wheel, pounding on the horn. There was a serious look on her face.

"C'mon everyone," she said. "Let's hit the road."

Crazy Diamond and Rachel walked towards the bus. Some of the other kids were already sitting down in there. Tegan and Stutter smiled at Rachel as she walked down the aisle. Rachel smiled back but it felt like a hollow gesture.

"I'm going to sit in the back by myself for a while," Rachel said to Crazy Diamond. "Look out the window and think."

"Alright," Crazy Diamond said, sitting down in the middle row. "Call me if you need me. I'll be here."

"I will."

Rachel sat down in the backseat, leaning her head against the cool glass.

"Where are we going?" Tegan called out. She was looking at Grandma Anna who turned around and shrugged her shoulders.

"You're in charge now," the old woman said. "You decide."

"Me?" Tegan said. "I'm in charge?"

"All of you," Grandma Anna said. "I just drive this thing. And I won't be around forever to drive it either. So start thinking about where you want to go."

The yellow school bus rolled away, heading north on the 101 towards Insterstate 5.

Rachel's face was pressed up against the window.

A row of palm trees lined the edge of the freeway. Giant telephone poles stood in the distance, their long, redundant wires stretching on for miles. Empty buildings played the part of desolate spectators. All these old familiar sights were ghosts – they would haunt the world in silence from now on.

Rachel leaned back in her seat. She ignored the empty chatter of the other kids as they discussed where they should go next. With a quick glance down the aisle, she made sure no one was looking at her. Then slowly, Rachel stretched out her hand and watched as the colored lights danced around her fingertips.

She thought back to her birthday party. It wasn't that long ago but it sure felt like a lifetime had passed since they'd all sat together on the seventh floor of the Rand that night. Rachel remembered the sloppy rendition of Happy Birthday, and the tin of birthday cake peaches with the green candle sticking out the top. But most of all, she remembered the feeling of being surrounded by friends and family.

Rachel recalled the wish she'd made that night while blowing out the candle.

It had come true.

But victory wasn't enough. She knew that now.

THE END

OTHER BOOKS BY MARK GILLESPIE

After the End Trilogy (Complete Box Set)

'Civic terror, apocalypse, gangs, horror, complete decline of civilization...read it and weep!' - Mallory A. Haws

The Future of London (Books 1-5)

THE BUTCH NOLAN SERIES

Nolan's Ark (Butch Nolan #1)

ManHunter (Butch Nolan #2)

Mad Max meets John Wick meets Clint Eastwood's spaghetti westerns in this rollercoaster ride of a post-apocalyptic action thriller...

DYSTOPIAVILLE

If Black Mirror did Books...

Shut Up and Die!

WaxWorld

Killing Floor

All Dystopiaville books are stand-alone novels/novellas that can be read in any order.

AFTER THE END TRILOGY

The Curse (After the End #1)

The Sinners (After the End #2)

The End War (After the End #3)

Complete Box Set

"A post-apocalyptic New York run by women...what could go wrong?

Margaret Atwood would be proud."

THE FUTURE OF LONDON

L-2011 (Future of London #1)

Mr Apocalypse (Future of London #2)

Ghosts of London (Future of London #3)

Sleeping Giants (Future of London #4)

Kojiro vs. The Vampire People (Future of London #5)

The Future of London Box Set (Books 1-3)

"Modern dystopian at its very best." - Kirsten McKenzie, author of Painted.

GRIMLOG (TALES OF TERROR)

Apex Predators

Air Nosferatu

"What's not to like about zombies and sharks, or zombie sharks?" - CJ (5 stars)

"Brilliantly fast-paced horror that was unputdownable." - Chantelle Atkins (5 stars)

JOIN THE READER LIST

Do you love Post-Apocalyptic, Dystopian and Horror fiction?

Mark's a busy author and he releases regularly in these genres so if you enjoy what you read here and want to be notified whenever there's a new book out, join the reader list. Just click the link below. It'll only take a minute.

www.markgillespieauthor.com

(*The sign up box is on the Home Page*)

You can also follow Mark on Bookbub.

WEBSITE/SOCIAL MEDIA

Mark Gillespie's author website
www.markgillespieauthor.com

Mark Gillespie on Facebook
www.facebook.com/markgillespieswritingstuff

Mark Gillespie on Twitter
www.twitter.com/MarkG_Author

Made in the USA
Monee, IL
23 November 2021

82831651R00300